REMEMBRANCE OF THINGS PAST

" When to the sessions of sweet silent thought
I summon up remembrance of things past . . ."

VOLUME III

WITHIN A
BUDDING GROVE

PART ONE

Marcel Proust's continuous novel *À la Recherche du Temps Perdu* (REMEMBRANCE OF THINGS PAST) was originally published in eight parts, the titles and dates of which were: I. *Du Côté de Chez Swann* (1913); II. *À l'Ombre des Jeunes Filles en Fleurs* (1918), awarded the Prix Goncourt in 1919; III. *Le Côté de Guermantes* I (1920); IV. *Le Côté de Guermantes* II, *Sodome et Gomorrhe* I (1921); V. *Sodome et Gomorrhe* II (1922); VI. *La Prisonnière* (1923); VII. *Albertine Disparue* (1925); VIII. *Le Temps Retrouvé* (1927).

Du Côté de Chez Swann has been published in English as SWANN'S WAY: *À l'Ombre des Jeunes Filles en Fleurs* as WITHIN A BUDDING GROVE: *Le Côté de Guermantes* as THE GUERMANTES WAY: *Sodome et Gomorrhe* as CITIES OF THE PLAIN: *La Prisonnière* as THE CAPTIVE: *Albertine Disparue* as THE SWEET CHEAT GONE: and *Le Temps Retrouvé* as TIME REGAINED. The first seven parts were translated by C. K. Scott Moncrieff; the eighth was first translated by Stephen Hudson but is now re-issued in a new translation by Andreas Mayor.

In the present uniform edition the volumes are as follows:—

VOL.

1. SWANN'S WAY. PART I
2. SWANN'S WAY. PART II
3. WITHIN A BUDDING GROVE. PART I
4. WITHIN A BUDDING GROVE. PART II
5. THE GUERMANTES WAY. PART I
6. THE GUERMANTES WAY. PART II
7. CITIES OF THE PLAIN. PART I
8. CITIES OF THE PLAIN. PART II
9. THE CAPTIVE. PART I
10. THE CAPTIVE. PART II
11. THE SWEET CHEAT GONE
12. TIME REGAINED

GILBERTE AT HOME

MARCEL PROUST

WITHIN A
BUDDING GROVE

PART ONE

Translated by
C. K. Scott Moncrieff

ILLUSTRATED BY
PHILIPPE JULLIAN

1972

CHATTO & WINDUS

LONDON

First published in English (cr. 8vo) 1924
Second impression 1924
First issued in the Phoenix Library 1929
First issued in the Uniform Edition
(12 vols.) 1941
Reprinted 1943, 1949, 1952 and 1956
Illustrated Edition 1957
Reprinted 1960, 1966, 1970, 1972

ISBN 0 7011 1052 X

Printed in Great Britain by
Redwood Press Limited
Trowbridge, Wiltshire

CONTENTS

*

THAT *men in armour may be born*
With serpents' teeth the field is sown;
Rains mould, winds bend, suns gild the corn
Too quickly ripe, too early mown.

I scan the quivering heads, behold
The features, catch the whispered breath
Of friends long garnered in the cold
Unopening granaries of death,

Whose names in solemn cadence ring
Across my slow oblivious page.
Their friendship was a finer thing
Than fame, or wealth, or honoured age,

And—while you live and I—shall last
Its tale of seasons with us yet
Who cherish, in the undying past,
The men we never can forget.

Bad Kissingen,   C. K. S. M.
    July 31, 1923.

ILLUSTRATIONS

*

WITHIN A BUDDING GROVE

MADAME SWANN AT HOME

MY mother, when it was a question of our having
M. de Norpois to dinner for the first time, having
expressed her regret that Professor Cottard was
away from home, and that she herself had quite ceased
to see anything of Swann, since either of these might have
helped to entertain the old Ambassador, my father replied that so eminent a guest, so distinguished a man of
science as Cottard could never be out of place at a dinner-
table, but that Swann, with his ostentation, his habit of
crying aloud from the house-tops the name of everyone
that he knew, however slightly, was an impossible vul-
garian whom the Marquis de Norpois would be sure to
dismiss as—to use his own epithet—a "pestilent" fellow.
Now, this attitude on my father's part may be felt to require a few words of explanation, inasmuch as some of
us, no doubt, remember a Cottard of distinct mediocrity
and a Swann by whom modesty and discretion, in all his
social relations, were carried to the utmost refinement of
delicacy. But in his case, what had happened was that,
to the original "young Swann" and also to the Swann of
the Jockey Club, our old friend had added a fresh personality (which was not to be his last) that of Odette's
husband. Adapting to the humble ambitions of that lady
the instinct, the desire, the industry which he had always
had, he had laboriously constructed for himself, a long

way beneath the old, a new position more appropriate to the companion who was to share it with him. In this he shewed himself another man. Since (while he continued to go, by himself, to the houses of his own friends, on whom he did not care to inflict Odette unless they had expressly asked that she should be introduced to them) it was a new life that he had begun to lead, in common with his wife, among a new set of people, it was quite intelligible that, in order to estimate the importance of these new friends and thereby the pleasure, the self-esteem that were to be derived from entertaining them, he should have made use, as a standard of comparison, not of the brilliant society in which he himself had moved before his marriage but of the earlier environment of Odette. And yet, even when one knew that it was with unfashionable officials and their faded wives, the wall-flowers of ministerial ball-rooms, that he was now anxious to associate, it was still astonishing to hear him, who in the old days, and even still, would so gracefully refrain from mentioning an invitation to Twickenham or to Marlborough House, proclaim with quite unnecessary emphasis that the wife of some Assistant Under-Secretary for Something had returned Mme. Swann's call. It will perhaps be objected here that what this really implied was that the simplicity of the fashionable Swann had been nothing more than a supreme refinement of vanity, and that, like certain other Israelites, my parents' old friend had contrived to illustrate in turn all the stages through which his race had passed, from the crudest and coarsest form of snobbishness up to the highest pitch of good manners. But the chief reason—and one which is applicable to humanity as a whole—was that our virtues them-

2

selves are not free and floating qualities over which we retain a permanent control and power of disposal ; they come to be so closely linked in our minds with the actions in conjunction with which we make it our duty to prac- tise them, that, if we are suddenly called upon to perform some action of a different order, it takes us by surprise, and without our supposing for a moment that it might in- volve the bringing of those very same virtues into play. Swann, in his intense consciousness of his new social sur- roundings, and in the pride with which he referred to them, was like those great artists—modest or generous by nature—who, if at the end of their career they take to cooking or to gardening, display a childlike gratification at the compliments that are paid to their dishes or their borders, and will not listen to any of the criticism which they heard unmoved when it was applied to their real achievements; or who, after giving away a canvas, cannot conceal their annoyance if they lose a couple of francs at dominoes.

As for Professor Cottard, we shall meet him again and can study him at our leisure, much later in the course of our story, with the " Mistress ", Mme. Verdurin, in her coun- try house La Raspelière. For the present, the following observations must suffice ; first of all, in the case of Swann the alteration might indeed be surprising, since it had been accomplished and yet was not suspected by me when I used to see Gilberte's father in the Champs-Elysées, where, moreover, as he never spoke to me, he could not very well have made any display of his political relations. It is true that, if he had done so, I might not at once have discerned his vanity, for the idea that one has long held of a person is apt to stop one's eyes and ears ; my mother, for three whole years, had no more noticed the salve with which one of her nieces used to paint her lips than if it had been wholly and invisibly dissolved in some clear liquid ; until one day a streak too much, or possibly something else, brought about the phenomenon known as super-saturation ; all the paint that had hitherto passed unperceived was now crystallised, and my mother, in the face of this sudden riot of colour, declared, in the best Combray manner, that it was a perfect scandal, and almost severed relations with her niece. With Cottard, on the contrary, the epoch in which we have seen him assisting at the first introduction of Swann to the Verdurins was now buried in the past ; whereas honours, offices and titles come with the passage of years; moreover, a man may be illiterate, and make stupid puns, and yet have a special gift, which no amount of general culture can replace—such as the gift of a great strategist or physician. And so it was not merely as an obscure practitioner, who had attained in course of time to European celebrity, that the rest of his profession regarded Cottard. The most intelligent of the younger doctors used to assert—for a year or two, that is to say, for fashions, being themselves begotten of the desire for change, are quick to change also —that if they themselves ever fell ill Cottard was the only one of the leading men to whom they would entrust their lives. No doubt they preferred, socially, to meet certain others who were better read, more artistic, with whom they could discuss Nietzsche and Wagner. When there was a musical party at Mme. Cottard's, on the evenings when she entertained—in the hope that it might one day make him Dean of the Faculty—the colleagues

and pupils of her husband, he, instead of listening, preferred to play cards in another room. Yet everybody
praised the quickness, the penetration, the unerring confidence with which, at a glance, he could diagnose disease. Thirdly, in considering the general impression
which Professor Cottard must have made on a man like
my father, we must bear in mind that the character which
a man exhibits in the latter half of his life is not always,
even if it is often his original character developed or
withered, attenuated or enlarged ; it is sometimes the exact
opposite, like a garment that has been turned. Except
from the Verdurins, who were infatuated with him, Cottard's hesitating manner, his excessive timidity and affability had, in his young days, called down upon him
endless taunts and sneers. What charitable friend counselled that glacial air? The importance of his professional standing made it all the more easy to adopt.
Wherever he went, save at the Verdurins', where he instinctively became himself again, he would assume a re-
pellent coldness, remain silent as long as possible, be per-
emptory when he was obliged to speak, and not forget
to say the most cutting things. He had every opportunity
of rehearsing this new attitude before his patients, who,
seeing him for the first time, were not in a position to
make comparisons, and would have been greatly surprised to learn that he was not at all a rude man by
nature. Complete impassivity was what he strove to attain, and even while visiting his hospital wards, when he
allowed himself to utter one of those puns which left
everyone, from the house physician to the junior student,
helpless with laughter, he would always make it without

5

moving a muscle of his face, while even that was no longer recognisable now that he had shaved off his beard and moustache.

But who, the reader has been asking, was the Marquis de Norpois. Well, he had been Minister Plenipotentiary before the War, and was actually an Ambassador on the Sixteenth of May ; in spite of which, and to the general astonishment, he had since been several times chosen to represent France on Extraordinary Missions,—even as Controller of the Public Debt in Egypt, where, thanks to his great capability as a financier, he had rendered important services—by Radical Cabinets under which a reactionary of the middle classes would have declined to serve, and in whose eyes M. de Norpois, in view of his past, his connexions and his opinions, ought presumably to have been suspect. But these advanced Ministers seemed to consider that, in making such an appointment, they were shewing how broad their own minds were, when the supreme interests of France were at stake, were raising themselves above the general run of politicians, were meriting, from the *Journal des Débats* itself, the title of "Statesmen", and were reaping direct advantage from the weight that attaches to an aristocratic name and the dramatic interest always aroused by an unexpected appointment. And they knew also that they could reap these advantages by making an appeal to M. de Norpois, without having to fear any want of political loyalty on his part, a fault against which his noble birth not only need not put them on their guard but offered a positive guarantee. And in this calculation the Government of the Republic were not mistaken. In the first place, because an aristocrat of a certain type, brought up from his cradle to

6

regard his name as an integral part of himself of which no accident can deprive him (an asset of whose value his peers, or persons of even higher rank, can form a fairly exact estimate), knows that he can dispense with the efforts (since they can in no way enhance his position) in which, without any appreciable result, so many public men of the middle class spend themselves,—to profess only the " right " opinions, to frequent only the " sound " people. Anxious, on the other hand, to increase his own importance in the eyes of the princely or ducal families which take immediate precedence of his own, he knows that he can do so by giving his name that complement which hitherto it has lacked, which will give it priority over other names heraldically its equals : such as political power, a literary or an artistic reputation, or a large fortune. And so what he saves by avoiding the society of the ineffective country squires, after whom all the professional families run helter-skelter, but of his intimacy with whom, were he to profess it, a prince would think nothing, he will lavish on the politicians who (free-masons, or worse, though they be) can advance him in Diplomacy or " back " him in an election, and on the artists or scientists whose patronage can help him to " arrive " in those departments in which they excel, on everyone, in fact, who is in a position to confer a fresh distinction or to " bring off " a rich marriage.

But in the character of M. de Norpois there was this predominant feature, that, in the course of a long career of diplomacy, he had become imbued with that negative, methodical, conservative spirit, called " governmental ", which is common to all Governments and, under every Government, particularly inspires its Foreign Office. He

7

had imbibed, during that career, an aversion, a dread, a contempt for the methods of procedure, more or less revolutionary and in any event quite incorrect, which are those of an Opposition. Save in the case of a few illiterates—high or low, it makes no matter—by whom no difference in quality is perceptible, what attracts men one to another is not a common point of view but a consanguinity of spirit. An Academician of the kind of Legouvé, and therefore an upholder of the classics, would applaud Maxime Ducamp's or Mezière's eulogy of Victor Hugo with more fervour than that of Boileau by Claudel. A common Nationalism suffices to endear Barrès to his electors, who scarcely distinguish between him and M. Georges Berry, but does not endear him to those of his brother Academicians who, with a similar outlook on politics but a different type of mind, will prefer to him even such open adversaries as M. Ribot and M. Deschanel, with whom, in turn, the most loyal Monarchists feel themselves more closely allied than with Maurras or Léon Daudet, although these also are living in the hope of a glorious Restoration. Miserly in the use of words, not only from a professional scruple of prudence and reserve, but because words themselves have more value, present more subtleties of definition to men whose efforts, protracted over a decade, to bring two countries to an understanding, are condensed, translated—in a speech or in a protocol—into a single adjective, colourless in all appearance, but to them pregnant with a world of meaning, M. de Norpois was considered very stiff, at the Commission, where he sat next to my father, whom everyone else congratulated on the astonishing way in which the old Ambassador unbent to him. My father was himself more astonished than anyone. For not being, as a rule, very affable, his company was little sought outside his own intimate circle, a limitation which he used modestly and frankly to avow. He realised that these overtures were an outcome, in the diplomat, of that point of view which everyone adopts for himself in making his choice of friends, from which all a man's intellectual qualities, his refinement, his affection are a far less potent recommendation of him, when at the same time he bores or irritates one, than are the mere straightforwardness and good-humour of another man whom most people would regard as frivolous or even fatuous. " De Norpois has asked me to dinner again ; it's quite extraordinary ; everyone on the Commission is amazed, as he never has any personal relations with any of us. I am sure he's going to tell me something thrilling, again, about the 'Seventy war." My father knew that M. de Norpois had warned, had perhaps been alone in warning the Emperor of the growing strength and bellicose designs of Prussia, and that Bismarck rated his intelligence most highly. Only the other day, at the Opera, during the gala performance given for King Theodosius, the newspapers had all drawn attention to the long conversation which that Monarch had held with M. de Norpois. " I must ask him whether the King's visit had any real significance," my father went on, for he was keenly interested in foreign politics. " I know old Norpois keeps very close as a rule, but when he's with me he opens out quite charmingly."

As for my mother, perhaps the Ambassador had not the type of mind towards which she felt herself most attracted. I should add that his conversation furnished so exhaustive a glossary of the superannuated forms of speech peculiar to a certain profession, class and period—a period which, for that profession and that class, might be said not to have altogether passed away—that I sometimes regret that I have not kept any literal record simply of the things that I have heard him say. I should thus have obtained an effect of old-fashioned courtesy by the same process and at as little expense as that actor at the Palais-Royal who, when asked where on earth he managed to find his astounding hats, answered, "I do not find my hats. I keep them." In a word, I suppose that my mother considered M. de Norpois a trifle "out-of-date", which was by no means a fault in her eyes, so far as manners were concerned, but attracted her less in the region—not, in this instance, of ideas, for those of M. de Norpois were extremely modern—but of idiom. She felt, however, that she was paying a delicate compliment to her husband when she spoke admiringly of the diplomat who had shewn so remarkable a predilection for him. By confirming in my father's mind the good opinion that he already had of M. de Norpois, and so inducing him to form a good opinion of himself also, she knew that she was carrying out that one of her wifely duties which consisted in making life pleasant and comfortable for her husband, just as when she saw to it that his dinner was perfectly cooked and served in silence. And as she was incapable of deceiving my father, she compelled herself to admire the old Ambassador, so as to be able to praise him with sincerity. Incidentally she could naturally, and did appreciate his kindness, his somewhat antiquated courtesy (so ceremonious that when, as he was walking along the street, his tall figure rigidly erect, he caught sight of my mother driving past, before raising his hat to her he would fling away the cigar that he had just lighted) ; his conversation, so elaborately circumspect, in which he referred as seldom as possible to himself and always considered what might interest the person to whom he was speaking ; his promptness in answering a letter, which was so astonishing that whenever my father, just after posting one himself to M. de Norpois, saw his handwriting upon an envelope, his first thought was always one of annoyance that their letters must, unfortunately, have crossed in the post ; which, one was led to suppose, bestowed upon him the special and luxurious privilege of extraordinary deliveries and collections at all hours of the day and night. My mother marvelled at his being so punctilious although so busy, so friendly although so much in demand, never realising that " although ", with such people, is invariably an unrecognised " because ", and that (just as old men are always wonderful for their age, and kings extraordinarily simple, and country cousins astonishingly well-informed) it was the same system of habits that enabled M. de Norpois to undertake so many duties and to be so methodical in answering letters, to go everywhere and to be so friendly when he came to us. Moreover she made the mistake which everyone makes who is unduly modest; she rated everything that concerned herself below, and consequently outside the range of other people's duties and engagements. The letter which it seemed to her so meritorious in my father's friend to have written us promptly, since in the course of the day he must have had ever so many letters to write, she excepted from that great number of letters, of which actually it was a unit ; in the same way she did not consider that dining with us was, for M. de Norpois, merely one of the innumerable activities of his social life ; she never guessed that the Ambassador had trained himself, long ago, to look upon dining-out as one of his diplomatic functions, and to display, at table, an inveterate charm which it would have been too much to have expected him specially to discard when he came to dine with us.

The evening on which M. de Norpois first appeared at our table, in a year when I still went to play in the Champs-Elysées, has remained fixed in my memory because the afternoon of the same day was that upon which I at last went to hear Berma, at a *matinée,* in *Phèdre,* and also because in talking to M. de Norpois I realised suddenly, and in a new and different way, how completely the feelings aroused in me by all that concerned Gilberte Swann and her parents differed from any that the same family could inspire in anyone else.

It was no doubt the sight of the depression in which I was plunged by the approach of the New Year holidays, in which, as she herself had informed me, I was to see nothing of Gilberte, that prompted my mother one day, in the hope of distracting my mind, to suggest, " If you are still so anxious to hear Berma, I think that your father would allow you perhaps to go ; your grandmother can take you."

But it was because M. de Norpois had told him that he ought to let me hear Berma, that it was an experience for a young man to remember in later life, that my father, who had hitherto been so resolutely opposed to my going and wasting my time, with the added risk of my falling ill again, on what he used to shock my grandmother by calling " futilities ", was now not far from regarding this manner of spending an afternoon as included, in some vague way, in the list of precious formulae for success in a brilliant career. My grandmother, who, in renouncing on my behalf the profit which, according to her, I should have derived from hearing Berma, had made a considerable sacrifice in the interests of my health, was surprised to find that this last had become of no account at a mere word from M. de Norpois. Reposing the unconquerable hopes of her rationalist spirit in the strict course of fresh air and early hours which had been prescribed for me, she now deplored, as something disastrous, this infringement that I was to make of my rules, and in a tone of despair protested, " How easily led you are ! " to my father, who replied angrily " What ! So it's you that are for not letting him go, now. That is really too much, after your telling us all day and every day that it would be so good for him."

M. de Norpois had also brought about a change in my father's plans in a matter of far greater importance to myself. My father had always meant me to become a diplomat, and I could not endure the thought that, even if I did have to stay for some years, first, at the Ministry, I should run the risk of being sent, later on, as Ambassador, to capitals in which no Gilberte dwelt. I should have preferred to return to the literary career that I had planned for myself, and had then abandoned, years before, in my wanderings along the Guermantes way. But my father had steadily opposed my devoting myself to literature, which he regarded as vastly inferior to diplomacy, refusing even to dignify it with the title of career, until the day when M. de Norpois, who had little love for the more recent generations of diplomatic agents, assured him that it was quite possible, by writing, to attract

13

as much attention, to receive as much consideration, to exercise as much influence, and at the same time to preserve more independence than in the Embassies.

"Well, well, I should never have believed it. Old Norpois doesn't at all disapprove of your idea of taking up writing," my father had reported. And as he had a certain amount of influence himself, he imagined that there was nothing that could not be "arranged", no problem for which a happy solution might not be found in the conversation of people who "counted". "I shall bring him back to dinner, one of these days, from the Commission. You must talk to him a little, and let him see what he thinks of you. Write something good that you can shew him ; he is an intimate friend of the editor of the *Deux-Mondes* ; he will get you in there ; he will arrange it all, the cunning old fox ; and, upon my soul, he seems to think that diplomacy, nowadays—— !"

My happiness in the prospect of not being separated from Gilberte made me desirous, but not capable, of writing something good which could be shewn to M. de Norpois. After a few laboured pages, weariness made the pen drop from my fingers ; I cried with anger at the thought that I should never have any talent, that I was not "gifted", that I could not even take advantage of the chance that M. de Norpois's coming visit was to offer me of spending the rest of my life in Paris. The recollection that I was to be taken to hear Berma alone distracted me from my grief. But just as I did not wish to see any storms except on those coasts where they raged with most violence, so I should not have cared to hear the great actress except in one of those classic parts in which Swann had told me that she touched the sublime. For when it is in the hope of making a priceless discovery that we desire to receive certain impressions from nature or from works of art, we have certain scruples about allowing our soul to gather, instead of these, other, inferior, impressions, which are liable to make us form a false estimate of the value of Beauty. Berma in *Andromaque*, in *Les Caprices de Marianne*, in *Phèdre*, was one of those famous spectacles which my imagination had so long desired. I should enjoy the same rapture as on the day when in a gondola I glided to the foot of the Titian of the Frari or the Carpaccios of San Giorgio dei Schiavoni, were I ever to hear Berma repeat the lines beginning,

> "On dit qu'un prompt départ vous éloigne de nous,
>   Seigneur,——"

I was familiar with them from the simple reproduction in black and white which was given of them upon the printed page; but my heart beat furiously at the thought—as of the realisation of a long-planned voyage—that I should at length behold them, bathed and brought to life in the atmosphere and sunshine of the voice of gold. A Carpaccio in Venice, Berma in *Phèdre*, masterpieces of pictorial or dramatic art which the glamour, the dignity attaching to them made so living to me, that is to say so indivisible, that if I had been taken to see Carpaccios in one of the galleries of the Louvre, or Berma in some piece of which I had never heard, I should not have experienced the same delicious amazement at finding myself at length, with wide-open eyes, before the unique and inconceivable object of so many thousand dreams. Then, while I waited, expecting to derive from Berma's playing the revelation of certain aspects of nobility and tragic grief, it seemed to me that whatever greatness, whatever truth there might be in her playing must be enhanced if the actress imposed it upon a work of real value, instead of what would, after all, be but embroidering a pattern of truth and beauty upon a commonplace and vulgar web.

Finally, if I went to hear Berma in a new piece, it would not be easy for me to judge of her art, of her diction, since I should not be able to differentiate between a text which was not already familiar and what she added to it by her intonations and gestures, an addition which would seem to me to be embodied in the play itself ; whereas the old plays, the classics which I knew by heart, presented themselves to me as vast and empty walls, reserved and made ready for my inspection, on which I should be able to appreciate without restriction the devices by which Berma would cover them, as with frescoes, with the perpetually fresh treasures of her inspiration. Unfortunately, for some years now, since she had retired from the great theatres, to make the fortune of one on the boulevards where she was the " star ", she had ceased to appear in classic parts ; and in vain did I scan the hoardings ; they never advertised any but the newest pieces, written specially for her by authors in fashion at the moment. When, one morning, as I stood searching the column of announcements to find the afternoon performances for the week of the New Year holidays, I saw there for the first time—at the foot of the bill, after some probably insignificant curtain-raiser, whose title was opaque to me because it had latent in it all the details of an action of which I was ignorant—two acts of *Phèdre* with Mme. Berma, and, on the following afternoons, *Le Demi-Monde, Les Caprices de Marianne,* names which, like that of *Phèdre,* were for me transparent, filled with light only, so familiar were those works to me, illuminated to their very depths by the revealing smile of art. They seemed to me to invest with a fresh nobility Mme. Berma herself when I read in the newspapers, after the programme of these performances, that it was she who had decided to shew herself once more to the public in some of her early creations. She was conscious, then, that certain stage-parts have an interest which survives the novelty of their first production or the success of a revival ; she regarded them, when interpreted by herself, as museum pieces which it might be instructive to set before the eyes of the generation which had admired her in them long ago, or of that which had never yet seen her in them. In thus advertising, in the middle of a column of plays intended only to while away an evening, this *Phèdre,* a title no longer than any of the rest, nor set in different type, she added something indescribable, as though a hostess, introducing you, before you all go in to dinner, to her other guests, were to mention, casually, amid the string of names which are the names of guests and nothing more, and without any change of tone:—" M. Anatole France."

The doctor who was attending me—the same who had forbidden me to travel—advised my parents not to let me go to the theatre ; I should only be ill again afterwards, perhaps for weeks, and should in the long run derive more pain than pleasure from the experience. The fear of this might have availed to stop me, if what I had anticipated from such a spectacle had been only a pleasure for which a subsequent pain could so compensate as to cancel it. But what I demanded from this performance—just as from the visit to Balbec, the visit to Venice for which I had so intensely longed—was something quite different from pleasure ; a series of verities pertaining to a world more real than that in which I lived, which, once acquired, could never be taken from me again by any of the trivial incidents—even though it were the cause of bodily suffering—of my otiose existence. At best, the pleasure which I was to feel during the performance appeared to me as the perhaps inevitable form of the perception of these truths ; and I hoped only that the illness which had been forecast for me would not begin until the play was finished, so that my pleasure should not be in any way compromised or spoiled. I implored my parents, who, after the doctor's visit, were no longer inclined to let me go to *Phèdre*. I repeated, all day long, to myself, the speech beginning,

"On dit qu'un prompt départ vous éloigne de nous,——"

seeking out every intonation that could be put into it, so as to be able better to measure my surprise at the way which Berma would have found of uttering the lines. Concealed, like the Holy of Holies, beneath the veil that screened her from my gaze, behind which I invested her, every moment, with a fresh aspect, according to which of the words of Bergotte—in the pamphlet that Gilberte had found for me—was passing through my mind ; " plastic nobility ", " Christian austerity " or " Jansenist pallor ", " Princess of Troezen and of Cleves " or " Mycenean drama ", " Delphic symbol ", " Solar myth " ; that divine Beauty, whom Berma's acting was to reveal to me, night and day, upon an altar perpetually illumined, sat en-

18

throned in the sanctuary of my mind, my mind for which not itself but my stern, my fickle parents were to decide whether or not it was to enshrine, and for all time, the perfections of the Deity unveiled, in the same spot where was now her invisible form. And with my eyes fixed upon that inconceivable image, I strove from morning to night to overcome the barriers which my family were putting in my way. But when those had at last fallen, when my mother—albeit this *matinée* was actually to coincide with the meeting of the Commission from which my father had promised to bring M. de Norpois home to dinner—had said to me, "Very well, we don't wish you to be unhappy ;—if you think that you will enjoy it so very much, you must go ; that's all ; " when this day of theatre-going, hitherto forbidden and unattainable, depended now only upon myself, then for the first time, being no longer troubled by the wish that it might cease to be impossible, I asked myself if it were desirable, if there were not other reasons than my parents' prohibition which should make me abandon my design. In the first place, whereas I had been detesting them for their cruelty, their consent made them now so dear to me that the thought of causing them pain stabbed me also with a pain through which the purpose of life shewed itself as the pursuit not of truth but of loving-kindness, and life itself seemed good or evil only as my parents were happy or sad. "I would rather not go, if it hurts you," I told my mother, who, on the contrary, strove hard to expel from my mind any lurking fear that she might regret my going, since that, she said, would spoil the pleasure that I should otherwise derive from *Phèdre,* and it was the thought of my pleasure that had induced my father and her to re-

verse their earlier decision. But then this sort of obligation to find a pleasure in the performance seemed to me
very burdensome. Besides, if I returned home ill, should
I be well again in time to be able to go to the Champs-
Elysées as soon as the holidays were over and Gilberte
returned ? Against all these arguments I set, so as to decide which course I should take, the idea, invisible
there behind its veil, of the perfections of Berma. I cast
into one pan of the scales "Making Mamma unhappy ", "risking not being able to go on the Champs-
Elysées ", and into the other, " Jansenist pallor ", " Solar
myth ", until the words themselves grew dark and clouded
in my mind's vision, ceased to say anything to me, lost
all their force ; and gradually my hesitations became so
painful that if I had now decided upon the theatre it
would have been only that I might bring them to an end,
and be delivered from them once and for all. It would
have been to fix a term to my sufferings, and no longer in
the expectation of an intellectual benediction, yielding to
the attractions of perfection, that I would let myself be
taken, not now to the Wise Goddess, but to the stern, implacable Divinity, featureless and unnamed, who had been
secretly substituted for her behind the veil. But suddenly everything was altered. My desire to go and hear
Berma received a fresh stimulus which enabled me to
await the coming of the *matinée* with impatience and with
joy ; having gone to take up, in front of the column on
which the playbills were, my daily station, as excruciat-
ing, of late, as that of a stylite saint, I had seen there,
still moist and wrinkled, the complete bill of *Phèdre*,
which had just been pasted up for the first time (and
on which, I must confess, the rest of the cast furnished

20

no additional attraction which could help me to decide). But it gave to one of the points between which my indecision wavered a form at once more concrete and—inasmuch as the bill was dated not from the day on which I read it but from that on which the performance would take place, and from the very hour at which the curtain would rise—almost imminent, well on the way, already, to its realisation, so that I jumped for joy before the column at the thought that on that day, and at that hour precisely, I should be sitting there in my place, ready to hear the voice of Berma ; and for fear lest my parents might not now be in time to secure two good seats for my grandmother and myself, I raced back to the house, whipped on by the magic words which had now taken the place, in my mind, of " Jansenist pallor " and " Solar myth " ;—" Ladies will not be admitted to the stalls in hats. The doors will be closed at two o'clock."

Alas ! that first *matinée* was to prove a bitter disappointment. My father offered to drop my grandmother and me at the theatre, on his way to the Commission. Before leaving the house he said to my mother : " See that you have a good dinner for us to-night ; you remember, I'm bringing de Norpois back with me." My mother had not forgotten. And all that day, and overnight, Françoise, rejoicing in the opportunity to devote herself to that art of the kitchen,—of which she was indeed a past-master, stimulated, moreover, by the prospect of having a new guest to feed, the consciousness that she would have to compose, by methods known to her alone, a dish of beef in jelly, had been living in the effervescence of creation ; since she attached the utmost importance to the intrinsic quality of the materials which were to enter into the fabric of her work, she had gone herself to the Halles to procure the best cuts of rump-steak, shin of beef, calves'-feet, as Michelangelo passed eight months in the mountains of Carrara choosing the most perfect blocks of marble for the monument of Julius II.—Françoise expended on these comings and goings so much ardour that Mamma, at the sight of her flaming cheeks, was alarmed lest our old servant should make herself ill with overwork, like the sculptor of the Tombs of the Medici in the quarries of Pietrasanta. And overnight Françoise had sent to be cooked in the baker's oven, shielded with breadcrumbs, like a block of pink marble packed in sawdust, what she called a " Nev'-York ham ". Believing the language to be less rich than it actually was in words, and her own ears less trustworthy, the first time that she heard anyone mention York ham she had thought, no doubt,—feeling it to be hardly conceivable that the dictionary could be so prodigal as to include at once a " York " and a " New York "—that she had misheard what was said, and that the ham was really called by the name already familiar to her. And so, ever since, the word York was preceded in her ears, or before her eyes when she read it in an advertisement, by the affix " New " which she pronounced " Nev' ". And it was with the most perfect faith that she would say to her kitchen-maid : " Go and fetch me a ham from Olida's. Madame told me especially to get a Nev'-York." On that particular day, if Françoise was consumed by the burning certainty of creative genius, my lot was the cruel anxiety of the seeker after truth. No doubt, so long as I had not yet heard Berma speak, I still felt some pleas-

ure. I felt it in the little square that lay in front of the
theatre, in which, in two hours' time, the bare boughs of
the chestnut trees would gleam with a metallic lustre as
the lighted gas-lamps shewed up every detail of their
structure ; before the attendants in the box-office, the selection of whom, their promotion, all their destiny depended upon the great artist—for she alone held power
in the theatre, where ephemeral managers followed one
after the other in an obscure succession—who took our
tickets without even glancing at us, so preoccupied were
they with their anxiety lest any of Mme. Berma's instructions had not been duly transmitted to the new members
of the staff, lest it was not clearly, everywhere, understood
that the hired applause must never sound for her, that the
windows must all be kept open so long as she was not on
the stage, and every door closed tight, the moment that
she appeared ; that a bowl of hot water must be concealed
somewhere close to her, to make the dust settle : and, for
that matter, at any moment now her carriage, drawn by
a pair of horses with flowing manes, would be stopping
outside the theatre, she would alight from it muffled in
furs, and, crossly acknowledging everyone's salute, would
send one of her attendants to find out whether a stage
box had been kept for her friends, what the temperature
was "in front", who were in the other boxes, if the programme sellers were looking smart ; theatre and public
being to her no more than a second, an outermost cloak
which she would put on, and the medium, the more or less
"good" conductor through which her talent would have
to pass. I was happy, too, in the theatre itself ; since I
had made the discovery that—in contradiction of the picture so long entertained by my childish imagination—

there was but one stage for everybody, I had supposed that I should be prevented from seeing it properly by the presence of the other spectators, as one is when in the thick of a crowd ; now I registered the fact that, on the contrary, thanks to an arrangement which is, so to speak, symbolical of all spectatorship, everyone feels himself to be the centre of the theatre ; which explained to me why, when Françoise had been sent once to see some melo-drama from the top gallery, she had assured us on her return that her seat had been the best in the house, and that instead of finding herself too far from the stage she had been positively frightened by the mysterious and liv-ing proximity of the curtain. My pleasure increased further when I began to distinguish behind the said low-ered curtain such confused rappings as one hears through the shell of an egg before the chicken emerges, sounds which speedily grew louder and suddenly, from that world which, impenetrable by our eyes, yet scrutinised us with its own, addressed themselves, and to us indubitably, in the imperious form of three consecutive hammer-blows as moving as any signals from the planet Mars. And— once this curtain had risen,—when on the stage a writing-table and a fireplace, in no way out of the ordinary, had indicated that the persons who were about to enter would be, not actors come to recite, as I had seen them once and heard them at an evening party, but real people, just living their lives at home, on whom I was thus able to spy without their seeing me—my pleasure still endured ; it was broken by a momentary uneasiness ; just as I was straining my ears in readiness before the piece began, two men entered the theatre from the side of the stage, who must have been very angry with each other, for they were talking so loud that in the auditorium, where there were at least a thousand people, we could hear every word, whereas in quite a small *café* one is obliged to call the waiter and ask what it is that two men, who appear to be quarrelling, are saying ; but at that moment, while I sat astonished to find that the audience was listening to them without protest, drowned as it was in a universal silence upon which broke, presently, a laugh here and there, I understood that these insolent fellows were the actors, and that the short piece known as the " curtain-raiser " had now begun. It was followed by an interval so long that the audience, who had returned to their places, grew impatient and began to stamp their feet. I was terrified at this ; for just as in the report of a criminal trial, when I read that some noble-minded person was coming, against his own interests, to testify on behalf of an innocent prisoner, I was always afraid that they would not be nice enough to him, would not shew enough gratitude, would not recompense him lavishly, and that he, in disgust, would then range himself on the side of injustice ; so now attributing to genius, in this respect, the same qualities as to virtue, I was afraid lest Berma, annoyed by the bad behaviour of so ill-bred an audience—in which, on the other hand, I should have liked her to recognise, with satisfaction, a few celebrities to whose judgment she would be bound to attach importance—should express her discontent and disdain by acting badly. And I gazed appealingly round me at these stamping brutes who were about to shatter, in their insensate rage, the rare and fragile impression which I had come to seek. The last moments of my pleasure were during the opening scenes of *Phèdre*. The heroine herself does not appear in these first scenes of the second act ; and yet, as soon as the curtain rose, and another curtain, of red velvet this time, was parted in the middle (a curtain which was used to halve the depth of the stage in all the plays in which the "star" appeared), an actress entered from the back who had the face and voice which, I had been told, were those of Berma. The cast must therefore have been changed ; all the trouble that I had taken in studying the part of the wife of Theseus was wasted. But a second actress now responded to the first. I must, then, have been mistaken in supposing that the first was Berma, for the second even more closely resembled her, and, more than the other, had her diction. Both of them, moreover, enriched their parts with noble gestures—which I could vividly distinguish, and could appreciate in their relation to the text, while they raised and let fall the lovely folds of their tunics—and also with skilful changes of tone, now passionate, now ironical, which made me realise the significance of lines that I had read to myself at home without paying sufficient attention to what they really meant. But all of a sudden, in the cleft of the red curtain that veiled her sanctuary, as in a frame, appeared a woman, and simultaneously with the fear that seized me, far more vexing than Berma's fear could be, lest someone should upset her by opening a window, or drown one of her lines by rustling a programme, or annoy her by applauding the others and by not applauding her enough ;—in my own fashion, still more absolute than Berma's, of considering from that moment theatre, audience, play and my own body only as an acoustic medium of no importance, save in the degree to which it was favourable to the inflexions of that voice,—I realised that the two actresses whom I had been for some minutes admiring bore not the least resemblance to her whom I had come to hear. But at the same time all my pleasure had ceased ; in vain might I strain towards Berma eyes, ears, mind, so as not to let one morsel escape me of the reasons which she would furnish for my admiring her, I did not succeed in gathering a single one. I could not even, as I could with her companions, distinguish in her diction and in her playing intelligent intonations, beautiful gestures. I listened to her as though I were reading *Phèdre,* or as though Phaedra herself had at that moment uttered the words that I was hearing, without its appearing that Berma's talent had added anything at all to them. I could have wished, so as to be able to explore them fully, so as to attempt to discover what it was in them that was beautiful, to arrest, to immobilise for a time before my senses every intonation of the artist's voice, every expression of her features ; at least I did attempt, by dint of my mental agility in having, before a line came, my attention ready and tuned to catch it, not to waste upon preparations any morsel of the precious time that each word, each gesture occupied, and, thanks to the intensity of my observation, to manage to penetrate as far into them as if I had had whole hours to spend upon them, by myself. But how short their duration was ! Scarcely had a sound been received by my ear than it was displaced there by another. In one scene, where Berma stands motionless for a moment, her arm raised to the level of a face bathed, by some piece of stagecraft, in a greenish light, before a back-cloth painted to represent the sea, the whole house broke out in applause ; but already the actress had moved, and the picture that I should have liked to study existed no longer. I told my grandmother that I could not see very well ; she handed me her glasses. Only, when one believes in the reality of a thing, making it visible by artificial means is not quite the same as feeling that it is close at hand. I thought now that it was no longer Berma at whom I was looking, but her image in a magnifying glass. I put the glasses down, but then possibly the image that my eye received of her, diminished by distance, was no more exact; which of the two Bermas was the real ? As for her speech to Hippolyte, I had counted enormously upon that, since, to judge by the ingenious significance which her companions were disclosing to me at every moment in less beautiful parts, she would certainly render it with intonations more surprising than any which, when reading the play at home, I had contrived to imagine ; but she did not attain to the heights which Œnone or Aricie would naturally have reached, she planed down into a uniform flow of melody the whole of a passage in which there were mingled together contradictions so striking that the least intelligent of tragic actresses, even the pupils of an academy could not have missed their effect ; besides which, she ran through the speech so rapidly that it was only when she had come to the last line that my mind became aware of the deliberate monotony which she had imposed on it throughout.

Then, at last, a sense of admiration did possess me, provoked by the frenzied applause of the audience. I mingled my own with theirs, endeavouring to prolong the general sound so that Berma, in her gratitude, should surpass herself, and I be certain of having heard her on one of her great days. A curious thing, by the way, was that the moment when this storm of public enthusiasm broke loose was, as I afterwards learned, that in which Berma reveals one of her richest treasures. It would appear that certain transcendent realities emit all around them a radiance to which the crowd is sensitive. So it is that when any great event occurs, when on a distant frontier an army is in jeopardy, or defeated, or victorious, the vague and conflicting reports which we receive, from which an educated man can derive little enlightenment, stimulate in the crowd an emotion by which that man is surprised, and in which, once expert criticism has informed him of the actual military situation, he recognises the popular perception of that " aura " which surrounds momentous happenings, and which may be visible hundreds of miles away. One learns of a victory either after the war is over, or at once, from the hilarious joy of one's hall porter. One discovers the touch of genius in Berma's acting a week after one has heard her, in the criticism of some review, or else on the spot, from the thundering acclamation of the stalls. But this immediate recognition by the crowd was mingled with a hundred others, all quite erroneous ; the applause came, most often, at wrong moments, apart from the fact that it was mechanically produced by the effect of the applause that had gone before, just as in a storm, once the sea is sufficiently disturbed, it will continue to swell, even after the wind has begun to subside. No matter ; the more I applauded, the better, it seemed to me, did Berma act. " I say," came from a woman sitting near me, of no great social pretensions, " she fairly gives it you, she does ; you'd think she'd do herself an injury, the way she runs about. I call that acting, don't you ? " And happy to find these reasons for Berma's superiority, though not

29

without a suspicion that they no more accounted for it than would for that of the Gioconda or of Benvenuto's Perseus a peasant's gaping "That's a good bit of work. It's all gold, look! Fine, ain't it?", I greedily imbibed the strong wine of this popular enthusiasm. I felt, all the same, when the curtain had fallen for the last time, disappointed that the pleasure for which I had so longed had been no greater, but at the same time I felt the need to prolong it, not to depart for ever, when I left the theatre, from this strange life of the stage which had, for a few hours, been my own, from which I should be tearing myself away, as though I were going into exile, when I returned to my own home, had I not hoped there to learn a great deal more about Berma from her admirer, to whom I was indebted already for the permission to go to *Phèdre,* M. de Norpois. I was introduced to him before dinner by my father, who summoned me into his study for the purpose. As I entered, the Ambassador rose, held out his hand, bowed his tall figure and fixed his blue eyes attentively on my face. As the foreign visitors who used to be presented to him, in the days when he still represented France abroad, were all more or less (even the famous singers) persons of note, with regard to whom he could tell, when he met them, that he would be able to say, later on, when he heard their names mentioned in Paris or in Petersburg, that he remembered perfectly the evening he had spent with them at Munich or Sofia, he had formed the habit of impressing upon them, by his affability, the pleasure with which he was making their acquaintance; but in addition to this, being convinced that in the life of European capitals, in contact at once with all the interesting personalities that passed through

them and with the manners and customs of the native
populations, one acquired a deeper insight than could be
gained from books into the intellectual movement throughout Europe, he would exercise upon each newcomer his
keen power of observation, so as to decide at once with
what manner of man he had to deal. The Government
had not for some time now entrusted to him a post abroad,
but still, as soon as anyone was introduced to him, his
eyes, as though they had not yet been informed of their
master's retirement, began their fruitful observation, while
by his whole attitude he endeavoured to convey that the
stranger's name was not unknown to him. And so, all the
time, while he spoke to me kindly and with the air of importance of a man who is conscious of the vastness of
his own experience, he never ceased to examine me with
a sagacious curiosity, and to his own profit, as though I
had been some exotic custom, some historic and instructive
building or some "star" upon his course. And in this
way he gave proof at once, in his attitude towards me, of
the majestic benevolence of the sage Mentor and of the
zealous curiosity of the young Anacharsis.

He offered me absolutely no opening to the *Revue des
Deux-Mondes*, but put a number of questions to me on
what I had been doing and reading ; asked what were my
own inclinations, which I heard thus spoken of for the
first time as though it might be a quite reasonable thing
to obey their promptings, whereas hitherto I had always
supposed it to be my duty to suppress them. Since they
attracted me towards Literature, he did not dissuade me
from that course ; on the contrary, he spoke of it with
deference, as of some venerable personage whose select
circle, in Rome or at Dresden, one remembers with pleas-

ure, and regrets only that one's multifarious duties in life enable one to revisit it so seldom. He appeared to be envying me, with an almost jovial smile, the delightful hours which, more fortunate than himself and more free, I should be able to spend with such a Mistress. But the very terms that he employed shewed me Literature as something entirely different from the image that I had formed of it at Combray, and I realised that I had been doubly right in abandoning my intention. Until now, I had reckoned only that I had not the "gift" for writing ; now M. de Norpois took from me the ambition also. I wanted to express to him what had been my dreams ; trembling with emotion, I was painfully apprehensive that all the words which I could utter would not be the sincerest possible equivalent of what I had felt, what I had never yet attempted to formulate ; that is to say that my words had no clear significance. Perhaps by a professional habit, perhaps by virtue of the calm that is acquired by every important personage whose advice is commonly sought, and who, knowing that he will keep the control of the conversation in his own hands, allows the other party to fret, to struggle, to take his time ; perhaps also to emphasise the dignity of his head (Greek, according to himself, despite his sweeping whiskers), M. de Norpois, while anything was being explained to him, would preserve a facial immobility as absolute as if you had been addressing some ancient and unhearing bust in a museum. Until suddenly, falling upon you like an auctioneer's hammer, or a Delphic oracle, the Ambassador's voice, as he replied to you, would be all the more impressive, in that nothing in his face had allowed you to guess what sort of impression you had made on him, or what opinion he was about to express.

" Precisely ; " he suddenly began, as though the case were now heard and judged, and after allowing me to writhe in increasing helplessness beneath those motionless eyes which never for an instant left my face. " There is the case of the son of one of my friends, which, *mutatis mutandis,* is very much like yours." He adopted in speaking of our common tendency the same reassuring tone as if it had been a tendency not to literature but to rheumatics, and he had wished to assure me that it would not necessarily prove fatal. " He too has chosen to leave the Quai d'Orsay, although the way had been paved for him there by his father, and without caring what people might say, he has settled down to write. And certainly, he's had no reason to regret it. He published two years ago— of course, he's much older than you, you understand—a book dealing with the Sense of the Infinite on the Western Shore of Victoria Nyanza, and this year he has brought out a little thing, not so important as the other, but very brightly, in places perhaps almost too pointedly written, on the Repeating Rifle in the Bulgarian Army ; and these have put him quite in a class by himself. He's gone pretty far already, and he's not the sort of man to stop half way ; I happen to know that (without any suggestion, of course, of his standing for election) his name has been mentioned several times, in conversation, and not at all unfavourably, at the Academy of Moral Sciences. And so, one can't say yet, of course, that he has reached the pinnacle of fame, still he has made his way, by sheer industry, to a very fine position indeed, and success—

which doesn't always come only to agitators and mischief-
makers and men who make trouble which is usually more
than they are prepared to take—success has crowned his
efforts."

My father, seeing me already, in a few years' time, an
Academician, was tasting a contentment which M. de
Norpois raised to the supreme pitch when, after a momentary hesitation in which he appeared to be calculating
the possible consequences of so rash an act, he handed
me his card and said : "Why not go and see him yourself ? Tell him, I sent you. He may be able to give you
some good advice," plunging me by his words into as
painful a state of anxiety as if he had told me that, next
morning, I was to embark as cabin-boy on board a sailing
ship, and to go round the world.

My Aunt Léonie had bequeathed to me, together with
all sorts of other things and much of her furniture, with
which it was difficult to know what to do, almost all her
unsettled estate—revealing thus after her death an affection for me which I had hardly suspected in her lifetime.
My father, who was trustee of this estate until I came of
age, now consulted M. de Norpois with regard to several
of the investments. He recommended certain stocks bearing a low rate of interest, which he considered particularly
sound, notably English consols and Russian four per cents.
"With absolutely first class securities such as those," said
M. de Norpois, "even if your income from them is nothing very great, you may be certain of never losing any of
your capital." My father then told him, roughly, what
else he had bought. M. de Norpois gave a just perceptible smile of congratulation ; like all capitalists, he regarded wealth as an enviable thing, but thought it more

34

delicate to compliment people upon their possessions only by a half-indicated sign of intelligent sympathy ; on the other hand, as he was himself immensely rich, he felt that he shewed his good taste by seeming to regard as considerable the meagre revenues of his friends, with a happy and comforting resilience to the superiority of his own. He made amends for this by congratulating my father, without hesitation, on the " composition " of his list of investments, selected " with so sure, so delicate, so fine a taste." You would have supposed, to hear him, that he attributed to the relative values of investments, and even to investments themselves something akin to aesthetic merit. Of one, comparatively recent and still little known, which my father mentioned, M. de Norpois, like the people who have always read the books of which, you imagine, you yourself alone have ever heard, said at once, " Ah, yes, I used to amuse myself for some time with watching it in the papers ; it was quite interesting," with the retrospective smile of a regular subscriber who has read the latest novel already, in monthly instalments, in his magazine. " It would not be at all a bad idea to apply for some of this new issue. It is distinctly attractive ; they are offering it at a most tempting discount." But when he came to some of the older investments, my father, who could not remember their exact names, which it was easy to confuse with others of the same kind, opened a drawer and shewed the securities themselves to the Ambassador. The sight of them enchanted me. They were ornamented with cathedral spires and allegorical figures, like the old, romantic editions that I had pored over as a child. All the products of one period have something in common ; the artists who illustrate the poetry of their generation are the same artists who are employed by the big financial houses. And nothing reminds me so much of the monthly parts of *Notre-Dame de Paris,* and of various books by Gérard de Nerval, that used to hang outside the grocer's door at Combray, than does, in its rectangular and flowery border, supported by recumbent river-gods, a "personal share" in the Water Company.

The contempt which my father had for my kind of intelligence was so far tempered by his natural affection for me that, in practice, his attitude towards anything that I might do was one of blind indulgence. And so he had no qualm about telling me to fetch a little "prose poem" which I had made up, years before, at Combray, while coming home from a walk. I had written it down in a state of exaltation which must, I felt certain, infect everyone who read it. But it was not destined to captivate M. de Norpois, for he handed it back to me without a word.

My mother, who had the most profound respect for all my father's occupations, came in now, timidly, to ask whether dinner might be served. She was afraid to interrupt a conversation in which she herself could have no part. And indeed my father was continually reminding the Marquis of some useful suggestion which they had decided to make at the next meeting of the Commission ; speaking in the peculiar tone always adopted, when in a strange environment by a pair of colleagues—as exclusive, in this respect, as two young men from the same college— whose professional routine has furnished them with a common fund of memories to which the others present have no access, and to which they are unwilling to refer before an audience.

But the absolute control over his facial muscles to which M. de Norpois had attained allowed him to listen without seeming to hear a word. At last my father became uneasy : " I had thought," he ventured, after an endless preamble, " of asking the advice of the Commission . . ." Then from the face of the noble virtuoso, who had been sitting inert as a player in an orchestra sits until the moment comes for him to begin his part, were uttered, with an even delivery, on a sharp note, and as though they were no more than the completion (but scored for a different voice) of the phrase that my father had begun, the words : " of which you will not hesitate, of course, to call a meeting ; more especially as the present members are all known to you personally, and there may be a change any day." This was not in itself a very remarkable ending. But the immobility that had preceded it made it detach itself with the crystal clarity, the almost malicious unexpectedness of those phrases in which the piano, silent until then, " takes up ", at a given moment, the violoncello to which one has just been listening, in a Mozart concerto.

" Well, did you enjoy your *matinée ?* " asked my father, as we moved to the dining-room ; meaning me to " shew off ", and with the idea that my enthusiasm would give M. de Norpois a good opinion of me. " He has just been to hear Berma. You remember, we were talking about it the other day," he went on, turning towards the diplomat, in the same tone of retrospective, technical, mysterious allusiveness as if he had been referring to a meeting of the Commission.

" You must have been enchanted, especially if you had never heard her before. Your father was alarmed at the effect that the little jaunt might have upon your health, which is none too good, I am told, none too robust. But I soon set his mind at rest. Theatres to-day are not what they were even twenty years ago. You have more or less comfortable seats now, and a certain amount of ventilation, although we have still a long way to go before we come up to Germany or England, which in that respect as in many others are immeasurably ahead of us. I have never seen Mme. Berma in *Phèdre,* but I have always heard that she is excellent in the part. You were charmed with her, of course ? "

M. de Norpois, a man a thousand times more intelligent than myself, must know that hidden truth which I had failed to extract from Berma's playing ; he knew, and would reveal it to me ; in answering his question I would implore him to let me know in what that truth consisted ; and he would tell me, and so justify me in the longing that I had felt to see and hear the actress. I had only a moment, I must make what use I could of it and bring my cross-examination to bear upon the essential points. But what were they ? Fastening my whole attention upon my own so confused impressions, with no thought of making M. de Norpois admire me, but only that of learning from him the truth that I had still to discover, I made no attempt to substitute ready-made phrases for the words that failed me—I stood there stammering, until finally, in the hope of provoking him into declaring what there was in Berma that was admirable, I confessed that I had been disappointed.

"What's that ? " cried my father, annoyed at the bad impression which this admission of my failure to appreciate the performance must make on M. de Norpois,

" What on earth do you mean ; you didn't enjoy it ? Why, your grandmother has been telling us that you sat there hanging on every word that Berma uttered, with your eyes starting out of your head ; that everyone else in the theatre seemed quite bored, beside you."

" Oh, yes, I was listening as hard as I could, trying to find out what it was that was supposed to be so wonderful about her. Of course, she's frightfully good, and all that . . ."

" If she is ' frightfully good ', what more do you want ? "

" One of the things that have undoubtedly contributed to the success of Mme. Berma," resumed M. de Norpois, turning with elaborate courtesy towards my mother, so as not to let her be left out of the conversation, and in conscientious fulfilment of his duty of politeness to the lady of the house, " is the perfect taste that she shews in selecting her parts ; thus she can always be assured of success, and success of the right sort. She hardly ever appears in anything trivial. Look how she has thrown herself into the part of Phèdre. And then, she brings the same good taste to the choice of her costumes, and to her acting. In spite of her frequent and lucrative tours in England and America, the vulgarity—I will not say of John Bull ; that would be unjust, at any rate to the England of the Victorian era—but of Uncle Sam has not infected her. No loud colours, no rant. And then that admirable voice, which has been of such service to her, with which she plays so delightfully—I should almost be tempted to describe it as a musical instrument ! "

My interest in Berma's acting had continued to grow ever since the fall of the curtain, because it was then no

longer compressed within the limits of reality ; but I felt
the need to find explanations for it ; moreover it had been
fixed with the same intensity, while Berma was on the
stage, upon everything that she offered, in the indivisi-
bility of a living whole, to my eyes and ears ; there was
nothing separate or distinct ; it welcomed, accordingly,
the discovery of a reasonable cause in these tributes paid
to the simplicity, to the good taste of the actress, it attracted them to itself by its power of absorption, seized
hold of them, as the optimism of a drunken man seizes
hold of the actions of his neighbour, in each of which he
finds an excuse for emotion. "He is right !" I told myself. "What a charming voice, what an absence of shrill-
ness, what simple costumes, what intelligence to have
chosen *Phèdre*. No ; I have not been disappointed !"

The cold beef, spiced with carrots, made its appearance,
couched by the Michelangelo of our kitchen upon enormous crystals of jelly, like transparent blocks of quartz.

"You have a chef of the first order, Madame," said M.
de Norpois, "and that is no small matter. I myself, who
have had, when abroad, to maintain a certain style in
housekeeping, I know how difficult it often is to find a
perfect master-cook. But this is a positive banquet that
you have set before us !"

And indeed Françoise, in the excitement of her ambition to make a success, for so distinguished a guest, of a
dinner the preparation of which had been obstructed by
difficulties worthy of her powers, had given herself such
trouble as she no longer took when we were alone, and had
recaptured her incomparable Combray manner.

"That is a thing you can't get in a chophouse,—in the
best of them, I mean ; a spiced beef in which the jelly

does not taste of glue and the beef has caught the flavour of the carrots ; it is admirable ! Allow me to come again," he went on, making a sign to shew that he wanted more of the jelly. " I should be interested to see how your Vatel managed a dish of quite a different kind ; I should like, for instance, to see him tackle a *bœuf Stroganoff.*"

M. de Norpois, so as to add his own contribution to the gaiety of the repast, entertained us with a number of the stories with which he was in the habit of regaling his colleagues in "the career", quoting now some ludicrous sentence uttered by a politician, an old offender, whose sentences were always long and packed with incoherent images, now some monumental epigram of a diplomat, sparkling with attic salt. But, to tell the truth, the criterion which for him set apart these two kinds of phrase in no way resembled that which I was in the habit of applying to literature. Most of the finer shades escaped me ; the words which he repeated with derision seemed to me not to differ very greatly from those which he found remarkable. He belonged to the class of men who, had we come to discuss the books that I liked, would have said ; "So you understand that, do you ? I must confess that I do not understand, I am not initiated," but I could have matched his attitude, for I did not grasp the wit or folly, the eloquence or pomposity which he found in a statement or a speech, and the absence of any perceptible reason for one's being badly and the other's well expressed made that sort of literature seem more mysterious, more obscure to me than any other. I could distinguish only that to repeat what everybody else was thinking was, in politics, the mark not of an inferior but of a superior mind. When

41

M. de Norpois made use of certain expressions which were "common form" in the newspapers, and uttered them with emphasis, one felt that they became an official pronouncement by the mere fact of his having employed them, and a pronouncement which would provoke a string of comment.

My mother was counting greatly upon the pineapple and truffle salad. But the Ambassador, after fastening for a moment on the confection the penetrating gaze of a trained observer, ate it with the inscrutable discretion of a diplomat, and without disclosing to us what he thought of it. My mother insisted upon his taking some more, which he did, but saying oniy, in place of the compliment for which she was hoping : "I obey, Madame, for I can see that it is, on your part, a positive ukase ! "

"We saw in the 'papers that you had a long talk with King Theodosius," my father ventured.

"Why, yes ; the King, who has a wonderful memory for faces, was kind enough to remember, when he noticed me in the stalls, that I had had the honour to meet him on several occasions at the Court of Bavaria, at a time when he had never dreamed of his oriental throne—to which, as you know, he was summoned by a European Congress, and indeed had grave doubts about accepting the invitation, regarding that particular sovereignty as unworthy of his race, the noblest, heraldically speaking, in the whole of Europe. An aide-de-camp came down to bid me pay my respects to his Majesty, whose command I hastened, naturally, to obey."

"And I trust, you are satisfied with the results of his visit ? "

"Enchanted ! One was justified in feeling some apprehension as to the manner in which a Sovereign who is still so young would handle a situation requiring tact, particularly at this highly delicate juncture. For my own part, I reposed entire confidence in the King's political sense. But I must confess that he far surpassed my expectations. The speech that he made at the Elysée, which, according to information that has come to me from a most authoritative source, was composed, from beginning to end, by himself, was fully deserving of the interest that it has aroused in all quarters. It was simply masterly ; a trifle daring, I quite admit, but with an audacity which, after all, has been fully justified by the event. Traditional diplomacy is all very well in its way, but in practice it has made his country and ours live in an hermetically sealed atmosphere in which it was no longer possible to breathe. Very well ! There is one method of letting in fresh air, obviously not one of the methods which one could officially recommend, but one which King Theodosius might allow himself to adopt—and that is to break the windows. Which he accordingly did, with a spontaneous good humour that delighted everybody, and also with an aptness in his choice of words in which one could at once detect the race of scholarly princes from whom he is descended through his mother. There can be no question that when he spoke of the ' affinities ' that bound his country to France, the expression, rarely as it may occur in the vocabulary of the Chancelleries, was a singularly happy one. You see that literary ability is no drawback, even in diplomacy, even upon a throne," he went on, turning for a moment to myself. "The community of interests had long been apparent, I quite admit, and the relations of the two Powers were excellent.

Still, it needed putting into words. The word was what we were all waiting for, it was chosen with marvellous aptitude ; you have seen the effect it had. For my part, I must confess I applauded openly."

" Your friend M. de Vaugoubert will be pleased, after preparing for the agreement all these years."

" All the more so that his Majesty, who is quite incorrigible, really, in some ways, had taken care to spring it on him as a surprise. And it did come as a complete surprise, incidentally, to everyone concerned, beginning with the Foreign Minister himself, who—I have heard—did not find it at all to his liking. It appears that someone spoke to him about it and that he replied, pretty sharply, and loud enough to be overheard by the people on either side of them : ' I have been neither consulted nor informed !' indicating clearly by that that he declined to accept any responsibility for the consequences. I must own that the incident has given rise to a great deal of comment, and I should not go so far as to deny," he went on with a malicious smile, " that certain of my colleagues, for whom the supreme law appears to be that of inertia, may have been shaken from their habitual repose. As for Vaugoubert, you are aware that he has been bitterly attacked for his policy of bringing that country into closer relations with France, which must have been more than ordinarily painful to him, he is so sensitive, such an exquisite nature. I can amply testify to that, since, for all that he is considerably my junior, I have had many dealings with him, we are friends of long standing and I know him intimately. Besides, who could help knowing him? His is a heart of crystal. Indeed, that is the one fault that there is to be found with him ; it is not necessary

44

for the heart of a diplomat to be as transparent as all that. Still, that does not prevent their talking of sending him to Rome, which would be a fine rise for him, but a pretty big plum to swallow. Between ourselves, I fancy that Vaugoubert, utterly devoid of ambition as he is, would be very well pleased, and would by no means ask for that cup to pass from him. For all we know, he may do wonders down there ; he is the chosen candidate of the Consulta, and for my part I can see him very well placed, with his artistic leanings, in the setting of the Farnese Palace and the Caracci Gallery. At least you would suppose that it was impossible for any one to hate him ; but there is a whole camarilla collected round King Theodosius which is more or less held in fief by the Wilhelmstrasse, whose inspiration its members dutifully absorb, and these men have done everything in their power to checkmate him. Not only has Vaugoubert had to face these backstairs intrigues, he has had to endure also the insults of a gang of hireling pamphleteers who later on, being like every subsidised journalist the most arrant cowards, have been the first to cry quits, but in the interval had not shrunk from hurling at our Representative the most fatuous accusations that the wit of irresponsible fools could invent. For a month and more Vaugoubert's enemies had been dancing round him, howling for his scalp," M. de Norpois detached this word with sharp emphasis. "But forewarned is forearmed ; as for their insults, he spurned them with his foot !" he went on with even more determination, and with so fierce a glare in his eye that for a moment we forgot our food. "In the words of a fine Arab proverb, 'The dogs may bark ; the caravan goes on !'"

After launching this quotation M. de Norpois paused and examined our faces, to see what effect it had had upon us. Its effect was great, the proverb being familiar to us already. It had taken the place, that year, among people who " really counted ", of " He who sows the wind shall reap the whirlwind ", which was sorely in need of a rest, not having the perennial freshness of " Working for the King of Prussia ". For the culture of these eminent men was an alternate, if not a tripartite and triennial culture. Of course, the use of quotations such as these, with which M. de Norpois excelled in jewelling his articles in the *Revue,* was in no way essential to their appearing solid and well-informed. Even without the ornament which the quotations supplied, it sufficed that M. de Norpois should write at a given point (as he never failed to write) : " The Court of St. James's was not the last to be sensible of the peril," or " Feeling ran high on the Singers' Bridge, which with anxious eyes was following the selfish but skilful policy of the Dual Monarchy," or " A cry of alarm sounded from Montecitorio," or yet again, " That everlasting double dealing which is so characteristic of the Ballplatz." By these expressions the profane reader had at once recognised and had paid deference to the diplomat *de carrière.* But what had made people say that he was something more than that, that he was endowed with a superior culture, had been his careful use of quotations, the perfect example of which, at that date, was still : " Give me a good policy and I will give you good finances, *to quote the favourite words of Baron Louis* " : for we had not yet imported from the Far East : " Victory is on the side that can hold out a quarter of an hour longer than the other, *as the Japanese say* ". This reputation for immense literary gifts, combined with a positive genius for intrigue which he kept concealed beneath a mask of indifference, had secured the election of M. de Norpois to the Académie des Sciences Morales. And there were some who even thought that he would not be out of place in the Académie Française, on the famous day when, wishing to indicate that it was only by drawing the Russian Alliance closer that we could hope to arrive at an understanding with Great Britain, he had not hesitated to write : "Be it clearly understood in the Quai d'Orsay, be it taught henceforward in all the manuals of geography, which appear to be incomplete in this respect, be his certificate of graduation remorselessly withheld from every candidate who has not learned to say, 'If all roads lead to Rome, nevertheless the way from Paris to London runs of necessity through St. Petersburgh.'"

"In short," M. de Norpois went on, addressing my father, "Vaugoubert has won himself considerable distinction from this affair, quite beyond anything on which he can have reckoned. He expected, you understand, a correctly worded speech (which, after the storm-clouds of recent years, would have been something to the good) but nothing more. Several persons who had the honour to be present have assured me that it is impossible, when one merely reads the speech, to form any conception of the effect that it produced when uttered—when articulated with marvellous clearness of diction by the King, who is a master of the art of public speaking and in that passage underlined every possible shade of meaning. I allowed myself, in this connexion, to listen to a little anecdote which brings into prominence once again that frank, boyish charm by which King Theodosius has won so many hearts. I am assured that, just as he uttered that word 'affinities', which was, of course, the startling innovation of the speech, and one that, as you will see, will provoke discussion in the Chancellories for years to come, his Majesty, anticipating the delight of our Ambassador, who was to find in that word the seal, the crown set upon all his labours, on his dreams, one might almost say, and, in a word, his marshal's baton, made a half turn towards Vaugoubert and fixing upon him his arresting gaze, so characteristic of the Oettingens, fired at him that admirably chosen word 'affinities', a positive treasure-trove, uttering it in a tone which made it plain to all his hearers that it was employed of set purpose and with full knowledge of the circumstances. It appears that Vaugoubert found some difficulty in mastering his emotion, and I must confess that, to a certain extent, I can well understand it. Indeed, a person who is entirely to be believed has told me, in confidence, that the King came up to Vaugoubert after the dinner, when his Majesty was holding an informal court, and was heard to say, 'Well, are you satisfied with your pupil, my dear Marquis?'

"One thing, however," M. de Norpois concluded, "is certain; and that is that a speech like that has done more than twenty years of negotiation towards bringing the two countries together, uniting their 'affinities', to borrow the picturesque expression of Theodosius II. It is no more than a word, if you like, but look what success it has had, how the whole of the European press is repeating it, what interest it has aroused, what a new note it has struck. Besides it is distinctly in the young Sovereign's manner. I will not go so far as to say that he

WITHIN A BUDDING GROVE

lights upon a diamond of that water every day. But it is
very seldom that, in his prepared speeches, or better still
in the impulsive flow of his conversation, he does not reveal his character—I was on the point of saying 'does
not affix his signature '—by the use of some incisive word.
I myself am quite free from any suspicion of partiality
in this respect, for I am stoutly opposed to all innova-
tions in terminology. Nine times out of ten they are
most dangerous."

"Yes, I was thinking, only the other day, that the
German Emperor's telegram could not be much to your
liking," said my father.

M. de Norpois raised his eyes to heaven, as who
should say, " Oh, that fellow ! " before he replied :   " In
the first place, it is an act of ingratitude. It is more than
a crime ; it is a blunder, and one of a crassness which I
can describe only as pyramidal ! Indeed, unless some
one puts a check on his activities, the man who has got rid
of Bismarck is quite capable of repudiating by degrees
the whole of the Bismarckian policy ; after which it will
be a leap in the dark."

"My husband tells me, sir, that you are perhaps going
to take him to Spain one summer ; that will be nice for
him ; I am so glad."

"Why, yes ; it is an idea that greatly attracts me ; I
amuse myself, planning a tour. I should like to go there
with you, my dear fellow. But what about you, Madame ; have you decided yet how you are going to spend
your holidays ? "

"I shall perhaps go with my son to Balbec, but I am
not certain."

"Oh, but Balbec is quite charming, I was down that

way a few years ago. They are beginning to build some
very pretty little villas there ; I think you'll like the
place. But may I ask what has made you choose
Balbec ? "

" My son is very anxious to visit some of the churches
in that neighbourhood, and Balbec church in particular.
I was a little afraid that the tiring journey there, and the
discomfort of staying in the place might be too much for
him. But I hear that they have just opened an excellent
hotel, in which he will be able to get all the comfort that
he requires."

" Indeed ! I must make a note of that, for a certain
person who will not turn up her nose at a comfortable
hotel."

" The church at Balbec is very beautiful, sir, is it
not ? " I inquired, repressing my sorrow at learning that
one of the attractions of Balbec consisted in its pretty
little villas.

" No, it is not bad ; but it cannot be compared for a
moment with such positive jewels in stone as the Cathedrals of Rheims and Chartres, or with what is to my mind
the pearl among them all, the Sainte-Chapelle here in
Paris."

" But, surely, Balbec church is partly romanesque, is it
not ? "

" Why, yes, it is in the romanesque style, which is to
say very cold and lifeless, with no hint in it anywhere of
the grace, the fantasy of the later gothic builders, who
worked their stone as if it had been so much lace. Balbec church is well worth a visit, if you are in those parts ;
it is decidedly quaint ; on a wet day, when you have noth-

ing better to do, you might look inside ; you will see the tomb of Tourville."

"Tell me, were you at the Foreign Ministry dinner last night ? " asked my father. " I couldn't go."

"No," M. de Norpois smiled, " I must confess that I renounced it for a party of a very different sort. I was dining with a lady whose name you may possibly have heard, the beautiful Mme. Swann." My mother checked an impulsive movement, for, being more rapid in perception than my father, she used to alarm herself on his account over things which only began to upset him a moment later. Anything unpleasant that might occur to him was discovered first by her, just as bad news from France is always known abroad sooner than among ourselves. But she was curious to know what sort of people the Swanns managed to entertain, and so inquired of M. de Norpois as to whom he had met there.

"Why, my dear lady, it is a house which (or so it struck me) is especially attractive to gentlemen. There were several married men there last night, but their wives were all, as it happened, unwell, and so had not come with them," replied the Ambassador with a mordancy sheathed in good-humour, casting on each of us a glance the gentleness and discretion of which appeared to be tempering while in reality they deftly intensified its malice.

"In all fairness," he went on, " I must add that women do go to the house, but women who belong rather—what shall I say—to the Republican world than to Swann's " (he pronounced it "Svann's") "circle. Still, you can never tell. Perhaps it will turn into a political or a literary salon some day. Anyhow, they appear to be quite happy as they are. Indeed, I feel that Swann advertises his happiness just a trifle too blatantly. He told us the names of all the people who had asked him and his wife out for the next week, people with whom there was no particular reason to be proud of being intimate, with a want of reserve, of taste, almost of tact which I was astonished to remark in so refined a man. He kept on repeating, 'We haven't a free evening!' as though that had been a thing to boast of, positively like a *parvenu*, and he is certainly not that. For Swann had always plenty of friends, women as well as men, and without seeming over-bold, without the least wish to appear indiscreet, I think I may safely say that not all of them, of course, nor even the majority of them, but one at least, who is a lady of the very highest rank, would perhaps not have shewn herself inexorably averse from the idea of entering upon relations with Mme. Swann, in which case it is safe to assume that more than one sheep of the social flock would have followed her lead. But it seems that there has been no indication on Swann's part of any movement in that direction.

"What do I see? A Nesselrode pudding! As well! I declare, I shall need a course at Carlsbad after such a Lucullus-feast as this.

"Possibly Swann felt that there would be too much resistance to overcome. The marriage—so much is certain —was not well received. There has been some talk of his wife's having money, but that is all humbug. Anyhow, the whole affair has been looked upon with disfavour. And then, Swann has an aunt who is excessively rich and in an admirable position socially, married to a man who, financially speaking, is a power. Not only has she refused

52

to meet Mme. Swann, she has actually started a campaign to force her friends and acquaintance to do the same. I do not mean to say that anyone who moves in a good circle in Paris has shewn any actual incivility to Mme. Swann. . . . No! A hundred times no! Quite apart from her husband's being eminently a man to take up the challenge. Anyhow, there is one curious thing about it, to see the immense importance that Swann, who knows so many and such exclusive people, attaches to a society of which the best that can be said is that it is extremely mixed. I myself, who knew him in the old days, must admit that I felt more astonished than amused at seeing a man so well-bred as he is, so much at home in the best houses, effusively thanking the Chief Secretary to the Minister of Posts for having come to them, and asking him whether Mme. Swann might *take the liberty* of calling upon his wife. He must feel something of an exile, don't you know; evidently, it's quite a different world. I don't think, all the same, that Swann is unhappy. It is true that for some years before the marriage she was always trying to blackmail him in a rather disgraceful way; she would take the child away whenever Swann refused her anything. Poor Swann, who is as unsophisticated as he is, for all that, sharp, believed every time that the child's disappearance was a coincidence, and declined to face the facts. Apart from that, she made such continual scenes that everyone expected that, from the day she attained her object and was safely married, nothing could possibly restrain her and that their life would be a hell on earth. Instead of which, just the opposite has happened. People are inclined to laugh at the way in which Swann speaks of his wife; it's become a standing joke. Of course, one could hardly expect that, conscious, more or less of being a—(you remember Molière's line) he would go and proclaim it *urbi et orbi ;* still that does not prevent one from finding a tendency in him to exaggerate when he declares that she makes an excellent wife. And yet that is not so far from the truth as people imagine. In her own way— which is not, perhaps, what all husbands would prefer, but then, between you and me, I find it difficult to believe that Swann, who has known her for ever so long and is far from being an utter fool, did not know what to expect— there can be no denying that she does seem to have a certain regard for him. I do not say that she is not flighty, and Swann himself has no fault to find with her for that, if one is to believe the charitable tongues which, as you may suppose, continue to wag. But she is distinctly grateful to him for what he has done for her, and, despite the fears that were everywhere expressed of the contrary, her temper seems to have become angelic."

This alteration was perhaps not so extraordinary as M. de Norpois professed to find it. Odette had not believed that Swann would ever consent to marry her ; each time that she made the suggestive announcement that some man about town had just married his mistress she had seen him stiffen into a glacial silence, or at the most, if she were directly to challenge him, asking : "Don't you think it very nice, a very fine thing that he has done, for a woman who sacrificed all her youth to him ?" had heard him answer dryly : "But I don't say that there's anything wrong in it. Everyone does what he himself thinks right." She came very near, indeed, to believing that (as he used to threaten in moments of anger) he was going to leave her altogether, for she had heard it said, not long since, by a woman sculptor, that " You cannot be surprised at anything men do, they're such brutes," and impressed by the profundity of this maxim of pessimism she had appropriated it for herself, and repeated it on every possible occasion with an air of disappointment which seemed to imply :   " After all, it's not impossible in any way ; it would be just my luck."   Meanwhile all the virtue had gone from the optimistic maxim which had hitherto guided Odette through life :   " You can do anything with men when they're in love with you, they're such idiots ! " a doctrine which was expressed on her face by the same tremor of an eyelid that might have accompanied such words as :   " Don't be frightened ; he won't break anything."   While she waited, Odette was tormented by the thought of what one of her friends, who had been married by a man who had not lived with her for nearly so long as Odette herself had lived with Swann, and had had no child by him, and who was now in a definitely respectable position, invited to the balls at the Elysée and so forth, must think of Swann's behaviour. A consultant more discerning than M. de Norpois would doubtless have been able to diagnose that it was this feeling of shame and humiliation that had embittered Odette, that the devilish characteristics which she displayed were no essential part of her, no irremediable evil, and so would easily have foretold what had indeed come to pass, namely that a new rule of life, the matrimonial, would put an end, with almost magic swiftness, to these painful incidents, of daily occurrence but in no sense organic. Practically everyone was surprised at the marriage, and this, in itself, is surprising. No doubt very few people understand the purely subjective nature of the phenomenon that we call love, or how it creates, so to speak, a fresh, a third, a supplementary person, distinct from the person whom the world knows by the same name, a person most of whose constituent elements are derived from ourself, the lover. And so there are very few who can regard as natural the enormous proportions that a creature comes to assume in our eyes who is not the same as the creature that they see. It would appear, none the less, that so far as Odette was concerned people might have taken into account the fact that if, indeed, she had never entirely understood Swann's mentality, at least she was acquainted with the titles, and with all the details of his studies, so much so that the name of Vermeer was as familiar to her as that of her own dressmaker ; while as for Swann himself she knew intimately those traits of character of which the rest of the world must remain ignorant or merely laugh at them, and only a mistress or a sister may gain possession of the revealing, cherished image ; and so strongly are we attached to such eccentricities, even to those of them which we are most anxious to correct, that it is because a woman comes in time to acquire an indulgent, an affectionately mocking familiarity, such as we ourselves have with them, or our relatives have, that amours of long standing have something of the sweetness and strength of family affection. The bonds that unite us to another creature receive their consecration when that creature adopts the same point of view as ourself in judging one of our imperfections. And among these special traits there were others, besides, which belonged as much to his intellect as to his character, which, all the same, because they had their roots in the latter, Odette had been able more easily to discern. She complained that when Swann turned author, when he published his essays, these characteristics were not to be found in them as they were in his letters, or in his conversation, where they abounded. She urged him to give them a more prominent place. She would have liked that because it was these things that she herself preferred in him, but since she preferred them because they were the things most typical of himself, she was perhaps not wrong in wishing that they might be found in his writings. Perhaps also she thought that his work, if endowed with more vitality, so that it ultimately brought him success, might enable her also to form what at the Verdurins' she had been taught to value above everything else in the world—a salon.

Among the people to whom this sort of marriage appeared ridiculous, people who in their own case would ask themselves, "What will M. de Guermantes think, what will Bréauté say when I marry Mlle. de Montmorency?", among the people who cherished that sort of social ideal would have figured, twenty years earlier, Swann himself, the Swann who had taken endless pains to get himself elected to the Jockey Club, and had reckoned at that time on making a brilliant marriage which, by consolidating his position, would have made him one of the most conspicuous figures in Paris. Only, the visions which a marriage like that suggests to the mind of the interested party need, like all visions, if they are not to fade away and be altogether lost, to receive sustenance from without. Your most ardent longing is to humiliate the man who has insulted you. But if you never hear of him again, having removed to some other place, your enemy will come to have no longer the slightest importance for you. If one has lost sight for a score of years of all the people on whose account one would have liked to be elected to the Jockey Club or the Institute, the prospect of becoming a member of one or other of those corporations will have ceased to tempt one. Now fully as much as retirement, ill-health or religious conversion, protracted relations with a woman will substitute fresh visions for the old. There was not on Swann's part, when he married Odette, any renunciation of his social ambitions, for from these ambitions Odette had long ago, in the spiritual sense of the word, detached him. Besides, had he not been so detached, his marriage would have been all the more creditable. It is because they imply the sacrifice of a more or less advantageous position to a purely private happiness that, as a general rule, "impossible" marriages are the happiest of all. (One cannot very well include among the "impossible" marriages those that are made for money, there being no instance on record of a couple, of whom the wife or even the husband has thus sold himself, who have not sooner or later been admitted into society, if only by tradition, and on the strength of so many precedents, and so as not to have two conflicting standards.) Perhaps, on the other hand, the artistic, if not the perverse side of Swann's nature would in any event have derived a certain amount of pleasure from coupling with himself, in one of those crossings of species such as Mendelians practise and mythology records, a creature of a different race, archduchess or prostitute, from contracting a royal alliance or from marrying beneath him. There had been but one person in all the world whose opinion he took into consideration whenever he thought of his possible marriage with Odette ; that was, and from no snobbish motive, the Duchesse de Guermantes. With whom Odette, on the contrary, was but little concerned, thinking only of those people whose position was immediately above her own, rather than in so vague an empyrean. But when Swann in his daydreams saw Odette as already his wife he invariably formed a picture of the moment in which he would take her—her, and above all her daughter—to call upon the Princesse des Laumes (who was shortly, on the death of her father-in-law, to become Duchesse de Guermantes). He had no desire to introduce them anywhere else, but his heart would soften as he invented—uttering their actual words to himself—all the things that the Duchess would say of him to Odette, and Odette to the Duchess, the affection that she would shew for Gilberte, spoiling her, making him proud of his child. He enacted to himself the scene of this introduction with the same precision in each of its imaginary details that people shew when they consider how they would spend, supposing they were to win it, a lottery prize the amount of which they have arbitrarily determined. In so far as a mental picture which accompanies one of our resolutions may be said to be its motive, so it might be said that if Swann married Odette it was in order to present her and Gilberte, without anyone's else being present, without, if need be, anyone's else ever coming to know of it, to the Duchesse de Guermantes. We shall see how this sole social ambition that he had entertained for his wife and daughter was precisely that one the realisation of which proved to be forbidden him by a veto so absolute that Swann died in the belief that the Duchess would never possibly come to know them. We shall see also that, on the contrary, the Duchesse de Guermantes did associate with Odette and Gilberte after the death of Swann. And doubtless he would have been wiser—seeing that he could attach so much importance to so small a matter—not to have formed too dark a picture of the future, in this connexion, but to have consoled himself with the hope that the meeting of the ladies might indeed take place when he was no longer there to enjoy it. The laborious process of causation which sooner or later will bring about every possible effect, including (consequently) those which one had believed to be most nearly impossible, naturally slow at times, is rendered slower still by our impatience (which in seeking to accelerate only obstructs it) and by our very existence, and comes to fruition only when we have ceased to desire it—have ceased, possibly, to live. Was not Swann conscious of this from his own experience, had there not been already, in his life, as it were a prefiguration of what was to happen after his death, a posthumous happiness in this marriage with this Odette whom he had passionately loved—even if she had not been pleasing to him at first sight—whom he had married when he no longer loved her, when the creature that, in Swann, had so longed to live, had so despaired of living all its life in company with Odette, when that creature was extinct?

I began next to speak of the Comte de Paris, to ask whether he was not one of Swann's friends, for I was afraid lest the conversation should drift away from him. "Why, yes!" replied M. de Norpois, turning towards me and fixing upon my modest person the azure gaze in which floated, as in their vital element, his immense capacity for work and his power of assimilation. And "Upon my word," he added, once more addressing my father, "I do not think that I shall be overstepping the bounds of the respect which I have always professed for the Prince (though without, you understand, maintaining any personal relations with him, which would inevitably compromise my position, unofficial as that may be), if I tell you of a little episode which is not without point ; no more than four years ago, at a small railway station in one of the countries of Central Europe, the Prince happened to set eyes on Mme. Swann. Naturally, none of his circle ventured to ask his Royal Highness what he thought of her. That would not have been seemly. But when her name came up by chance in conversation, by certain signs—imperceptible, if you like, but quite unmistakable —the Prince appeared willing enough to let it be understood that his impression of her had, in a word, been far from unfavourable."

"But there could have been no possibility, surely, of her being presented to the Comte de Paris ? " inquired my father.

"Well, we don't know ; with Princes one never does know," replied M. de Norpois. "The most exalted, those who know best how to secure what is due to them, are as often as not the last to let themselves be embarrassed by the decrees of popular opinion, even by those for which there is most justification, especially when it is a question of their rewarding a personal attachment to themselves. Now it is certain that the Comte de Paris has always most graciously recognised the devotion of Swann, who is, for that matter, a man of character, in spite of it all."

"And what was your own impression, your Excellency ? Do tell us ! " my mother asked, from politeness as well as from curiosity.

All the energy of the old connoisseur broke through the habitual moderation of his speech as he answered : "Quite excellent !"

And knowing that the admission that a strong impression has been made on one by a woman takes its place, provided that one makes it in a playful tone, in a certain category of the art of conversation that is highly appreciated, he broke into a little laugh that lasted for several seconds, moistening the old diplomat's blue eyes and making his nostrils, with their network of tiny scarlet veins, quiver. "She is altogether charming !"

"Was there a writer of the name of Bergotte at this dinner, sir ?" I asked timidly, still trying to keep the conversation to the subject of the Swanns.

"Yes, Bergotte was there," replied M. de Norpois, inclining his head courteously towards me, as though in his desire to be pleasant to my father he attached to everything connected with him a real importance, even to the questions of a boy of my age who was not accustomed to see such politeness shewn to him by persons of his. "Do you know him ?" he went on, fastening on me that clear gaze, the penetration of which had won the praise of Bismarck.

"My son does not know him, but he admires his work immensely," my mother explained.

"Good heavens !" exclaimed M. de Norpois, inspiring me with doubts of my own intelligence far more serious than those that ordinarily distracted me, when I saw that what I valued a thousand thousand times more than myself, what I regarded as the most exalted thing in the world, was for him at the very foot of the scale of admiration. "I do not share your son's point of view.

Bergotte is what I call a flute-player : one must admit that he plays on it very agreeably, although with a great deal of mannerism, of affectation. But when all is said, it is no more than that, and that is nothing very great. Nowhere does one find in his enervated writings anything that could be called construction. No action—or very little—but above all no range. His books fail at the foundation, or rather they have no foundation at all. At a time like the present, when the ever-increasing complexity of life leaves one scarcely a moment for reading, when the map of Europe has undergone radical alterations, and is on the eve, very probably, of undergoing others more drastic still, when so many new and threatening problems are arising on every side, you will allow me to suggest that one is entitled to ask that a writer should be something else than a fine intellect which makes us forget, amid otiose and byzantine discussions of the merits of pure form, that we may be overwhelmed at any moment by a double tide of barbarians, those from without and those from within our borders. I am aware that this is a blasphemy against the sacrosanct school of what these gentlemen term 'Art for Art's sake', but at this period of history there are tasks more urgent than the manipulation of words in a harmonious manner. Not that Bergotte's manner is not now and then quite attractive. I have no fault to find with that, but taken as a whole, it is all very precious, very thin, and has very little virility. I can now understand more easily, when I bear in mind your altogether excessive regard for Bergotte, the few lines that you shewed me just now, which it would have been unfair to you not to overlook, since you yourself told me, in all simplicity, that they were merely a childish scrib-

bling." (I had, indeed, said so, but I did not think anything of the sort.) "For every sin there is forgiveness,
and especially for the sins of youth. After all, others
as well as yourself have such sins upon their conscience,
and you are not the only one who has believed himself to
be a poet in his day. But one can see in what you have
shewn me the evil influence of Bergotte. You will not, of
course, be surprised when I say that there was in it none
of his good qualities, since he is a past-master in the art—
incidentally quite superficial—of handling a certain style
of which, at your age, you cannot have acquired even the
rudiments. But already there is the same fault, that
paradox of stringing together fine-sounding words and
only afterwards troubling about what they mean. That
is putting the cart before the horse, even in Bergotte's
books. All those chinese puzzles of form, all these deli-
quescent mandarin subtleties seem to me to be quite futile.
Given a few fireworks, let off prettily enough by an
author, and up goes the shout of genius. Works of genius
are not so common as all that ! Bergotte cannot place
to his credit—does not carry in his baggage, if I may use
the expression—a single novel that is at all lofty in its
conception, any of those books which one keeps in a special corner of one's library. I do not discover one such
in the whole of his work. But that does not exclude the
fact that, with him, the work is infinitely superior to the
author. Ah ! there is a man who justifies the wit who
insisted that one ought never to know an author except
through his books. It would be impossible to imagine
an individual who corresponded less to his—more pretentious, more pompous, less fitted for human society.
Vulgar at some moments, at others talking like a book,

and not even like one of his own, but like a boring book, which his, to do them justice, are not—such is your Bergotte. He has the most confused mind, alembicated, what our ancestors called a *diseur de phébus,* and he makes the things that he says even more unpleasant by the manner in which he says them. I forget for the moment whether it is Loménie or Sainte-Beuve who tells us that Vigny repelled people by the same eccentricity. But Bergotte has never given us a *Cinq-Mars,* or a *Cachet Rouge,* certain pages of which are regular anthology pieces."

Paralysed by what M. de Norpois had just said to me with regard to the fragment which I had submitted to him, and remembering at the same time the difficulties that I experienced when I attempted to write an essay or merely to devote myself to serious thought, I felt conscious once again of my intellectual nullity and that I was not born for a literary life. Doubtless in the old days at Combray certain impressions of a very humble order, or a few pages of Bergotte used to plunge me into a state of musing which had appeared to me to be of great value. But this state was what my poem in prose reflected; there could be no doubt that M. de Norpois had at once grasped and had seen through the fallacy of what I had discovered to be beautiful simply by a mirage that must be entirely false since the Ambassador had not been taken in by it. He had shewn me, on the other hand, what an infinitely unimportant place was mine when I was judged from outside, objectively, by the best-disposed and most intelligent of experts. I felt myself to be struck speechless, overwhelmed ; and my mind, like a fluid which is without dimensions save those of the vessel that is provided for it, just as it had been expanded a moment ago so as to fill all the vast capacity of genius, contracted now was entirely contained in the straitened mediocrity in which M. de Norpois had of a sudden enclosed and sealed it.

"Our first introduction—I speak of Bergotte and myself—— " he resumed, turning to my father, " was somewhat beset with thorns (which is, after all, only another way of saying that it was not lacking in points). Bergotte—some years ago, now—paid a visit to Vienna while I was Ambassador there ; he was presented to me by the Princess Metternich, came and wrote his name, and expected to be asked to the Embassy. Now, being in a foreign country as the Representative of France, to which he has after all done some honour by his writings, to a certain extent (let us say, to be quite accurate, to a very slight extent), I was prepared to set aside the unfavourable opinion that I hold of his private life. But he was not travelling alone, and he actually let it be understood that he was not to be invited without his companion. I trust that I am no more of a prude than most men, and, being a bachelor, I was perhaps in a position to throw open the doors of the Embassy a little wider than if I had been married and the father of a family. Nevertheless, I must admit that there are depths of degradation to which I should hesitate to descend, while these are rendered more repulsive still by the tone, not moral, merely—let us be quite frank and say moralising,—that Bergotte takes up in his books, where one finds nothing but perpetual and, between ourselves, somewhat wearisome analyses, torturing scruples, morbid remorse, and all for the merest peccadilloes, the most trivial naughtinesses (as one knows from one's own experience), while all the time he is shewing such an utter lack of conscience and so much cynicism in his private life. To cut a long story short, I evaded the responsibility, the Princess returned to the charge, but without success. So that I do not suppose that I appear exactly in the odour of sanctity to the gentleman, and I am not sure how far he appreciated Swann's kindness in inviting him and myself on the same evening. Unless of course it was he who asked for the invitation. One can never tell, for really he is not normal. Indeed that is his sole excuse."

"And was Mme. Swann's daughter at the dinner?" I asked M. de Norpois, taking advantage, to put this question, of a moment in which, as we all moved towards the drawing-room, I could more easily conceal my emotion than would have been possible at table, where I was held fast in the glare of the lamplight.

M. de Norpois appeared to be trying for a moment to remember : then, "Yes, you mean a young person of fourteen or fifteen? Yes, of course, I remember now that she was introduced to me before dinner as the daughter of our Amphitryon. I may tell you that I saw but little of her ; she retired to bed early. Or else she went out to see a friend—I forget. But I can see that you are very intimate with the Swann household."

"I play with Mlle. Swann in the Champs-Elysées, and she is delightful."

"Oh! so that is it, is it? But I assure you, I thought her charming. I must confess to you, however, that I do not believe that she will ever be anything like her mother, if I may say as much without wounding you in a vital spot."

"I prefer Mlle. Swann's face, but I admire her mother,

too, enormously ; I go for walks in the Bois simply in the hope of seeing her pass."

" Ah ! But I must tell them that ; they will be highly flattered."

While he was uttering these words, and for a few seconds after he had uttered them, M. de Norpois was still in the same position as anyone else who, hearing me speak of Swann as an intelligent man, of his family as respectable stockbrokers, of his house as a fine house, imagined that I would speak just as readily of another man equally intelligent, of other stockbrokers equally respectable, of another house equally fine ; it was the moment in which a sane man who is talking to a lunatic has not yet perceived that his companion is mad. M. de Norpois knew that there was nothing unnatural in the pleasure which one derived from looking at pretty women, that it was a social convention, when anyone spoke to you of a pretty woman with any fervour, to pretend to think that he was in love with her, and to promise to further his designs. But in saying that he would speak of me to Gilberte and her mother (which would enable me, like an Olympian deity who has taken on the fluidity of a breath of wind, or rather the aspect of the old greybeard whose form Minerva borrows, to penetrate, myself, unseen, into Mme. Swann's drawing-room, to attract her attention, to occupy her thoughts, to arouse her gratitude for my admiration, to appear before her as the friend of an important person, to seem to her worthy to be invited by her in the future and to enter into the intimate life of her family), this important person who was going to make use, in my interests, of the great influence which he must have with Mme. Swann inspired in me suddenly an affec-

tion so compelling that I had difficulty in restraining myself from kissing his gentle hands, white and crumpled,
which looked as though they had been left lying too long
in water. I even sketched in the air an outline of that
impulsive movement, but this I supposed that I alone had
observed. For it is difficult for any of us to calculate exactly on what scale his words or his gestures are apparent
to others. Partly from the fear of exaggerating our own
importance, and also because we enlarge to enormous proportions the field over which the impressions formed by
other people in the course of their lives are obliged to ex-
tend, we imagine that the accessories of our speech and
attitudes scarcely penetrate the consciousness, still less remain in the memory of those with whom we converse. It
is, we may suppose, to a prompting of this sort that crim-
inals yield when they " touch up " the wording of a statement already made, thinking that the new variant cannot be confronted with any existing version. But it is
quite possible that, even in what concerns the millennial
existence of the human race, the philosophy of the journalist, according to which everything is destined to oblivion, is less true than a contrary philosophy which would
predict the conservation of everything. In the same
newspaper in which the moralist of the " Paris column "
says to us of an event, of a work of art, all the more
forcibly of a singer who has enjoyed her " crowded
hour " : " Who will remember this in ten years' time ? "
overleaf does not the report of the Académie des In-
scriptions speak often of a fact, in itself of smaller importance, of a poem of little merit, which dates from the epoch
of the Pharaohs and is now known again in its entirety ?
Is it not, perhaps, just the same in our brief life on earth ?

And yet, some years later, in a house in which M. de Norpois, who was also calling there, had seemed to me the most solid support that I could hope to find, because he was the friend of my father, indulgent, inclined to wish us all well, and besides, by his profession and upbringing, trained to discretion, when, after the Ambassador had gone, I was told that he had alluded to an evening long ago when he had seen the moment in which I was just going to kiss his hands, not only did I colour up to the roots of my hair but I was stupefied to learn how different from all that I had believed were not only the manner in which M. de Norpois spoke of me but also the constituents of his memory : this tittle-tattle enlightened me as to the incalculable proportions of absence and presence of mind, of recollection and forgetfulness which go to form the human intelligence ; and I was as marvellously surprised as on the day on which I read for the first time, in one of Maspero's books, that we had an exact list of the sportsmen whom Assurbanipal used to invite to his hunts, a thousand years before the Birth of Christ.

"Oh, sir," I assured M. de Norpois, when he told me that he would inform Gilberte and her mother how much I admired them, "if you would do that, if you would speak of me to Mme. Swann, my whole life would not be long enough for me to prove my gratitude, and that life would be all at your service. But I feel bound to point out to you that I do not know Mme. Swann, and that I have never been introduced to her."

I had added these last words from a scruple of conscience, and so as not to appear to be boasting of an acquaintance which I did not possess. But while I was uttering them I felt that they were already superfluous, for from the beginning of my speech of thanks, with its chilling ardour, I had seen flitting across the face of the Ambassador an expression of hesitation and dissatisfaction, and in his eyes that vertical, narrow, slanting look (like, in the drawing of a solid body in perspective, the receding line of one of its surfaces), that look which one addresses to the invisible audience whom one has within oneself at the moment when one is saying something that one's other audience, the person whom one has been addressing—myself, in this instance—is not meant to hear. I realised in a flash that these phrases which I had pronounced, which, feeble as they were when measured against the flood of gratitude that was coursing through me, had seemed to me bound to touch M. de Norpois and to confirm his decision upon an intervention which would have given him so little trouble and me so much joy, were perhaps (out of all those that could have been chosen, with diabolical malice, by persons anxious to do me harm) the only ones that could result in making him abandon his intention. Indeed, when he heard me speak, just as at the moment when a stranger with whom we have been exchanging—quite pleasantly—our impressions, which we might suppose to be similar to his, of the passers-by, whom we have agreed in regarding as vulgar, reveals suddenly the pathological abyss that divides him from us by adding carelessly, as he runs his hand over his pocket : " What a pity, I haven't got my revolver here ; I could have picked off the lot ! " M. de Norpois, who knew that nothing was less costly or more easy than to be commended to Mme. Swann and taken to her house, and saw that to me, on the contrary, such favours bore so high a price and were consequently, no doubt, of great difficulty, thought that the desire, apparently normal, which I had expressed must cloak some different thought, some suspect intention, some pre-existent fault, on account of which, in the certainty of displeasing Mme. Swann, no one hitherto had been willing to undertake the responsibility for conveying a message to her from me. And I understood that this office was one which he would never discharge, that he might see Mme. Swann daily, for years to come, without ever mentioning my name. He did indeed ask her, a few days later, for some information which I required, and charged my father to convey it to me. But he had not thought it his duty to tell her at whose instance he was inquiring. So she would never discover that I knew M. de Norpois and that I hoped so greatly to be asked to her house ; and this was perhaps a less misfortune than I supposed. For the second of these discoveries would probably not have added much to the efficacy, in any event uncertain, of the first. In Odette the idea of her own life and of her home awakened no mysterious disturbance ; a person who knew her, who came to see her, did not seem to her a fabulous creature such as he seemed to me who would have flung a stone through Swann's windows if I could have written upon it that I knew M. de Norpois ; I was convinced that such a message, even when transmitted in so brutal a fashion, would have done far more to exalt me in the eyes of the lady of the house than it would have prejudiced her against me. But even if I had been capable of understanding that the mission which M. de Norpois did not perform must have remained futile, nay, more than that, might even have damaged my credit with the Swanns, I should not have had the courage, had he shewn himself consenting, to release the Ambassador from it, and to renounce the pleasure—however fatal its consequences might prove—of feeling that my name and my person were thus brought for a moment into Gilberte's presence, in her unknown life and home.

After M. de Norpois had gone my father cast an eye over the evening paper ; I dreamed once more of Berma. The pleasure which I had found in listening to her required to be made complete, all the more because it had fallen far short of what I had promised myself ; and so it at once assimilated everything that was capable of giving it nourishment, those merits, for instance, which M. de Norpois had admitted that Berma possessed, and which my mind had absorbed at one draught, like a dry lawn when water is poured on it. Then my father handed me the newspaper, pointing me out a paragraph which ran more or less as follows :—

> The performance of *Phèdre*, given this afternoon before an enthusiastic audience, which included the foremost representatives of society and the arts, as well as the principal critics, was for Mme. Berma, who played the heroine, the occasion of a triumph as brilliant as any that she has known in the course of her phenomenal career. We shall discuss more fully in a later issue this performance, which is indeed an event in the history of the stage ; for the present we need only add that the best qualified judges are unanimous in the pronouncement that such an interpretation sheds an entirely new light on the part of Phèdre, which is one of the finest and most studied of Racine's creations, and that it constitutes the purest and most exalted manifestation of dramatic art which it has been the privilege of our generation to witness.

Immediately my mind had conceived this new idea of " the purest and most exalted manifestation of dramatic art ", it, the idea, sped to join the imperfect pleasure which I had felt in the theatre, added to it a little of what was lacking, and their combination formed something so exalting that I cried out within myself : "What a great artist !" It may doubtless be argued that I was not absolutely sincere. But let us bear in mind, rather, the numberless writers who, dissatisfied with the page which they have just written, if they read some eulogy of the genius of Chateaubriand, or evoke the spirit of some great artist whose equal they aspire to be, by humming to themselves, for instance, a phrase of Beethoven, the melancholy of which they compare with what they have been trying to express in prose, are so filled with that idea of genius that they add it to their own productions, when they think of them once again, see them no longer in the light in which at first they appeared, and, hazarding an act of faith in the value of their work, say to themselves : "After all !" without taking into account that, into the total which determines their ultimate satisfaction, they have introduced the memory of marvellous pages of Chateaubriand which they assimilate to their own, but of which, in cold fact, they are not the authors ; let us bear in mind the numberless men who believe in the love of a mistress on the evidence only of her betrayals ; all those, too, who are sustained by the alternative hopes, either of an incomprehensible survival of death, when they think, inconsolable husbands, of the wives whom they have lost but have not ceased to love, or, artists, of the posthumous glory which they may thus enjoy ; or else the hope of complete extinction which comforts them when their thoughts turn to the misdeeds that otherwise they must expiate after death ; let us bear in mind also the travellers who come home enraptured by the general beauty of a tour of which, from day to day, they have felt nothing but the tedious incidents ; and let us then declare whether, in the communal life that is led by our ideas in the enclosure of our minds, there is a single one of those that make us most happy which has not first sought, a very parasite, and won from an alien but neighbouring idea the greater part of the strength that it originally lacked.

My mother appeared none too well pleased that my father no longer thought of "the career" for myself. I fancy that, anxious before all things that a definite rule of life should discipline the eccentricity of my nervous system, what she regretted was not so much seeing me abandon diplomacy as the prospect of my devoting myself to literature. But "Let him alone !" my father protested ; "the main thing is that a man should find pleasure in his work. He is no longer a child. He knows pretty well now what he likes, it is not at all probable that he will change, and he is quite capable of deciding for himself what will make him happy in life." That evening, as I waited for the time to arrive when, thanks to the freedom of choice which they allowed me, I should or should not begin to be happy in life, my father's words caused me great uneasiness. At all times his unexpected kindnesses had, when they were manifested, prompted in me so keen a desire to kiss, above where his beard began, his glowing cheeks, that if I did not yield to that desire, it was simply because I was afraid of annoying him. And on that day, as an author becomes alarmed when he sees the fruits of

75

his own meditation, which do not appear to him to be of great value since he does not separate them from himself, oblige a publisher to choose a kind of paper, to employ a fount of type finer, perhaps, than they deserve, I asked myself whether my desire to write was of sufficient importance to justify my father in dispensing so much generosity. But apart from that, when he spoke of my inclinations as no longer liable to change, he awakened in me two terrible suspicions. The first was that (at a time when, every day, I regarded myself as standing upon the threshold of a life which was still intact and would not enter upon its course until the following morning) my existence was already begun, and that, furthermore, what was yet to follow would not differ to any extent from what had already elapsed. The second suspicion, which was nothing more, really, than a variant of the first, was that I was not situated somewhere outside the realm of Time, but was subject to its laws, just like the people in novels who, for that reason, used to plunge me in such depression when I read of their lives, down at Combray, in the fastness of my wicker sentry-box. In theory one is aware that the earth revolves, but in practice one does not perceive it, the ground upon which one treads seems not to move, and one can live undisturbed. So it is with Time in one's life. And to make its flight perceptible novelists are obliged, by wildly accelerating the beat of the pendulum, to transport the reader in a couple of minutes over ten, or twenty, or even thirty years. At the top of one page we have left a lover full of hope ; at the foot of the next we meet him again, a bowed old man of eighty, painfully dragging himself on his daily walk about the courtyard of an almshouse, scarcely replying to what is said to him, oblivious of the past. In saying of me, " He is no longer a child ", " His tastes will not change now ", and so forth, my father had suddenly made me apparent to myself in my position in Time, and caused me the same kind of depression as if I had been, not yet the enfeebled old pensioner, but one of those heroes of whom the author, in a tone of indifference which is particularly galling, says to us at the end of a book : " He very seldom comes up now from the country. He has finally decided to end his days there."

Meanwhile my father, so as to forestall any criticism that we might feel tempted to make of our guest, said to my mother : " Upon my word, old Norpois was rather ' typical ', as you call it, this evening, wasn't he ? When he said that it would not have been ' seemly ' to ask the Comte de Paris a question, I was quite afraid you would burst out laughing."

" Not at all ! " answered my mother. " I was delighted to see a man of his standing, and age too, keep that sort of simplicity, which is really a sign of straightforwardness and good-breeding."

" I should think so, indeed ! That does not prevent his having a shrewd and discerning mind ; I know him well, I see him at the Commission, remember, where he is very different from what he was here," exclaimed my father, who was glad to see that Mamma appreciated M. de Norpois, and anxious to persuade her that he was even superior to what she supposed, because a cordial nature exaggerates a friend's qualities with as much pleasure as a mischievous one finds in depreciating them. " What was it that he said, again—'With Princes one never does know.' . . . ? "

"Yes, that was it. I noticed it at the time ; it was very neat. You can see that he has a vast experience of life."

" The astonishing thing is that he should have been dining with the Swanns, and that he seems to have found quite respectable people there, officials even. How on earth can Mme. Swann have managed to catch them ? "

" Did you notice the malicious way he said : 'It is a house which is especially attractive to gentlemen !' ? "

And each of them attempted to reproduce the manner in which M. de Norpois had uttered these words, as they might have attempted to capture some intonation of Bressant's voice or of Thiron's in *L'Aventurière* or in the *Gendre de M. Poirier.* But of all his sayings there was none so keenly relished as one was by Françoise, who, years afterwards, even, could not " keep a straight face " if we reminded her that she had been qualified by the Ambassador as " a chef of the first order ", a compliment which my mother had gone in person to transmit to her, as a War Minister publishes the congratulations addressed to him by a visiting Sovereign after the grand review. I, as it happened, had preceded my mother to the kitchen. For I had extorted from Françoise, who though opposed to war was cruel, that she would cause no undue suffering to the rabbit which she had to kill, and I had had no report yet of its death. Françoise assured me that it had passed away as peacefully as could be desired, and very swiftly. " I have never seen a beast like it ; it died without uttering a word ; you would have thought it was dumb." Being but little versed in the language of beasts

I suggested that the rabbit had not, perhaps, a cry like the chicken's. "Just wait till you see," said Françoise, filled with contempt for my ignorance, "if rabbits don't cry every bit as much as chickens. Why, they are far noisier." She received the compliments of M. de Norpois with the proud simplicity, the joyful and (if but for the moment) intelligent expression of an artist when someone speaks to him of his art. My mother had sent her when she first came to us to several of the big restaurants to see how the cooking there was done. I had the same pleasure, that evening, in hearing her dismiss the most famous of them as mere cookshops that I had had long ago, when I learned with regard to theatrical artists that the hierarchy of their merits did not at all correspond to that of their reputations. "The Ambassador," my mother told her, "assured me that he knows no place where he can get cold beef and *soufflés* as good as yours." Françoise, with an air of modesty and of paying just homage to the truth, agreed, but seemed not at all impressed by the title "Ambassador"; she said of M. de Norpois, with the friendliness due to a man who had taken her for a chef : "He's a good old soul, like me." She had indeed hoped to catch sight of him as he arrived, but knowing that Mamma hated their standing about behind doors and in windows, and thinking that Mamma would get to know from the other servants or from the porter that she had been keeping watch (for Françoise saw everywhere nothing but "jealousies" and "tale-bearings", which played the same grim and unending part in her imagination as do for others of us the intrigues of the Jesuits or the Jews), she had contented herself with a peep from the kitchen window, "so as not to have words with Madame," and beneath the momentary aspect of M. de Norpois had " thought it was Monsieur Legrand," because of what she called his " agelity " and in spite of their having not a single point in common. " Well," inquired my mother, " and how do you explain that nobody else can make a jelly as well as you—when you choose ? " " I really couldn't say how that becomes about," replied Françoise, who had established no very clear line of demarcation between the verb "to come ", in certain of its meanings at least, and the verb "to become ". She was speaking the truth, if not the whole truth, being scarcely more capable—or desirous—of revealing the mystery which ensured the superiority of her jellies or her creams than a leader of fashion the secrets of her toilet or a great singer those of her song. Their explanations tell us little ; it was the same with the recipes furnished by our cook. " They do it in too much of a hurry," she went on, alluding to the great restaurants, " and then it's not all done together. You want the beef to become like a sponge, then it will drink up all the juice to the last drop. Still, there was one of those Cafés where I thought they did know a little bit about cooking. I don't say it was altogether my jelly, but it was very nicely done, and the *soufflés* had plenty of cream." " Do you mean Henry's ? " asked my father (who had now joined us), for he greatly enjoyed that restaurant in the Place Gaillon where he went regularly to club dinners. " Oh, dear no ! " said Françoise, with a mildness which cloaked her profound contempt. " I meant a little restaurant. At that Henry's it's all very good, sure enough, but it's not a restaurant, it's more like a—soup-kitchen." " Weber's, then ? " " Oh, no, sir, I meant a good restaurant. Weber's, that's in the Rue Royale ; that's not a restaurant, it's a drinking-shop. I don't know that the food they give you there is even served. I think they don't have any table-cloths ; they just shove it down in front of you like that, with a take it or leave it." "Ciro's ?" "Oh ! there I should say they have the cooking done by ladies of the world." ("World" meant for Françoise the under-world.) "Lord ! They need that to fetch the boys in." We could see that, with all her air of simplicity, Françoise was for the celebrities of her profession a more disastrous " comrade " than the most jealous, the most infatuated of actresses. We felt, all the same, that she had a proper feeling for her art and a respect for tradition ; for she went on : "No, I mean a restaurant where they looked as if they kept a very good little family table. It's a place of some consequence, too. Plenty of custom there. Oh, they raked in the coppers there, all right." Françoise, being an economist, reckoned in coppers, where your plunger would reckon in gold. ' "Madame knows the place well enough, down there to the right along the main boulevards, a little way back." The restaurant of which she spoke with this blend of pride and good-humoured tolerance was, it turned out, the Café Anglais.

When New Year's Day came, I first of all paid a round of family visits with Mamma who, so as not to tire me, had planned them beforehand (with the aid of an itinerary drawn up by my father) according to districts rather than to degrees of kinship. But no sooner had we entered the drawing-room of the distant cousin whose claim to being visited first was that her house was at no distance from ours, than my mother was horrified to see standing there, his present of *marrons glacés* or *déguisés* in his hand, the bosom friend of the most sensitive of all my uncles, to whom he would at once go and report that we had not begun our round with him. And this uncle would certainly be hurt; he would have thought it quite natural that we should go from the Madeleine to the Jardin des Plantes, where he lived, before stopping at Saint-Augustin, on our way to the Rue de l'Ecole de Médecine.

Our visits ended (my grandmother had dispensed us from the duty of calling on her, since we were to dine there that evening), I ran all the way to the Champs-Elysées to give to our own special stall-keeper, with instructions to hand it over to the person who came to her several times a week from the Swanns to buy gingerbread, the letter which, on the day when my friend had caused me so much anxiety, I had decided to send her at the New Year, and in which I told her that our old friendship was vanishing with the old year, that I would forget, now, my old sorrows and disappointments, and that, from this first day of January, it was a new friendship that we were going to cement, one so solid that nothing could destroy it, so wonderful that I hoped that Gilberte would go out of her way to preserve it in all its beauty, and to warn me in time, as I promised to warn her, should either of us detect the least sign of a peril that might endanger it. On our way home Françoise made me stop at the corner of the Rue Royale, before an open-air stall from which she selected for her own stock of presents photographs of Pius IX and Raspail, while for myself I purchased one of Berma. The innumerable admiration which that artist excited gave an air almost of poverty to this one face that she had to respond with, unalterable and precarious as are the garments of people who have not a " change ", this

face on which she must continually expose to view only
the tiny dimple upon her upper lip, the arch of her eyebrows, a few other physical peculiarities always the same,
which, when it came to that, were at the mercy of a burn
or a blow. This face, moreover, could not in itself have
seemed to me beautiful, but it gave me the idea, and consequently the desire to kiss it by reason of all the kisses
that it must have received, for which, from its page in the
album, it seemed still to be appealing with that coquettishly tender gaze, that artificially ingenuous smile. For
our Berma must indeed have felt for many young men
those longings which she confessed under cover of the personality of Phaedra, longings of which everything, even
the glamour of her name which enhanced her beauty and
prolonged her youth, must render the gratification so
easy to her. Night was falling; I stopped before a
column of playbills, on which was posted that of the piece
in which she was to appear on January 1. A moist and
gentle breeze was blowing. It was a time of day and year
that I knew; I suddenly felt a presentiment that New
Year's Day was not a day different from the rest, that
it was not the first day of a new world, in which I might,
by a chance that had never yet occurred, that was still
intact, make Gilberte's acquaintance afresh, as at the
Creation of the World, as though the past had no longer
any existence, as though there had been obliterated, with
the indications which I might have preserved for my
future guidance, the disappointments which she had sometimes brought me; a new world in which nothing should
subsist from the old—save one thing, my desire that Gilberte should love me. I realised that if my heart hoped
for such a reconstruction, round about it, of a universe

that had not satisfied it before, it was because my heart had not altered, and I told myself that there was no reason why Gilberte's should have altered either ; I felt that this new friendship was the same, just as there is no boundary ditch between their fore-runners and those new years which our desire for them, without being able to reach and so to modify them, invests, unknown to themselves, with distinctive names. I might dedicate this new year, if I chose, to Gilberte, and as one bases a religious system upon the blind laws of nature, endeavour to stamp New Year's Day with the particular image that I had formed of it ; but in vain, I felt that it was not aware that people called it New Year's Day, that it was passing in a wintry dusk in a manner that was not novel to me ; in the gentle breeze that floated about the column of play-bills I had recognised, I had felt reappear the eternal, the universal substance, the familiar moisture, the unheeding fluidity of the old days and years.

I returned to the house. I had spent the New Year's Day of old men, who differ on that day from their juniors, not because people have ceased to give them presents but because they themselves have ceased to believe in the New Year. Presents I had indeed received, but not that present which alone could bring me pleasure, namely a line from Gilberte. I was young still, none the less, since I had been able to write her one, by means of which I hoped, in telling her of my solitary dreams of love and longing, to arouse similar dreams in her. The sadness of men who have grown old lies in their no longer even thinking of writing such letters, the futility of which their experience has shewn.

After I was in bed, the noises of the street, unduly pro-

longed upon this festive evening, kept me awake. I
thought of all the people who were ending the night in
pleasure, of the lover, the troop, it might be, of debauchees
who would be going to meet Berma at the stage-door after
the play that I had seen announced for this evening. I
was not even able, so as to calm the agitation which that
idea engendered in me during my sleepless night, to assure
myself that Berma was not, perhaps, thinking about love,
since the lines that she was reciting, which she had long
and carefully rehearsed, reminded her at every moment
that love is an exquisite thing, as of course she already
knew, and knew so well that she displayed its familiar
pangs—only enriched with a new violence and an unsus-
pected sweetness—to her astonished audience ; and yet
each of them had felt those pangs himself. I lighted my
candle again, to look once more upon her face. At the
thought that it was, no doubt, at that very moment being
caressed by those men whom I could not prevent from
giving to Berma and receiving from her joys superhuman
but vague, I felt an emotion more cruel than voluptuous, a
longing that was aggravated presently by the sound of a
horn, as one hears it on the nights of the Lenten carnival
and often of other public holidays, which, because it then
lacks all poetry, is more saddening, coming from a toy
squeaker, than " at evening, in the depth of the woods."
At that moment, a message from Gilberte would perhaps
not have been what I wanted. Our desires cut across one
another's paths, and in this confused existence it is but
rarely that a piece of good fortune coincides with the desire that clamoured for it.

I continued to go to the Champs-Elysées on fine days,
along streets whose stylish pink houses seemed to be

washed (because exhibitions of water-colours were then at the height of fashion) in a lightly floating atmosphere. It would be untrue to say that in those days the palaces of Gabriel struck me as being of greater beauty, or even of another epoch than the adjoining houses. I found more style, and should have supposed more antiquity if not in the Palais de l'Industrie at any rate in the Trocadéro. Plunged in a restless sleep, my adolescence embodied in one uniform vision the whole of the quarter through which it might be strolling, and I had never dreamed that there could be an eighteenth century building in the Rue Royale, just as I should have been astonished to learn that the Porte-Saint-Martin and the Porte-Saint-Denis, those glories of the age of Louis XIV, were not contemporary with the most recently built tenements in the sordid regions that bore their names. Once only one of Gabriel's palaces made me stop for more than a moment ; that was because, night having fallen, its columns, dematerialised by the moonlight, had the appearance of having been cut out in pasteboard, and by recalling to me a scene in the operetta *Orphée aux Enfers* gave me for the first time an impression of beauty.

Meanwhile Gilberte never came to the Champs-Elysées. And yet it was imperative that I should see her, for I could not so much as remember what she was like. The questing, anxious, exacting way that we have of looking at the person we love, our eagerness for the word which shall give us or take from us the hope of an appointment for the morrow, and, until that word is uttered, our alternative if not simultaneous imaginings of joy and of despair, all these make our observation, in the beloved object's presence, too tremulous to be able to carry away a clear im-

pression of her. Perhaps, also, that activity of all the
senses at once which endeavours to learn from the visible
aspect alone what lies behind it is over-indulgent to the
thousand forms, to the changing fragrance, to the movements of the living person whom as a rule, when we are
not in love, we regard as fixed in one permanent position.
Whereas the beloved model does not stay still ; and our
mental photographs of her are always blurred. I did not
rightly know how Gilberte's features were composed, save
in the heavenly moments when she disclosed them to me ;
I could remember nothing but her smile. And not being
able to see again that beloved face, despite every effort
that I might make to recapture it, I would be disgusted to
find, outlined in my memory with a maddening precision
of detail, the meaningless, emphatic faces of the man with
the wooden horses and of the barley-sugar woman ; just
as those who have lost a dear friend whom they never see
even while they are asleep, are exasperated at meeting incessantly in their dreams any number of insupportable
creatures whom it is quite enough to have known in the
waking world. In their inability to form any image of
the object of their grief they are almost led to assert that
they feel no grief. And I was not far from believing that,
since I could not recall the features of Gilberte, I had forgotten Gilberte herself, and no longer loved her. At
length she returned to play there almost every day, setting before me fresh pleasures to desire, to demand of her
for the morrow, indeed making my love for her every day,
in this sense, a new love. But an incident was to change
once again, and abruptly, the manner in which, at about
two o'clock every afternoon, the problem of my love confronted me. Had M. Swann intercepted the letter that I

had written to his daughter, or was Gilberte merely con-
fessing to me long after the event, and so that I should be
more prudent in future, a state of things already long
established? As I was telling her how greatly I admired
her father and mother, she assumed that vague air, full
of reticence and kept secrets, which she invariably wore
when anyone spoke to her of what she was going to do,
her walks, drives, visits—then suddenly expressed it with :
" You know, they can't abide you ! " and, slipping from
me like the Undine that she was, burst out laughing.
Often her laughter, out of harmony with her words,
seemed, as music seems, to be tracing an invisible surface
on another plane. M. and Mme. Swann did not require
Gilberte to give up playing with me, but they would have
been just as well pleased, she thought, if we had never
begun. They did not look upon our relations with a
kindly eye ; they believed me to be a young person of low
moral standard and imagined that my influence over their
daughter must be evil. This type of unscrupulous young
man whom the Swanns thought that I resembled, I pictured him to myself as detesting the parents of the girl he
loved, flattering them to their faces but, when he was alone
with her, making fun of them, urging her on to disobey
them and, when once he had completed his conquest,
not allowing them even to set eyes on her again. With
these characteristics (though they are never those under
which the basest of scoundrels recognises himself) how
vehemently did my heart contrast the sentiments that did
indeed animate it with regard to Swann, so passionate,
on the contrary, that I never doubted that, were he to
have the least suspicion of them, he must repent of his
condemnation of me as of a judicial error. All that I felt

about him I made bold to express to him in a long letter which I entrusted to Gilberte, with the request that she would deliver it. She consented. Alas ! so he saw in me an even greater impostor than I had feared; those sentiments which I had supposed myself to be portraying, in sixteen pages, with such amplitude of truth, so he had suspected them ; in short, the letter that I had written him, as ardent and as sincere as the words that I had uttered to M. de Norpois, met with no more success. Gilberte told me next day, after taking me aside behind a clump of laurels, along a little path by which we sat down on a couple of chairs, that as he read my letter, which she had now brought back to me, her father had shrugged his shoulders, with : " All this means nothing ; it only goes to prove how right I was." I, who knew the purity of my intentions, the goodness of my soul, was furious that my words should not even have impinged upon the surface of Swann's ridiculous error. For it was an error ; of that I had then no doubt. I felt that I had described with such accuracy certain irrefutable characteristics of my generous sentiments that, if Swann had not at once reconstructed these from my indications, had not come to ask my forgiveness and to admit that he had been mistaken, it must be because these noble sentiments he had never himself experienced, which would make him incapable of understanding the existence of them in other people.

Well, perhaps it was simply that Swann knew that generosity is often no more than the inner aspect which our egotistical feelings assume when we have not yet named and classified them. Perhaps he had recognised in the sympathy that I expressed for him simply an effect—and the strongest possible proof—of my love for Gilberte, by which, and not by any subordinate veneration of himself, my subsequent actions would be irresistibly controlled. I was unable to share his point of view, since I had not succeeded in abstracting my love from myself, in forcing it back into the common experience of humanity, and thus suffering, experimentally, its consequences ; I was in despair. I was obliged to leave Gilberte for a moment ; Françoise had called me. I must accompany her into a little pavilion covered in a green trellis, not unlike one of the disused toll-houses of old Paris, in which had recently been installed what in England they call a lavatory but in France, by an ill-informed piece of anglomania, "water-closets ". The old, damp walls at the entrance, where I stood waiting for Françoise, emitted a chill and fusty smell which, relieving me at once of the anxieties that Swann's words, as reported by Gilberte, had just awakened in me, pervaded me with a pleasure not at all of the same character as other pleasures, which leave one more unstable than before, incapable of retaining them, of possessing them, but, on the contrary, with a consistent pleasure on which I could lean for support, delicious, soothing, rich with a truth that was lasting, unexplained and certain. I should have liked, as long ago in my walks along the Guermantes way, to endeavour to penetrate the charm of this impression which had seized hold of me, and, remaining there motionless, to interrogate this antiquated emanation which invited me not to enjoy the pleasure which it was offering me only as an " extra ", but to descend into the underlying reality which it had not yet disclosed to me. But the tenant of the establishment, an elderly dame with painted cheeks and an auburn wig, was speaking to me. Françoise thought her " very well-

THE CHAMPS ELYSEES

to-do indeed." Her "missy" had married what Françoise called "a young man of family," which meant that
he differed more, in her eyes, from a workman than, in
Saint-Simon's, a duke did from a man "risen from the
dregs of the people." No doubt the tenant, before entering upon her tenancy, had met with reverses. But Françoise was positive that she was a "marquise", and belonged to the Saint-Ferréol family. This "marquise"
warned me not to stand outside in the cold, and even
opened one of her doors for me, saying : "Won't you
go inside for a minute ? Look, here's a nice, clean one,
and I shan't charge *you* anything." Perhaps she just
made this offer in the spirit in which the young ladies at
Gouache's, when we went in there to order something,
used to offer me one of the sweets which they kept on the
counter under glass bells, and which, alas, Mamma would
never allow me to take ; perhaps with less innocence, like
an old florist whom Mamma used to have in to replenish
her flower-stands, who rolled languishing eyes at me as
she handed me a rose. In any event, if the "marquise"
had a weakness for little boys, when she threw open to
them the hypogean doors of those cubicles of stone in
which men crouch like sphinxes, she must have been
moved to that generosity less by the hope of corrupting
them than by the pleasure which all of us feel in displaying a needless prodigality to those whom we love, for I
have never seen her with any other visitor except an old
park-keeper.

A moment later I said good-bye to the "marquise", and
went out accompanied by Françoise, whom I left to return
to Gilberte. I caught sight of her at once, on a chair,
behind the clump of laurels. She was there so as not to

be seen by her friends : they were playing at hide-and-seek. I went and sat down by her side. She had on a flat cap which drooped forwards over her eyes, giving her the same "underhand", brooding, crafty look which I had remarked in her that first time at Combray. I asked her if there was not some way for me to have it out with her father, face to face. Gilberte said that she had suggested that to him, but that he had not thought it of any use. "Look," she went on, "don't go away without your letter ; I must run along to the others, as they haven't caught me."

Had Swann appeared on the scene then before I had recovered it, this letter, by the sincerity of which I felt that he had been so unreasonable in not letting himself be convinced, perhaps he would have seen that it was he who had been in the right. For as I approached Gilberte, who, leaning back in her chair, told me to take the letter but did not hold it out to me, I felt myself so irresistibly attracted by her body that I said to her :

"Look ! You try to stop me from getting it ; we'll see which is the stronger."

She thrust it behind her back ; I put my arms round her neck, raising the plaits of hair which she wore over her shoulders, either because she was still of an age for that or because her mother chose to make her look a child for a little longer so that she herself might still seem young ; and we wrestled, locked together. I tried to pull her towards me, she resisted ; her cheeks, inflamed by the effort, were as red and round as two cherries ; she laughed as though I were tickling her ; I held her gripped between my legs like a young tree which I was trying to climb ; and, in the middle of my gymnastics, when I was already out of breath with the muscular exercise and the heat of the game, I felt, as it were a few drops of sweat wrung from me by the effort, my pleasure express itself in a form which I could not even pause for a moment to analyse ; immediately I snatched the letter from her. Whereupon Gilberte said, good-naturedly :

" You know, if you like, we might go on wrestling for a little."

Perhaps she was dimly conscious that my game had had another object than that which I had avowed, but too dimly to have been able to see that I had attained it. And I, who was afraid that she had seen (and a slight recoil, as though of offended modesty which she made and checked a moment later made me think that my fear had not been unfounded), agreed to go on wrestling, lest she should suppose that I had indeed no other object than that, after which I wished only to sit quietly by her side.

On my way home I perceived, I suddenly recollected the impression, concealed from me until then, towards which, without letting me distinguish or recognise it, the cold, almost sooty smell of the trellised pavilion had borne me. It was that of my uncle Adolphe's little sitting-room at Combray, which had indeed exhaled the same odour of humidity. But I could not understand, and I postponed the attempt to discover why the recollection of so trivial an impression had given me so keen a happiness. It struck me, however, that I did indeed deserve the contempt of M. de Norpois ; I had preferred, hitherto, to all other writers, one whom he styled a mere " flute-player " and a positive rapture had been conveyed to me, not by any important idea, but by a mouldy smell.

For some time past, in certain households, the name

of the Champs-Elysées, if a visitor mentioned it, would be greeted by the mother of the family with that air of contempt which mothers keep for a physician of established reputation whom they have (or so they make out) seen make too many false diagnoses to have any faith left in him ; people insisted that these gardens were not good for children, that they knew of more than one sore throat, more than one case of measles and any number of feverish chills for which the Champs must be held responsible. Without venturing openly to doubt the maternal affection of Mamma, who continued to let me play there, several of her friends deplored her inability to see what was as plain as daylight.

Neurotic subjects are perhaps less addicted than any, despite the time-honoured phrase, to " listening to their insides " : they can hear so many things going on inside themselves, by which they realise later that they did wrong to let themselves be alarmed, that they end by paying no attention to any of them. Their nervous systems have so often cried out to them for help, as though from some serious malady, when it was merely because snow was coming, or because they had to change their rooms, that they have acquired the habit of paying no more heed to these warnings than a soldier who in the heat of battle perceives them so little that he is capable, although dying, of carrying on for some days still the life of a man in perfect health. One morning, bearing arranged within me all my regular disabilities, from whose constant, internal circulation I kept my mind turned as resolutely away as from the circulation of my blood, I had come running into the dining-room where my parents were already at table, and—having assured myself, as usual, that to feel cold may mean not that one ought to warm oneself but that, for instance, one has received a scolding, and not to feel hungry that it is going to rain, and not that one ought not to eat anything—had taken my place between them when, in the act of swallowing the first mouthful of a particularly tempting cutlet, a nausea, a giddiness stopped me, the feverish reaction of a malady that had already begun, the symptoms of which had been masked, retarded by the ice of my indifference, but which obstinately refused the nourishment that I was not in a fit state to absorb. Then, at the same moment, the thought that they would stop me from going out if they saw that I was unwell gave me, as the instinct of self-preservation gives a wounded man, the strength to crawl to my own room, where I found that I had a temperature of 104, and then to get ready to go to the Champs-Elysées. Through the languid and vulnerable shell which encased them, my eager thoughts were urging me towards, were clamouring for the soothing delight of a game of prisoner's base with Gilberte, and an hour later, barely able to keep on my feet, but happy in being by her side, I had still the strength to enjoy it.

Françoise, on our return, declared that I had been "taken bad", that I must have caught a "hot and cold", while the doctor, who was called in at once, declared that he "preferred" the "severity", the "virulence" of the rush of fever which accompanied my congestion of the lungs, and would be no more than "a fire of straw", to other forms, more "insidious" and "septic". For some time now I had been liable to choking fits, and our doctor, braving the disapproval of my grandmother, who could see me already dying a drunkard's death, had recommended me to take, as well as the caffeine which had been prescribed to help me to breathe, beer, champagne or brandy when I felt an attack coming. These attacks would subside, he told me, in the " euphoria " brought about by the alcohol. I was often obliged, so that my grandmother should allow them to give it to me, instead of dissembling, almost to make a display of my state of suffocation. On the other hand, as soon as I felt an attack coming, never being quite certain what proportions it would assume, I would grow distressed at the thought of my grandmother's anxiety, of which I was far more afraid than of my own sufferings. But at the same time my body, either because it was too weak to keep those sufferings secret, or because it feared lest, in their ignorance of the imminent disaster, people might demand of me some exertion which it would have found impossible or dangerous, gave me the need to warn my grandmother of my attacks with a punctiliousness into which I finally put a sort of physiological scruple. Did I perceive in myself a disturbing symptom which I had not previously observed, my body was in distress so long as I had not communicated it to my grandmother. Did she pretend to pay no attention, it made me insist. Sometimes I went too far ; and that dear face, which was no longer able always to control its emotion as in the past, would allow an expression of pity to appear, a painful contraction. Then my heart was wrung by the sight of her grief ; as if my kisses had had power to expel that grief, as if my affection could give my grandmother as much joy as my recovery, I flung myself into her arms. And its scruples being at the same time calmed by the certainty that she now knew the discomfort that I felt, my body offered no opposition to my reassuring her. I protested that this discomfort had been nothing, that I was in no sense to be pitied, that she might be quite sure that I was now happy ; my body had wished to secure exactly the amount of pity that it deserved, and, provided that someone knew that it 'had a pain' in its right side, it could see no harm in my declaring that this pain was of no consequence and was not an obstacle to my happiness ; for my body did not pride itself on its philosophy ; that was outside its province. Almost every day during my convalesence I passed through these crises of suffocation. One evening, after my grandmother had left me comparatively well, she returned to my room very late and, seeing me struggling for breath, "Oh, my poor boy," she exclaimed, her face quivering with sympathy, "you are in dreadful pain." She left me at once ; I heard the outer gate open, and in a little while she came back with some brandy which she had gone out to buy, since there was none in the house. Presently I began to feel better. My grandmother, who was rather flushed, seemed "put out" about something, and her eyes had a look of weariness and dejection.

"I shall leave you alone now, and let you get the good of this improvement," she said, rising suddenly to go. I detained her, however, for a kiss, and could feel on her cold cheek something moist, but did not know whether it was the dampness of the night air through which she had just passed. Next day, she did not come to my room until the evening, having had, she told me, to go out. I considered that this shewed a surprising indifference to my welfare, and I had to restrain myself so as not to reproach her with it.

As my chokings had persisted long after any congestion remained that could account for them, my parents asked for a consultation with Professor Cottard. It is not enough that a physician who is called in to treat cases of this sort should be learned. Brought face to face with symptoms which may or may not be those of three or four different complaints, it is in the long run his instinct, his eye that must decide with which, despite the more or less similar appearance of them all, he has to deal. This mysterious gift does not imply any superiority in the other departments of the intellect, and a creature of the utmost vulgarity, who admires the worst pictures, the worst music, in whose mind there is nothing out of the common, may perfectly well possess it. In my case, what was physically evident might equally well have been due to nervous spasms, to the first stages of tuberculosis, to asthma, to a toxi-alimentary dyspnoea with renal insufficiency, to chronic bronchitis, or to a complex state into which more than one of these factors entered. Now, nervous spasms required to be treated firmly, and discouraged, tuberculosis with infinite care and with a " feeding-up " process which would have been bad for an arthritic condition such as asthma, and might indeed have been dangerous in a case of toxi-alimentary dyspnoea, this last calling for a strict diet which, in return, would be fatal to a tuberculous patient. But Cottard's hesitations were brief and his prescriptions imperious. " Purges ; violent and drastic purges ; milk for some days, nothing but milk. No meat. No alcohol." My mother murmured that I needed, all the same, to be " built up ", that my nerves were already weak, that drenching me like a horse and restricting my diet would make me worse. I could see in

Cottard's eyes, as uneasy as though he were afraid of missing a train, that he was asking himself whether he had not allowed his natural good-humour to appear. He was trying to think whether he had remembered to put on his mask of coldness, as one looks for a mirror to see whether one has not forgotten to tie one's tie. In his uncertainty, and, so as, whatever he had done, to put things right, he replied brutally : " I am not in the habit of repeating my instructions. Give me a pen. Now remember, milk ! Later on, when we have got the crises and the agrypnia by the throat, I should like you to take a little clear soup, and then a little broth, but always with milk ; *au lait !* You'll enjoy that, since Spain is all the rage just now ; *ollé, ollé !* " His pupils knew this joke well, for he made it at the hospital whenever he had to put a heart or liver case on a milk diet. " After that, you will gradually return to your normal life. But whenever there is any coughing or choking—purges, injections, bed, milk ! " He listened with icy calm, and without uttering a word, to my mother's final objections, and as he left us without having condescended to explain the reasons for this course of treatment, my parents concluded that it had no bearing on my case, and would weaken me to no purpose, and so they did not make me try it. Naturally they sought to conceal their disobedience from the Professor, and to succeed in this avoided all the houses in which he was likely to be found. Then, as my health became worse, they decided to make me follow out Cottard's prescriptions to the letter ; in three days my " rattle " and cough had ceased, I could breathe freely. Whereupon we realised that Cottard, while finding, as he told us later on, that I was distinctly asthmatic, and still more inclined to "imagine things", had seen that what was really the matter with me at the moment was intoxication, and that by loosening my liver and washing out my kidneys he would get rid of the congestion of my bronchial tubes and thus give me back my breath, my sleep and my strength. And we realised that this imbecile was a clinical genius. At last I was able to get up. But they spoke of not letting me go any more to the Champs-Elysées. They said that it was because the air there was bad ; but I felt sure that this was only a pretext so that I should not see Mlle. Swann, and I forced myself to repeat the name of Gilberte all the time, like the native tongue which peoples in captivity endeavour to preserve among themselves so as not to forget the land that they will never see again. Sometimes my mother would stroke my forehead with her hand, saying : "So little boys don't tell Mamma their troubles any more ?" And Françoise used to come up to me every day with : "What a face, to be sure ! If you could just see yourself ! Anyone would think there was a corpse in the house." It is true that, if I had simply had a cold in the head, Françoise would have assumed the same funereal air. These lamentations pertained rather to her "class" than to the state of my health. I could not at the time discover whether this pessimism was due to sorrow or to satisfaction. I decided provisionally that it was social and professional.

One day, after the postman had called, my mother laid a letter upon my bed. I opened it carelessly, since it could not bear the one signature that would have made me happy, the name of Gilberte, with whom I had no relations outside the Champs-Elysées. And lo, at the foot of the page, embossed with a silver seal representing a man's head in a helmet, and under him a scroll with the device *Per viam rectam,* beneath a letter written in a large and flowing hand, in which almost every word appeared to be underlined, simply because the crosses of the 't's ran not across but over them, and so drew a line beneath the corresponding letters of the word above, it was indeed Gilberte's signature and nothing else that I saw. But because I knew that to be impossible upon a letter addressed to myself, the sight of it, unaccompanied by any belief in it, gave me no pleasure. For a moment it merely struck an impression of unreality on everything round about me. With lightning rapidity the impossible signature danced about my bed, the fireplace, the four walls. I saw everything sway, as one does when one falls from a horse, and I asked myself whether there was not an existence altogether different from the one I knew, in direct contradiction of it, but itself the true existence, which, being suddenly revealed to me, filled me with that hesitation which sculptors, in representing the Last Judgment, have given to the awakening dead who find themselves at the gates of the next world. "My dear Friend," said the letter, "I hear that you have been very ill and have given up going to the Champs-Elysées. I hardly ever go there either because there has been such an enormous lot of illness. But I'm having my friends to tea here every Monday and Friday. Mamma asks me to tell you that it will be a great pleasure to us all if you will come too, as soon as you are well again, and we can have some more nice talks here, just like the Champs-Elysées. Good-bye, dear friend ; I hope that your parents will allow you to come to tea very often. With all my kindest regards. GILBERTE."

While I was reading these words, my nervous system was receiving, with admirable promptitude, the news that a piece of great good fortune had befallen me. But my mind, that is to say myself, and in fact the party principally concerned, was still in ignorance. Such good fortune, coming from Gilberte, was a thing of which I had never ceased to dream ; a thing wholly in my mind, it was, as Leonardo says of painting, *cosa mentale*. Now, a sheet of paper covered with writing is not a thing that the mind assimilates at once. But as soon as I had finished reading the letter, I thought of it, it became an object of my dreams, became, it also, *cosa mentale*, and I loved it so much already that every few minutes I must read it, kiss it again. Then at last I was conscious of my happiness.

Life is strewn with these miracles, for which people who are in love can always hope. It is possible that this one had been artificially brought about by my mother who, seeing that for some time past I had lost all interest in life, may have suggested to Gilberte to write to me, just as, when I was little and went first to the sea-side, so as to give me some pleasure in bathing, which I detested because it took away my breath, she used secretly to hand to the man who was to " dip " me marvellous boxes made of shells, and branches of coral, which I believed that I myself had discovered lying at the bottom of the sea. However, with every occurrence which, in our life and among its contrasted situations, bears any relation to love, it is best to make no attempt to understand it, since in so far as these are inexorable, as they are unlooked-for, they appear to be governed by magic rather than by rational laws. When a multi-millionaire—who for all his millions is quite a charming person—sent packing by a poor and unattractive woman with whom he has been living, calls to his aid, in his desperation, all the resources of wealth, and brings every worldly influence to bear without succeeding in making her take him back, it is wiser for him, in the face of the implacable obstinacy of his mistress, to suppose that Fate intends to crush him, and to make him die of an affection of the heart, than to seek any logical explanation. These obstacles, against which lovers have to contend, and which their imagination, over-excited by suffering, seeks in vain to analyse, are contained, as often as not, in some peculiar characteristic of the woman whom they cannot bring back to themselves, in her stupidity, in the influence acquired over her, the fears suggested to her by people whom the lover does not know, in the kind of pleasures which, at the moment, she is demanding of life, pleasures which neither her lover nor her lover's wealth can procure for her. In any event, the lover is scarcely in a position to discover the nature of these obstacles, which her womanly cunning hides from him and his own judgment, falsified by love, prevents him from estimating exactly. They may be compared with those tumours which the doctor succeeds in reducing, but without having traced them to their source. Like them these obstacles remain mysterious but are temporary. Only they last, as a rule, longer than love itself. And as that is not a disinterested passion, the lover who is no longer in love does not seek to know why the woman, neither rich nor virtuous, with whom he was in love refused obstinately for years to let him continue to keep her.

Now the same mystery which often veils from our eyes the reason for a catastrophe, when love is in question, envelops just as frequently the suddenness of certain happy solutions, such as had come to me with Gilberte's letter. Happy, or at least seemingly happy, for there are few solutions that can really be happy when we are dealing with a sentiment of such a kind that every satisfaction which we can bring to it does no more, as a rule, than dislodge some pain. And yet sometimes a respite is granted us, and we have for a little while the illusion that we are healed.

So far as concerns this letter, at the foot of which Françoise declined to recognise Gilberte's name, because the elaborate capital 'G' leaning against the undotted 'i' looked more like an 'A', while the final syllable was indefinitely prolonged by a waving flourish, if we persist in looking for a rational explanation of the sudden reversal of her attitude towards me which it indicated, and which made me so radiantly happy, we may perhaps find that I was to some extent indebted for it to an incident which I should have supposed, on the contrary, to be calculated to ruin me for ever in the sight of the Swann family. A short while back, Bloch had come to see me at a time when Professor Cottard, whom, now that I was following his instructions, we were again calling in, happened to be in my room. As his examination of me was over, and he was sitting with me simply as a visitor because my parents had invited him to stay to dinner, Bloch was allowed to come in. While we were all talking, Bloch having mentioned that he had heard it said that Mme. Swann was very fond of me, by a lady with whom he had been dining the day before, who was herself very intimate with Mme. Swann, I should have liked to reply that he was most certainly mistaken, and to establish the fact (from the same scruple of conscience that had made me proclaim it to M. de Norpois, and for fear of Mme. Swann's taking me for a liar) that I did not know her and had never spoken to her. But I had not the courage to correct Bloch's mistake, because I could see quite well that it was deliberate, and that, if he invented something that Mme. Swann could not possibly have said, it was simply to let us know (what he considered flattering to himself, and was not true either) that he had been dining with one of that lady's friends. And so it fell out that, whereas M. de Norpois, on learning that I did not know but would very much like to know Mme. Swann, had taken great care to avoid speaking to her about me, Cottard, who was her doctor also, having gathered from what he had heard Bloch say that she knew me quite well and thought highly of me, concluded that to remark, when next he saw her, that I was a charming young fellow and a great friend of his could not be of the smallest use to me and would be of advantage to himself, two reasons which made him decide to speak of me to Odette whenever an opportunity arose.

Thus at length I found my way into that abode from which was wafted even on to the staircase the scent that Mme. Swann used, though it was embalmed far more sweetly still by the peculiar, disturbing charm that emanated from the life of Gilberte. The implacable porter, transformed into a benevolent Eumenid, adopted the custom, when I asked him if I might go upstairs, of indicating to me, by raising his cap with a propitious hand, that he gave ear to my prayer. Those windows which, seen from outside, used to interpose between me and the treasures within, which were not intended for me, a polished, distant and superficial stare, which seemed to me the very stare of the Swanns themselves, it fell to my lot, when in the warm weather I had spent a whole afternoon with Gilberte in her room, to open them myself, so as to let in a little air, and even to lean over the sill of one of them by her side, if it was her mother's "at home" day, to watch the visitors arrive who would often, raising their heads as they stepped out of their carriages, greet me with a wave of the hand, taking me for some nephew of their hostess. At such moments Gilberte's plaits used to brush my cheek. They seemed to me, in the fineness of their grain, at once natural and supernatural, and in the strength of their constructed tracery, a matchless work of art, in the composition of which had been used the very grass of Paradise. To a section of them, even infinitely minute, what celestial herbary would I not have given as a reliquary. But since I never hoped to obtain an actual fragment of those plaits, if at least I had been able to have their photograph, how far more precious than one of a sheet of flowers traced by Vinci's pencil! To acquire one of these, I stooped—with friends of the Swanns, and even with photographers—to servilities which did not procure for me what I wanted, but tied me for life to a number of extremely tiresome people.

Gilberte's parents, who for so long had prevented me from seeing her, now—when I entered the dark hall in which hovered perpetually, more formidable and more to be desired than, at Versailles of old, the apparition of the King, the possibility of my encountering them, in which too, invariably, after butting into an enormous hat-stand with seven branches, like the Candlestick in Holy Writ, I would begin bowing confusedly before a footman,

seated among the skirts of his long grey coat upon
the wood-box, whom in the dim light I had mistaken for
Mme. Swann—Gilberte's parents, if one of them happened
to be passing at the moment of my arrival, so far from
seeming annoyed would come and shake hands with a
smile, and say :

"How d'e do ? " (They both pronounced it in the
same clipped way, which, you may well imagine, once I
was back at home, I made an incessant and delightful
practice of copying.) "Does Gilberte know you're here ?
She does ? Then I'll leave you to her."

Better still, the tea-parties themselves to which Gilberte invited her friends, parties which for so long had
seemed to me the most insurmountable of the barriers
heaped up between her and myself, became now an opportunity for uniting us of which she would inform me
in a few lines, written (because I was still a comparative
stranger) upon sheets that were always different. One
was adorned with a poodle embossed in blue, above a
fantastic inscription in English with an exclamation mark
after it ; another was stamped with an anchor, or with
the monogram G. S. preposterously elongated in a rec-
tangle which ran from top to bottom of the page, or else
with the name Gilberte, now traced across one corner in
letters of gold which imitated my friend's signature and
ended in a flourish, beneath an open umbrella printed in
black, now enclosed in a monogram in the shape of a
Chinaman's hat, which contained all the letters of the
word in capitals without its being possible to make out a
single one of them. At last, as the series of different
writing-papers which Gilberte possessed, numerous as it
might be, was not unlimited, after a certain number of

weeks I saw reappear the sheet that bore (like the first letter she had written me) the motto *Per viam rectam,* and over it the man's head in a helmet, set in a medallion of tarnished silver. And each of them was chosen, on one day rather than another, by virtue of a certain ritual, as I then supposed, but more probably, as I now think, because she tried to remember which of them she had already used, so as never to send the same one twice to any of her correspondents, of those at least whom she took special pains to please, save at the longest possible intervals. As, on account of the different times of their lessons, some of the friends whom Gilberte used to invite to her parties were obliged to leave just as the rest were arriving, while I was still on the stairs I could hear escaping from the hall a murmur of voices which, such was the emotion aroused in me by the imposing ceremony in which I was to take part, long before I had reached the landing, broke all the bonds that still held me to my past life, so that I did not even remember that I was to take off my muffler as soon as I felt too hot, and to keep an eye on the clock so as not to be late in getting home. That staircase, besides, all of wood, as they were built about that time in certain houses, in keeping with that Henri II style which had for so long been Odette's ideal though she was shortly to lose interest in it, and furnished with a placard, to which there was no equivalent at home, on which one read the words : "NOTICE. The lift must not be taken downstairs", seemed to me a thing so marvellous that I told my parents that it was an ancient staircase brought from ever so far away by M. Swann. My regard for the truth was so great that I should not have hesitated to give them this information even if I had known it to be false, for it alone could enable them to feel for the dignity of the Swanns' staircase the same respect that I felt myself. It was just as, when one is talking to some ignorant person who cannot understand in what the genius of a great physician consists, it is as well not to admit that he does not know how to cure a cold in the head. But since I had no power of observation, since, as a general rule, I never knew either the name or the nature of things that were before my eyes, and could understand only that when they were connected with the Swanns they must be extraordinary, I was by no means certain that in notifying my parents of the artistic value and remote origin of the staircase I was guilty of falsehood. It did not seem certain ; but it must have seemed probable, for I felt myself turn very red when my father interrupted me with : " I know those houses ; I have been in one ; they are all alike ; Swann just has several floors in one ; it was Berlier built them all." He added that he had thought of taking a flat in one of them, but that he had changed his mind, finding that they were not conveniently arranged, and that the landings were too dark. So he said ; but I felt instinctively that my mind must make the sacrifices necessary to the glory of the Swanns and to my own happiness, and by a stroke of internal authority, in spite of what I had just heard, I banished for ever from my memory, as a good Catholic banishes Renan's *Vie de Jésus*, the destroying thought that their house was just an ordinary flat in which we ourselves might have been living.

Meanwhile on those tea-party days, pulling myself up the staircase step by step, reason and memory already cast off like outer garments, and myself no more now than the sport of the basest reflexes, I would arrive in the zone in which the scent of Mme. Swann greeted my nostrils. I felt that I could already behold the majesty of the chocolate cake, encircled by plates heaped with little cakes, and by tiny napkins of grey damask with figures on them, as required by convention but peculiar to the Swanns. But this unalterable and governed whole seemed, like Kant's necessary universe, to depend on a supreme act of free will. For when we were all together in Gilberte's little sitting-room, suddenly she would look at the clock and exclaim :

"I say ! It's getting a long time since luncheon, and we aren't having dinner till eight. I feel as if I could eat something. What do you say ? "

And she would make us go into the dining-room, as sombre as the interior of an Asiatic Temple painted by Rembrandt, in which an architectural cake, as gracious and sociable as it was imposing, seemed to be enthroned there in any event, in case the fancy seized Gilberte to discrown it of its chocolate battlements and to hew down the steep brown slopes of its ramparts, baked in the oven like the bastions of the palace of Darius. Better still, in proceeding to the demolition of that Babylonitish pastry, Gilberte did not consider only her own hunger ; she inquired also after mine, while she extracted for me from the crumbling monument a whole glazed slab jewelled with scarlet fruits, in the oriental style. She asked me even at what o'clock my parents were dining, as if I still knew, as if the disturbance that governed me had allowed to persist the sensation of satiety or of hunger, the notion of dinner or the picture of my family in my empty memory and paralysed stomach. Alas, its paralysis was but momentary. The cakes that I took without noticing them, a time would come when I should have to digest them. But that time was still remote. Meanwhile Gilberte was making " my " tea. I went on drinking it indefinitely, whereas a single cup would keep me awake for twenty-four hours. Which explains why my mother used always to say : " What a nuisance it is ; he can never go to the Swanns' without coming home ill." But was I aware even, when I was at the Swanns', that it was tea that I was drinking ? Had I known, I should have taken it just the same, for even supposing that I had recovered for a moment the sense of the present, that would not have restored to me the memory of the past or the apprehension of the future. My imagination was incapable of reaching to the distant time in which I might have the idea of going to bed, and the need to sleep.

Gilberte's girl friends were not all plunged in that state of intoxication in which it is impossible to make up one's mind. Some of them refused tea ! Then Gilberte would say, using a phrase highly fashionable that year : " I can see I'm not having much of a success with my tea ! " And to destroy more completely any idea of ceremony, she would disarrange the chairs that were drawn up round the table, with: "We look just like a wedding breakfast. Good lord, what fools servants are ! "

She nibbled her cake, perched sideways upon a cross-legged seat placed at an angle to the table. And then, just as though she could have had all those cakes at her disposal without having first asked leave of her mother, when Mme. Swann, whose "day" coincided as a rule with Gilberte's tea-parties, had shewn one of her visitors to the door, and came sweeping in, a moment later, dressed sometimes in blue velvet, more often in a black satin gown draped with white lace, she would say with an air of astonishment : " I say, that looks good, what you've got there. It makes me quite hungry to see you all eating cake."

" But, Mamma, do ! We invite you ! " Gilberte would answer.

" Thank you, no, my precious ; what would my visitors say ? I've still got Mme. Trombert and Mme. Cottard and Mme. Bontemps ; you know dear Mme. Bontemps never pays very short visits, and she has only just come. What would all those good people say if I never went back to them ? If no one else calls, I'll come in again and have a chat with you (which will be far more amusing) after they've all gone. I really think I've earned a little rest ; I have had forty-five different people to-day, and forty-two of them told me about Gérôme's picture ! But you must come along one of these days," she turned to me, " and take ' your ' tea with Gilberte. She will make it for you just as you like it, as you have it in your own little ' studio '," she went on, flying off to her visitors, as if it had been something as familiar to me as my own habits (such as the habit that I should have had of taking tea, had I ever taken it ; as for my " studio ", I was uncertain whether I had one or not) that I had come to seek in this mysterious world. " When can you come ? To-morrow ? We will make you ' toast ' every bit as good as you get at Colombin's. No ? You are horrid ! "— for, since she also had begun to form a salon, she had borrowed Mme. Verdurin's mannerisms, and notably her tone of petulant autocracy. " Toast " being as incompre-

hensible to me as "Colombin's", this further promise
could not add to my temptation. It will appear stranger
still, now that everyone uses such expressions—and perhaps even at Combray they are creeping in—that I had
not at first understood of whom Mme. Swann was speaking when I heard her sing the praises of our old "nurse".
I did not know any English ; I gathered, however, as she
went on that the word was intended to denote Françoise.
I who, in the Champs-Elysées, had been so terrified of the
bad impression that she must make, I now learned from
Mme. Swann that it was all the things that Gilberte had
told them about my "nurse" that had attracted her husband and her to me. "One feels that she is so devoted
to you ; she must be nice ! " (At once my opinion of
Françoise was diametrically changed. By the same
token, to have a governess equipped with a waterproof
and a feather in her hat no longer appeared quite so essential.) Finally I learned from some words which Mme.
Swann let fall with regard to Mme. Blatin (whose good
nature she recognised but dreaded her visits) that personal relations with that lady would have been of less
value to me than I had supposed, and would not in any
way have improved my standing with the Swanns.

If I had now begun to explore, with tremors of reverence and joy the faery domain which, against all probability, had opened to me its hitherto locked approaches,
this was still only in my capacity as a friend of Gilberte.
The kingdom into which I was received was itself contained within another, more mysterious still, in which
Swann and his wife led their supernatural existence and
towards which they made their way, after taking my hand
in theirs, when they crossed the hall at the same moment

as myself but in the other direction. But soon I was to penetrate also to the heart of the Sanctuary. For instance, Gilberte might be out when I called, but M. or Mme. Swann was at home. They would ask who had rung, and on being told that it was myself would send out to ask me to come in for a moment and talk to them, desiring me to use in one way or another, and with this or that object in view, my influence over their daughter. I reminded myself of that letter, so complete, so convincing, which I had written to Swann only the other day, and which he had not deigned even to acknowledge. I marvelled at the impotence of the mind, the reason and the heart to effect the least conversion, to solve a single one of those difficulties which, in the sequel, life, without one's so much as knowing what steps it has taken, so easily unravels. My new position as the friend of Gilberte, endowed with an excellent influence over her, entitling me now to enjoy the same favours as if, having had as a companion at some school where they had always put me at the head of my class the son of a king, I had owed to that accident the right of informal entry into the palace and to audiences in the throne-room, Swann, with an infinite benevolence and as though he were not overburdened with glorious occupations, would make me go into his library and there let me for an hour on end respond in stammered monosyllables, timid silences broken by brief and incoherent bursts of courage, to utterances of which my emotion prevented me from understanding a single word; would shew me works of art and books which he thought likely to interest me, things as to which I had no doubt, before seeing them, that they infinitely surpassed in beauty anything that the Louvre

possessed or the National Library, but at which I found it
impossible to look. At such moments I should have been
grateful to Swann's butler, had he demanded from me my
watch, my tie-pin, my boots, and made me sign a deed
acknowledging him as my heir : in the admirable words
of a popular expression of which, as of the most famous
epics, we do not know who was the author, although, like
those epics, and with all deference to Wolff and his theory,
it most certainly had an author, one of those inventive,
modest souls such as we come across every year, who
light upon such gems as "putting a name to a face",
though their own names they never let us learn, I did not
know what I was doing. All the greater was my astonishment, when my visit was prolonged, at finding to what
a zero of realisation, to what an absence of happy ending
those hours spent in the enchanted dwelling led me. But
my disappointment arose neither from the inadequacy of
the works of art that were shewn to me nor from the impossibility of fixing upon them my distracted gaze. For
it was not the intrinsic beauty of the objects themselves
that made it miraculous for me to be sitting in Swann's
library, it was the attachment to those objects—which
might have been the ugliest in the world—of the particular
feeling, melancholy and voluptuous, which I had for so
many years localised in that room and which still impregnated it ; similarly the multitude of mirrors, of silver-
backed brushes, of altars to Saint Anthony of Padua,
carved and painted by the most eminent artists, her
friends, counted for nothing in the feeling of my own unworthiness and of her regal benevolence which was
aroused in me when Mme. Swann received me for a moment in her own room, in which three beautiful and im-

pressive creatures, her principal and second and third maids, smilingly prepared for her the most marvellous toilets, and towards which, on the order conveyed to me by the footman in knee-breeches that Madame wished to say a few words to me, I would make my way along the tortuous path of a corridor all embalmed, far and near, by the precious essences which exhaled without ceasing from her dressing-room a fragrance exquisitely sweet.

When Mme. Swann had returned to her visitors, we could still hear her talking and laughing, for even with only two people in the room, and as though she had to cope with all the " good friends " at once, she would raise her voice, ejaculate her words, as she had so often in the " little clan " heard its " Mistress " do, at the moments when she " led the conversation ". The expressions which we have borrowed from other people being those which, for a time at least, we are fondest of using, Mme. Swann used to select at one time those which she had learned from distinguished people whom her husband had not managed to prevent her from getting to know (it was from them that she derived the mannerism which consists in suppressing the article or demonstrative pronoun, in French, before an adjective qualifying a person's name), at another time others more plebeian (such as " It's a mere nothing ! " the favourite expression of one of her friends), and used to make room for them in all the stories which, by a habit formed among the "little clan ", she loved to tell about people. She would follow these up automatically with, " I do love that story ! " or " Do admit, it's a very *good* story ! " which came to her, through her husband, from the Guermantes, whom she did not know.

Mme. Swann had left the dining-room, but her husband, who had just returned home, made his appearance among us in turn. "Do you know if your mother is alone, Gilberte?" "No, Papa, she has still some people." "What, still? At seven o'clock! It's appalling! The poor woman must be absolutely dead. It's odious." (At home I had always heard the first syllable of this word pronounced with a long 'o', like "ode", but M. and Mme. Swann made it short, as in "odd".) "Just think of it; ever since two o'clock this afternoon!" he went on, turning to me. "And Camille tells me that between four and five he let in at least a dozen people. Did I say a dozen? I believe he told me fourteen. No, a dozen; I don't remember. When I came home I had quite forgotten it was her 'day', and when I saw all those carriages outside the door I thought there must be a wedding in the house. And just now, while I've been in the library for a minute, the bell has never stopped ringing; upon my word, it's given me quite a headache. And are there a lot of them in there still?" "No; only two." "Who are they, do you know?" "Mme. Cottard and Mme. Bontemps." "Oh! the wife of the Chief Secretary to the Minister of Posts." "I know her husband's a clerk in some Ministry or other, but I don't know what he does." Gilberte assumed a babyish manner.

"What's that? You silly child, you talk as if you were two years old. What do you mean; 'a clerk in some Ministry or other' indeed! He is nothing less than Chief Secretary, chief of the whole show, and what's more —what on earth am I thinking of? Upon my word, I'm getting as stupid as yourself; he is not the Chief Secretary, he's the Permanent Secretary."

" I don't know, I'm sure ; does that mean a lot, being Permanent Secretary ? " answered Gilberte, who never let slip an opportunity of displaying her own indifference to anything that gave her parents cause for vanity. (She may, of course, have considered that she only enhanced the brilliance of such an acquaintance by not seeming to attach any undue importance to it.)

" I should think it did ' mean a lot ' ! " exclaimed Swann, who preferred to this modesty, which might have left me in doubt, a more explicit mode of speech. " Why it means simply that he's the first man after the Minister. In fact, he's more important than the Minister, because it is he that does all the work. Besides, it appears that he has immense capacity, a man quite of the first rank, a most distinguished individual. He's an Officer of the Legion of Honour. A delightful man, he is, and very good-looking too."

(This man's wife, incidentally, had married him against everyone's wishes and advice because he was a ' charming creature '. He had, what may be sufficient to constitute a rare and delicate whole, a fair, silky beard, good features, a nasal voice, powerful lungs and a glass eye.)

" I may tell you," he added, turning again to me, " that I am greatly amused to see that lot serving in the present Government, because they are Bontemps of the Bontemps-Chenut family, typical old-fashioned middle-class people, reactionary, clerical, tremendously straitlaced. Your grandfather knew quite well—at least by name and by sight he must have known old Chenut, the father, who never tipped the cabmen more than a ha'penny, though he was a rich enough man for those days, and the Baron Bréau-Chenut. All their money went in the Union

Générale smash—you're too young to remember that, of course—and, gad ! they've had to get it back as best they could."

"He's the uncle of a little girl who used to come to my lessons, in a class a long way below mine, the famous 'Albertine'. She's certain to be dreadfully 'fast' when she's older, but just now she's the quaintest spectacle."

"She is amazing, this daughter of mine. She knows everyone."

"I don't know her. I only used to see her going about, and hear them calling 'Albertine' here, and 'Albertine' there. But I do know Mme. Bontemps, and I don't like her much either."

"You are quite wrong ; she is charming, pretty, intelligent. In fact, she's quite clever. I shall go in and say how d'ye do to her, and ask her if her husband thinks we're going to have war, and whether we can rely on King Theodosius. He's bound to know, don't you think, since he's in the counsels of the gods."

It was not thus that Swann used to talk in days gone by ; but which of us cannot call to mind some royal princess of limited intelligence who let herself be carried off by a footman, and then, ten years later, tried to get back into society, and found that people were not very willing to call upon her ; have we not found her spontaneously adopting the language of all the old bores, and, when we referred to some duchess who was at the height of fashion, heard her say : " She came to see me only yesterday," or " I live a very quiet life." So that it is superfluous to make a study of manners, since we can deduce them all from psychological laws.

The Swanns shared this eccentricity of people who have

not many friends ; a visit, an invitation, a mere friendly word from some one ever so little prominent were for them events to which they aspired to give full publicity. If bad luck would have it that the Verdurins were in London when Odette gave a rather smart dinner-party, arrangements were made by which some common friend was to "cable" a report to them across the Channel. Even the complimentary letters and telegrams received by Odette the Swanns were incapable of keeping to themselves. They spoke of them to their friends, passed them from hand to hand. Thus the Swanns' drawing-room reminded one of a seaside hotel where telegrams containing the latest news are posted up on a board.

Still, people who had known the old Swann not merely outside society, as I had known him, but in society, in that Guermantes set which, with certain concessions to Highnesses and Duchesses, was almost infinitely exacting in the matter of wit and charm, from which banishment was sternly decreed for men of real eminence whom its members found boring or vulgar,—such people might have been astonished to observe that their old Swann had ceased to be not only discreet when he spoke of his acquaintance, but difficult when he was called upon to enlarge it. How was it that Mme. Bontemps, so common, so ill-natured, failed to exasperate him ? How could he possibly describe her as attractive ? The memory of the Guermantes set must, one would suppose, have prevented him ; as a matter of fact it encouraged him. There was certainly among the Guermantes, as compared with the great majority of groups in society, taste, indeed a refined taste, but also a snobbishness from which there arose the possibility of a momentary interruption in the exercise

of that taste. If it were a question of some one who was
not indispensable to their circle, of a Minister for Foreign
Affairs, a Republican and inclined to be pompous, or of
an Academician who talked too much, their taste would
be brought to bear heavily against him, Swann would
condole with Mme. de Guermantes on having had to sit
next to such people at dinner at one of the Embassies, and
they would a thousand times rather have a man of
fashion, that is to say a man of the Guermantes kind,
good for nothing, but endowed with the wit of the Guermantes, some one who was " of the same chapel " as themselves. Only, a Grand Duchess, a Princess of the Blood,
should she dine often with Mme. de Guermantes, would
soon find herself enrolled in that chapel also, without
having any right to be there, without being at all so endowed. But with the simplicity of people in society, from
the moment they had her in their houses they went out of
their way to find her attractive, since they were unable to
say that it was because she was attractive that they invited her. Swann, coming to the rescue of Mme. de
Guermantes, would say to her after the Highness had
gone : " After all, she's not such a bad woman ; really,
she has quite a sense of the comic. I don't suppose for
a moment that she has mastered the *Critique of Pure
Reason* ; still, she is not unattractive." " Oh, I do so entirely agree with you ! " the Duchess would respond.
" Besides, she was a little frightened of us all ; you will
see that she can be charming." " She is certainly a great
deal less devastating than Mme. X——" (the wife of the
talkative Academician, and herself a remarkable woman)
" who quotes twenty volumes at you." " Oh, but
there isn't any comparison between them." The faculty

of saying such things as these, and of saying them sincerely, Swann had acquired from the Duchess, and had never lost. He made use of it now with reference to the people who came to his house. He forced himself to distinguish, and to admire in them the qualities that every human being will display if we examine him with a prejudice in his favour, and not with the distaste of the nice-minded ; he extolled the merits of Mme. Bontemps, as he had once extolled those of the Princesse de Parme, who must have been excluded from the Guermantes set if there had not been privileged terms of admission for certain Highnesses, and if, when they presented themselves for election, no consideration had indeed been paid except to wit and charm. We have seen already, moreover, that Swann had always an inclination (which he was now putting into practice, only in a more lasting fashion) to exchange his social position for another which, in certain circumstances, might suit him better. It is only people incapable of analysing, in their perception, what at first sight appears indivisible who believe that one's position is consolidated with one's person. One and the same man, taken at successive points in his life, will be found to breathe, at different stages on the social ladder, in atmospheres that do not of necessity become more and more refined ; whenever, in any period of our existence, we form or re-form associations with a certain environment, and feel that we can move at ease in it and are made comfortable, we begin quite naturally to make ourselves fast to it by putting out roots and tendrils.

In so far as Mme. Bontemps was concerned, I believe also that Swann, in speaking of her with so much emphasis, was not sorry to think that my parents would hear that she had been to see his wife. To tell the truth, in our house the names of the people whom Mme. Swann was gradually getting to know pricked our curiosity more than they aroused our admiration. At the name of Mme. Trombert, my mother exclaimed : " Ah ! That's a new recruit, and one who will bring in others." And as though she found a similarity between the somewhat summary, rapid and violent manner in which Mme. Swann acquired her friends, as it were by conquest, and a Colonial expedition, Mamma went on to observe : " Now that the Tromberts have surrendered, the neighbouring tribes will not be long in coming in." If she had passed Mme. Swann in the street, she would tell us when she came home : " I saw Mme. Swann in all her war-paint ; she must have been embarking on some triumphant offensive against the Massachutoes, or the Cingalese, or the Tromberts." And so with all the new people whom I told her that I had seen in that somewhat composite and artificial society, to which they had often been brought with great difficulty and from widely different surroundings, Mamma would at once divine their origin, and, speaking of them as of trophies dearly bought, would say : " Brought back from an Expedition against the so-and-so ! "

As for Mme. Cottard, my father was astonished that Mme. Swann could find anything to be gained by getting so utterly undistinguished a woman to come to her house, and said : " In spite of the Professor's position, I must say that I cannot understand it." Mamma, on the other hand, understood quite well ; she knew that a great deal of the pleasure which a woman finds in entering a class of society different from that in which she has previously lived would be lacking if she had no means of keeping her

old associates informed of those others, relatively more
brilliant, with whom she has replaced them. Therefore,
she requires an eye-witness who may be allowed to penetrate this new, delicious world (as a buzzing, browsing insect bores its way into a flower) and will then, as the
course of her visits may carry her, spread abroad, or so
at least one hopes, with the tidings, a latent germ of envy
and of wonder. Mme. Cottard, who might have been
created on purpose to fill this part, belonged to that special
category in a visiting list which Mamma (who inherited
certain facets of her father's turn of mind) used to call
the "Tell Sparta" people. Besides—apart from another reason which did not come to our knowledge until
many years later—Mme. Swann, in inviting this good-
natured, reserved and modest friend, had no need to fear
lest she might be introducing into her drawing-room, on
her brilliant "days", a traitor or a rival. She knew
what a vast number of homely blossoms that busy
worker, armed with her plume and card-case, could visit
in a single afternoon. She knew the creature's power
of dissemination, and, basing her calculations upon the
law of probability, was led to believe that almost certainly some intimate of the Verdurins would be bound
to hear, within two or three days, how the Governor
of Paris had left cards upon her, or that M. Verdurin
himself would be told how M. Le Hault de Pressagny,
the President of the Horse Show, had taken them, Swann
and herself, to the King Theodosius gala ; she imagined
the Verdurins as informed of these two events, both so
flattering to herself and of these alone, because the particular materialisations in which we embody and pursue
fame are but few in number, by the default of our own

minds which are incapable of imagining at one time all the forms which, none the less, we hope—in a general way—that fame will not fail simultaneously to assume for our benefit.

Mme. Swann had, however, met with no success outside what was called the "official world". Smart women did not go to her house. It was not the presence there of Republican "notables" that frightened them away. In the days of my early childhood, conservative society was to the last degree worldly, and no "good" house would ever have opened its doors to a Republican. The people who lived in such an atmosphere imagined that the impossibility of ever inviting an "opportunist"—still more, a "horrid radical"—to their parties was something that would endure for ever, like oil-lamps and horse-drawn omnibuses. But, like a kaleidoscope which is every now and then given a turn, society arranges successively in different orders elements which one would have supposed to be immovable, and composes a fresh pattern. Before I had made my first Communion, ladies on the "right side" in politics had had the stupefaction of meeting, while paying calls, a smart Jewess. These new arrangements of the kaleidoscope are produced by what a philosopher would call a "change of criterion". The Dreyfus case brought about another, at a period rather later than that in which I began to go to Mme. Swann's, and the kaleidoscope scattered once again its little scraps of colour. Everything Jewish, even the smart lady herself, fell out of the pattern, and various obscure nationalities appeared in its place. The most brilliant drawing-room in Paris was that of a Prince who was an Austrian and ultra-Catholic. If instead of the Dreyfus case there had come a war with Germany, the base of the kaleidoscope would have been turned in the other direction, and its pattern reversed. The Jews having shewn, to the general astonishment, that they were patriots also, would have kept their position, and no one would have cared to go any more, or even to admit that he had ever gone to the Austrian Prince's. All this does not, however, prevent the people who move in it from imagining, whenever society is stationary for the moment, that no further change will occur, just as in spite of having witnessed the birth of the telephone they decline to believe in the aeroplane. Meanwhile the philosophers of journalism are at work, castigating the preceding epoch, and not only the kind of pleasures in which it indulged, which seem to them to be the last word in corruption, but even the work of its artists and philosophers, which have no longer the least value in their eyes, as though they were indissolubly linked to the successive moods of fashionable frivolity. The one thing that does not change is that at any and every time it appears that there have been " great changes ". At the time when I went to Mme. Swann's the Dreyfus storm had not yet broken, and some of the more prominent Jews were extremely powerful. None more so than Sir Rufus Israels, whose wife, Lady Israels, was Swann's aunt. She had not herself any intimate acquaintance so distinguished as her nephew's, while he, since he did not care for her, had never much cultivated her society, although he was, so far as was known, her heir. But she was the only one of Swann's relatives who had any idea of his social position, the others having always remained in the state of ignorance, in that respect, which had long been our own.

When, from a family circle, one of its members emigrates into "high society"—which to him appears a feat without parallel until after the lapse of a decade he observes that it has been performed in other ways and for different reasons by more than one of the men whom he knew as boys—he draws round about himself a zone of shadow, a *terra incognita,* which is clearly visible in its minutest details to all those who inhabit it with him, but is darkest night and nothingness to those who may not penetrate it but touch its fringe without the least suspicion of its existence in their midst. There being no news agency to furnish Swann's lady cousins with intelligence of the people with whom he consorted, it was (before his appalling marriage, of course) with a smile of condescension that they would tell one another, over family dinner-tables, that they had spent a "virtuous" Sunday in going to see "cousin Charles", whom (regarding him as a "poor relation" who was inclined to envy their prosperity,) they used wittily to name, playing upon the title of Balzac's story, "Le Cousin Bête". Lady Israels, however, was letter-perfect in the names and quality of the people who lavished upon Swann a friendship of which she was frankly jealous. Her husband's family, which almost equalled the Rothschilds in importance, had for several generations managed the affairs of the Orleans Princes. Lady Israels, being immensely rich, exercised a wide influence, and had employed it so as to ensure that no one whom she knew should be "at home" to Odette. One only had disobeyed her, in secret, the Comtesse de Marsantes. And then, as ill luck would have it, Odette having gone to call upon Mme. de Marsantes, Lady Israels had entered the room almost at her heels. Mme. de

Marsantes was on tenter-hooks. With the craven impotence of those who are at liberty to act as they choose, she did not address a single word to Odette, who thus found little encouragement to press farther the invasion of a world which, moreover, was not at all that into which she would have liked to be welcomed. In this complete detachment of the Faubourg Saint-Germain, Odette continued to be regarded as the illiterate " light woman ", utterly different from the respectable ladies, " well up " in all the minutest points of genealogy, who endeavoured to quench by reading biographies and memoirs their thirst for the aristocratic relations with which real life had omitted to provide them. And Swann, for his part, continued no doubt to be the lover in whose eyes all these peculiarities of an old mistress would appear lovable or at least inoffensive, for I have often heard his wife profess what were really social heresies, without his attempting (whether from lingering affection for her, loss of regard for society or weariness of the effort to make her perfect) to correct them. It was perhaps also another form of the simplicity which for so long had misled us at Combray, and which now had the effect that, while he continued to know, on his own account at least, many highly distinguished people, he did not make a point, in conversation in his wife's drawing-room, of our seeming to feel that they were of the smallest importance. They had, indeed, less than ever for Swann, the centre of gravity of his life having been displaced. In any case, Odette's ignorance of social distinctions was so dense that if the name of the Princesse de Guermantes were mentioned in conversation after that of the Duchess, her cousin, " So those ones are Princes, are they ? " she would exclaim ;

"Why, they've gone up a step." Were anyone to say "the Prince", in speaking of the Duc de Chartres, she would put him right with, "The Duke, you mean ; he is Duc de Chartres, not Prince." As for the Duc d'Orléans, son of the Comte de Paris : "That's funny ; the son is higher than the father !" she would remark, adding, for she was afflicted with anglomania, "Those *Royalties* are so dreadfully confusing !"—while to someone who asked her from what province the Guermantes family came she replied, "From the Aisne."

But, so far as Odette was concerned, Swann was quite blind, not merely to these deficiencies in her education but to the general mediocrity of her intelligence. More than that ; whenever Odette repeated a silly story Swann would sit listening to his wife with a complacency, a merriment, almost an admiration into which some survival of his desire for her must have entered ; while in the same conversation, anything subtle, anything deep even that he himself might say would be listened to by Odette with an habitual lack of interest, rather curtly, with impatience, and would at times be sharply contradicted. And we must conclude that this enslavement of refinement by vulgarity is the rule in many households, when we think, conversely, of all the superior women who yield to the blandishments of a boor, merciless in his censure of their most delicate utterances, while they go into ecstasies, with the infinite indulgence of love, over the feeblest of his witticisms. To return to the reasons which prevented Odette, at this period, from making her way into the Faubourg Saint-Germain, it must be observed that the latest turn of the social kaleidoscope had been actuated by a series of scandals. Women to whose houses one had been going with entire confidence had been discovered to be common prostitutes, if not British spies. One would, therefore, for some time to come expect people (so, at least, one supposed) to be, before anything else, in a sound position, regular, settled, accountable. Odette represented simply everything with which one had just severed relations, and was incidentally to renew them at once (for men, their natures not altering from day to day, seek in every new order a continuance of the old) but to renew them by seeking it under another form which would allow one to be innocently taken in, and to believe that it was no longer the same society as before the disaster. However, the scapegoats of that society and Odette were too closely alike. People who move in society are very short-sighted ; at the moment in which they cease to have any relations with the Israelite ladies whom they have known, while they are asking themselves how they are to fill the gap thus made in their lives, they perceive, thrust into it as by the windfall of a night of storm, a new lady, an Israelite also ; but by virtue of her novelty she is not associated in their minds with her predecessors, with what they are convinced that they must abjure. She does not ask that they shall respect her God. They take her up. There was no question of anti-semitism at the time when I used first to visit Odette. But she was like enough to it to remind people of what they wished, for a while, to avoid.

As for Swann himself, he was still a frequent visitor of several of his former acquaintance, who, of course, were all of the very highest rank. And yet when he spoke to us of the people whom he had just been to see I noticed that, among those whom he had known in the old days, the choice that he made was dictated by the same kind of taste, partly artistic partly historic, that inspired him as a collector. And remarking that it was often some great lady or other of waning reputation, who interested him because she had been the mistress of Liszt or because one of Balzac's novels was dedicated to her grandmother (as he would purchase a drawing if Chateaubriand had written about it) I conceived a suspicion that we had, at Combray, replaced one error, that of regarding Swann as a mere stockbroker, who did not go into society, by another, when we supposed him to be one of the smartest men in Paris. To be a friend of the Comte de Paris meant nothing at all. Is not the world full of such " friends of Princes ", who would not be received in any house that was at all " exclusive " ? Princes know themselves to be princes, and are not snobs ; besides, they believe themselves to be so far above everything that is not of their blood royal that great nobles and " business men " appear, in the depths beneath them, to be practically on a level.

But Swann went farther than this; not content with seeking in society, such as it was, when he fastened upon the names which, inscribed upon its roll by the past, were still to be read there, a simple artistic and literary pleasure, he indulged in the slightly vulgar diversion of arranging as it were social nosegays by grouping heterogeneous elements, bringing together people taken at hazard, here, there and everywhere. These experiments in the lighter side (or what was to Swann the lighter side) of sociology did not stimulate an identical reaction, with any regularity, that is to say, in each of his wife's friends. " I'm thinking of asking the Cottards to meet the

Duchesse de Vendôme," he would laughingly say to Mme. Bontemps, in the appetised tone of an epicure who has thought of, and intends to try the substitution, in a sauce, of cayenne pepper for cloves. But this plan, which was, in fact, to appear quite humorous, in an archaic sense of the word, to the Cottards, had also the power of infuriating Mme. Bontemps. She herself had recently been presented by the Swanns to the Duchesse de Vendôme, and had found this as agreeable as it seemed to her natural. The thought of winning renown from it at the Cottards', when she related to them what had happened, had been by no means the least savoury ingredient of her pleasure. But like those persons recently decorated who, their investiture once accomplished, would like to see the fountain of honour turned off at the main, Mme. Bontemps would have preferred that, after herself, no one else in her own circle of friends should be made known to the Princess. She denounced (to herself, of course) the licentious taste of Swann who, in order to gratify a wretched aesthetic whim, was obliging her to scatter to the winds, at one swoop, all the dust that she would have thrown in the eyes of the Cottards when she told them about the Duchesse de Vendôme. How was she even to dare to announce to her husband that the Professor and his wife were in their turn to partake of this pleasure, of which she had boasted to him as though it were unique. And yet, if the Cottards could only be made to know that they were being invited not seriously but for the amusement of their host! It is true that the Bontemps had been invited for the same reason, but Swann, having acquired from the aristocracy that eternal "Don Juan" spirit which, in treating with two women of no importance, makes each of them believe that it is she alone who is seriously loved, had spoken to Mme. Bontemps of the Duchesse de Vendôme as of a person whom it was clearly laid down that she must meet at dinner. "Yes, we're determined to have the Princess here with the Cottards," said Mme. Swann a few weeks later ; "My husband thinks that we might get something quite amusing out of that conjunction." For if she had retained from the "little nucleus" certain habits dear to Mme. Verdurin, such as that of shouting things aloud so as to be heard by all the faithful, she made use, at the same time, of certain expressions, such as "conjunction", which were dear to the Guermantes circle, of which she thus felt unconsciously and at a distance, as the sea is swayed by the moon, the attraction, though without being drawn perceptibly closer to it. "Yes, the Cottards and the Duchesse de Vendôme. Don't you think that might be rather fun ?" asked Swann. "I think they'll be exceedingly ill-assorted, and it can only lead to a lot of bother ; people oughtn't to play with fire, is what I say !" snapped Mme. Bontemps, furious. She and her husband were, all the same, invited, as was the Prince d'Agrigente, to this dinner, which Mme. Bontemps and Cottard had each two alternative ways of describing, according to whom they were telling about it. To one set Mme. Bontemps for her part, and Cottard for his would say casually, when asked who else had been of the party : "Only the Prince d'Agrigente ; it was all quite intimate." But there were others who might, alas, be better informed (once, indeed, some one had challenged Cottard with : "But weren't the Bontemps there too ?" "Oh, I forgot them," Cottard had blushingly admitted to the tactless ques-

tioner whom he ever afterwards classified among slan-
derers and speakers of evil). For these the Bontemps
and Cottards had each adopted, without any mutual arrangement, a version the framework of which was identical
for both parties, their own names alone changing places.
" Let me see ; " Cottard would say, " there were our host
and hostess, the Duc and Duchesse de Vendôme—" (with
a satisfied smile) " Professor and Mme. Cottard, and,
upon my soul, heaven only knows how they got there, for
they were about as much in keeping as hairs in the soup,
M. and Mme. Bontemps ! " Mme. Bontemps would recite an exactly similar " piece ", only it was M. and Mme.
Bontemps who were named with a satisfied emphasis between the Duchesse de Vendôme and the Prince d'Agrigente, while the " also ran ", whom finally she used to ac-
cuse of having invited themselves, and who completely
spoiled the party, were the Cottards.

When he had been paying calls Swann would often come
home with little time to spare before dinner. At that
point in the evening, six o'clock, when in the old days he
had felt so wretched, he no longer asked himself what
Odette might be about, and was hardly at all concerned to
hear that she had people still with her, or had gone out.
He recalled at times that he had once, years ago, tried
to read through its envelope a letter addressed by Odette
to Forcheville. But this memory was not pleasing to him,
and rather than plumb the depth of shame that he felt
in it he preferred to indulge in a little grimace, twisting
up the corners of his mouth and adding, if need be, a
shake of the head which signified " What does it all matter ? " In truth, he considered now that the hypothesis
by which he had often been brought to a standstill in

days gone by, according to which it was his jealous imagination alone that blackened what was in reality the
innocent life of Odette—that this hypothesis (which after
all was beneficent, since, so long as his amorous malady
had lasted, it had diminished his sufferings by making
them seem imaginary) was not the truth, that it was his
jealousy that had seen things in the right light, and that if
Odette had loved him better than he supposed, she had
deceived him more as well. Formerly, while his sufferings were still keen, he had vowed that, as soon as he
should have ceased to love Odette, and so to be afraid
either of vexing her or of making her believe that he loved
her more than he did, he would afford himself the satisfaction of elucidating with her, simply from his love of
truth and as a historical point, whether or not she had
had Forcheville in her room that day when he had rung
her bell and rapped on her window without being let in,
and she had written to Forcheville that it was an uncle
of hers who had called. But this so interesting problem,
of which he was waiting to attempt the solution only until
his jealousy should have subsided, had precisely lost all
interest in Swann's eyes when he had ceased to be jealous.
Not immediately, however. He felt no other jealousy now
with regard to Odette than what the memory of that day,
that afternoon spent in knocking vainly at the little house
in the Rue Lapérouse, had continued to excite in him ;
as though his jealousy, not dissimilar in that respect from
those maladies which appear to have their seat, their centre of contagion less in certain persons than in certain
places, in certain houses, had had for its object not so
much Odette herself as that day, that hour in the irrevocable past when Swann had beaten at every entrance

to her house in turn. You would have said that that day, that hour alone had caught and preserved a few last fragments of the amorous personality which had once been Swann's, and that there alone could he now recapture them. For a long time now it had made no matter to him that Odette had been false to him, and was false still. And yet he had continued for some years to seek out old servants of Odette, so strongly in him persisted the painful curiosity to know whether on that day, so long ago, at six o'clock, Odette had been in bed with Forcheville. Then that curiosity itself had disappeared, without, however, his abandoning his investigations. He continued the attempt to discover what no longer interested him, because his old ego though it had shrivelled to the extreme of decrepitude still acted mechanically, following the course of preoccupations so utterly abandoned that Swann could not now succeed even in forming an idea of that anguish—so compelling once that he had been unable to foresee his ever being delivered from it, that only the death of her whom he loved (death which, as will be shewn later on in this story, by a cruel example, in no way diminishes the sufferings caused by jealousy) seemed to him capable of making smooth the road, then insurmountably barred to him, of his life.

But to bring to light, some day, those passages in the life of Odette to which he owed his sufferings had not been Swann's only ambition ; he had in reserve that also of wreaking vengeance for his sufferings when, being no longer in love with Odette, he should no longer be afraid of her ; and the opportunity of gratifying this second ambition had just occurred, for Swann was in love with another woman, a woman who gave him—grounds for jeal-

ousy, no, but who did all the same make him jealous, because he was not capable, now, of altering his way of making love, and it was the way he had used with Odette that
must serve him now for another. To make Swann's jealousy revive it was not essential that this woman should be
unfaithful, it sufficed that for any reason she was separated from him, at a party for instance, where she was
presumably enjoying herself. That was enough to reawaken in him the old anguish, that lamentable and inconsistent excrescence of his love, which held Swann ever
at a distance from what she really was, like a yearning
to attain the impossible (what this young woman really
felt for him, the hidden longing that absorbed her days,
the secret places of her heart), for between Swann and her
whom he loved this anguish piled up an unyielding mass
of already existing suspicions, having their cause in
Odette, or in some other perhaps who had preceded
Odette, allowing this now ageing lover to know his mistress of the moment only in the traditional and collective
phantasm of the "woman who made him jealous", in
which he had arbitrarily incarnated his new love. Often,
however, Swann would charge his jealousy with the offence of making him believe in imaginary infidelities ; but
then he would remember that he had given Odette the
benefit of the same argument and had in that been wrong.
And so everything that the young woman whom he loved
did in those hours when he was not with her appeared
spoiled of its innocence in his eyes. But whereas at that
other time he had made a vow that if ever he ceased
to love her whom he did not then imagine to be his future wife, he would implacably exhibit to her an indifference that would at length be sincere, so as to avenge his

pride that had so long been trampled upon by her—of those reprisals which he might now enforce without risk to himself (for what harm could it do him to be taken at his word and deprived of those intimate moments with Odette that had been so necessary to him once), of those reprisals he took no more thought ; with his love had vanished the desire to shew that he was in love no longer. And he who, when he was suffering at the hands of Odette, would have looked forward so keenly to letting her see one day that he had fallen to a rival, now that he was in a position to do so took infinite precautions lest his wife should suspect the existence of this new love.

*
* *

It was not only in those tea-parties, on account of which I had formerly had the sorrow of seeing Gilberte leave me and go home earlier than usual, that I was henceforth to take part, but the engagements that she had with her mother, to go for a walk or to some afternoon party, which by preventing her from coming to the Champs-Elysées had deprived me of her, on those days when I loitered alone upon the lawn or stood before the wooden horses,— to these outings M. and Mme. Swann henceforth admitted me, I had a seat in their landau, and indeed it was me that they asked if I would rather go to the theatre, to a dancing lesson at the house of one of Gilberte's friends, to some social gathering given by friends of her parents (what Odette called " a little meeting ") or to visit the tombs at Saint-Denis.

On days when I was going anywhere with the Swanns

I would arrive at the house in time for *déjeuner,* which Mme. Swann called " le lunch " ; as one was not expected before half-past twelve, while my parents in those days had their meal at a quarter past eleven, it was not until they had risen from the table that I made my way towards that sumptuous quarter, deserted enough at any hour, but more particularly just then, when everyone had gone indoors. Even on winter days of frost, if the weather held, tightening every few minutes the knot of a gorgeous necktie from Charvet's and looking to see that my varnished boots were not getting dirty, I would roam to and fro among the avenues, waiting until twenty-seven minutes past the hour. I could see from afar in the Swanns' little garden-plot the sunlight glittering like hoar frost from the bare-boughed trees. It is true that the garden boasted but a pair of them. The unusual hour presented the scene in a new light. Into these pleasures of nature (intensified by the suppression of habit and indeed by my physical hunger) the thrilling prospect of sitting down to luncheon with Mme. Swann was infused ; it did not diminish them, but taking command of them trained them to its service ; so that if, at this hour when ordinarily I did not perceive them, I seemed now to be discovering the fine weather, the cold, the wintry sunlight, it was all as a sort of preface to the creamed eggs, as a patina, a cool and coloured glaze applied to the decoration of that mystic chapel which was the habitation of Mme. Swann, and in the heart of which there were, by contrast, so much warmth, so many scents and flowers.

At half-past twelve I would finally make up my mind to enter that house which, like an immense Christmas stocking, seemed ready to bestow upon me supernatural delights. (The French name "Noël" was, by the way, unknown to Mme. Swann and Gilberte, who had substituted for it the English "Christmas", and would speak of nothing but "Christmas pudding", what people had given them as "Christmas presents" and of going away— the thought of which maddened me with grief—"for Christmas". At home even, I should have thought it degrading to use the word "Noël", and always said "Christmas", which my father considered extremely silly.)

I encountered no one at first but a footman who after leading me through several large drawing-rooms shewed me into one that was quite small, empty, its windows beginning to dream already in the blue light of afternoon ; I was left alone there in the company of orchids, roses and violets, which, like people who are kept waiting in a room beside you but do not know you, preserved a silence which their individuality as living things made all the more impressive, and received coldly the warmth of a glowing fire of coals, preciously displayed behind a screen of crystal, in a basin of white marble over which it spilled, now and again, its perilous rubies.

I had sat down, but I rose hurriedly on hearing the door opened ; it was only another footman, and then a third, and the minute result that their vainly alarming entrances and exits achieved was to put a little more coal on the fire or water in the vases. They departed, I found myself alone, once that door was shut which Mme. Swann was surely soon going to open. Of a truth, I should have been less ill at ease in a magician's cave than in this little waiting-room where the fire appeared to me to be performing alchemical transmutations as in Klingsor's laboratory. Footsteps sounded afresh, I did not rise, it was sure to be just another footman ; it was M. Swann. "What ! All by yourself ? What is one to do ; that poor wife of mine has never been able to remember what time means ! Ten minutes to one. She gets later every day. And you'll see, she will come sailing in without the least hurry, and imagine she's in heaps of time." And as he was still subject to neuritis, and as he was becoming a trifle ridiculous, the fact of possessing so unpunctual a wife, who came in so late from the Bois, forgot everything at her dressmaker's and was never in time for luncheon made Swann anxious for his digestion but flattered his self-esteem.

He shewed me his latest acquisitions and explained their interest to me, but my emotion, added to the unfamiliarity of being still without food at this hour, sweeping through my mind left it void, so that while able to speak I was incapable of hearing. Anyhow, so far as the works of art in Swann's possession were concerned, it was enough for me that they were contained in his house, formed a part there of the delicious hour that preceded luncheon. The Gioconda herself might have appeared there without giving me any more pleasure than one of Mme. Swann's indoor gowns, or her scent bottles.

I continued to wait, alone or with Swann, and often with Gilberte, come in to keep us company. The arrival of Mme. Swann, prepared for me by all those majestic apparitions, must (so it seemed to me) be something truly immense. I strained my ears to catch the slightest sound. But one never finds quite as high as one has been expecting a cathedral, a wave in a storm, a dancer's leap in the air ; after those liveried footmen, suggesting the chorus whose processional entry upon the stage leads up to and at the same time diminishes the final appearance of the queen, Mme. Swann, creeping furtively in, with a little otter-skin coat, her veil lowered to cover a nose pink-tipped by the cold, did not fulfil the promises lavished, while I had been waiting, upon my imagination.

But if she had stayed at home all morning, when she arrived in the drawing-room it would be clad in a wrapper of *crêpe-de-Chine,* brightly coloured, which seemed to me more exquisite than any of her dresses.

Sometimes the Swanns decided to remain in the house all afternoon, and then, as we had had luncheon so late, very soon I must watch setting, beyond the garden-wall, the sun of that day which had seemed to me bound to be different from other days ; then in vain might the serv-ants bring in lamps of every size and shape, burning each upon the consecrated altar of a console, a card-table, a corner-cupboard, a bracket, as though for the celebration of some strange and secret rite ; nothing extraordinary transpired in the conversation, and I went home disap-pointed, as one often is in one's childhood after the mid-night mass.

But my disappointment was scarcely more than mental. I was radiant with happiness in this house where Gil-berte, when she was still not with us, was about to appear and would bestow on me in a moment, and for hours to come, her speech, her smiling and attentive gaze, just as I had caught it, that first time, at Combray. At the most I was a trifle jealous when I saw her so often dis-appear into vast rooms above, reached by a private staircase. Obliged myself to remain in the drawing-room, like a man in love with an actress who is confined to his stall "in front" and wonders anxiously what is going on behind the scenes, in the green-room, I put to Swann, with regard to this other part of the house questions artfully veiled, but in a tone from which I could not quite succeed in banishing the note of uneasiness. He explained to me that the place to which Gilberte had gone was the linen-room, offered himself to shew it to me, and promised me that whenever Gilberte had occasion to go there again he would insist upon her taking me with her. By these last words and the relief which they brought me Swann at once annihilated for me one of those terrifying interior perspectives at the end of which a woman with whom we are in love appears so remote. At that moment I felt for him an affection which I believed to be deeper than my affection for Gilberte. For he, being the master over his daughter, was giving her to me, whereas she, she withheld herself now and then, I had not the same direct control over her as I had indirectly through Swann. Besides, it was she whom I loved and could not, therefore look upon without that disturbance, without that desire for something more which destroys in us, in the presence of one whom we love, the sensation of loving.

As a rule, however, we did not stay indoors, we went out. Sometimes, before going to dress, Mme. Swann would sit down at the piano. Her lovely hands, escaping from the pink, or white, or, often, vividly coloured sleeves of her *crêpe-de-Chine* wrapper, drooped over the keys with that same melancholy which was in her eyes but was not in her heart. It was on one of those days that she happened to play me the part of Vinteuil's sonata that contained the little phrase of which Swann had been so fond But often one listens and hears nothing, if it is a piece of music at all complicated to which one is listening for the first time. And yet when, later on, this sonata had been played over to me two or three times I found that I knew it quite well. And so it is not wrong to speak of hearing a thing for the first time. If one had indeed, as one supposes, received no impression from the first hearing, the second, the third would be equally "first hearings" and there would be no reason why one should understand it any better after the tenth. Probably what is wanting, the first time, is not comprehension but memory. For our memory, compared to the complexity of the impressions which it has to face while we are listening, is infinitesimal, as brief as the memory of a man who in his sleep thinks of a thousand things and at once forgets them, or as that of a man in his second childhood who cannot recall, a minute afterwards, what one has just been saying to him. Of these multiple impressions our memory is not capable of furnishing us with an immediate picture. But that picture gradually takes shape, and, with regard to works which we have heard more than once, we are like the schoolboy who has read several times over before going to sleep a lesson which he supposed himself not to know, and finds that he can repeat it by heart next morning. It was only that I had not, until then, heard a note of the sonata, and where Swann and his wife could make out a distinct phrase that was as far beyond the range of my perception as a name which one endeavours to recall and in place of which one discovers only a void, a void from which, an hour later, when one is not thinking about them, will spring of their own accord, in one continuous flight, the syllables that one has solicited in vain. And not only does one not seize at once and retain an impression of works that are really great, but even in the content of any such work (as befell me in the case of Vinteuil's sonata) it is the least valuable parts that one at first perceives. Thus it was that I was mistaken not only in thinking that this work held nothing further in store for me (so that for a long time I made no effort to hear it again) from the moment in which Mme. Swann had played over to me its most famous passage ; I was in this respect as stupid as people are who expect to feel no astonishment when they stand in Venice before the front of Saint Mark's, because photography has already acquainted them with the outline of its domes. Far more than that, even when I had heard the sonata played from beginning to end, it remained almost wholly invisible to me, like a monument of which its distance or a haze in the atmosphere allows us to catch but a faint and fragmentary glimpse. Hence the depression inseparable from one's knowledge of such works, as of everything that acquires reality in time. When the least obvious beauties of Vinteuil's sonata were revealed to me, already, borne by the force of habit beyond the reach of my sensibility, those that I had from the first distinguished and preferred in it were beginning to escape, to avoid me. Since I was able only in successive moments to enjoy all the pleasures that this sonata gave me, I never possessed it in its entirety : it was like life itself. But, less disappointing than life is, great works of art do not begin by giving us all their best. In Vinteuil's sonata the beauties that one discovers at once are those also of which one most soon grows tired, and for the same reason, no doubt, namely that they are less different from what one already knows. But when those first apparitions have withdrawn, there is left for

our enjoyment some passage which its composition, too
new and strange to offer anything but confusion to our
mind, had made indistinguishable and so preserved intact ; and this, which we have been meeting every day and
have not guessed it, which has thus been held in reserve
for us, which by the sheer force of its beauty has become
invisible and has remained unknown, this comes to us last
of all. But this also must be the last that we shall
relinquish. And we shall love it longer than the rest
because we have taken longer to get to love it. The
time, moreover, that a person requires—as I required in
the matter of this sonata—to penetrate a work of any
depth is merely an epitome, a symbol, one might say,
of the years, the centuries even that must elapse before
the public can begin to cherish a masterpiece that is really
new. So that the man of genius, to shelter himself from
the ignorant contempt of the world, may say to himself
that, since one's contemporaries are incapable of the necessary detachment, works written for posterity should be
read by posterity alone, like certain pictures which one
cannot appreciate when one stands too close to them.
But, as it happens, any such cowardly precaution to avoid
false judgments is doomed to failure ; they are inevitable.
The reason for which a work of genius is not easily admired from the first is that the man who has created it is
extraordinary, that few other men resemble him. It was
Beethoven's Quartets themselves (the Twelfth, Thir-
teenth, Fourteenth and Fifteenth) that devoted half a
century to forming, fashioning and enlarging a public for
Beethoven's Quartets, marking in this way, like every
great work of art, an advance if not in artistic merit at
least in intellectual society, largely composed to-day of

what was not to be found when the work first appeared, that is to say of persons capable of enjoying it. What artists call posterity is the posterity of the work of art. It is essential that the work (leaving out of account, for brevity's sake, the contingency that several men of genius may at the same time be working along parallel lines to create a more instructed public in the future, a public from which other men of genius shall reap the benefit) shall create its own posterity. For if the work were held in reserve, were revealed only to posterity, that audience, for that particular work, would be not posterity but a group of contemporaries who were merely living half-a-century later in time. And so it is essential that the artist (and this is what Vinteuil had done), if he wishes his work to be free to follow its own course, shall launch it, wherever he may find sufficient depth, confidently outward bound towards the future. And yet this interval of time, the true perspective in which to behold a work of art, if leaving it out of account is the mistake made by bad judges, taking it into account is at times a dangerous precaution of the good. No doubt one can easily imagine, by an illusion similar to that which makes everything on the horizon appear equidistant, that all the revolutions which have hitherto occurred in painting or in music did at least shew respect for certain rules, whereas that which immediately confronts us, be it impressionism, a striving after discord, an exclusive use of the Chinese scale, cubism, futurism or what you will, differs outrageously from all that have occurred before. Simply because those that have occurred before we are apt to regard as a whole, forgetting that a long process of assimilation has melted them into a continuous substance, varied of course but, taking it as a whole, homogeneous, in which Hugo blends with Molière. Let us try to imagine the shocking incoherence that we should find, if we did not take into account the future, and the changes that it must bring about, in a horoscope of our own riper years, drawn and presented to us in our youth. Only horoscopes are not always accurate, and the necessity, when judging a work of art, of including the temporal factor in the sum total of its beauty introduces, to our way of thinking, something as hazardous, and consequently as barren of interest, as every prophecy the non-fulfilment of which will not at all imply any inadequacy on the prophet's part, for the power to summon possibilities into existence or to exclude them from it is not necessarily within the competence of genius ; one may have had genius and yet not have believed in the future of railways or of flight, or, although a brilliant psychologist, in the infidelity of a mistress or of a friend whose treachery persons far less gifted would have foreseen.

If I did not understand the sonata, it enchanted me to hear Mme. Swann play. Her touch appeared to me (like her wrappers, like the scent of her staircase, her cloaks, her chrysanthemums) to form part of an individual and mysterious whole, in a world infinitely superior to that in which the mind is capable of analysing talent. " Attractive, isn't it, that Vinteuil sonata ? " Swann asked me. " The moment when night is darkening among the trees, when the arpeggios of the violin call down a cooling dew upon the earth. You must admit that it is rather charming ; it shews all the static side of moonlight, which is the essential part. It is not surprising that a course of radiant heat such as my wife is taking, should act on the muscles, since moonlight can prevent the leaves from stirring. That is what he expresses so well in that little phrase, the Bois de Boulogne plunged in a cataleptic trance. By the sea it is even more striking, because you have there the faint response of the waves, which, of course, you can hear quite distinctly, since nothing else dares to move. In Paris it is the other way ; at the most, you may notice unfamiliar lights among the old buildings, the sky brightened as though by a colourless and harmless conflagration, that sort of vast variety show of which you get a hint here and there. But in Vinteuil's little phrase, and in the whole sonata for that matter, it is not like that ; the scene is laid in the Bois ; in the *gruppetto* you can distinctly hear a voice saying : ' I can almost see to read the paper ! ' " These words from Swann might have falsified, later on, my impression of the sonata, music being too little exclusive to inhibit absolutely what other people suggest that we should find in it. But I understood from other words which he let fall that this nocturnal foliage was simply that beneath whose shade in many a restaurant on the outskirts of Paris he had listened on many an evening to the little phrase. In place of the profound significance that he had so often sought in it, what it recalled now to Swann were the leafy boughs, arranged, wreathed, painted round about it (which it gave him the desire to see again because it seemed to him to be their inner, their hidden self, as it were their soul) ; was the whole of one spring season which he had not been able to enjoy before, not having had— feverish and moody as he then was—enough strength of body and mind for its enjoyment, which, as one puts by for an invalid the dainties that he has not been able to eat, it had kept in store for him. The charm that he had been made to feel by certain evenings in the Bois, a charm of which Vinteuil's sonata served to remind him, he could not have recaptured by questioning Odette, although she, as well as the little phrase, had been his companion there. But Odette had been merely his companion, by his side, not (as the phrase had been) within him, and so had seen nothing—nor would she, had she been a thousand times as comprehending, have seen anything of that vision which for no one among us (or at least I was long under the impression that this rule admitted no exception) can be made externally visible. "It is rather charming, don't you think," Swann continued, "that sound can give a reflection, like water, or glass. It is curious, too, that Vinteuil's phrase now shews me only the things to which I paid no attention then. Of my troubles, my loves of those days it recalls nothing, it has altered all my values." "Charles, I don't think that's very polite to me, what you're saying." "Not polite? Really, you women are superb! I was simply trying to explain to this young man that what the music shews—to me, at least—is not for a moment 'Free-will' or 'In Tune with the Infinite', but shall we say old Verdurin in his frock coat in the palm-house at the Jardin d'Acclimatation. Hundreds of times, without my leaving this room, the little phrase has carried me off to dine with it at Armenonville. Gad, it is less boring, anyhow, than having to go there with Mme. de Cambremer." Mme. Swann laughed. "That is a lady who is supposed to have been violently in love with Charles," she explained, in the same tone in which, shortly before, when we were speaking of Vermeer of Delft, of whose existence I had been surprised to find her

conscious, she had answered me with : " I ought to explain that M. Swann was very much taken up with that
painter at the time he was courting me. Isn't that so,
Charles dear ? " " You're not to start saying things
about Mme. de Cambremer ! " Swann checked her, secretly flattered. " But I'm only repeating what I've
been told. Besides, it seems that she's an extremely clever
woman ; I don't know her myself. I believe she's very
pushing, which surprises me rather in a clever woman.
But everyone says that she was quite mad about you ;
there's no harm in repeating that." Swann remained silent as a deaf-mute which was in a way a confirmation of
what she had said, and a proof of his own fatuity.
" Since what I'm playing reminds you of the Jardin d'Acclimatation," his wife went on, with a playful semblance
of being offended, " we might take him there some day in
the carriage, if it would amuse him. It's lovely there just
now, and you can recapture your fond impressions !
Which reminds me, talking of the Jardin d'Acclimatation,
do you know, this young man thought that we were de-
votedly attached to a person whom I cut, as a matter of
fact, whenever I possibly can, Mme. Blatin ! I think it is
rather crushing for us, that she should be taken for a
friend of ours. Just fancy, dear Dr. Cottard, who never
says a harsh word about anyone, declares that she's positively contagious." " A frightful woman ! The one
thing to be said for her is that she is exactly like Savon-
arola. She is the very image of that portrait of Savon-
arola, by Fra Bartolommeo." This mania which Swann
had for finding likenesses to people in pictures was de-
fensible, for even what we call individual expression is—
as we so painfully discover when we are in love and would

fain believe in the unique reality of the beloved—something diffused and general, which can be found existing at different periods. But if one had listened to Swann, the processions of the Kings of the East, already so anachronistic when Benozzo Gozzoli introduced in their midst various Medici, would have been even more so, since they would have included the portraits of a whole crowd of men, contemporaries not of Gozzoli but of Swann, subsequent, that is to say not only by fifteen centuries to the Nativity but by four more to the painter himself. There was not missing from those trains, according to Swann, a single living Parisian of any note, any more than there was from that act in one of Sardou's plays, in which, out of friendship for the author and for the leading lady, and also because it was the fashion, all the best known men in Paris, famous doctors, politicians, barristers, amused themselves, each on a different evening, by "walking on". " But what has she got to do with the Jardin d'Acclimatation ? " " Everything ! " " What ? You don't suggest that she's got a sky-blue behind, like the monkeys ? " " Charles, you really are too dreadful ! I was thinking of what the Cingalese said to her. Do tell him, Charles ; it really is a gem." " Oh, it's too silly. You know, Mme. Blatin loves asking people questions, in a tone which she thinks friendly, but which is really overpowering." " What our good friends on the Thames call ' patronising'," interrupted Odette. " Exactly. Well, she went the other day to the Jardin d'Acclimatation, where they have some blackamoors—Cingalese, I think I heard my wife say ; she is much ' better up' in ethnology than I am." " Now, Charles, you're not to make fun of poor me." " I've no intention of making fun, I assure you.

Well, to continue, she went up to one of these black fellows with 'Good morning, nigger!'..." "Oh, it's too absurd!" "Anyhow, this classification seems to have displeased the black. 'Me nigger,' he shouted, (quite furious, don't you know), to Mme. Blatin, 'me nigger; you, old cow!'" "I do think that's so delightful! I adore that story. Do say it's a good one. Can't you see old Blatin standing there, and hearing him: 'Me nigger; you, old cow'?" I expressed an intense desire to go there and see these Cingalese, one of whom had called Mme. Blatin an old cow. They did not interest me in the least. But I reflected that in going to the Jardin d'Acclimatation, and again on our way home, we should pass along that Allée des Acacias in which I had loved so, once, to gaze on Mme. Swann, and that perhaps Coquelin's mulatto friend, to whom I had never managed to exhibit myself in the act of saluting her, would see me there, seated at her side, as the victoria swept by.

During those minutes in which Gilberte, having gone to "get ready", was not in the room with us, M. and Mme. Swann would take delight in revealing to me all the rare virtues of their child. And everything that I myself observed seemed to prove the truth of what they said. I remarked that, as her mother had told me, she had not only for her friends but for the servants, for the poor, the most delicate attentions carefully thought out, a desire to give pleasure, a fear of causing annoyance, translated into all sorts of trifling actions which must often have meant great inconvenience to her. She had done some "work" for our stall-keeper in the Champs-Elysées, and went out in the snow to give it to her with her own hands, so as not to lose a day. "You have no idea how kind-hearted she is, she won't let it be seen," her father assured me. Young as she was, she appeared far more sensible already than her parents. When Swann boasted of his wife's grand friends Gilberte would turn away, and remain silent, but without any air of reproaching him, for it seemed inconceivable to her that her father could be subjected to the slightest criticism. One day, when I had spoken to her of Mlle. Vinteuil, she said to me :

" I shall never know her, for a very good reason, and that is that she was not nice to her father, by what one hears, she gave him a lot of trouble. You can't understand that any more than I, can you ; I'm sure you could no more live without your papa than I could, which is quite natural after all. How can one ever forget a person one has loved all one's life ? "

And once when she was making herself particularly endearing to Swann, as I mentioned this to her when he was out of the room :

"Yes, poor Papa, it is the anniversary of his father's death, just now. You can understand what he must be feeling ; you do understand, don't you ; you and I feel the same about things like that. So I just try to be a little less naughty than usual." "But he doesn't ever think you naughty. He thinks you're quite perfect." "Poor Papa, that's because he's far too good himself."

But her parents were not content with singing the praises of Gilberte—that same Gilberte, who, even before I had set eyes on her, used to appear to me standing before a church, in a landscape of the Ile-de-France, and later, awakening in me not dreams now but memories, was embowered always in a hedge of pink hawthorn, in the little lane that I took when I was going the Méséglise way. Once when I had asked Mme. Swann (and had made an effort to assume the indifferent tone of a friend of the family, curious to know the preferences of a child), which among all her playmates Gilberte liked the best, Mme. Swann replied : "But you ought to know a great deal better than I do. You are in her confidence, her great favourite, her 'chum', as the English say."

It appears that in a coincidence as perfect as this was, when reality is folded over to cover the ideal of which we have so long been dreaming, it completely hides that ideal, absorbing it in itself, as when two geometrical figures that are congruent are made to coincide, so that there is but one, whereas we would rather, so as to give its full significance to our enjoyment, preserve for all those separate points of our desire, at the very moment in which we succeed in touching them, and so as to be quite certain that they are indeed themselves, the distinction of being intangible. And our thought cannot even reconstruct the old state so as to confront the new with it, for it has no longer a clear field : the acquaintance that we have made, the memory of those first, unhoped-for moments, the talk to which we have listened are there now to block the passage of our consciousness, and as they control the outlets of our memory far more than those of our imagination, they react more forcibly upon our past, which we are no longer able to visualise without taking them into account, than upon the form, still un-shaped, of our future. I had been able to believe, year after year, that the right to visit Mme. Swann was a vague and fantastic privilege to which I should never attain ; after I had spent a quarter of an hour in her drawing-room, it was the period in which I did not yet know her that was become fantastic and vague like a possibility which the realisation of an alternative possibility has made impossible. How was I ever to dream again of her dining-room as of an inconceivable place, when I could not make the least movement in my mind without crossing the path of that inextinguishable ray cast backwards to infinity, even into my own most distant past, by the lobster *à l'Américaine* which I had just been eating. And Swann must have observed in his own case a similar phenomenon ; for this house in which he entertained me might be regarded as the place into which had flowed, to coincide and be lost in one another, not only the ideal dwelling that my imagination had constructed, but another still, that which his jealous love, as inventive as any fantasy of mine, had so often depicted to him, that dwelling common to Odette and himself which had appeared so inaccessible once, on evenings when Odette had taken him home with Forcheville to drink orangeade with her ; and what had flowed in to be absorbed, for him, in the walls and furniture of the dining-room in which we now sat down to luncheon was that unhoped-for paradise in which, in the old days, he could not without a pang imagine that he would one day be saying to *their* butler those very words, " Is Madame ready yet ? " which I now heard him utter with a touch of impatience mingled with self-satisfaction. No more than, probably, Swann himself could I succeed in knowing my own happiness, and when Gilberte once broke out : " Who would ever have said that the little girl you watched playing prisoners' base, without daring to speak to her, would one day be your greatest friend, and you would go to her house whenever you liked ? " she spoke of a change the occurrence of which I could verify only by observing it from without, finding no trace of it within myself, for it was composed of two separate states on both of which I could not, without their ceasing to be distinct from one another, succeed in keeping my thoughts fixed at one and the same time.

And yet this house, because it had been so passionately desired by Swann, must have kept for him some of its attraction, if I was to judge by myself for whom it had not lost all its mystery. That singular charm in which I had for so long supposed the life of the Swanns to be bathed I had not completely exorcised from their house on making my own way into it; I had made it, that charm, recoil, overpowered as it must be by the sight of the stranger, the pariah that I had been, to whom now Mme. Swann pushed forward graciously for him to sit in it an armchair exquisite, hostile, scandalised; but all round me that charm, in my memory, I can still distinguish. Is it because, on those days on which M. and Mme. Swann invited me to luncheon, to go out afterwards with them and Gilberte, I imprinted with my gaze,—while I sat waiting for them there alone—on the carpet, the sofas, the tables, the screens, the pictures, the idea engraved upon my mind that Mme. Swann, or her husband, or Gilberte was about to enter the room? Is it because those objects have dwelt ever since in my memory side by side with the Swanns, and have gradually acquired something of their personal character? Is it because, knowing that the Swanns passed their existence among all those things, I made of all of them as it were emblems of the private lives, of those habits of the Swanns from which I had too long been excluded for them not to continue to appear strange to me, even when I was allowed the privilege of sharing in them ? However it may be, always when I think of that drawing-room which Swann (not that the criticism implied on his part any intention to find fault with his wife's taste) found so incongruous—because, while it was still planned and carried out in the style, half conservatory half studio, which had been that of the rooms in which he had first known Odette, she had, none the less, begun to replace in its medley a quantity of the Chinese ornaments, which she now felt to be rather gimcrack, a trifle dowdy, by a swarm of little chairs and stools and things upholstered in old Louis XIV silks ; not to mention the works of art brought by Swann himself from his house on the Quai d'Orléans—it has kept in my memory, on the contrary, that composite, heterogeneous room, a cohesion, a unity, an individual charm never possessed even by the most complete, the least spoiled of such collections that the past has bequeathed to us, or the most modern, alive and stamped with the imprint of a living personality ; for we alone can, by our belief that they have an existence of their own, give to certain of the things that we see a soul which they afterwards keep, which they develop in our minds. All the ideas that I had formed of the hours, different from those that exist for other men, passed by the Swanns in that house which was to their life what the body is to the soul, and must give expression to its singularity, all those ideas were rearranged, amalgamated—equally disturbing and indefinite throughout—in the arrangement of the furniture, the thickness of the carpets, the position of the windows, the ministrations of the servants. When, after luncheon, we went in the sunshine to drink our coffee in the great bay window of the drawing-room, while Mme.

Swann was asking me how many lumps of sugar I took, it was not only the silk-covered stool which she pushed towards me that emitted, with the agonising charm that I had long ago felt—first among the pink hawthorn and then beside the clump of laurels—in the name of Gilberte, the hostility that her parents had shewn to me, which this little piece of furniture seemed to have so well understood, to have so completely shared that I felt myself unworthy, and found myself almost reluctant to set my feet on its defenceless cushion ; a personality, a soul was latent there which linked it secretly to the light of two o'clock in the afternoon, so different from any other light, in the gulf in which there played about our feet its sparkling tide of gold out of which the bluish crags of sofas and vaporous carpet beaches emerged like enchanted islands ; and there was nothing, even to the painting by Rubens hung above the chimneypiece, that was not endowed with the same quality and almost the same intensity of charm as the laced boots of M. Swann, and that hooded cape, the like of which I had so dearly longed to wear, whereas now Odette would beg her husband to go and put on another, so as to appear more smart, whenever I did them the honour of driving out with them. She too went away to change her dress—not heeding my protestations that no " outdoor " clothes could be nearly so becoming as the marvellous garment of *crêpe-de-Chine* or silk, old rose, cherry-coloured, Tiepolo pink, white, mauve, green, red or yellow, plain or patterned, in which Mme. Swann had sat down to luncheon and which she was now going to take off. When I assured her that she ought to go out in that costume, she laughed, either in scorn of my ignorance or from delight in my compliment. She apologised for having so many wrappers, explaining that they were the only kind of dress in which she felt comfortable, and left us, to go and array herself in one of those regal toilets which imposed their majesty on all beholders, and yet among which I was sometimes summoned to decide which of them I preferred that she should put on.

In the Jardin d'Acclimatation, how proud I was when we had left the carriage to be walking by the side of Mme. Swann! While she strolled carelessly on, letting her cloak stream on the air behind her, I kept eyeing her with an admiring gaze to which she coquettishly responded in a lingering smile. And now, were we to meet one or other of Gilberte's friends, boy or girl, who saluted us from afar, I would in my turn be looked upon by them as one of those happy creatures whose lot I had envied, one of those friends of Gilberte who knew her family and had a share in that other part of her life, the part which was not spent in the Champs-Elysées.

Often upon the paths of the Bois or the Jardin we passed, we were greeted by some great lady who was Swann's friend, whom he perchance did not see, so that his wife must rally him with a "Charles! Don't you see Mme. de Montmorency?" And Swann, with that amicable smile, bred of a long and intimate friendship, bared his head, but with a slow sweeping gesture, with a grace peculiarly his own. Sometimes the lady would stop, glad of an opportunity to shew Mme. Swann a courtesy which would involve no tiresome consequences, by which they all knew that she would never seek to profit, so thoroughly had Swann trained her in reserve. She had none the less acquired all the manners of polite society, and however smart, however stately the lady might be,

Mme. Swann was invariably a match for her ; halting for
a moment before the friend whom her husband had recognised and was addressing, she would introduce us, Gilberte
and myself, with so much ease of manner, would remain
so free, so tranquil in her exercise of courtesy, that it
would have been hard to say, looking at them both,
which of the two was the aristocrat. The day on which
we went to inspect the Cingalese, on our way home we
saw coming in our direction, and followed by two others
who seemed to be acting as her escort, an elderly but
still attractive woman cloaked in a dark mantle and
capped with a little bonnet tied beneath her chin with a
pair of ribbons. "Ah ! Here is someone who will interest you !" said Swann. The old lady, who had come
within a few yards of us, now smiled at us with a caressing
sweetness. Swann doffed his hat. Mme. Swann swept to
the ground in a curtsey and made as if to kiss the hand
of the lady, who, standing there like a Winterhalter portrait, drew her up again and kissed her cheek. "There,
there ; will you put your hat on, you !" she scolded Swann
in a thick and almost growling voice, speaking like an
old and familiar friend. "I am going to present you to
Her Imperial Highness," Mme. Swann whispered. Swann
drew me aside for a moment while his wife talked of the
weather and of the animals recently added to the Jardin
d'Acclimatation, with the Princess. "That is the Princesse Mathilde ; " he told me, "you know who' I mean,
the friend of Flaubert, Sainte-Beuve, Dumas. Just fancy,
she's the niece of Napoleon I. She had offers of marriage
from Napoleon III and the Emperor of Russia. Isn't
that interesting ? Talk to her a little. But I hope she
won't keep us standing here for an hour ! . . . I met

Taine the other day," he went on, addressing the Princess, "and he told me that your Highness was vexed with him." "He's behaved like a perfect peeg !" she said gruffly, pronouncing the word *cochon* as though she referred to Joan of Arc's contemporary, Bishop Cauchon. "After his article on the Emperor I left my card on him with p. p. c. on it." I felt the surprise that one feels on opening the Correspondence of that Duchesse d'Orléans who was by birth a Princess Palatine. And indeed Princesse Mathilde, animated by sentiments so entirely French, expressed them with a straightforward bluntness that recalled the Germany of an older generation, and was inherited, doubtless, from her Wurtemberg mother. This somewhat rude and almost masculine frankness she softened, as soon as she began to smile, with an Italian languor. And the whole person was clothed in a dress so typically " Second Empire " that—for all that the Princess wore it simply and solely, no doubt, from attachment to the fashions that she had loved when she was young—she seemed to have deliberately planned to avoid the slightest discrepancy in historic colour, and to be satisfying the expectations of those who looked to her to evoke the memory of another age. I whispered to Swann to ask her whether she had known Musset. "Very slightly, sir," was the answer, given in a tone which seemed to feign annoyance at the question, and of course it was by way of a joke that she called Swann " Sir ", since they were intimate friends. " I had him to dine once. I had invited him for seven o'clock. At half-past seven, as he had not appeared, we sat down to dinner. He arrived at eight, bowed to me, took his seat, never opened his lips, went off after dinner without letting me hear the sound of his voice. Of course, he was dead drunk. That hardly encouraged me to make another attempt." We were standing a little way off, Swann and I. "I hope this little audience is not going to last much longer," he muttered, "the soles of my feet are hurting. I cannot think why my wife keeps on making conversation. When we get home it will be she that complains of being tired, and she knows I simply cannot go on standing like this." For Mme. Swann, who had had the news from Mme. Bontemps, was in the course of telling the Princess that the Government, having at last begun to realise the depth of its depravity, had decided to send her an invitation to be present on the platform in a few days' time, when the Tsar Nicholas was to visit the Invalides. But the Princess who, in spite of appearances, in spite of the character of her circle, which consisted mainly of artists and literary people, had remained at heart and shewed herself, whenever she had to take action, the niece of Napoleon, replied : "Yes, Madame, I received it this morning, and I sent it back to the Minister, who must have had it by now. I told him that I had no need of an invitation to go to the Invalides. If the Government desires my presence there, it will not be on the platform, it will be in our vault, where the Emperor's tomb is. I have no need of a card to admit me there. I have my keys. I go in and out when I choose. The Government has only to let me know whether it wishes me to be present or not. But if I do go to the Invalides, it will be down below there or nowhere at all." At that moment we were saluted, Mme. Swann and I, by a young man who greeted her without stopping, and whom I was not aware that she knew ; it was Bloch. I inquired about him, and was told that he had been introduced to her by Mme. Bontemps, and that he was employed in the Minister's secretariat, which was news to me. Anyhow, she could not have seen him often—or perhaps she had not cared to utter the name, hardly "smart" enough for her liking, of Bloch, for she told me that he was called M. Moreul. I assured her that she was mistaken, that his name was Bloch. The Princess gathered up the train that flowed out behind her, while Mme. Swann gazed at it with admiring eyes. "It is only a fur that the Emperor of Russia sent me," she explained, "and as I have just been to see him I put it on, so as to shew him that I'd managed to have it made up as a mantle." "I hear that Prince Louis has joined the Russian Army ; the Princess will be very sad at losing him," went on Mme. Swann, not noticing her husband's signals of distress. "That was a fine thing to do. As I said to him, ' Just because there's been a soldier, before, in the family, that's no reason ! ' " replied the Princess, alluding with this abrupt simplicity to Napoleon the Great. But Swann could hold out no longer. "Ma'am, it is I that am going to play the Prince, and ask your permission to retire ; but, you see, my wife has not been so well, and I do not like her to stand still for any time." Mme. Swann curtseyed again, and the Princess conferred upon us all a celestial smile, which she seemed to have summoned out of the past, from among the graces of her girlhood, from the evenings at Compiègne, a smile which glided, sweet and unbroken, over her hitherto so sullen face ; then she went on her way, followed by the two ladies in waiting, who had confined themselves, in the manner of interpreters, of children's or invalids' nurses, to punctuating our conversation with insignificant sentences and superfluous explanations. "You should go and write your name in her book, one day this week," Mme. Swann counselled me. "One doesn't leave cards upon these 'Royalties', as the English call them, but she will invite you to her house if you put your name down."

Sometimes in those last days of winter we would go, before proceeding on our expedition, into one of the small picture-shows that were being given at that time, where Swann, as a collector of mark, was greeted with special deference by the dealers in whose galleries they were held. And in that still wintry weather the old longing to set out for the South of France and Venice would be reawakened in me by those rooms in which a springtime, already well advanced, and a blazing sun cast violet shadows upon the roseate Alpilles and gave the intense transparency of emeralds to the Grand Canal. If the weather were inclement, we would go to a concert or a theatre, and afterwards to one of the fashionable tea-rooms. There, whenever Mme. Swann had anything to say to me which she did not wish the people at the next table, or even the waiters who brought our tea to understand, she would say it in English, as though that had been a secret language known to our two selves alone. As it happened everyone in the place knew English—I only had not yet learned the language, and was obliged to say so to Mme. Swann in order that she might cease to make, on the people who were drinking tea or were serving us with it, remarks which I guessed to be uncomplimentary without either my understanding or the person referred to losing a single word.

Once, in the matter of an afternoon at the theatre, Gilberte gave me a great surprise. It was precisely the day of which she had spoken to me some time back, on which fell the anniversary of her grandfather's death. We were to go, she and I, with her governess, to hear selections from an opera, and Gilberte had dressed with a view to attending this performance, and wore the air of indifference with which she was in the habit of treating whatever we might be going to do, with the comment that it might be anything in the world, no matter what, provided that it amused me and had her parents' approval. Before luncheon, her mother drew us aside to tell us that her father was vexed at the thought of our going to a theatre on that day. This seemed to me only natural. Gilberte remained impassive, but grew pale with an anger which she was unable to conceal ; still she uttered not a word. When M. Swann joined us his wife took him to the other end of the room and said something in his ear. He called Gilberte, and they went together into the next room. We could hear their raised voices. And yet I could not bring myself to believe that Gilberte, so submissive, so loving, so thoughtful, would resist her father's appeal, on such a day and for so trifling a matter. At length Swann reappeared with her, saying : "You heard what I said. Now you may do as you like."

Gilberte's features remained compressed in a frown throughout luncheon, after which we retired to her room. Then suddenly, without hesitating and as though she had never at any point hesitated over her course of action : "Two o'clock !" she exclaimed, "You know the concert begins at half-past." And she told her governess to make haste.

"But," I reminded her, "won't your father be cross with you?"

"Not the least little bit!"

"Surely, he was afraid it would look odd, because of the anniversary."

"What difference can it make to me what people think? I think it's perfectly absurd to worry about other people in matters of sentiment. We feel things for ourselves, not for the public. Mademoiselle has very few pleasures; she's been looking forward to going to this concert. I am not going to deprive her of it just to satisfy public opinion."

"But, Gilberte," I protested, taking her by the arm, "it is not to satisfy public opinion, it is to please your father."

"You are not going to pass remarks upon my conduct, I hope," she said sharply, plucking her arm away.

* *
*

A favour still more precious than their taking me with them to the Jardin d'Acclimatation, the Swanns did not exclude me even from their friendship with Bergotte, which had been at the root of the attraction that I had found in them when, before I had even seen Gilberte, I reflected that her intimacy with that godlike elder would have made her, for me, the most passionately enthralling of friends, had not the disdain that I was bound to inspire in her forbidden me to hope that she would ever take me, in his company, to visit the towns that he loved.

And lo, one day, came an invitation from Mme. Swann to
a big luncheon-party. I did not know who else were to
be the guests. On my arrival I was disconcerted, as I
crossed the hall, by an alarming incident. Mme. Swann
seldom missed an opportunity of adopting any of those
customs which pass as fashionable for a season, and then,
failing to find support, are speedily abandoned (as, for instance, many years before, she had had her " private han-
som ", or now had, printed in English upon a card inviting you to luncheon, the words, " To meet ", followed by
the name of some more or less important personage).
Often enough these usages implied nothing mysterious and
required no initiation. Take, for instance, a minute innovation of those days, imported from England ; Odette
had made her husband have some visiting cards printed
on which the name Charles Swann was preceded by
" Mr.". After the first visit that I paid her, Mme. Swann
had left at my door one of these " pasteboards ", as she
called them. No one had ever left a card on me before ; I
felt at once so much pride, emotion, gratitude that, scrap-
ing together all the money I possessed, I ordered a superb
basket of camellias and had it sent to Mme. Swann. I
implored my father to go and leave a card on her, but
first, quickly, to have some printed on which his name
should bear the prefix " Mr. ". He vouchsafed neither of
my prayers ; I was in despair for some days, and then
asked myself whether he might not after all have been
right. But this use of " Mr. ", if it meant nothing, was at
least intelligible. Not so with another that was revealed
to me on the occasion of this luncheon-party, but revealed without any indication of its purport. At the moment when I was about to step from the hall into the

drawing-room the butler handed me a thin, oblong envelope upon which my name was inscribed. In my surprise I thanked him ; but I eyed the envelope with misgivings. I no more knew what I was expected to do with it than a foreigner knows what to do with one of those little utensils that they lay by his place at a Chinese banquet. I noticed that it was gummed down ; I was afraid of appearing indiscreet, were I to open it then and there ; and so I thrust it into my pocket with an air of knowing all about it. Mme. Swann had written to me a few days before, asking me to come to luncheon with "just a few people". There were, however, sixteen of us, among whom I never suspected for a moment that I was to find Bergotte. Mme. Swann, who had already "named" me, as she called it, to several of her guests, suddenly, after my name, in the same tone that she had used in uttering it (in fact, as though we were merely two of the guests at her party, who ought each to feel equally flattered on meeting the other), pronounced that of the sweet Singer with the snowy locks. The name Bergotte made me jump like the sound of a revolver fired at me point blank, but instinctively, for appearance's sake, I bowed ; there, straight in front of me, as by one of those conjurers whom we see standing whole and unharmed, in their frock coats, in the smoke of a pistol shot out of which a pigeon has just fluttered, my salute was returned by a young common little thick-set peering person, with a red nose curled like a snail-shell and a black tuft on his chin. I was cruelly disappointed, for what had just vanished in the dust of the explosion was not only the feeble old man, of whom no vestige now remained ; there was also the beauty of an immense work which I had contrived to enshrine in the frail and hallowed organism that I had constructed, like a temple, expressly for itself, but for which no room was to be found in the squat figure, packed tight with blood-vessels, bones, muscles, sinews, of the little man with the snub nose and black beard who stood before me. All the Bergotte whom I had slowly and delicately elaborated for myself, drop by drop, like a stalactite, out of the transparent beauty of his books, ceased (I could see at once) to be of any use, the moment I was obliged to include in him the snail-shell nose and to utilise the little black beard ; just as we must reject as worthless the solution of a problem the terms of which we have not read in full, having failed to observe that the total must amount to a specified figure. The nose and beard were elements similarly ineluctable, and all the more aggravating in that, while forcing me to reconstruct entirely the personage of Bergotte, they seemed further to imply, to produce, to secrete incessantly a certain quality of mind, alert and self-satisfied, which was not in the picture, for such a mind had no connexion whatever with the sort of intelligence that was diffused throughout those books, so intimately familiar to me, which were permeated by a gentle and godlike wisdom. Starting from them, I should never have arrived at that snail-shell nose ; but starting from the nose, which did not appear to be in the slightest degree ashamed of itself, but stood out alone there like a grotesque ornament fastened on his face, I must proceed in a diametrically opposite direction from the work of Bergotte, I must arrive, it would seem, at the mentality of a busy and preoccupied engineer, of the sort who when you accost them in the street think it correct to say :

"Thanks, and you?" before you have actually inquired of them how they are, or else, if you assure them that you have been charmed to make their acquaintance, respond with an abbreviation which they imagine to be effective, intelligent and up-to-date, inasmuch as it avoids any waste of precious time on vain formalities: "Same here!" Names are, no doubt, but whimsical draughtsmen, giving us of people as well as of places sketches so little like the reality that we often experience a kind of stupor when we have before our eyes, in place of the imagined, the visible world (which, for that matter, is not the true world, our senses being little more endowed than our imagination with the art of portraiture, so little, indeed, that the final and approximately lifelike pictures which we manage to obtain of reality are at least as different from the visible world as that was from the imagined). But in Bergotte's case, my preconceived idea of him from his name troubled me far less than my familiarity with his work, to which I was obliged to attach, as to the cord of a balloon, the man with the little beard, without knowing whether it would still have the strength to raise him from the ground. It seemed quite clear, however, that it really was he who had written the books that I had so greatly enjoyed, for Mme. Swann having thought it incumbent upon her to tell him of my admiration for one of these, he shewed no surprise that she should have mentioned this to him rather than to any other of the party, nor did he seem to regard her action as due to a misapprehension, but, swelling out the frock coat which he had put on in honour of all these distinguished guests with a body distended in anticipation of the coming meal, while his mind was completely occupied by other, more real and more important considerations, it was only as at some finished episode in his early life, as though one had made an allusion to a costume of the Duc de Guise which he had worn, one season, at a fancy dress ball, that he smiled as he bore his mind back to the idea of his books ; which at once began to fall in my estimation (dragging down with them the whole value of Beauty, of the world, of life itself), until they seemed to have been merely the casual amusement of a man with a little beard. I told myself that he must have taken great pains over them, but that, if he had lived upon an island surrounded by beds of pearl-oysters, he would instead have devoted himself to, and would have made a fortune out of the pearling trade. His work no longer appeared to me so inevitable. And then I asked myself whether originality did indeed prove that great writers were gods, ruling each one over a kingdom that was his alone, or whether all that was not rather make-believe, whether the differences between one man's book and another's were not the result of their respective labours rather than the expression of a radical and essential difference between two contrasted personalities.

Meanwhile we had taken our places at the table. By the side of my plate I found a carnation, the stalk of which was wrapped in silver paper. It embarrassed me less than the envelope that had been handed to me in the hall, which, however, I had completely forgotten. This custom, strange as it was to me, became more intelligible when I saw all the male guests take up the similar carnations that were lying by their plates and slip them into the buttonholes of their coats. I did as they had done, with the air of spontaneity that a free-thinker assumes in church, who is not familiar with the order of service but rises when everyone else rises and kneels a moment after everyone else is on his knees. Another usage, equally strange to me but less ephemeral, disquieted me more. On the other side of my plate was a smaller plate, on which was heaped a blackish substance which I did not then know to be caviare. I was ignorant of what was to be done with it but firmly determined not to let it enter my mouth.

Bergotte was sitting not far from me and I could hear quite well everything that he said. I understood then the impression that M. de Norpois had formed of him. He had indeed a peculiar " organ " ; there is nothing that so much alters the material qualities of the voice as the presence of thought behind what one is saying ; the resonance of one's diphthongs, the energy of one's labials are profoundly affected—in fact, one's whole way of speaking. His seemed to me to differ entirely from his way of writing, and even the things that he said from those with which he filled his books. But the voice issues from behind a mask through which it is not powerful enough to make us recognise, at first sight, a face which we have seen uncovered in the speaker's literary style. At certain points in the conversation, when Bergotte, by force of habit, began to talk in a way which no one but M. de Norpois would have thought affected or unpleasant, it was a long time before I discovered an exact correspondence with the parts of his books in which his form became so poetic and so musical. At those points he could see in what he was saying a plastic beauty independent of whatever his sentences might mean, and as human speech reflects the human soul, though without expressing it as does literary style, Bergotte appeared almost to be talking nonsense, intoning certain words and, if he were secretly pursuing, beneath them, a single image, stringing them together uninterruptedly on one continuous note, with a wearisome monotony. So that a pretentious, emphatic and monotonous opening was a sign of the rare aesthetic value of what he was saying, and an effect, in his conversation, of the same power which, in his books, produced that harmonious flow of imagery. I had had all the more difficulty in discovering this at first since what he said at such moments, precisely because it was the authentic utterance of Bergotte, had not the appearance of being Bergotte's. It was an abundant crop of clearly defined ideas, not included in that "Bergotte manner" which so many story-tellers had appropriated to themselves ; and this dissimilarity was probably but another aspect—made out with difficulty through the stream of conversation, as an eclipse is seen through a smoked glass —of the fact that when one read a page of Bergotte it was never just what would have been written by any of those lifeless imitators who, nevertheless, in newspapers and in books, adorned their prose with so many "Bergottish" images and ideas. This difference in style arose from the fact that what was meant by "Bergottism" was, first and foremost, a priceless element of truth hidden in the heart of everything, whence it was extracted by that great writer, by virtue of his genius, and that this extraction, and not simply the perpetration of "Bergottisms", was my sweet Singer's aim in writing. Though, it must be added, he continued to perpetrate them in spite of himself, and because he was Bergotte, so that, in one sense, every fresh beauty in his work was the little drop of

Bergotte buried at the heart of a thing which he had dis-
tilled from it. But if, for that reason, each of those
beauties was related to all the rest, and had a "family
likeness", yet each remained separate and individual, as
was the act of discovery that had brought it to the light
of day ; new, and consequently different from what was
called the Bergotte manner, which was a loose synthesis of
all the "Bergottisms" already invented and set forth by
him in writing, with no indication by which men who
lacked genius might forecast what would be his next discovery. So it is with all great writers, the beauty of their
language is as incalculable as that of a woman whom we
have never seen ; it is creative, because it is applied to
an external object of which, and not of their language or
its beauty, they are thinking, to which they have not yet
given expression. An author of memorials of our time,
wishing to write without too obviously seeming to be writing like Saint-Simon, might, on occasion, give us the first
line of his portrait of Villars : "He was a rather tall
man, dark . . . with an alert, open, expressive physiognomy," but what law of determinism could bring him to
the discovery of Saint-Simon's next line, which begins with
"and, to tell the truth, a trifle mad" ? The true variety
is in this abundance of real and unexpected elements, in
the branch loaded with blue flowers which thrusts itself
forward, against all reason, from the spring hedgerow that
seemed already overcharged with blossoms, whereas the
purely formal imitation of variety (and one might advance the same argument for all the other qualities of
style) is but a barren uniformity, that is to say the very
antithesis of variety, and cannot, in the work of imitators,

give the illusion or recall other examples of variety save to a reader who has not acquired the sense of it from the masters themselves.

And so—just as Bergotte's way of speaking would no doubt have been charming if he himself had been merely an amateur repeating imitations of Bergotte, whereas it was attached to the mind of Bergotte, at work and in action, by essential ties which the ear did not at once distinguish—so it was because Bergotte applied that mind with precision to the reality which pleased him that his language had in it something positive, something over-rich, disappointing those who expected to hear him speak only of the " eternal torrent of forms," and of the " mystic thrills of beauty ". Moreover the quality, always rare and new, of what he wrote was expressed in his conversation by so subtle a manner of approaching a question, ignoring every aspect of it that was already familiar, that he appeared to be seizing hold of an unimportant detail, to be quite wrong about it, to be speaking in paradox, so that his ideas seemed as often as not to be in confusion, for each of us finds lucidity only in those ideas which are in the same state of confusion as his own. Besides, as all novelty depends upon the elimination, first, of the stereotyped attitude to which we have grown accustomed, and which has seemed to us to be reality itself, every new conversation, as well as all original painting and music, must always appear laboured and tedious. It is founded upon figures of speech with which we are not familiar, the speaker appears to us to be talking entirely in metaphors ; and this wearies us, and gives us the impression of a want of truth. (After all, the old forms of speech must in their time have been images difficult to follow when the listener was not yet cognisant of the universe which they depicted. But he has long since decided that this must be the real universe, and so relies confidently upon it.) So when Bergotte—and his figures appear simple enough to-day—said of Cottard that he was a mannikin in a bottle, always trying to rise to the surface, and of Brichot that " to him even more than to Mme. Swann the arrangement of his hair was a matter for anxious deliberation, because, in his twofold preoccupation over his profile and his reputation, he had always to make sure that it was so brushed as to give him the air at once of a lion and of a philosopher," one immediately felt the strain, and sought a foothold upon something which one called more concrete, meaning by that more ordinary. These unintelligible words, issuing from the mask that I had before my eyes, it was indeed to the writer whom I admired that they must be attributed, and yet they could not have been inserted among his books, in the form of a puzzle set in a series of different puzzles, they occupied another plane and required a transposition by means of which, one day, when I was repeating to myself certain phrases that I had heard Bergotte use, I discovered in them the whole machinery of his literary style, the different elements of which I was able to recognise and to name in this spoken discourse which had struck me as being so different.

From a less immediate point of view the special way, a little too meticulous, too intense, that he had of pronouncing certain words, certain adjectives which were constantly recurring in his conversation, and which he never uttered without a certain emphasis, giving to each of their syllables a separate force and intoning the last syllable (as for instance the word *visage,* which he always used in preference to *figure,* and enriched with a number of superfluous v's and s's and g's, which seemed all to explode from his outstretched palm at such moments) corresponded exactly to the fine passages in which, in his prose, he brought those favourite words into the light, preceded by a sort of margin and composed in such a way in the metrical whole of the phrase that the reader was obliged, if he were not to make a false quantity, to give to each of them its full value. And yet one did not find in the speech of Bergotte a certain luminosity which in his books, as in those of some other writers, often modified in the written phrase the appearance of its words. This was doubtless because that light issues from so profound a depth that its rays do not penetrate to our spoken words in the hours in which, thrown open to others by the act of conversation, we are to a certain extent closed against ourselves. In this respect, there were more intonations, there was more accent in his books than in his talk ; an accent independent of the beauty of style, which the author himself has possibly not perceived, for it is not separable from his most intimate personality. It was this accent which, at the moments when, in his books, Bergotte was entirely natural, gave a rhythm to the words—often at such times quite insignificant—that he wrote. This accent is not marked on the printed page, there is nothing there to indicate it, and yet it comes of its own accord to his phrases, one cannot pronounce them in any other way, it is what was most ephemeral and at the same time most profound in the writer, and it is what will bear witness to his true nature, what will say whether, despite all the austerity that he has expressed he was gentle, despite all his sensuality sentimental.

Certain peculiarities of elocution, faint traces of which were to be found in Bergotte's conversation, were not exclusively his own ; for when, later on, I came to know his brothers and sisters, I found those peculiarities much more accentuated in their speech. There was something abrupt and harsh in the closing words of a light and spirited utterance, something faint and dying at the end of a sad one. Swann, who had known the Master as a boy, told me that in those days one used to hear on his lips, just as much as on his brothers' and sisters', those inflexions, almost a family type, shouts of violent merriment interspersed with murmurings of a long-drawn melancholy, and that in the room in which they all played together he used to perform his part, better than any of them, in their symphonies, alternately deafening and subdued. However characteristic it may be, the sound that escapes from human lips is fugitive and does not survive the speaker. But it was not so with the pronunciation of the Bergotte family. For if it is difficult ever to understand, even in the *Meistersinger,* how an artist can invent music by listening to the twittering of birds, yet Bergotte had transposed and fixed in his written language that manner of dwelling on words which repeat themselves in shouts of joy, or fall, drop by drop, in melancholy sighs. There are in his books just such closing phrases where the accumulated sounds are prolonged (as in the last chords of the overture of an opera which cannot come to an end, and repeats several times over its supreme cadence before the conductor finally lays down his baton), in which, later on, I was to find a musical equivalent for those phonetic ' brasses ' of the Bergotte family. But in his own case, from the moment in which he transferred them to his books, he ceased instinctively to make use of them in his speech. From the day on which he had begun to write—all the more markedly, therefore, in the later years in which I first knew him—his voice had lost this orchestration for ever.

These young Bergottes—the future writer and his brothers and sisters—were doubtless in no way superior, far from it, to other young people, more refined, more intellectual than themselves, who found the Bergottes rather " loud ", that is to say a trifle vulgar, irritating one by the witticisms which characterised the tone, at once pretentious and puerile, of their household. But genius, and even what is only great talent, spring less from seeds of intellect and social refinement superior to those of other people than from the faculty of transposing, and so transforming them. To heat a liquid over an electric lamp one requires to have not the strongest lamp possible, but one of which the current can cease to illuminate, can be diverted so as instead of light to give heat. To mount the skies it is not necessary to have the most powerful of motors, one must have a motor which, instead of continuing to run along the earth's surface, intersecting with a vertical line the horizontal which it began by following, is capable of converting its speed into ascending force. Similarly the men who produce works of genius are not those who live in the most delicate atmosphere, whose conversation is most brilliant or their culture broadest, but those who have had the power, ceasing in a moment to live only for themselves, to make use of their personality as of a mirror, in such a way that their life, however un-important it may be socially, and even, in a sense, in-tellectually speaking, is reflected by it, genius consisting in the reflective power of the writer and not in the intrinsic quality of the scene reflected. The day on which young Bergotte succeeded in shewing to the world of his readers the tasteless household in which he had passed his child-hood, and the not very amusing conversations between himself and his brothers, on that day he climbed far above the friends of his family, more intellectual and more distinguished than himself; they in their fine Rolls Royces might return home expressing due contempt for the vulgarity of the Bergottes; but he, with his modest engine which had at last left the ground, he soared above their heads.

But there were other characteristics of his elocution which it was not with the members of his family, but with certain contemporary writers that he must share. Younger men, who were beginning to repudiate him as a master and disclaimed any intellectual affinity to him in themselves, displayed their affinity without knowing it when they made use of the same adverbs, the same prepositions that he incessantly repeated, when they constructed their sentences in the same way, spoke in the same quiescent, lingering tone, by a reaction from the eloquent, easy language of an earlier generation. Per-haps these young men—we shall come across some of whom this may be said—had never known Bergotte. But his way of thinking, inoculated into them, had led them to those alterations of syntax and of accent which bear a necessary relation to originality of mind. A relation which, incidentally, requires to be traced. Thus Bergotte, if he owed nothing to any man for his manner of writing, derived his manner of speaking from one of his early associates, a marvellous talker to whose ascendancy he had succumbed, whom he imitated, unconsciously, in his conversation, but who himself, being less gifted, had never written any really outstanding book. So that if one had been in quest of originality in speech, Bergotte must have been labelled a disciple, a writer at second-hand, whereas, influenced by his friend only so far as talk went, he had been original and creative in his writings. Doubtless again, so as to distinguish himself from the previous generation, too fond as it had been of abstractions, of weighty commonplaces, when Bergotte wished to speak favourably of a book, what he would bring into prominence, what he would quote with approval would always be some scene that furnished the reader with an image, some picture that had no rational significance. " Ah, yes ! " he would exclaim, " it is quite admirable ! There is a little girl in an orange shawl. It is excellent ! " or again, " Oh, yes, there is a passage in which there is a regiment marching along the street ; yes, it is excellent ! " As for style, he was not altogether of his time (though he remained quite exclusively of his race, abominating Tolstoy, George Eliot, Ibsen and Dostoievsky), for the word that always came to his lips when he wished to praise the style of any writer was " mild ". " Yes, you know I like Chateaubriand better in *Atala* than in *René ;* he seems to me to be ' milder '." He said the word like a doctor who, when his patient assures him that milk will give him indigestion, answers, " But, you know, it's very ' mild '." And it is true that there was in Bergotte's style a kind of harmony similar to that for which the ancients used to praise certain of their orators in terms which we now find it hard to understand, accustomed as we are to our own modern tongues in which effects of that kind are not sought.

He would say also, with a shy smile, of pages of his own for which some one had expressed admiration : " I think it is more or less true, more or less accurate ; it may be of some value perhaps," but he would say this simply from modesty, as a woman to whom one has said that her dress, or her daughter is charming replies, " It is comfortable," or " She is a good girl." But the constructive instinct was too deeply implanted in Bergotte for him not to be aware that the sole proof that he had built usefully and on the lines of truth lay in the pleasure that his work had given, to himself first of all and afterwards to his readers. Only many years later, when he no longer had any talent, whenever he wrote anything with which he was not satisfied, so as not to have to suppress it, as he ought to have done, so as to be able to publish it with a clear conscience he would repeat, but to himself this time : " After all, it is more or less accurate, it must be of some value to the country." So that the phrase murmured long ago among his admirers by the insincere voice of modesty came in the end to be whispered in the secrecy of his heart by the uneasy tongue of pride. And the same words which had served Bergotte as an unwanted excuse for the excellence of his earliest works became as it were an ineffective consolation to him for the hopeless mediocrity of the latest.

A kind of austerity of taste which he had, a kind of determination to write nothing of which he could not say that it was " mild ", which had made people for so many years regard him as a sterile and precious artist, a chiseller of exquisite trifles, was on the contrary the secret of his strength, for habit forms the style of the writer just as much as the character of the man, and the author who has more than once been patient to attain, in the expression of his thoughts, to a certain kind of attractiveness, in so doing lays down unalterably the boundaries of his talent, just as if he yields too often to pleasure, to laziness, to the fear of being put to trouble, he will find himself describing in terms which no amount of revision can modify, the forms of his own vices and the limits of his virtue.

If, however, despite all the analogies which I was to perceive later on between the writer and the man, I had not at first sight, in Mme. Swann's drawing-room, believed that this could be Bergotte, the author of so many divine books, who stood before me, perhaps I was not altogether wrong, for he himself did not, in the strict sense of the word, "believe" it either. He did not believe it because he shewed a great assiduity in the presence of fashionable people (and yet he was not a snob), of literary men and journalists who were vastly inferior to himself. Of course he had long since learned, from the suffrage of his readers, that he had genius, compared to which social position and official rank were as nothing. He had learned that he had genius, but he did not believe it because he continued to simulate deference towards mediocre writers in order to succeed, shortly, in becoming an Academician, whereas the Academy and the Faubourg Saint-Germain have no more to do with that part of the Eternal Mind which is the author of the works of Bergotte than with the law of causality or the idea of God.

That also he knew, but as a kleptomaniac knows, without profiting by the knowledge, that it is wrong to steal. And the man with the little beard and snail-shell nose knew and used all the tricks of the gentleman who pockets your spoons, in his efforts to reach the coveted academic chair, or some duchess or other who could dispose of several votes at the election, but while on his way to them he would endeavour to make sure that no one who would consider the pursuit of such an object a vice in him should see what he was doing. He was only half-successful ; one could hear, alternating with the speech of the true Bergotte, that of the other Bergotte, ambitious, utterly selfish, who thought it not worth his while to speak of any but his powerful, rich or noble friends, so as to enhance his own position, he who in his books, when he was really himself, had so well portrayed the charm, pure as a mountain spring, of poverty.

As for those other vices to which M. de Norpois had alluded, that almost incestuous love, which was made still worse, people said, by a want of delicacy in the matter of money, if they contradicted, in a shocking manner, the tendency of his latest novels, in which he shewed everywhere a regard for what was right and proper so painfully rigid that the most innocent pleasures of their heroes were poisoned by it, and that even the reader found himself turning their pages with a sense of acute discomfort, and asked himself whether it was possible to go on living even the quietest of lives, those vices did not at all prove, supposing that they were fairly imputed to Bergotte, that his literature was a lie and all his sensitiveness mere play-acting. Just as in pathology certain conditions similar in appearance are due, some to an excess others to an insufficiency of tension, of secretion and so forth, so there may be vice arising from supersensitiveness just as much as from the lack of it. Perhaps it is only in really vicious lives that the moral problem can arise in all its disquieting strength. And of this problem the artist finds a solution in the terms not of his own personal life but of what is for him the true life, a general, a literary solution. As the great Doctors of the Church began often, without losing their virtue, by acquainting themselves with the sins of all mankind, out of which they extracted their own personal sanctity, so great artists often, while being thoroughly wicked, make use of their vices in order to arrive at a conception of the moral law that is binding upon us all. It is the vices (or merely the weaknesses and follies) of the circle in which they live, the meaningless conversation, the frivolous or shocking lives of their daughters, the infidelity of their wives, or their own misdeeds that writers have most often castigated in their books, without, however, thinking it necessary to alter their domestic economy or to improve the tone of their households. And this contrast had never before been so striking as it was in Bergotte's time, because, on the one hand, in proportion as society grew more corrupt, our notions of morality were increasingly exalted, while on the other hand the public were now told far more than they had ever hitherto known about the private lives of literary men ; and on certain evenings in the theatre people would point out the author whom I had so greatly admired at Combray, sitting at the back of a box the mere composition of which seemed an oddly humorous, or perhaps keenly ironical commentary upon— a brazen-faced denial of the thesis which he had just been maintaining in his latest book. Not that anything which this or that casual informant could tell me was of much use in helping me to settle the question of the goodness or wickedness of Bergotte. An intimate friend would furnish proofs of his hardheartedness ; then a stranger would cite some instance (touching, since he had evidently wished it to remain hidden) of his real depth of feeling. He had behaved cruelly to his wife. But in a village inn, where he had gone to spend the night, he had stayed on to watch over a poor woman who had tried to drown herself, and when he was obliged to continue his journey had left a large sum of money with the landlord, so that he should not turn the poor creature out, but see that she got proper attention. Perhaps the more the great writer was developed in Bergotte at the expense of the little man with the beard, so much the more his own personal life was drowned in the flood of all the lives that he imagined, until he no longer felt himself obliged to perform certain practical duties, for which he had substituted the duty of imagining those other lives. But at the same time, because he imagined the feelings of others as completely as if they had been his own, whenever he was obliged, for any reason, to talk to some person who had been unfortunate (that is to say in a casual encounter) he would, in doing so, take up not his own personal standpoint but that of the sufferer himself, a standpoint in which he would have been horrified by the speech of those who continued to think of their own petty concerns in the presence of another's grief. With the result that he gave rise everywhere to justifiable rancour and to undying gratitude.

Above all, he was a man who in his heart of hearts

loved nothing really except certain images and (like a miniature set in the floor of a casket) the composing and painting of them in words. For a trifle that some one had sent him, if that trifle gave him the opportunity of introducing one or two of these images, he would be prodigal in the expression of his gratitude, while shewing none whatever for an expensive present. And if he had had to plead before a tribunal, he would inevitably have chosen his words not for the effect that they might have on the judge but with an eye to certain images which the judge would certainly never have perceived.

That first day on which I met him with Gilberte's parents, I mentioned to Bergotte that I had recently been to hear Berma in *Phèdre ;* and he told me that in the scene in which she stood with her arm raised to the level of her shoulder—one of those very scenes that had been greeted with such applause—she had managed to suggest with great nobility of art certain classical figures which, quite possibly, she had never even seen, a Hesperid carved in the same attitude upon a metope at Olympia, and also the beautiful primitive virgins on the Erechtheum.

" It may be sheer divination, and yet I fancy that she visits the museums. It would be interesting to ' establish ' that." (" Establish " was one of those regular Bergotte expressions, and one which various young men who had never met him had caught from him, speaking like him by some sort of telepathic suggestion.)

" Do you mean the Caryatides ? " asked Swann.

" No, no," said Bergotte, " except in the scene where she confesses her passion to Œnone, where she moves her hand exactly like Hegeso on the stele in the Ceramicus, it is a far more primitive art that she revives. I was refer-

ring to the Korai of the old Erechtheum, and I admit that
there is perhaps nothing quite so remote from the art of
Racine, but there are so many things already in *Phèdre,*
. . . that one more . . . Oh, and then, yes, she is really
charming, that little sixth century Phaedra, the rigidity of
the arm, the lock of hair 'frozen into marble', yes, you
know, it is wonderful of her to have discovered all that.
There is a great deal more antiquity in it than in most
of the books they are labelling 'antique' this year."

As Bergotte had in one of his volumes addressed a
famous invocation to these archaic statues, the words that
he was now uttering were quite intelligible to me and gave
me a fresh reason for taking an interest in Berma's acting.
I tried to picture her again in my mind, as she had looked
in that scene in which I remembered that she had raised
her arm to the level of her shoulder. And I said to myself, " There we have the Hesperid of Olympia ; there we
have the sister of those adorable suppliants on the Acrop-
olis ; there is indeed nobility in art ! " But if these considerations were to enhance for me the beauty of Berma's
gesture, Bergotte should have put them into my head before the performance. Then, while that attitude of the
actress was actually existing in flesh and blood before my
eyes, at that moment in which the thing that was happening had still the substance of reality, I might have tried
to extract from it the idea of archaic sculpture. But of
Berma in that scene all that I retained was a memory
which was no longer liable to modification, slender as a
picture which lacks that abundant perspective of the
present tense where one is free to delve and can always
discover something new, a picture to which one cannot retrospectively give a meaning that is not subject to verifica-

tion and correction from without. At this point Mme.
Swann joined in the conversation, asking me whether Gilberte had remembered to give me what Bergotte had
written about *Phèdre,* and adding, " My daughter is such
a scatter-brain ! " Bergotte smiled modestly and protested that they were only a few pages, of no importance.
" But it is perfectly charming, that little pamphlet, that
little ' tract ' of yours ! " Mme. Swann assured him, to
shew that she was a good hostess, to make the rest of us
think that she had read Bergotte's essay, and also because
she liked not merely to flatter Bergotte, but to make a
selection for herself out of what he wrote, to control his
writing. And it must be admitted that she did inspire
him, though not in the way that she supposed. But when
all is said there is, between what constituted the smartness
of Mme. Swann's drawing-room and a whole side of Bergotte's work, so close a correspondence that either of them
might serve, among elderly men to-day, as a commentary
upon the other.

I let myself go in telling him what my impressions had
been. Often Bergotte disagreed, but he allowed me to go
on talking. I told him that I had liked the green light
which was turned on when Phèdre raised her arm.
" Ah ! The designer will be glad to hear that ; he is a
real artist. I shall tell him you liked it, because he is
very proud of that effect. I must say, myself, that I do
not care for it very much, it drowns everything in a sort
of aqueous vapour, little Phèdre standing there looks too
like a branch of coral on the floor of an aquarium. You
will tell me, of course, that it brings out the cosmic aspect
of the play. That is quite true. All the same, it would
be more appropriate if the scene were laid in the Court of

MADAME SWANN AT HOME

Neptune. Oh yes, of course, I know the Vengeance of Neptune does come into the play. I don't suggest for a moment that we should think only of Port-Royal, but after all the story that Racine tells us is not the 'Loves of the Sea-Urchins'. Still, it is what my friend wished to have, and it is very well done, right or wrong, and it's really quite pretty when you come to look at it. Yes, so you liked that, did you; you understood what it meant, of course; we feel the same about it, don't we, really; it is a trifle unbalanced, what he's done, you agree with me, but on the whole it is very clever of him." And so, when Bergotte had to express an opinion which was the opposite of my own, he in no way reduced me to silence, to the impossibility of framing any reply, as M. de Norpois would have done. This does not prove that Bergotte's opinions were of less value than the Ambassador's; far from it. A powerful idea communicates some of its strength to him who challenges it. Being itself a part of the riches of the universal Mind, it makes its way into, grafts itself upon the mind of him whom it is employed to refute, slips in among the ideas already there, with the help of which, gaining a little ground, he completes and corrects it; so that the final utterance is always to some extent the work of both parties to a discussion. It is to ideas which are not, properly speaking, ideas at all, to ideas which, founded upon nothing, can find no support, no kindred spirit among the ideas of the adversary, that he, grappling with something which is not there, can find no word to say in answer. The arguments of M. de Norpois (in the matter of art) were unanswerable simply because they were without reality.

Since Bergotte did not sweep aside my objections, I con-

fessed to him that they had won the scorn of M. de Norpois. " But he's an old parrot ! " was the answer. " He
keeps on pecking you because he imagines all the time that
you're a piece of cake, or a slice of cuttle-fish." " What's
that ? " asked Swann. " Are you a friend of Norpois ? "
" He's as dull as a wet Sunday," interrrupted his wife,
who had great faith in Bergotte's judgment, and was no
doubt afraid that M. de Norpois might have spoken ill of
her to us. " I tried to make him talk after dinner ; I
don't know if it's his age or his indigestion, but I found
him too sticky for words. I really thought I should have
to ' dope ' him." " Yes, isn't he ? " Bergotte chimed in.
" You see, he has to keep his mouth shut half the time so
as not to use up all the stock of inanities that hold his
shirt-front down and his white waistcoat up." " I think
that Bergotte and my wife are both very hard on him,"
came from Swann, who took the " line ", in his own house,
of a plain, sensible man. " I quite see that Norpois cannot interest you very much, but from another point of
view," (for Swann made a hobby of collecting scraps of
" real life ") " he is quite remarkable, quite a remarkable
instance of a lover. When he was Secretary at Rome,"
he went on, after making sure that Gilberte could not hear
him, " he had, here in Paris, a mistress with whom he was
madly in love, and he found time to make the double
journey every week, so as to see her for a couple of hours.
She was, as it happens, a most intelligent woman, and is
quite attractive to this day ; she is a dowager now.
And he has had any number of others since then. I'm
sure I should have gone stark mad if the woman I was in
love with lived in Paris and I was kept shut up in Rome.
Nervous men ought always to love, as the lower orders

say, 'beneath' them, so that their women have a material inducement to do what they tell them." As he spoke, Swann realised that I might be applying this maxim to himself and Odette, and as, even among superior beings, at the moment when you and they seem to be soaring together above the plane of life, their personal pride is still basely human, he was seized by a violent ill-will towards me. But this was made manifest only in the uneasiness of his glance. He said nothing more to me at the time. Not that this need surprise us. When Racine (according to a story the truth of which has been exploded, though the theme of it may be found recurring every day in Parisian life) made an allusion to Scarron in front of Louis XIV, the most powerful monarch on earth said nothing to the poet that evening. It was on the following day, only, that he fell.

But as a theory requires to be stated as a whole, Swann, after this momentary irritation, and after wiping his eyeglass, finished saying what was in his mind in these words, words which were to assume later on in my memory the importance of a prophetic warning, which I had not had the sense to take : "The danger of that kind of love, however, is that the woman's subjection calms the man's jealousy for a time but also makes it more exacting. After a little he will force his mistress to live like one of those prisoners whose cells they keep lighted day and night, to prevent their escaping. And that generally ends in trouble."

I reverted to M. de Norpois. "You must never trust him ; he has the most wicked tongue !" said Mme. Swann in an accent which seemed to me to indicate that M. de Norpois had been "saying things" about her, especially as Swann looked across at his wife with an air of rebuke, as though to stop her before she went too far.

Meanwhile Gilberte, who had been told to go and get ready for our drive, stayed to listen to the conversation, and hovered between her mother and her father, leaning affectionately against his shoulder. Nothing, at first sight, could be in greater contrast to Mme. Swann, who was dark, than this child with her red hair and golden skin. But after looking at them both for a moment one saw in Gilberte many of the features—for instance, the nose cut short with a sharp, unfaltering decision by the unseen sculptor whose chisel repeats its work upon successive generations—the expression, the movements of her mother ; to take an illustration from another form of art, she made one think of a portrait that was not a good likeness of Mme. Swann, whom the painter, to carry out some whim of colouring, had posed in a partial disguise, dressed to go out to a party in Venetian "character". And as not merely was she wearing a fair wig, but every atom of a swarthier complexion had been discharged from her flesh which, stripped of its veil of brownness, seemed more naked, covered simply in rays of light shed by an internal sun, this "make-up" was not just superficial but was incarnate in her ; Gilberte had the appearance of embodying some fabulous animal or of having assumed a mythological disguise. This reddish skin was so exactly that of her father that nature semed to have had, when Gilberte was being created, to solve the problem of how to reconstruct Mme. Swann piecemeal, without any material at her disposal save the skin of M. Swann. And nature had utilised this to perfection, like a master carver who makes a point of leaving the grain, the knots of his wood in evid-

ence.   On Gilberte's face, at the corner of a perfect reproduction of Odette's nose, the skin was raised so as to
preserve intact the two beauty spots of M. Swann.   It was
a new variety of Mme. Swann that was thus obtained,
growing there by her side like a white lilac-tree beside a
purple.   At the same time it did not do to imagine the
boundary line between these two likenesses as definitely
fixed.   Now and then, when Gilberte smiled, one could
distinguish the oval of her father's cheek upon her
mother's face, as though some one had mixed them together to see what would result from the blend ; this oval
grew distinct, as an embryo grows into a living shape, it
lengthened obliquely, expanded, and a moment later had
disappeared.   In Gilberte's eyes there was the frank and
honest gaze of her father ; this was how she had looked
at me when she gave me the agate marble and said " Keep
it, to remind yourself of our friendship."   But were one
to put a question to Gilberte, to ask her what she had
been doing, then one saw in those same eyes the embar-
rassment, the uncertainty, the prevarication, the misery
that Odette used in the old days to shew, when Swann
asked her where she had been and she gave him one of
those lying answers which, in those days, drove the lover
to despair and now made him abruptly change the conversation, as an incurious and prudent husband.   Often
in the Champs-Elysées I was disturbed by seeing this
look on Gilberte's face.   But as a rule my fears were unfounded.   For in her, a purely physical survival of her
mother, this look (if nothing else) had ceased to have any
meaning.   It was when she had been to her classes, when
she must go home for some lesson that Gilberte's pupils
executed that movement which, in time past, in the eyes

of Odette, had been caused by the fear of disclosing that
she had, during the day, opened the door to one of
her lovers, or was at that moment in a hurry to be at
some trysting-place. So one could see the two natures
of M. and Mme. Swann ebb and flow, encroaching
alternately one upon the other in the body of this Me-
lusine.

It is, of course, common knowledge that a child takes
after both its father and its mother. And yet the dis-
tribution of the merits and defects which it inherits is so
oddly planned that, of two good qualities which seemed inseparable in one of the parents you will find but one in the
child, and allied to that very fault in the other parent
which seemed most irreconcilable with it. Indeed, the in-
carnation of a good moral quality in an incompatible
physical blemish is often one of the laws of filial resemblance. Of two sisters, one will combine with the proud
bearing of her father the mean little soul of her mother ;
the other, abundantly endowed with the paternal intelligence, will present it to the world in the aspect which
her mother has made familiar ; her mother's shapeless
nose and scraggy bosom are become the bodily covering
of talents which you had learned to distinguish beneath a
superb presence. With the result that of each of the sisters one can say with equal justification that it is she who
takes more after one or other of her parents. It is true
that Gilberte was an only child, but there were, at the
least, two Gilbertes. The two natures, her father's and
her mother's, did more than just blend themselves in her ;
they disputed the possession of her—and yet one cannot
exactly say that, which would let it be thought that a
third Gilberte was in the meantime suffering by being the

prey of the two others. Whereas Gilberte was alternately
one and the other, and at any given moment no more
than one of the two, that is to say incapable, when she was
not being good, of suffering accordingly, the better Gilberte not being able at the time, on account of her momentary absence, to detect the other's lapse from virtue.
And so the less good of the two was free to enjoy pleasures of an ignoble kind. When the other spoke to you
from the heart of her father, she held broad views, you
would have liked to engage with her upon a fine and beneficent enterprise ; you told her so, but, just as your arrangements were being completed, her mother's heart
would already have resumed its control ; hers was the
voice that answered ; and you were disappointed and
vexed—almost baffled, as in the face of a substitution of
one person for another—by an unworthy thought, an insincere laugh, in which Gilberte saw no harm, for they
sprang from what she herself at that moment was. Indeed, the disparity was at times so great between these
two Gilbertes that you asked yourself, though without
finding an answer, what on earth you could have said
or done to her, last time, to find her now so different.
When she herself had arranged to meet you somewhere,
not only did she fail to appear, and offer no excuse afterwards, but, whatever the influence might have been that
had made her change her mind, she shewed herself in so
different a character when you did meet her that you
might well have supposed that, taken in by a likeness
such as forms the plot of the *Menaechmi,* you were now
talking to some one not the person who had so politely
expressed her desire to see you, had she not shewn signs
of an ill-humour which revealed that she felt herself to

be in the wrong, and wished to avoid the necessity of an explanation.

"Now then, run along and get ready ; you're keeping us waiting," her mother reminded her.

"I'm so happy here with my little Papa ; I want to stay just for a minute," replied Gilberte, burying her head beneath the arm of her father, who passed his fingers lovingly through her bright hair.

Swann was one of those men who, having lived for a long time amid the illusions of love, have seen the prosperity that they themselves brought to numberless women increase the happiness of those women without exciting in them any gratitude, any tenderness towards their benefactors ; but in their child they believe that they can feel an affection which, being incarnate in their own name, will enable them to remain in the world after their death. When there should no longer be any Charles Swann, there would still be a Mlle. Swann, or a Mme. something-else, *née* Swann, who would continue to love the vanished father. Indeed, to love him too well, perhaps, Swann may have been thinking, for he acknowledged Gilberte's caress with a "Good girl !" in that tone, made tender by our apprehension, to which, when we think of the future, we are prompted by the too passionate affection of a creature who is destined to survive us. To conceal his emotion, he joined in our talk about Berma. He pointed out to me, but in a detached, a listless tone, as though he wished to remain to some extent unconcerned in what he was saying, with what intelligence, with what an astonishing fitness the actress said to Œnone, "You knew it !" He was right. That intonation at least had a value that was really intelligible, and might therefore have satisfied my desire to find incontestable reasons for admiring Berma. But it was by the very fact of its clarity that it did not at all content me. Her intonation was so ingenious, so definite in intention and in its meaning, that it seemed to exist by itself, so that any intelligent actress might have learned to use it. It was a fine idea ; but whoever else should conceive it as fully must possess it equally. It remained to Berma's credit that she had discovered it, but is one entitled to use the word " discover " when the object in question is something that would not be different if one had been given it, something that does not belong essentially to one's own nature seeing that some one else may afterwards reproduce it ?

"Upon my soul, your presence among us does raise the tone of the conversation ! " Swann observed to me, as though to excuse himself to Bergotte ; for he had formed the habit, in the Guermantes set, of entertaining great artists as if they were just ordinary friends whom one seeks only to make eat the dishes that they like, play the games, or, in the country, indulge in whatever form of sport they please. " It seems to me that we're talking a great deal of art," he went on. " But it's so nice, I do love it ! " said Mme. Swann, throwing me a look of gratitude, as well from good nature as because she had not abandoned her old aspirations towards a more intellectual form of conversation. After this it was to others of the party, and principally to Gilberte that Bergotte addressed himself. I had told him everything that I felt with a freedom which had astonished me, and was due to the fact that, having acquired with him, years before (in the course of all those hours of solitary reading, in which he was to me merely the better part of myself), the habit of sincerity, of frankness, of confidence, I was less frightened by him than by a person with whom I should have been talking for the first time. And yet, for the same reason, I was greatly disturbed by the thought of the impression that I must have been making on him, the contempt that I had supposed he would feel for my ideas dating not from that afternoon but from the already distant time in which I had begun to read his books in our garden at Combray. And yet I ought perhaps to have reminded myself that, since it was in all sincerity, abandoning myself to the train of my thoughts, that I had felt, on the one hand, so intensely in sympathy with the work of Bergotte and on the other hand, in the theatre, a disappointment the reason of which I did not know, those two instinctive movements which had both carried me away could not be so very different from one another, but must be obedient to the same laws ; and that that mind of Bergotte which I had loved in his books could not be anything entirely foreign and hostile to my disappointment and to my in-ability to express it. For my intelligence must be a uniform thing, perhaps indeed there exists but a single intelligence, in which everyone in the world participates, towards which each of us from the position of his own separate body turns his eyes, as in a theatre where, if everyone has his own separate seat, there is on the other hand but a single stage. Of course, the ideas which I was tempted to seek to disentangle were probably not those whose depths Bergotte usually sounded in his books. But if it were one and the same intelligence which we had, he and I, at our disposal, he must, when he heard me express those ideas, be reminded of them, cherish them, smile upon them, keeping probably, in spite of what I

supposed, before his mind's eye a whole world of intelligence other than that an excerpt of which had passed
into his books, an excerpt upon which I had based my imagination of his whole mental universe. Just as priests,
having the widest experience of the human heart, are best
able to pardon the sins which they do not themselves
commit, so genius, having the widest experience of the
human intelligence, can best understand the ideas most
directly in opposition to those which form the foundation
of its own writings. I ought to have told myself all this
(though, for that matter, it was none too consoling a
thought, for the benevolent condescension of great minds
has as a corollary the incomprehension and hostility of
small ; and one derives far less happiness from the friendliness of a great writer, which one finds expressed, failing
a more intimate association, in his books, than suffering
from the hostility of a woman whom one did not choose
for her intelligence but cannot help loving). I ought to
have told myself all this, but I did not ; I was convinced
that I had appeared a fool to Bergotte, when Gilberte
whispered in my ear :

"You can't think how delighted I am, because you
have made a conquest of my great friend Bergotte. He's
been telling Mamma that he found you extremely intelligent."

"Where are we going ?" I asked her. "Oh, wherever you like ; you know, it's all the same to me." But
since the incident that had occurred on the anniversary of
her grandfather's death I had begun to ask myself whether
Gilberte's character was not other than I had supposed,
whether that indifference to what was to be done, that
wisdom, that calm, that gentle and constant submission

did not indeed conceal passionate longings which her self-esteem would not allow to be visible and which she disclosed only by her sudden resistance whenever by any chance they were frustrated.

As Bergotte lived in the same neighbourhood as my parents, we left the house together ; in the carriage he spoke to me of my health. "Our friends were telling me that you had been ill. I am very sorry. And yet, after all, I am not too sorry, because I can see quite well that you are able to enjoy the pleasures of the mind, and they are probably what mean most to you, as to everyone who has known them."

Alas, what he was saying, how little, I felt, did it apply to myself, whom all reasoning, however exalted it might be, left cold, who was happy only in moments of pure idleness, when I was comfortable and well ; I felt how purely material was everything that I desired in life, and how easily I could dispense with the intellect. As I made no distinction among my pleasures between those that came to me from different sources, of varying depth and permanence, I was thinking, when the moment came to answer him, that I should have liked an existence in which I was on intimate terms with the Duchesse de Guermantes, and often came across, as in the old toll-house in the Champs-Elysées, a chilly smell that would remind me of Combray. But in this ideal existence which I dared not confide to him the pleasures of the mind found no place.

"No, sir, the pleasures of the mind count for very little with me ; it is not them that I seek after ; indeed I don't even know that I have ever tasted them."

"You really think not ?" he replied. "Well, it may

be, no, wait a minute now, yes, after all that must be
what you like best, I can see it now clearly, I am certain
of it."

As certainly, he did not succeed in convincing me ; and
yet I was already feeling happier, less restricted. After
what M. de Norpois had said to me, I had regarded my
moments of dreaming, of enthusiasm, of self-confidence as
purely subjective and barren of truth. But according to
Bergotte, who appeared to understand my case, it seemed
that it was quite the contrary, that the symptom I ought
to disregard was, in fact, my doubts, my disgust with myself. Moreover, what he had said about M. de Norpois
took most of the sting out of a sentence from which I
had supposed that no appeal was possible.

"Are you being properly looked after ?" Bergotte asked
me. "Who is treating you ?" I told him that I had
seen, and should probably go on seeing Cottard. "But
that's not at all the sort of man you want !" he told me.
"I know nothing about him as a doctor. But I've met
him at Mme. Swann's. The man's an imbecile. Even
supposing that that doesn't prevent his being a good doctor, which I hesitate to believe, it does prevent his being a
good doctor for artists, for men of intelligence. People
like you must have suitable doctors, I would almost go
so far as to say treatment and medicines specially adapted
to themselves. Cottard will bore you, and that alone will
prevent his treatment from having any effect. Besides,
the proper course of treatment cannot possibly be the
same for you as for any Tom, Dick or Harry. Nine
tenths of the ills from which intelligent people suffer
spring from their intellect. They need at least a doctor
who understands their disease. How do you expect that

Cottard should be able to treat you ; he has made allow-
ances for the difficulty of digesting sauces, for gastric
trouble, but he has made no allowance for the effect of
reading Shakespeare. So that his calculations are inac-
curate in your case, the balance is upset ; you see, always
the little bottle-imp bobbing up again. He will find that
you have a dilated stomach ; he has no need to examine
you for it, since he has it already in his eye. You can
see it there, reflected in his glasses." This manner of
speaking tired me greatly ; I said to myself, with the
stupidity of common sense : " There is no more any
dilated stomach reflected in Professor Cottard's glasses
than there are inanities stored behind the white waistcoat
of M. de Norpois." " I should recommend you, instead,"
went on Bergotte, " to consult Dr. du Boulbon, who is
quite an intelligent man." " He is a great admirer of
your books," I replied. I saw that Bergotte knew this,
and I decided that kindred spirits soon come together, that
one has few really " unknown friends ". What Bergotte
had said to me with respect to Cottard impressed me,
while running contrary to everything that I myself believed. I was in no way disturbed by finding my doctor
a bore ; I expected of him that, thanks to an art the laws
of which were beyond me, he should pronounce on the
subject of my health an infallible oracle, after consultation of my entrails. And I did not at all require that,
with the aid of an intellect, in which I easily outstripped
him, he should seek to understand my intellect, which I
pictured to myself merely as a means, of no importance in
itself, of trying to attain to certain external verities. I
doubted greatly whether intellectual people required a
different form of hygiene from imbeciles, and I was quite

prepared to submit myself to the latter kind. " I'll tell you who does need a good doctor, and that is our friend Swann," said Bergotte. And on my asking whether he was ill, " Well, don't you see, he's typical of the man who has married a whore, and has to swallow a hundred serpents every day, from women who refuse to meet his wife, or men who were there before him. You can see them in his mouth, writhing. Just look, any day you're there, at the way he lifts his eyebrows when he comes in, to see who's in the room." The malice with which Bergotte spoke thus to a stranger of the friends in whose house he had so long been received as a welcome guest was as new to me as the almost amorous tone which, in that house, he had constantly been adopting to speak to them. Certainly a person like my great-aunt, for instance, would have been incapable of treating any of us with that politeness which I had heard Bergotte lavishing upon Swann. Even to the people whom she liked, she enjoyed saying disagreeable things. But behind their backs she would never have uttered a word to which they might not have listened. There was nothing less like the social "world" than our society at Combray. The Swanns' house marked a stage on the way towards it, towards its inconstant tide. If they had not yet reached the open sea, they were certainly in the lagoon. " This is all between ourselves," said Bergotte as he left me outside my own door. A few years later I should have answered : " I never repeat things." That is the ritual phrase of society, from which the slanderer always derives a false reassurance. It is what I should have said then and there to Bergotte, for one does not invent all one's speeches, especially when one is acting merely as a card in the social pack. But I did not yet know the formula. What my great-aunt, on the other hand, would have said on a similar occasion was : "If you don't wish it to be repeated, why do you say it ?" That is the answer of the unsociable, of the quarrelsome. I was nothing of that sort : I bowed my head in silence.

Men of letters who were in my eyes persons of considerable importance had had to plot for years before they succeeded in forming with Bergotte relations which continued to the end to be but dimly literary, and never emerged beyond the four walls of his study, whereas I, I had now been installed among the friends of the great writer, at the first attempt and without any effort, like a man who, instead of standing outside in a crowd for hours in order to secure a bad seat in a theatre, is shown in at once to the best, having entered by a door that is closed to the public. If Swann had thus opened such a door to me, it was doubtless because, just as a king finds himself naturally inviting his children's friends into the royal box, or on board the royal yacht, so Gilberte's parents received their daughter's friends among all the precious things that they had in their house, and the even more precious intimacies that were enshrined there. But at that time I thought, and perhaps was right in thinking that this friendliness on Swann's part was aimed indirectly at my parents. I seemed to remember having heard once at Combray that he had suggested to them that, in view of my admiration for Bergotte, he should take me to dine with him, and that my parents had declined, saying that I was too young, and too easily excited to "go out" yet. My parents, no doubt, represented to certain other people (precisely those who seemed to me the most marvellous) something quite different from what they were to me, so that, just as when the lady in pink had paid my father a tribute of which he had shewn himself so unworthy, I should have wished them to understand what an inestimable present I had just received, and to testify their gratitude to that generous and courteous Swann who had offered it to me, or to them rather, without seeming any more to be conscious of its value than is, in Luini's fresco, the charming Mage with the arched nose and fair hair, to whom, it appeared, Swann had at one time been thought to bear a striking resemblance.

Unfortunately, this favour that Swann had done me, which, as I entered the house, before I had even taken off my greatcoat, I reported to my parents, in the hope that it would awaken in their hearts an emotion equal to my own, and would determine them upon some immense and decisive act of politeness towards the Swanns, did not appear to be greatly appreciated by them. "Swann introduced you to Bergotte ? An excellent friend for you, charming society ! " cried my father, ironically. "It only wanted that ! " Alas, when I had gone on to say that Bergotte was by no means inclined to admire M. de Norpois :

"I dare say !" retorted my father. "That simply proves that he's a foolish and evil-minded fellow. My poor boy, you never had much common sense, still, I'm sorry to see you fall among a set that will finish you off altogether."

Already the mere fact of my frequenting the Swanns had been far from delighting my parents. This introduction to Bergotte seemed to them a fatal but natural consequence of an original mistake, namely their own weakness in controlling me, which my grandfather would have called a " want of circumspection ". I felt that I had only, in order to complete their ill humour, to tell them that this perverse fellow who did not appreciate M. de Norpois had found me extremely intelligent. For I had observed that whenever my father decided that anyone, one of my school friends for instance, was going astray— as I was at that moment—if that person had the approval of somebody whom my father did not rate high, he would see in this testimony the confirmation of his own stern judgment. The evil merely seemed to him more pronounced. I could hear him already exclaiming, " Of course, it all hangs together," an expression that terrified me by the vagueness and vastness of the reforms the introduction of which into my quiet life it seemed to threaten. But since, were I not to tell them what Bergotte had said of me, even then nothing could efface the impression my parents had formed, that this should be made slightly worse mattered little. Besides, they seemed to me so unfair, so completely mistaken, that not only had I not any hope, I had scarcely any desire to bring them to a more equitable point of view. At the same time, feeling, as the words came from my lips, how alarmed they would be by the thought that I had found favour in the sight of a person who dismissed clever men as fools and had earned the contempt of all decent people, praise from whom, since it seemed to me a thing to be desired, would only encourage me in wrongdoing, it was in faltering tones and with a slightly shamefaced air that, coming to the end of my story, I flung them the bouquet of : " He told the Swanns that he had found me extremely intelligent." Just as a poisoned dog, in a field, rushes, without knowing why, straight to the grass which is the precise antidote to the toxin that he has swallowed, so I, without in the least suspecting it, had said the one thing in the world that was capable of overcoming in my parents this prejudice with respect to Bergotte, a prejudice which all the best reasons that I could have urged, all the tributes that I could have paid him must have proved powerless to defeat. Instantly the situation changed.

"Oh ! He said that he found you intelligent," repeated my mother. "I am glad to hear that, because he is a man of talent."

"What ! He said that, did he ? " my father joined in. "I don't for a moment deny his literary distinction, before which the whole world bows ; only it is a pity that he should lead that scarcely reputable existence to which old Norpois made a guarded allusion, when he was here," he went on, not seeing that against the sovran virtue of the magic words which I had just repeated the depravity of Bergotte's morals was little more able to contend than the falsity of his judgment.

"But, my dear," Mamma interrupted, "we've no proof that it's true. People say all sorts of things. Besides, M. de Norpois may have the most perfect manners in the world, but he's not always very good-natured, especially about people who are not exactly his sort."

"That's quite true ; I've noticed it myself," my father admitted.

"And then, too, a great deal ought to be forgiven Bergotte, since he thinks well of my little son," Mamma went on, stroking my hair with her fingers and fastening upon me a long and pensive gaze.

My mother had not, indeed, awaited this verdict from Bergotte before telling me that I might ask Gilberte to tea whenever I had friends coming. But I dared not do so for two reasons. The first was that at Gilberte's there was never anything else to drink but tea. Whereas at home Mamma insisted on there being a pot of chocolate as well. I was afraid that Gilberte might regard this as "common"; and so conceive a great contempt for us. The other reason was a formal difficulty, a question of procedure which I could never succeed in settling. When I arrived at Mme. Swann's she used to ask me : "And how is your mother ?" I had made several overtures to Mamma to find out whether she would do the same when Gilberte came to us, a point which seemed to me more serious than, at the Court of Louis XIV, the use of "Monseigneur". But Mamma would not hear of it for a moment.

"Certainly not. I do not know Mme. Swann."

"But neither does she know you."

"I never said she did, but we are not obliged to behave in exactly the same way about everything. I shall find other ways of being civil to Gilberte than Mme. Swann has with you."

But I was unconvinced, and preferred not to invite Gilberte.

Leaving my parents, I went upstairs to change my clothes and on emptying my pockets came suddenly upon the envelope which the Swanns' butler had handed me before shewing me into the drawing-room. I was now alone. I opened it ; inside was a card on which I was told the name of the lady whom I ought to have "taken in" to luncheon.

It was about this period that Bloch overthrew my conception of the world and opened for me fresh possibilities of happiness (which, for that matter, were to change later on into possibilities of suffering), by assuring me that, in contradiction of all that I had believed at the time of my walks along the Méséglise way, women never asked for anything better than to make love. He added to this service a second, the value of which I was not to appreciate until much later ; it was he who took me for the first time into a disorderly house. He had indeed told me that there were any number of pretty women whom one might enjoy. But I could see them only in a vague outline for which those houses were to enable me to substitute actual human features. So that if I owed to Bloch—for his " good tidings " that beauty and the enjoyment of beauty were not inaccessible things, and that we have acted foolishly in renouncing them for all time— a debt of gratitude of the same kind that we owe to an optimistic physician or philosopher who has given us reason to hope for length of days in this world and not to be entirely cut off from it when we shall have passed beyond the veil, the houses of assignation which I began to frequent some years later—by furnishing me with specimens of beauty, by allowing me to add to the beauty of women that element which we are powerless to invent, which is something more than a mere summary of former beauties, that present indeed divine, the one present that we cannot bestow upon ourselves, before which faint and fail all the logical creations of our intellect, and which we can seek from reality alone : an individual charm—deserved to be ranked by me with those other benefactors more recent in origin but of comparable utility (before

finding which we used to imagine without any warmth
the seductive charms of Mantegna, of Wagner, of Siena,
by studying other painters, hearing other composers, visiting other cities) : namely illustrated editions of the history
of painting, symphonic concerts and handbooks to 'Mediaeval Towns'. But the house to which Bloch led me,
(and which he himself, for that matter, had long ceased
to visit) was of too humble a grade, its denizens were too
inconspicuous and too little varied to be able to satisfy
my old or to stimulate new curiosities. The mistress of
this house knew none of the women with whom one asked
her to negotiate, and was always suggesting others whom
one did not want. She boasted to me of one in particular,
one of whom, with a smile full of promise (as though this
had been a great rarity and a special treat) she would
whisper : " She is a Jewess ! Doesn't that make you
want to ? " (That, by the way, was probably why the
girl's name was Rachel.) And with a silly and affected
excitement which, she hoped, would prove contagious, and
which ended in a hoarse gurgle, almost of sensual satisfaction : " Think of that, my boy, a Jewess ! Wouldn't
that be lovely ? Rrrr ! " This Rachel, of whom I
caught a glimpse without her seeing me, was dark and
not good looking, but had an air of intelligence, and would
pass the tip of her tongue over her lips as she smiled, with
a look of boundless impertinence at the " boys " who
were introduced to her and whom I could hear making
conversation. Her small and narrow face was framed in
short curls of black hair, irregular as though they were
outlined in pen-strokes upon a wash-drawing in Indian
ink. Every evening I promised the old woman who
offered her to me with a special insistence, boasting of

her superior intelligence and her education, that I would
not fail to come some day on purpose to make the acquaintance of Rachel, whom I had nicknamed " Rachel
when from the Lord ". But the first evening I had heard
her, as she was leaving the house, say to the mistress :
" That's settled then ; I shall be free to-morrow, if you
have anyone you won't forget to send for me."

And these words had prevented me from recognising her
as a person because they had made me classify her at once
in a general category of women whose habit, common to
all of them, was to come there in the evening to see
whether there might not be a louis or two to be earned.
She would simply vary her formula, saying indifferently :
" If you want me " or " If you want anybody ".

The mistress, who was not familiar with Halévy's
opera, did not know why I always called the girl " Rachel
when from the Lord ". But failure to understand a joke
has never yet made anyone find it less amusing, and it
was always with a whole-hearted laugh that she would
say to me :

" Then there's nothing doing to-night ? When am I
going to fix you up with ' Rachel when from the Lord ' ?
Why do you always say that, ' Rachel when from the
Lord ' ? Oh, that's very smart, that is. I'm going to
make a match of you two. You won't be sorry for it,
you'll see."

Once I was just making up my mind, but she was " in
the press ", another time in the hands of the hairdresser,
an elderly gentleman who never did anything for the
women except pour oil on their loosened hair and then
comb it. And I grew tired of waiting, even though several
of the humbler frequenters of the place (working girls,

they called themselves, but they always seemed to be out of work), had come to mix drinks for me and to hold long conversations to which, despite the gravity of the subjects discussed, the partial or total nudity of the speakers gave an attractive simplicity. I ceased moreover to go to this house because, anxious to present a token of my good-will to the woman who kept it and was in need of furniture, I had given her several pieces, notably a big sofa, which I had inherited from my aunt Léonie. I used never to see them, for want of space had prevented my parents from taking them in at home, and they were stored in a warehouse. But as soon as I discovered them again in the house where these women were putting them to their own uses, all the virtues that one had imbibed in the air of my aunt's room at Combray became apparent to me, tortured by the cruel contact to which I had abandoned them in their helplessness ! Had I outraged the dead, I should not have suffered such remorse. I returned no more to visit their new mistress, for they seemed to me to be alive, and to be appealing to me, like those objects, apparently inanimate, in a Persian fairy-tale, in which are embodied human souls that are undergoing martyrdom and plead for deliverance. Besides, as our memory presents things to us, as a rule, not in their chronological sequence but as it were by a reflexion in which the order of the parts is reversed, I remembered only long afterwards that it was upon that same sofa that, many years before, I had tasted for the first time the sweets of love with one of my girl cousins, with whom I had not known where to go until she somewhat rashly suggested our taking advantage of a moment in which aunt Léonie had left her room.

A whole lot more of my aunt Léonie's things, and notably a magnificent set of old silver plate, I sold, in spite of my parents' warnings, so as to have more money to spend, and to be able to send more flowers to Mme. Swann who would greet me, after receiving an immense basket of orchids, with: " If I were your father, I should have you up before the magistrate for this." How was I to suppose that one day I might regret more than anything the loss of my silver plate, and rank certain other pleasures more highly than that (which would have shrunk perhaps into none at all) of bestowing favours upon Gilberte's parents. Similarly, it was with Gilberte in my mind, and so as not to be separated from her, that I had decided not to enter a career of diplomacy abroad. It is always thus, impelled by a state of mind which is destined not to last, that we make our irrevocable decisions. I could scarcely imagine that that strange substance which was housed in Gilberte, and from her permeated her parents and her home, leaving me indifferent to all things else, could be liberated from her, could migrate into another person. The same substance, unquestionable, and yet one that would have a wholly different effect on me. For a single malady goes through various evolutions, and a delicious poison can no longer be taken with the same impunity when, with the passing of the years, the heart's power of resistance has diminished.

My parents meanwhile would have liked to see the intelligence that Bergotte had discerned in me made manifest in some remarkable achievement. When I still did not know the Swanns I thought that I was prevented from working by the state of agitation into which I was thrown by the impossibility of seeing Gilberte when I chose.

But, now that their door stood open to me, scarcely had I sat down at my desk than I would rise and run to them. And after I had left them and was at home again, my isolation was apparent only, my mind was powerless to swim against the stream of words on which I had allowed myself mechanically to be borne for hours on end. Sitting alone, I continued to fashion remarks such as might have pleased or amused the Swanns, and to make this pastime more entertaining I myself took the parts of those absent players, I put to myself imagined questions, so chosen that my brilliant epigrams served merely as happy answers to them. Though conducted in silence, this exercise was none the less a conversation and not a meditation, my solitude a mental society in which it was not I myself but other imaginary speakers who controlled my choice of words, and in which I felt as I formulated, in place of the thoughts that I believed to be true, those that came easily to my mind, and involved no introspection from without, that kind of pleasure, entirely passive, which sitting still affords to anyone who is burdened with a sluggish digestion.

Had I been less firmly resolved upon setting myself definitely to work, I should perhaps have made an effort to begin at once. But since my resolution was explicit, since within twenty-four hours, in the empty frame of that long morrow in which everything was so well arranged because I myself had not yet entered it, my good intentions would be realised without difficulty, it was better not to select an evening on which I was ill-disposed for a beginning for which the following days were not, alas, to shew themselves any more propitious. But I was reasonable. It would have been puerile, on the part of one who had waited now for years, not to put up with a post-ponement of two or three days. Confident that by the day after next I should have written several pages, I said not a word more to my parents of my decision ; I pre-ferred to remain patient for a few hours and then to bring to a convinced and comforted grandmother a sample of work that was already under way. Unfortunately the morrow was not that vast, external day to which I in my fever had looked forward. When it drew to a close, my laziness and my painful struggle to overcome certain internal obstacles had simply lasted twenty-four hours longer. And at the end of several days, my plans not having matured, I had no longer the same hope that they would be realised at once, no longer the courage, therefore, to subordinate everything else to their realisation : I be-gan again to keep late hours, having no longer, to oblige me to go to bed early on any evening, the certain hope of seeing my work begun next morning. I needed, before I could recover my creative energy, several days of relaxa-tion, and the only time that my grandmother ventured, in a gentle and disillusioned tone, to frame the reproach : " Well, and that work of yours ; aren't we even to speak of it now ? " I resented her intrusion, convinced that in her inability to see that my mind was irrevocably made up, she had further and perhaps for a long time postponed the execution of my task, by the shock which her denial of justice to me had given my nerves, since until I had recovered from that shock I should not feel inclined to begin my work. She felt that her scepticism had charged blindly into my intention. She apologised, kissing me : " I am sorry ; I shall not say anything again," and, so that I should not be discouraged, assured me that, from the day on which I should be quite well again, the work would come of its own accord from my superfluity of strength.

Besides, I said to myself, in spending all my time with the Swanns, am I not doing exactly what Bergotte does? To my parents it seemed almost as though, idle as I was, I was leading, since it was spent in the same drawing-room with a great writer, the life most favourable to the growth of talent. And yet the assumption that anyone can be dispensed from having to create that talent for himself, from within himself, and can acquire it from some one else, is as impossible as it would be to suppose that a man can keep himself in good health, in spite of neglecting all the rules of hygiene and of indulging in the worst excesses, merely by dining out often in the company of a physician. The person, by the way, who was most completely taken in by this illusion, which misled me as well as my parents, was Mme. Swann. When I explained to her that I was unable to come, that I must stay at home and work, she looked as though she were thinking that I made a great fuss about nothing, that there was something foolish as well as ostentatious in what I had said.

"But Bergotte is coming, isn't he? Do you mean that you don't think it good, what he writes? It will be better still, very soon," she went on, "for he is more pointed, he concentrates more in newspaper articles than in his books, where he is apt to spread out too much. I've arranged that in future he's to do the leading articles in the *Figaro*. He'll be distinctly the 'right man in the right place' there." And, finally, "Come! He will tell you, better than anyone, what you ought to do."

And so, just as one invites a gentleman ranker to meet

his colonel, it was in the interests of my career, and as though masterpieces of literature arose out of " getting to know " people, that she told me not to fail to come to dinner with her next day, to meet Bergotte.

And so there was not from the Swanns any more than from my parents, that is to say from those who, at different times, had seemed bound to place obstacles in my way, any further opposition to that pleasant existence in which I might see Gilberte as often as I chose, with enjoyment if not with peace of mind. There can be no peace of mind in love, since the advantage one has secured is never anything but a fresh starting-point for further desires. So long as I had not been free to go to her, having my eyes fixed upon that inaccessible goal of happiness, I could not so much as imagine the fresh grounds for anxiety that lay in wait for me there. Once the resistance of her parents was broken, and the problem solved at last, it began to set itself anew, and always in different terms. Each evening, on arriving home, I reminded myself that I had things to say to Gilberte of prime importance, things upon which our whole friendship hung, and these things were never the same. But at least I was happy, and no further menace arose to threaten my happiness. One was to appear, alas, from a quarter in which I had never detected any peril, namely from Gilberte and myself. And yet I ought to have been tormented by what, on the contrary, reassured me, by what I mistook for happiness. We are, when we love, in an abnormal state, capable of giving at once to an accident, the most simple to all appearance and one that may at any moment occur, a serious aspect which that accident by itself would not bear. What makes us so happy is the presence in our heart of an unstable element which we are perpetually arranging to keep in position, and of which we cease almost to be aware so long as it is not displaced. Actually, there is in love a permanent strain of suffering which happiness neutralises, makes conditional only, procrastinates, but which may at any moment become what it would long since have been had we not obtained what we were seeking, sheer agony.

On several occasions I felt that Gilberte was anxious to put off my visits. It is true that when I was at all anxious to see her I had only to get myself invited by her parents who were increasingly persuaded of my excellent influence over her. "Thanks to them," I used to think, "my love is running no risk ; the moment I have them on my side, I can set my mind at rest ; they have full authority over Gilberte." Until, alas, I detected certain signs of impatience which she allowed to escape her when her father made me come to the house, almost against her will, and asked myself whether what I had regarded as a protection for my happiness was not in fact the secret reason why that happiness could not endure.

The last time that I called to see Gilberte, it was raining ; she had been asked to a dancing lesson in the house of some people whom she knew too slightly to be able to take me there with her. In view of the dampness of the air I had taken rather more caffeine than usual. Perhaps on account of the weather, or because she had some objection to the house in which this party was being given, Mme. Swann, as her daughter was leaving the room, called her back in the sharpest of tones : "Gilberte !" and pointed to me, to indicate that I had come there to see her and that she ought to stay with me. This

" Gilberte ! " had been uttered, or shouted rather, with the best of intentions towards myself, but from the way in which Gilberte shrugged her shoulders as she took off her outdoor clothes I divined that her mother had unwittingly hastened the gradual evolution, which until then it had perhaps been possible to arrest, which was gradually drawing away from me my friend. " You don't need to go out dancing every day," Odette told her daughter, with a sagacity acquired, no doubt, in earlier days, from Swann. Then, becoming once more Odette, she began speaking to her daughter in English. At once it was as though a wall had sprung up to hide from me a part of the life of Gilberte, as though an evil genius had spirited my friend far away. In a language that we know, we have substituted for the opacity of sounds, the perspicuity of ideas. But a language which we do not know is a fortress sealed, within whose walls she whom we love is free to play us false, while we, standing without, desperately alert in our impotence, can see, can prevent nothing. So this conversation in English, at which, a month earlier, I should merely have smiled, interspersed with a few proper names in French which did not fail to accentuate, to give a point to my uneasiness, had, when conducted within a few feet of me by two motionless persons, the same degree of cruelty, left me as much abandoned and alone as the forcible abduction of my companion. At length Mme. Swann left us. That day, perhaps from resentment against myself, the unwilling cause of her not going out to enjoy herself, perhaps also because, guessing her to be angry with me, I was precautionally colder than usual with her, the face of Gilberte, divested of every sign of joy, bleak, bare, pillaged, seemed all afternoon to be devoting a melancholy regret to the pas-de-quatre in which my arrival had prevented her from going to take part, and to be defying every living creature, beginning with myself, to understand the subtle reasons that had determined in her a sentimental attachment to the boston. She confined herself to exchanging with me, now and again, on the weather, the increasing violence of the rain, the fastness of the clock, a conversation punctuated with silences and monosyllables, in which I lashed myself on, with a sort of desperate rage, to the destruction of those moments which we might have devoted to friendship and happiness. And on each of our remarks was stamped, as it were, a supreme harshness, by the paroxysm of their stupefying unimportance, which at the same time consoled me, for it prevented Gilberte from being taken in by the banality of my observations and the indifference of my tone. In vain was my polite : " I thought, the other day, that the clock was slow, if anything ; " she evidently understood me to mean : "How tiresome you are being ! " Obstinately as I might protract, over the whole length of that rain-sodden afternoon, the dull cloud of words through which no fitful ray shone, I knew that my coldness was not so unalterably fixed as I pretended, and that Gilberte must be fully aware that if, after already saying it to her three times, I had hazarded a fourth repetition of the statement that the evenings were drawing in, I should have had difficulty in restraining myself from bursting into tears. When she was like that, when no smile filled her eyes or unveiled her face, I cannot describe the devastating monotony that stamped her melancholy eyes and sullen features. Her face, grown almost livid, reminded me then of those dreary beaches where the sea, ebbing far out, wearies one with its faint shimmering, everywhere the same, fixed in an immutable and low horizon. At length, as I saw no sign in Gilberte of the happy change for which I had been waiting now for some hours, I told her that she was not being nice. "It is you that are not being nice," was her answer. "Oh, but surely——" I asked myself what I could have done, and, finding no answer, put the question to her. "Naturally, you think yourself nice!" she said to me with a laugh, and went on laughing. Whereupon I felt all the anguish that there was for me in not being able to attain to that other, less perceptible plane of her mind which her laughter indicated. It seemed, that laughter, to mean: "No, no, I'm not going to let myself be moved by anything that you say, I know you're madly in love with me, but that leaves me neither hot nor cold, for I don't care a rap for you." But I told myself that, after all, laughter was not a language so well defined that I could be certain of understanding what this laugh really meant. And Gilberte's words were affectionate. "But how am I not being nice," I asked her, "tell me; I will do anything you want." "No; that wouldn't be any good. I can't explain." For a moment I was afraid that she thought that I did not love her, and this was for me a fresh agony, no less keen, but one that required treatment by a different conversational method. "If you knew how much you were hurting me you would tell me." But this pain which, had she doubted my love for her, must have rejoiced her, seemed instead to make her more angry. Then, realising my mistake, making up my mind to pay no more attention to what she said, letting her (without bothering to believe her) assure me: "I do love you, indeed I do ; you will see one day," (that day on which the guilty are convinced that their innocence will be made clear, and which, for some mysterious reason, never happens to be the day on which their evidence is taken), I had the courage to make a sudden resolution not to see her again, and without telling her of it yet since she would not have believed me.

Grief that is caused one by a person with whom one is in love can be bitter, even when it is interpolated among preoccupations, occupations, pleasures in which that person is not directly involved and from which our attention is diverted only now and again to return to it. But when such a grief has its birth—as was now happening—at a moment when the happiness of seeing that person fills us to the exclusion of all else, the sharp depression that then affects our spirits, sunny hitherto, sustained and calm, lets loose in us a raging tempest against which we know not whether we are capable of struggling to the end. The tempest that was blowing in my heart was so violent that I made my way home baffled, battered, feeling that I could recover my breath only by retracing my steps, by returning, upon whatever pretext, into Gilberte's presence. But she would have said to herself : " Back again ! Evidently I can go to any length with him ; he will come back every time, and the more wretched he is when he leaves me the more docile he'll be." Besides, I was irresistibly drawn towards her in thought, and those alternative orientations, that mad careering between them of the compass-needle within me persisted after I had reached home, and expressed themselves in the mutually contradictory letters to Gilberte which I began to draft.

I was about to pass through one of those difficult crises which we generally find that we have to face at various stages in life, and which, for all that there has been no change in our character, in our nature (that nature which itself creates our loves, and almost creates the women whom we love, even to their faults), we do not face in the same way on each occasion, that is to say at every age. At such moments our life is divided, and so to speak distributed over a pair of scales, in two counterpoised pans which between them contain it all. In one there is our desire not to displease, not to appear too humble to the creature whom we love without managing to understand her, but whom we find it more convenient at times to appear almost to disregard, so that she shall not have that sense of her own indispensability which may turn her from us ; in the other scale there is a feeling of pain— and one that is not localised and partial only—which cannot be set at rest unless, abandoning every thought of pleasing the woman and of making her believe that we can dispense with her, we go at once to find her. When we withdraw from the pan in which our pride lies a small quantity of the will-power which we have weakly allowed to exhaust itself with increasing age, when we add to the pan that holds our suffering a physical pain which we have acquired and have let grow, then, instead of the courageous solution that would have carried the day at one-and-twenty, it is the other, grown too heavy and insufficiently balanced, that crushes us down at fifty. All the more because situations, while repeating themselves, tend to alter, and there is every likelihood that, in middle life or in old age, we shall have had the grim satisfaction of complicating our love by an intrusion of habit which adolescence, repressed by other demands upon it, less master of itself, has never known.

I had just written Gilberte a letter in which I allowed the tempest of my wrath to thunder, not however without throwing her the lifebuoy of a few words disposed as though by accident on the page, by clinging to which my friend might be brought to a reconciliation ; a moment later, the wind having changed, they were phrases full of love that I addressed to her, chosen for the sweetness of certain forlorn expressions, those " nevermores " so touching to those who pen them, so wearisome to her who will have to read them, whether she believe them to be false and translate " nevermore " by " this very evening, if you want me," or believe them to be true and so to be breaking the news to her of one of those final separations which make so little difference to our lives when the other person is one with whom we are not in love. But since we are incapable, while we are in love, of acting as fit predecessors of the next persons whom we shall presently have become, and who will then be in love no longer, how are we to imagine the actual state of mind of a woman whom, even when we are conscious that we are of no account to her, we have perpetually represented in our musings as uttering, so as to lull us into a happy dream or to console us for a great sorrow, the same speeches that she would make if she loved us. When we come to examine the thoughts, the actions of a woman whom we love, we are as completely at a loss as must have been, face to face with the phenomena of nature, the world's first natural philosophers, before their science had been elaborated and had cast a ray of light over the unknown. Or, worse still, we are like a person in whose mind the law of causality barely exists, a person who would be incapable, therefore, of establishing any connexion between one phenomenon and another, to whose eyes the spectacle of the world would appear unstable as a dream. Of course I made efforts to emerge from this incoherence, to find reasons for things. I tried even to be " objective " and, to that end, to bear well in mind the disproportion that existed between the importance which Gilberte had in my eyes and that, not only which I had in hers, but which she herself had in the eyes of other people, a disproportion which, had I failed to remark it, would have involved my mistaking mere friendliness on my friend's part for a passionate avowal, and a grotesque and debasing display on my own for the simple and graceful movement with which we are attracted towards a pretty face. But I was afraid also of falling into the contrary error, in which I should have seen in Gilberte's unpunctuality in keeping an appointment an irremediable hostility. I tried to discover between these two perspectives, equally distorting, a third which would enable me to see things as they really were ; the calculations I was obliged to make with that object helped to take my mind off my sufferings ; and whether in obedience to the laws of arithmetic or because I had made them give me the answer that I desired, I made up my mind that next day I would go to the Swanns', happy, but happy in the same way as people who, having long been tormented by the thought of a journey which they have not wished to make, go no farther than to the station and return home to unpack their boxes. And since, while one is hesitating, the bare

idea of a possible resolution (unless one has rendered
that idea sterile by deciding that one will make no
resolution) develops, like a seed in the ground, the
lineaments, every detail of the emotions that will be born
from the performance of the action, I told myself that
it had been quite absurd of me to be as much hurt by
the suggestion that I should not see Gilberte again as
if I had really been about to put that suggestion into
practice, and that since, on the contrary, I was to end
by returning to her side, I might have saved myself the
expense of all those vain longings and painful acceptances.
But this resumption of friendly relations lasted only so
long as it took me to reach the Swanns'; not because
their butler, who was really fond of me, told me that
Gilberte had gone out (a statement the truth of which
was confirmed, as it happened, the same evening, by people who had seen her somewhere), but because of the
manner in which he said it. "Sir, the young lady is not
at home ; I can assure you, sir, that I am speaking the
truth. If you wish to make any inquiries I can fetch the
young lady's maid. You know very well, sir, that I would
do everything in my power to oblige you, and that if the
young lady was at home I would take you to her at once."
These words being of the only kind that is really important, that is to say spontaneous, the kind that gives us
a radiograph shewing the main points, at any rate, of the
unimaginable reality which would be wholly concealed beneath a prepared speech, proved that in Gilberte's household there was an impression that I bothered her with
my visits ; and so, scarcely had the man uttered them
before they had aroused in me a hatred of which I preferred to make him rather than Gilberte the victim ; he

drew upon his own head all the angry feelings that I might have had for my friend ; freed from these complications, thanks to his words, my love subsisted alone ; but his words had, at the same time, shewn me that I must cease for the present to attempt to see Gilberte. She would be certain to write to me, to apologise. In spite of which, I should not return at once to see her, so as to prove to her that I was capable of living without her. Besides, once I had received her letter, Gilberte's society was a thing with which I should be more easily able to dispense for a time, since I should be certain of finding her ready to receive me whenever I chose. All that I needed in order to support with less pain the burden of a voluntary separation was to feel that my heart was rid of the terrible uncertainty whether we were not irreconcilably sundered, whether she had not promised herself to another, left Paris, been taken away by force. The days that followed resembled the first week of that old New Year which I had had to spend alone, without Gilberte. But when that week had dragged to its end, then for one thing my friend would be coming again to the Champs-Elysées, I should be seeing her as before ; I had been sure of that ; for another thing, I had known with no less certainty that so long as the New Year holidays lasted it would not be worth my while to go to the Champs-Elysées, which meant that during that miserable week, which was already ancient history, I had endured my wretchedness with a quiet mind because there was blended in it neither fear nor hope. Now, on the other hand, it was the latter of these which, almost as much as my fear of what might happen, rendered intolerable the burden of my grief. Not having had any letter from Gil-

berte that evening, I had attributed this to her careless-
ness, to her other occupations, I did not doubt that I
should find something from her in the morning's post.
This I awaited, every day, with a beating heart which
subsided, leaving me utterly prostrate, when I had found
in it only letters from people who were not Gilberte, or
else nothing at all, which was no worse, the proofs of another's friendship making all the more cruel those of her
indifference. I transferred my hopes to the afternoon
post. Even between the times at which letters were delivered I dared not leave the house, for she might be sending hers by a messenger. Then, the time coming at last
when neither the postman nor a footman from the
Swanns' could possibly appear that night, I must procras-
tinate my hope of being set at rest, and thus, because I
believed that my sufferings were not destined to last, I
was obliged, so to speak, incessantly to renew them. My
disappointment was perhaps the same, but instead of
just uniformly prolonging, as in the old days, an initial
emotion, it began again several times daily, starting each
time with an emotion so frequently renewed that it ended
—it, so purely physical, so instantaneous a state—by becoming stabilised, so consistently that the strain of waiting
having hardly time to relax before a fresh reason for waiting supervened, there was no longer a single minute in the
day in which I was not in that state of anxiety which it is
so difficult to bear even for an hour. So my punishment
was infinitely more cruel than in those New Year holidays
long ago, because this time there was in me, instead of
the acceptance, pure and simple, of that punishment, the
hope, at every moment, of seeing it come to an end. And
yet at this state of acceptance I ultimately arrived ; then

I understood that it must be final, and I renounced Gilberte for ever, in the interests of my love itself and because I hoped above all that she would not retain any contemptuous memory of me. Indeed, from that moment, so that she should not be led to suppose any sort of lover's spite on my part, when she made appointments for me to see her I used often to accept them and then, at the last moment, write to her that I was prevented from coming, but with the same protestations of my disappointment that I should have made to anyone whom I had not wished to see. These expressions of regret, which we keep as a rule for people who do not matter, would do more, I imagined, to persuade Gilberte of my indifference than would the tone of indifference which we affect only to those whom we love. When, better than by mere words, by a course of action indefinitely repeated, I should have proved to her that I had no appetite for seeing her, perhaps she would discover once again an appetite for seeing me. Alas ! I was doomed to failure ; to attempt, by ceasing to see her, to reawaken in her that inclination to see me was to lose her for ever ; first of all, because, when it began to revive, if I wished it to last I must not give way to it at once ; besides, the most agonising hours would then have passed ; it was at this very moment that she was indispensable to me, and I should have liked to be able to warn her that what presently she would have to assuage, by the act of seeing me again, would be a grief so far diminished as to be no longer (what a moment ago it would still have been), nor the thought of putting an end to it, a motive towards surrender, reconciliation, further meetings. And then again, later on, when I should at last be able safely to confess to Gilberte (so far would her liking for me have regained its strength) my liking for her, the latter, not having been able to resist the strain of so long a separation, would have ceased to exist ; Gilberte would have become im- material to me. I knew this, but I could not explain it to her ; she would have assumed that if I was pretending that I should cease to love her if I remained for too long without seeing her, that was solely in order that she might summon me back to her at once. In the meantime, what made it easier for me to sentence myself to this separation was the fact that (in order to make it quite clear to her that despite my protestations to the contrary it was my own free will and not any conflicting engage- ment, not the state of my health that prevented me from seeing her), whenever I knew beforehand that Gilberte would not be in the house, was going out somewhere with a friend and would not be home for dinner, I went to see Mme. Swann who had once more become to me what she had been at the time when I had such difficulty in seeing her daughter and (on days when the latter was not coming to the Champs-Elysées) used to repair to the Allée des Acacias. In this way I should be hearing about Gilberte, and could be certain that she would in due course hear about me, and in terms which would shew her that I was not interested in her. And I found, as all those who suffer find, that my melancholy condition might have been worse. For being free at any time to enter the habitation in which Gilberte dwelt, I constantly reminded myself, for all that I was firmly resolved to make no use of that privilege, that if ever my pain grew too sharp there was a way of making it cease. I was not unhappy, save only from day to day. And even that is

an exaggeration. How many times in an hour (but now
without that anxious expectancy which had strained every
nerve of me in the first weeks after our quarrel, before I
had gone again to the Swanns') did I not repeat to myself the words of the letter which, one day soon, Gilberte
would surely send, would perhaps even bring to me herself. The perpetual vision of that imagined happiness
helped me to endure the desolation of my real happiness.
With women who do not love us, as with the " missing ",
the knowledge that there is no hope left does not prevent
our continuing to wait for news. We live on tenter-
hooks, starting at the slightest sound ; the mother whose
son has gone to sea on some perilous voyage of discovery
sees him in imagination every moment, long after the
fact of his having perished has been established, striding
into the room, saved by a miracle and in the best of
health. And this strain of waiting, according to the
strength of her memory and the resistance of her bodily
organs, either helps her on her journey through the years,
at the end of which she will be able to endure the knowledge that her son is no more, to forget gradually and to
survive his loss, or else it kills her.

On the other hand, my grief found consolation in the
idea that my love must profit by it. Each visit that I
paid to Mme. Swann without seeing Gilberte was a cruel
punishment, but I felt that it correspondingly enhanced
the idea that Gilberte had of me.

Besides, if I always took care, before going to see Mme.
Swann, that there should be no risk of her daughter's appearing, that arose, it is true, from my determination to
break with her, but no less perhaps from that hope of
reconciliation which overlay my intention to renounce her

(very few of such intentions are absolute, at least in a continuous form, in this human soul of ours, one of whose laws, confirmed by the unlooked-for wealth of illustration that memory supplies, is intermittence), and hid from me all that in it was unbearably cruel. As for that hope, I saw clearly how far it was chimerical. I was like a pauper who moistens his dry crust with fewer tears if he assures himself that, at any moment, a total stranger is perhaps going to leave him the whole of his fortune. We are all of us obliged, if we are to make reality endurable, to nurse a few little follies in ourselves. Now my hope remained more intact—while at the same time our separation became more effectual—if I refrained from meeting Gilberte. If I had found myself face to face with her in her mother's drawing-room, we might perhaps have uttered irrevocable words which would have rendered our breach final, killed my hope and, on the other hand, by creating a fresh anxiety, reawakened my love and made resignation harder.

Ever so long ago, before I had even thought of breaking with her daughter, Mme. Swann had said to me : " It is all very well your coming to see Gilberte ; I should like you to come sometimes for my sake, not to my ' kettle-drums ', which would bore you because there is such a crowd, but on the other days, when you will always find me at home if you come fairly late." So that I might be thought, when I came to see her, to be yielding only after a long resistance to a desire which she had expressed in the past. And very late in the afternoon, when it was quite dark, almost at the hour at which my parents would be sitting down to dinner, I would set out to pay Mme. Swann a visit, in the course of which I knew that I should not see Gilberte, and yet should be thinking only of her. In that quarter, then looked upon as remote, of a Paris darker than Paris is to-day, where even in the centre there was no electric light in the public thoroughfares and very little in private houses, the lamps of a drawing-room situated on the ground level, or but slightly raised above it, as were the rooms in which Mme. Swann generally received her visitors, were enough to lighten the street, and to make the passer-by raise his eyes, connecting with their glow, as with its apparent though hidden cause, the presence outside the door of a string of smart broughams. This passer-by was led to believe, not without a certain emotion, that a modification had been effected in this mysterious cause, when he saw one of the carriages begin to move ; but it was merely a coachman who, afraid of his horses' catching cold, started them now and again on a brisk walk, all the more impressive because the rubber-tired wheels gave the sound of their hooves a background of silence from which it stood out more distinct and more explicit.

The " winter-garden ", of which in those days the passer-by generally caught a glimpse, in whatever street he might be walking, if the drawing-room did not stand too high above the pavement, is to be seen to-day only in photogravures in the gift-books of P. J. Stahl, where, in contrast to the infrequent floral decorations of the Louis XVI drawing-rooms now in fashion—a single rose or a Japanese iris in a long-necked vase of crystal into which it would be impossible to squeeze a second—it seems, because of the profusion of indoor plants which people had then, and of the absolute want of style in their arrangement, as though it must have responded in the ladies whose houses it adorned to some living and delicious passion for botany rather than to any cold concern for lifeless decoration. It suggested to one, only on a larger scale, in the houses of those days, those tiny, portable hothouses laid out on New Year's morning beneath the lighted lamp—for the children were always too impatient to wait for daylight—among all the other New Year's presents but the loveliest of them all, consoling them with its real plants which they could tend as they grew for the bareness of the winter soil ; and even more than those little houses themselves, those winter gardens were like the hothouse that the children could see there at the same time, portrayed in a delightful book, another of their presents, and one which, for all that it was given not to them but to Mlle. Lili, the heroine of the story, enchanted them to such a pitch that even now, when they are almost old men and women, they ask themselves whether, in those fortunate years, winter was not the loveliest of the seasons. And inside there, beyond the winter-garden, through the various kinds of arborescence which from the street made the lighted window appear like the glass front of one of those children's playthings, pictured or real, the passer-by, drawing himself up on tiptoe, would generally observe a man in a frock coat, a gardenia or a carnation in his buttonhole, standing before a seated lady, both vaguely outlined, like two intaglios cut in a topaz, in the depths of the drawing-room atmosphere clouded by the samovar—then a recent importation—with steam which may very possibly be escaping from it still to-day, but to which, if it does, we are grown so accustomed now that no one notices it. Mme. Swann attached great importance to her

" tea " ; she thought that she shewed her originality and
expressed her charm when she said to a man, " You will
find me at home any day, fairly late ; come to tea ! " so
that she allowed a sweet and delicate smile to accompany
the words which she pronounced with a fleeting trace of
English accent, and which her listener duly noted, bowing
solemnly in acceptance, as though the invitation had been
something important and uncommon which commanded
deference and required attention. There was another
reason, apart from those given already, for the flowers'
having more than a merely ornamental part in Mme.
Swann's drawing-room, and this reason pertained not to
the period, but, in some degree, to the former life of
Odette. A great courtesan, such as she had been, lives
largely for her lovers, that is to say at home, which means
that she comes in time to live for her home. The things
that one sees in the house of a " respectable " woman,
things which may of course appear to her also to be of
importance, are those which are in any event of the utmost importance to the courtesan. The culminating point
of her day is not the moment in which she dresses herself for all the world to see, but that in which she un-
dresses herself for a man. She must be as smart in her
wrapper, in her nightgown, as in her outdoor attire.
Other women display their jewels, but as for her, she lives
in the intimacy of her pearls. This kind of existence im-
poses on her as an obligation and ends by giving her a
fondness for luxury which is secret, that is to say which
comes near to being disinterested. Mme. Swann extended
this to include her flowers. There was always beside her
chair an immense bowl of crystal filled to the brim with
Parma violets or with long white daisy-petals scattered

upon the water, which seemed to be testifying, in the eyes
of the arriving guest, to some favourite and interrupted
occupation, such as the cup of tea which Mme. Swann
would, for her own amusement, have been drinking
there by herself ; an occupation more intimate still and
more mysterious, so much so that one felt oneself impelled to apologise on seeing the flowers exposed there by
her side, as one would have apologised for looking at the
title of the still open book which would have revealed to
one what had just been read by—and so, perhaps, what
was still in the mind of Odette. And unlike the book the
flowers were living things ; it was annoying, when one entered the room to pay Mme. Swann a visit, to discover
that she was not alone, or if one came home with her not
to find the room empty, so prominent a place in it, enig-
matic and intimately associated with hours in the life of
their mistress of which one knew nothing, did those flowers
assume which had not been made ready for Odette's
visitors but, as it were, forgotten there by her, had held
and would hold with her again private conversations which
one was afraid of disturbing, the secret of which one tried
in vain to read, fastening one's eyes on the moist purple,
the still liquid water-colour of the Parma violets. By the
end of October Odette would begin to come home with
the utmost punctuality for tea, which was still known, at
that time, as " five-o'clock tea ", having once heard it said,
and being fond of repeating that if Mme. Verdurin had
been able to form a salon it was because people were always certain of finding her at home at the same hour.
She imagined that she herself had one also, of the same
kind, but freer, *senza rigore* as she used to say. She saw
herself figuring thus as a sort of Lespinasse, and believed

that she had founded a rival salon by taking from the du Deffant of the little group several of her most attractive men, notably Swann himself, who had followed her in her secession and into her retirement, according to a version for which one can understand that she had succeeded in gaining credit among her more recent friends, ignorant of what had passed, though without convincing herself. But certain favourite parts are played by us so often before the public and rehearsed so carefully when we are alone that we find it easier to refer to their fictitious testimony than to that of a reality which we have almost entirely forgotten. On days on which Mme. Swann had not left the house, one found her in a wrapper of *crêpe-de-Chine,* white as the first snows of winter, or, it might be, in one of those long pleated garments of *mousseline-de-soie,* which seemed nothing more than a shower of white or rosy petals, and would be regarded to-day as hardly suitable for winter, though quite wrongly. For these light fabrics and soft colours gave to a woman—in the stifling warmth of the drawing-rooms of those days, with their heavily curtained doors, rooms of which the most effective thing that the society novelists of the time could find to say was that they were " exquisitely cushioned "— the same air of coolness that they gave to the roses which were able to stay in the room there by her side, despite the winter, in the glowing flesh tints of their nudity, as though it were already spring. By reason of the muffling of all sound in the carpets, and of the remoteness of her cosy retreat, the lady of the house, not being apprised of your entry as she is to-day, would continue to read almost until you were standing before her chair, which enhanced still further that sense of the romantic, that charm of a sort

239

REMEMBRANCE OF THINGS PAST

of secret discovery, which we find to-day in the memory
of those gowns, already out of fashion even then, which
Mme. Swann was perhaps alone in not having discarded,
and which give us the feeling that the woman who wore
them must have been the heroine of a novel because most
of us have scarcely set eyes on them outside the pages
of certain of Henry Gréville's tales. Odette had, at
this time, in her drawing-room, when winter began,
chrysanthemums of enormous size and of a variety of
colours such as Swann, in the old days, certainly never
saw in her drawing-room in the Rue La Pérouse. My
admiration for them—when I went to pay Mme. Swann
one of those melancholy visits during which, prompted by
my sorrow, I discovered in her all the mystical poetry of
her character as the mother of that Gilberte to whom she
would say on the morrow: "Your friend came to see
me yesterday,"—sprang, no doubt, from my sense that,
rose-pale like the Louis XIV silk that covered her chairs,
snow-white like her *crêpe-de-Chine* wrapper, or of a
metallic red like her samovar, they superimposed upon the
decoration of the room another, a supplementary scheme
of decoration, as rich, as delicate in its colouring, but one
which was alive and would last for a few days only.
But I was touched to find that these chrysanthemums appeared less ephemeral than, one might almost say, lasting,
when I compared them with the tones, as pink, as cop-
pery, which the setting sun so gorgeously displays amid
the mists of a November afternoon, and which, after seeing them, before I had entered the house, fade from the
sky, I found again inside, prolonged, transposed on to the
flaming palette of the flowers. Like the fires caught and
fixed by a great colourist from the impermanence of the

atmosphere and the sun, so that they should enter and
adorn a human dwelling, they invited me, those chrysanthemums, to put away all my sorrows and to taste with
a greedy rapture during that "tea-time" the too fleeting
joys of November, of which they set ablaze all around me
the intimate and mystical glory. Alas, it was not in the
conversations to which I must listen that I could hope to
attain to that glory ; they had but little in common with
it. Even with Mme. Cottard, and although it was growing late, Mme. Swann would assume her most caressing
manner to say : "Oh, no, it's not late, really ; you
mustn't look at the clock ; that's not the right time ; it's
stopped ; you can't possibly have anything else to do now,
why be in such a hurry ?" as she pressed a final tartlet
upon the Professor's wife, who was gripping her card-case
in readiness for flight.

"One simply can't tear oneself away from this house !"
observed Mme. Bontemps to Mme. Swann, while Mme.
Cottard, in her astonishment at hearing her own thought
put into words, exclaimed : "Why, that's just what I
always say myself, what I tell my own little judge, in the
court of conscience !" winning the applause of the gentlemen from the Jockey Club, who had been profuse in their
salutations, as though confounded at such an honour's
being done them, when Mme. Swann had introduced them
to this common and by no means attractive little woman,
who kept herself, when confronted with Odette's brilliant
friends, in reserve, if not on what she herself called "the
defensive", for she always used stately language to describe the simplest happenings. "I should never have
suspected it," was Mme. Swann's comment, "three
Wednesdays running you've played me false." "That's

quite true, Odette ; it's simply ages, it's an eternity since I saw you last. You see, I plead guilty ; but I must tell you," she went on with a vague suggestion of outraged modesty, for although a doctor's wife she would never have dared to speak without periphrasis of rheumatism or of a chill on the kidneys, " that I have had a lot of little troubles. As we all have, I dare say. And besides that I've had a crisis among my masculine domestics. I'm sure, I'm no more imbued with a sense of my own authority than most ladies ; still I've been obliged, just to make an example you know, to give my Vatel notice ; I believe he was looking out anyhow for a more remunerative place. But his departure nearly brought about the resignation of my entire ministry. My own maid refused to stay in the house a moment longer ; oh, we have had some Homeric scenes. However I held fast to the reins through thick and thin ; the whole affair's been a perfect lesson, which won't be lost on me, I can tell you. I'm afraid I'm boring you with all these stories about servants, but you know as well as I do what a business it is when one is obliged to set about rearranging one's household.

" Aren't we to see anything of your delicious child ? " she wound up. " No, my delicious child is dining with a friend," replied Mme. Swann, and then, turning to me : " I believe she's written to you, asking you to come and see her to-morrow. And your babies ? " she went on to Mme. Cottard. I breathed a sigh of relief. These words by which Mme. Swann proved to me that I could see Gilberte whenever I chose gave me precisely the comfort which I had come to seek, and which at that time made my visits to Mme. Swann so necessary. " No, I'm afraid not ; I shall write to her, anyhow, this evening. Gilberte and I never seem to see one another now," I added, pretending to attribute our separation to some mysterious agency, which gave me a further illusion of being in love, supported as well by the affectionate way in which I spoke of Gilberte and she of me. " You know, she's simply devoted to you," said Mme. Swann. " Really, you won't come to-morrow ? " Suddenly my heart rose on wings ; the thought had just struck me—"After all, why shouldn't I, since it's her own mother who suggests it ? " But with the thought I fell back into my old depression. I was afraid now lest, when she saw me again, Gilberte might think that my indifference of late had been feigned, and it seemed wiser to prolong our separation. During these asides Mme. Bontemps had been complaining of the insufferable dulness of politicians' wives, for she pretended to find everyone too deadly or too stupid for words, and to deplore her husband's official position. " Do you mean to say you can shake hands with fifty doctors' wives, like that, one after the other ? " she exclaimed to Mme. Cottard, who, unlike her, was full of the kindest feelings for everybody and of determination to do her duty in every respect. " Ah ! you're a law-abiding woman ! You see, in my case, at the Ministry, don't you know, I simply have to keep it up, of course. It's too much for me, I can tell you ; you know what those officials' wives are like, it's all I can do not to put my tongue out at them. And my niece Albertine is just like me. You really wouldn't believe the impudence that girl has. Last week, on my ' day ', I had the wife of the Under Secretary of State for Finance, who told us that she knew nothing at all about cooking. ' But surely, ma'am,' my niece chipped in with her most winning smile, ' you ought to know everything

about it, after all the dishes your father had to wash.' "
" Oh, I do love that story ; I think it's simply exquisite ! "
cried Mme. Swann. " But certainly on the Doctor's consultation days you should make a point of being ' at
home', among your flowers and books and all your pretty
things," she urged Mme. Cottard. " Straight out like
that ! Bang ! Right in the face ; bang ! She made no
bones about it, I can tell you ! And she'd never said a
word to me about it, the little wretch ; she's as cunning
as a monkey. You are lucky to be able to control yourself ; I do envy people who can hide what is in their
minds." " But I've no need to do that, Mme. Bontemps,
I'm not so hard to please," Mme. Cottard gently expos-
tulated. " For one thing, I'm not in such a privileged
position," she went on, slightly raising her voice as was
her custom, as though she were underlining the point of
her remark, whenever she slipped into the conversation
any of those delicate courtesies, those skilful flatteries
which won her the admiration and assisted the career of
her husband. " And besides I'm only too glad to do anything that can be of use to the Professor."

" But, my dear, it isn't what one's glad to do ; it's what
one is able to do ! I expect you're not nervous. Do you
know, whenever I see the War Minister's wife making
faces, I start copying her at once. It's a dreadful thing
to have a temperament like mine."

" To be sure, yes," said Mme. Cottard, " I've heard
people say that she had a twitch; my husband knows
someone else who occupies a very high position, and it's
only natural, when gentlemen get talking together . . ."

" And then, don't you know, it's just the same with the
Chief of the Registry ; he's a hunchback. Whenever he

comes to see me, before he's been in the room five minutes my fingers are itching to stroke his hump. My husband says I'll cost him his place. What if I do ! A fig for the Ministry ! Yes, a fig for the Ministry ! I should like to have that printed as a motto on my notepaper. I can see I am shocking you ; you're so frightfully proper, but I must say there's nothing amuses me like a little devilry now and then. Life would be dreadfully monotonous without it."

And she went on talking about the Ministry all the time, as though it had been Mount Olympus. To change the conversation, Mme. Swann turned to Mme. Cottard : "But you're looking very smart to-day. Redfern *fecit ?* "

"No, you know, I always swear by Rauthnitz. Besides, it's only an old thing I've had done up." "Not really ! It's charming ! "

"Guess how much. . . . No, change the first figure ! "

"You don't say so ! Why, that's nothing ; it's given away ! Three times that at least, I should have said." "You see how history comes to be written," apostrophised the doctor's wife. And pointing to a neck-ribbon which had been a present from Mme. Swann ; "Look, Odette ! Do you recognise this ? "

Through the gap between a pair of curtains a head peeped with ceremonious deference, making a playful pretence of being afraid of disturbing the party ; it was Swann. "Odette, the Prince d'Agrigente is with me in the study. He wants to know if he may pay his respects to you. What am I to tell him ? " "Why, that I shall be delighted," Odette would reply, secretly flattered, but without losing anything of the composure which came to her all the more easily since she had always, even in her "fast" days, been accustomed to entertain men of fashion. Swann disappeared to deliver the message, and would presently return with the Prince, unless in the meantime Mme. Verdurin had arrived. When he married Odette Swann had insisted on her ceasing to frequent the little clan. (He had several good reasons for this stipulation, though, had he had none, he would have made it just the same in obedience to a law of ingratitude which admits no exception, and proves that every "go-between" is either lacking in foresight or else singularly disinterested.) He had conceded only that Odette and Mme. Verdurin might exchange visits once a year, and even this seemed excessive to some of the "faithful", indignant at the insult offered to the "Mistress" who for so many years had treated Odette and even Swann himself as the spoiled children of her house. For if it contained false brethren who "failed" upon certain evenings in order that they might secretly accept an invitation from Odette, ready, in the event of discovery, with the excuse that they were curious to meet Bergotte (although the Mistress assured them that he never went to the Swanns', and even if he did had no vestige of talent, really—in spite of which she was making the most strenuous efforts, to quote one of her favourite expressions, to "attract" him), the little group had its "die-hards" also. And these, though ignorant of those conventional refinements which often dissuade people from the extreme attitude one would have liked to see them adopt in order to annoy some one else, would have wished Mme. Verdurin, but had never managed to prevail upon her to sever all connexion with Odette, and thus deprive her of the satisfaction of saying, with a mocking laugh : "We go to the Mistress's very seldom now, since the Schism. It was all very well while my husband was still a bachelor, but when one is married, you know, it isn't always so easy. . . . If you must know, M. Swann can't abide old Ma Verdurin, and he wouldn't much like the idea of my going there regularly, as I used to. And I, as a dutiful spouse, don't you see . . . ?" Swann would accompany his wife to their annual evening there but would take care not to be in the room when Mme. Verdurin came to call. And so, if the "Mistress" was in the drawing-room, the Prince d'Agrigente would enter it alone. Alone, too, he was presented to her by Odette, who preferred that Mme. Verdurin should be left in ignorance of the names of her humbler guests, and so might, seeing more than one strange face in the room, be led to believe that she was mixing with the cream of the aristocracy, a device which proved so far successful that Mme. Verdurin said to her husband, that evening, with profound contempt : "Charming people, her friends ! I met all the fine flower of the Reaction !" Odette was living, with respect to Mme. Verdurin, under a converse illusion. Not that the latter's salon had ever begun, at that time, to develop into what we shall one day see it to have become. Mme. Verdurin had not yet reached the period of incubation in which one dispenses with one's big parties, where the few brilliant specimens recently acquired would be lost in too numerous a crowd, and prefers to wait until the generative force of the ten righteous whom one has succeeded in attracting shall have multiplied those ten seventy-fold. As Odette was not to be long now in doing, Mme. Verdurin did indeed entertain the idea of "Society" as her final objective, but her zone of attack was as yet so restricted, and moreover so remote from that in which Odette had some chance of arriving at an identical goal, of breaking the line of defence, that the latter remained absolutely ignorant of the strategic plans which the "Mistress" was elaborating. And it was with the most perfect sincerity that Odette, when anyone spoke to her of Mme. Verdurin as a snob, would answer, laughing, "Oh, no, quite the opposite ! For one thing, she never gets a chance of being a snob ; she doesn't know anyone. And then, to do her justice, I must say that she seems quite pleased not to know anyone. No, what she likes are her Wednesdays, and people who talk well." And in her hearts of hearts she envied Mme. Verdurin (for all that she did not despair of having herself, in so eminent a school, succeeded in acquiring them) those arts to which the "Mistress" attached such paramount importance, albeit they did but discriminate between shades of the Non-existent, sculpture the void, and were, properly speaking, the Arts of Nonentity : to wit those, in the lady of a house, of knowing how to "bring people together", how to "group", to "draw out", to "keep in the background", to act as a "connecting link".

In any case, Mme. Swann's friends were impressed when they saw in her house a lady of whom they were accustomed to think only as in her own, in an inseparable setting of her guests, amid the whole of her little group which they were astonished to behold thus suggested, summarised, assembled, packed into a single armchair in the bodily form of the "Mistress", the hostess turned visitor, muffled in her cloak with its grebe trimming, as shaggy as the white skins that carpeted that drawing-room embowered in which Mme. Verdurin was a drawing-room in herself. The more timid among the women thought it prudent to retire, and using the plural, as people do when they mean to hint to the rest of the room that it is wiser not to tire a convalescent who is out of bed for the first time : " Odette," they murmured, " we are going to leave you." They envied Mme. Cottard, whom the " Mistress " called by her Christian name. " Can I drop you anywhere ? " Mme. Verdurin asked her, unable to bear the thought that one of the faithful was going to remain behind instead of following her from the room. " Oh, but this lady has been so very kind as to say, she'll take me," replied Mme. Cottard, not wishing to appear to be forgetting, when approached by a more illustrious personage, that she had accepted the offer which Mme. Bontemps had made of driving her home behind her cockaded coachman. " I must say that I am always specially grateful to the friends who are so kind as to take me with them in their vehicles. It is a regular godsend to me, who have no Automedon." " Especially," broke in the " Mistress ", who felt that she must say something, since she knew Mme. Bontemps slightly and had just invited her to her Wednesdays, " as at Mme. de Crécy's house you're not very near home. Oh, good gracious, I shall never get into the way of saying Mme. Swann ! " It was a recognised pleasantry in the little clan, among those who were not over endowed with wit, to pretend that they could never grow used to saying " Mme. Swann." " I have been so accustomed to saying Mme. de Crécy that I nearly went wrong again ! " Only Mme. Verdurin, when she spoke to Odette, was not content with the nearly, but went wrong on purpose. "Don't you feel afraid, Odette, living out in the wilds like this? I'm sure I shouldn't feel at all comfortable, coming home after dark. Besides, it's so damp. It can't be at all good for your husband's eczema. You haven't rats in the house, I hope!" "Oh, dear no. What a horrid idea!" "That's a good thing; I was told you had. I'm glad to know it's not true, because I have a perfect horror of the creatures, and I should never have come to see you again. Good-bye, my dear child, we shall meet again soon; you know what a pleasure it is to me to see you. You don't know how to put your chrysanthemums in water," she went on, as she prepared to leave the room, Mme. Swann having risen to escort her. "They are Japanese flowers; you must arrange them the same way as the Japanese." "I do not agree with Mme. Verdurin, although she is the Law and the Prophets to me in all things! There's no one like you, Odette, for finding such lovely chrysanthemums, or chrysanthema rather, for it seems that's what we ought to call them now," declared Mme. Cottard as soon as the "Mistress" had shut the door behind her. "Dear Mme. Verdurin is not always very kind about other people's flowers," said Odette sweetly. "Whom do you go to, Odette," asked Mme. Cottard, to forestall any further criticism of the "Mistress". "Lemaître? I must confess, the other day in Lemaître's window I saw a huge, great pink bush which made me do something quite mad." But modesty forbade her to give any more precise details as to the price of the bush, and she said merely that the Professor, "and you know, he's not at all a quick-tempered man," had "waved his sword in

the air " and told her that she " didn't know what money
meant." " No, no, I've no regular florist except Debac."
" Nor have I," said Mme. Cottard, " but I confess that
I am unfaithful to him now and then with Lachaume."
" Oh, you forsake him for Lachaume, do you ; I must
tell Debac that," retorted Odette, always anxious to shew
her wit, and to lead the conversation in her own house,
where she felt more at her ease than in the little clan.
" Besides, Lachaume is really becoming too dear ; his
prices are quite excessive, don't you know ; I find his
prices impossible ! " she added, laughing.

Meanwhile Mme. Bontemps, who had been heard a
hundred times to declare that nothing would induce her to
go to the Verdurins', delighted at being asked to the
famous Wednesdays, was planning in her own mind how
she could manage to attend as many of them as possible.
She was not aware that Mme. Verdurin liked people not
to miss a single one ; also she was one of those people
whose company is but little sought, who, when a hostess
invites them to a series of parties, do not accept and go
to them without more ado, like those who know that it
is always a pleasure to see them, whenever they have a
moment to spare and feel inclined to go out ; people of
her type deny themselves it may be the first evening and
the third, imagining that their absence will be noticed,
and save themselves up for the second and fourth, unless
it should happen that, having heard from a trustworthy
source that the third is to be a particularly brilliant party,
they reverse the original order, assuring their hostess that
" most unfortunately, we had another engagement last
week." So Mme. Bontemps was calculating how many
Wednesdays there could still be left before Easter, and by

what means she might manage to secure one extra, and yet not appear to be thrusting herself upon her hostess. She relied upon Mme. Cottard, whom she would have with her in the carriage going home, to give her a few hints. "Oh, Mme. Bontemps, I see you getting up to go; it is very bad of you to give the signal for flight like that! You owe me some compensation for not turning up last Thursday. . . . Come, sit down again, just for a minute. You can't possibly be going anywhere else before dinner. Really, you won't let yourself be tempted?" went on Mme. Swann, and, as she held out a plate of cakes, "You know, they're not at all bad, these little horrors. They don't look nice, but just taste one, I know you'll like it." "On the contrary, they look quite delicious," broke in Mme. Cottard. "In your house, Odette, one is never short of victuals. I have no need to ask to see the trade-mark; I know you get everything from Rebattet. I must say that I am more eclectic. For sweet biscuits and everything of that sort I repair, as often as not, to Bourbonneux. But I agree that they simply don't know what an ice means. Rebattet for everything iced, and syrups and sorbets; they're past-masters. As my husband would say, they're the *ne plus ultra.*" "Oh, but we just make these in the house. You won't, really?" "I shan't be able to eat a scrap of dinner," pleaded Mme. Bontemps, "but I will just sit down again for a moment; you know, I adore talking to a clever woman like you." "You will think me highly indiscreet, Odette, but I should so like to know what you thought of the hat Mme. Trombert had on. I know, of course, that big hats are the fashion just now. All the same, wasn't it just the least little bit exaggerated? And compared to the hat she came to see me in the other day, the one she had on just now was microscopic ! " " Oh no, I am not at all clever," said Odette, thinking that this sounded well. " I am a perfect simpleton, I believe everything people say, and worry myself to death over the least thing." And she insinuated that she had, just at first, suffered terribly from the thought of having married a man like Swann, who had a separate life of his own and was unfaithful to her. Meanwhile the Prince d'Agrigente, having caught the words " I am not at all clever ", thought it incumbent on him to protest ; unfortunately he had not the knack of repartee. " Tut, tut, tut, tut ! " cried Mme. Bontemps, " Not clever ; you ! " " That's just what I was saying to myself—' What do I hear ? '," the Prince clutched at this straw, " My ears must have played me false ! " " No, I assure you," went on Odette, " I am really just an ordinary woman, very easily shocked, full of prejudices, living in my own little groove and dreadfully ignorant." And then, in case he had any news of the Baron de Charlus, " Have you seen our dear Baronet ? " she asked him. " You, ignorant ! " cried Mme. Bontemps. " Then I wonder what you'd say of the official world, all those wives of Excellencies who can talk of nothing but their frocks. . . . Listen to this, my friend ; not more than a week ago I happened to mention *Lohengrin* to the Education Minister's wife. She stared at me, and said ' *Lohengrin?* Oh, yes, the new review at the Folies-Bergères. I hear it's a perfect scream ! ' What do you say to that, eh ? You can't help yourself ; when people say things like that it makes your blood boil. I could have struck her. Because I have a bit of a temper of my own. What do you say, sir ; " she turned to me,

" was I not right ? " " Listen," said Mme. Cottard, " people can't help answering a little off the mark when they're asked a thing like that point blank, without any warning. I know something about it, because Mme. Verdurin also has a habit of putting a pistol to your head." " Speaking of Mme. Verdurin," Mme. Bontemps asked Mme. Cottard, " do you know who will be there on Wednesday ? Oh, I've just remembered that we've accepted an invitation for next Wednesday. You wouldn't care to dine with us on Wednesday week ? We could go on together to Mme. Verdurin's. I should never dare to go there by myself ; I don't know why it is, that great lady always terrifies me." " I'll tell you what it is," replied Mme. Cottard, " what frightens you about Mme. Verdurin is her organ. But you see everyone can't have such a charming organ as Mme. Swann. Once you've found your tongue, as the ' Mistress ' says, the ice will soon be broken. For she's a very easy person, really, to get on with. But I can quite understand what you feel ; it's never pleasant to find oneself for the first time in a strange country." " Won't you dine with us, too ? " said Mme. Bontemps to Mme. Swann. " After dinner we could all go to the Verdurins together, ' do a Verdurin ' ; and even if it means that the ' Mistress ' will stare me out of countenance and never ask me to the house again, once we are there we'll just sit by ourselves and have a quiet talk, I'm sure that's what I should like best." But this assertion can hardly have been quite truthful, for Mme. Bontemps went on to ask : " Who do you think will be there on Wednesday week ? What will they be doing ? There won't be too big a crowd, I hope ! " " I certainly shan't be there," said Odette. " We shall just look in for a minute on the last Wednesday of all. If you don't mind waiting till then——" But Mme. Bontemps did not appear to be tempted by the proposal.

Granted that the intellectual distinction of a house and its smartness are generally in inverse rather than direct ratio, one must suppose, since Swann found Mme. Bontemps attractive, that any forfeiture of position once accepted has the consequence of making us less particular with regard to the people among whom we have resigned ourselves to finding entertainment, less particular with regard to their intelligence as to everything else about them. And if this be true, men, like nations, must see their culture and even their language disappear with their independence. One of the effects of this indulgence is to aggravate the tendency which after a certain age we have towards finding pleasure in speeches that are a homage to our own turn of mind, to our weaknesses, an encouragement to us to yield to them ; that is the age at which a great artist prefers to the company of original minds that of pupils who have nothing in common with him save the letter of his doctrine, who listen to him and offer incense ; at which a man or woman of mark, who is living entirely for love, will find that the most intelligent person in a gathering is one perhaps of no distinction, but one who has shewn by some utterance that he can understand and approve what is meant by an existence devoted to gallantry, and has thus pleasantly excited the voluptuous instincts of the lover or mistress ; it was the age, too, at which Swann, in so far as he had become the husband of Odette, enjoyed hearing Mme. Bontemps say how silly it was to have nobody in one's house but duchesses (concluding from that, quite the contrary of what he would have decided in the old days at the Verdurins', that she was a good creature, extremely sensible and not at all a snob) and telling her stories which made her "die, laughing" because she had not heard them before, although she always "saw the point" at once, liked flattering her for his own amusement. "Then the Doctor is not mad about flowers, like you?" Mme. Swann asked Mme. Cottard. "Oh, well, you know, my husband is a sage; he practises moderation in all things. Yes, I must admit, he has a passion." Her eye aflame with malice, joy, curiosity, "And what is that, pray?" inquired Mme. Bontemps. Quite simply Mme. Cottard answered her, "Reading." "Oh, that's a very restful passion in a husband!" cried Mme. Bontemps suppressing an impish laugh. "When the Doctor gets a book in his hands, you know!" "Well, that needn't alarm you much . . ." "But it does, for his eyesight. I must go now and look after him, Odette, and I shall come back on the very first opportunity and knock at your door. Talking of eyesight, have you heard that the new house Mme. Verdurin has just bought is to be lighted by electricity? I didn't get that from my own little secret service, you know, but from quite a different source; it was the electrician himself, Mildé, who told me. You see, I quote my authorities! Even the bedrooms, he says, are to have electric lamps with shades which will filter the light. It is evidently a charming luxury, for those who can afford it. But it seems that our contemporaries must absolutely have the newest thing if it's the only one of its kind in the world. Just fancy, the sister-in-law of a friend of mine has had the telephone installed in her house! She can order things from her tradesmen without having to go out of doors ! I confess that I've made the most bare-faced stratagems to get permission to go there one day, just to speak into the instrument. It's very tempting, but more in a friend's house than at home. I don't think I should like to have the telephone in my establishment. Once the first excitement is over, it must be a perfect racket going on all the time. Now, Odette, I must be off ; you're not to keep Mme. Bontemps any longer, she's looking after me. I must absolutely tear myself away ; you're making me behave in a nice way, I shall be getting home after my husband ! "

And for myself also it was time to return home, before I had tasted those wintry delights of which the chrysan-themums had seemed to me to be the brilliant envelope. These pleasures had not appeared, and yet Mme. Swann did not look as though she expected anything more. She allowed the servants to carry away the tea-things, as who should say "Time, please, gentlemen ! " And at last she did say to me : "Really, must you go ? Very well ; good-bye ! " I felt that I might have stayed there without encountering those unknown pleasures, and that my unhappiness was not the cause of my having to forego them. Were they to be found, then, situated not upon that beaten track of hours which leads one always to the moment of departure, but rather upon some cross-road unknown to me along which I ought to have digressed ? At least, the object of my visit had been attained ; Gilberte would know that I had come to see her parents when she was not at home, and that I had, as Mme. Cottard had incessantly assured me, "made a complete conquest, first shot, of Mme. Verdurin," whom, she added, she had never seen "make so much" of anyone. ("You and she must have hooked atoms.") She would know that I had spoken of her as was fitting, with affection, but that I had not that incapacity for living without our seeing one another which I believed to be at the root of the boredom that she had shewn at our last meetings. I had told Mme. Swann that I should not be able to see Gilberte again. I had said this as though I had finally decided not to see her any more. And the letter which I was going to send Gilberte would be framed on those lines. Only to myself, to fortify my courage, I proposed no more than a supreme and concentrated effort, lasting a few days only. I said to myself : "This is the last time that I shall refuse to meet her ; I shall accept the next invitation." To make our separation less difficult to realise, I did not picture it to myself as final. But I knew very well that it would be.

The first of January was exceptionally painful to me that winter. So, no doubt, is everything that marks a date and an anniversary when we are unhappy. But if our unhappiness is due to the loss of some dear friend, our suffering consists merely in an unusually vivid comparison of the present with the past. There was added to this, in my case, the unexpressed hope that Gilberte, having intended to leave me to take the first steps towards a reconciliation, and discovering that I had not taken them, had been waiting only for the excuse of New Year's Day to write to me, saying : "What is the matter ? I am madly in love with you ; come, and let us explain things properly ; I cannot live without seeing you." As the last days of the old year went by, such a letter began to seem probable. It was, perhaps, nothing of the sort, but to make us believe that such a thing is probable the desire, the need that we have for it suffices. The soldier is convinced that a certain interval of time, capable of being indefinitely prolonged, will be allowed him before the bullet finds him, the thief before he is taken, men in general before they have to die. That is the amulet which preserves people—and sometimes peoples—not from danger but from the fear of danger, in reality from the belief in danger, which in certain cases allows them to brave it without their actually needing to be brave. It is confidence of this sort, and with as little foundation, that sustains the lover who is counting upon a reconciliation, upon a letter. For me to cease to expect a letter it would have sufficed that I should have ceased to wish for one. However unimportant one may know that one is in the eyes of her whom one still loves, one attributes to her a series of thoughts (though their sum-total be indifference) the intention to express those thoughts, a complication of her inner life in which one is the constant object possibly of her antipathy but certainly of her attention. But to imagine what was going on in Gilberte's mind I should have required simply the power to anticipate on that New Year's Day what I should feel on the first day of any of the years to come, when the attention or the silence or the affection or the coldness of Gilberte would pass almost unnoticed by me and I should not dream, should not even be able to dream of seeking a solution of problems which would have ceased to perplex me. When we are in love, our love is too big a thing for us to be able altogether to contain it within us. It radiates towards the beloved object, finds in her a surface which arrests it, forcing it to return to its starting-point, and it is this shock of the repercussion of our own affec-

tion which we call the other's regard for ourselves, and
which pleases us more then than on its outward journey
because we do not recognise it as having originated in ourselves. New Year's Day rang out all its hours without
there coming to me that letter from Gilberte. And as I
received a few others containing greetings tardy or retarded by the overburdening of the mails at that season,
on the third and fourth of January I hoped still, but my
hope grew hourly more faint. Upon the days that followed I gazed through a mist of tears. This undoubtedly
meant that, having been less sincere than I thought in my
renunciation of Gilberte, I had kept the hope of a letter
from her for the New Year. And seeing that hope ex-
hausted before I had had time to shelter myself behind
another, I suffered as would an invalid who had emptied
his phial of morphia without having another within his
reach. But perhaps also in my case—and these two explanations are not mutually exclusive, for a single feeling
is often made up of contrary elements—the hope that I
entertained of ultimately receiving a letter had brought
to my mind's eye once again the image of Gilberte, had
reawakened the emotions which the expectation of finding
myself in her presence, the sight of her, her way of treating me had aroused in me before. The immediate possibility of a reconciliation had suppressed in me that
faculty the immense importance of which we are apt to
overlook : the faculty of resignation. Neurasthenics find
it impossible to believe the friends who assure them that
they will gradually recover their peace of mind if they
will stay in bed and receive no letters, read no newspapers.
They imagine that such a course will only exasperate
their twitching nerves. And similarly lovers, who look

upon it from their enclosure in a contrary state of mind, who have not begun yet to make trial of it, are unable to believe in the healing power of renunciation.

In consequence of the violence of my palpitations, my doses of caffeine were reduced ; the palpitations ceased. Whereupon I asked myself whether it was not to some extent the drug that had been responsible for the anguish that I had felt when I came near to quarrelling with Gilberte, an anguish which I had attributed, on every recurrence of it, to the distressing prospect of never seeing my friend again or of running the risk of seeing her only when she was a prey to the same ill-humour. But if this medicine had been at the root of the sufferings which my imagination must in that case have interpreted wrongly (not that there would be anything extraordinary in that, seeing that, among lovers, the most acute mental suffering assumes often the physical identity of the woman with whom they are living), it had been, in that sense, like the philtre which, long after they have drunk of it, continues to bind Tristan to Isolde. For the physical improvement which the reduction of my caffeine effected almost at once did not arrest the evolution of that grief which my absorption of the toxin had perhaps—if it had not created it— at any rate contrived to render more acute.

Only, as the middle of the month of January approached, once my hopes of a letter on New Year's Day had been disappointed, once the additional disturbance that had come with their disappointment had grown calm, it was my old sorrow, that of " before the holidays ", which began again. What was perhaps the most cruel thing about it was that I myself was its architect, unconscious, wilful, merciless and patient. The one thing that mattered, my relations with Gilberte, it was I who was labouring to make them impossible by gradually creating out of this prolonged separation from my friend, not indeed her indifference, but what would come to the same thing in the end, my own. It was to a slow and painful suicide of that part of me which was Gilberte's lover that I was goading myself with untiring energy, with a clear sense not only of what I was presently doing but of what must result from it in the future ; I knew not only that after a certain time I should cease to love Gilberte, but also that she herself would regret it and that the attempts which she would then make to see me would be as vain as those that she was making now, no longer because I loved her too well but because I should certainly be in love with some other woman whom I should continue to desire, to wait for, through hours of which I should not dare to divert any particle of a second to Gilberte who would be nothing to me then. And no doubt at that very moment in which (since I was determined not to see her again, unless after a formal request for an explanation or a full confession of love on her part, neither of which was in the least degree likely to come to me now) I had already lost Gilberte, and loved her more than ever, and could feel all that she was to me better than in the previous year when, spending all my afternoons in her company, or as many as I chose, I believed that no peril threatened our friendship,—no doubt at that moment the idea that I should one day entertain identical feelings for another was odious to me, for that idea carried me away beyond the range of Gilberte, my love and my sufferings. My love, my sufferings in which through my tears I attempted to discern precisely what Gilberte was, and was

obliged to recognise that they did not pertain exclusively
to her but would, sooner or later, be some other woman's
portion. So that—or such, at least, was my way of thinking then—we are always detached from our fellow-
creatures ; when a man loves one of them he feels that
his love is not labelled with their two names, but may be
born again in the future, may have been born already
in the past for another and not for her. And in the time
when he is not in love, if he makes up his mind philosophi-
cally as to what it is that is inconsistent in love, he will
find that the love of which he can speak unmoved he
did not, at the moment of speaking, feel, and therefore
did not know, knowledge in these matters being intermittent and not outlasting the actual presence of the sentiment. That future in which I should not love Gilberte,
which my sufferings helped me to divine although my
imagination was not yet able to form a clear picture of
it, certainly there would still have been time to warn Gilberte that it was gradually taking shape, that its coming
was, if not imminent, at least inevitable, if she herself,
Gilberte, did not come to my rescue and destroy in the
germ my nascent indifference. How often was I not on
the point of writing, or of going to Gilberte to tell her :
"Take care. My mind is made up. What I am doing
now is my supreme effort. I am seeing you now for the
last time. Very soon I shall have ceased to love you."
But to what end ? By what authority should I have
reproached Gilberte for an indifference which, not that I
considered myself guilty on that count, I too manifested
towards everything that was not herself ? The last time !
To me, that appeared as something of immense significance, because I was in love with Gilberte. On her it

would doubtless have made just as much impression as those letters in which our friends ask whether they may pay us a visit before they finally leave the country, an offer which, like those made by tiresome women who are in love with us, we decline because we have pleasures of our own in prospect. The time which we have at our disposal every day is elastic ; the passions that we feel expand it, those that we inspire contract it ; and habit fills up what remains.

Besides, what good would it have done if I had spoken to Gilberte ; she would not have understood me. We imagine always when we speak that it is our own ears, our own mind that are listening. My words would have come to her only in a distorted form, as though they had had to pass through the moving curtain of a waterfall before they reached my friend, unrecognisable, giving a foolish sound, having no longer any kind of meaning. The truth which one puts into one's words does not make a direct path for itself, is not supported by irresistible evidence. A considerable time must elapse before a truth of the same order can take shape in the words themselves. Then the political opponent who, despite all argument, every proof that he has advanced to damn the votary of the rival doctrine as a traitor, will himself have come to share the hated conviction by which he who once sought in vain to disseminate it is no longer bound. Then the masterpiece of literature which for the admirers who read it aloud seemed to make self-evident the proofs of its excellence, while to those who listened it presented only a senseless or commonplace image, will by these too be proclaimed a masterpiece, but too late for the author to learn of their discovery. Similarly in love the barriers, do what one may,

cannot be broken down from without by him whom they
maddeningly exclude ; it is when he is no longer concerned
with them that suddenly, as the result of an effort directed
from elsewhere, accomplished within the heart of her
who did not love him, those barriers which he has charged
without success will fall to no advantage. If I had come
to Gilberte to tell her of my future indifference and the
means of preventing it, she would have assumed from
my action that my love for her, the need that I had
of her, were even greater than I had supposed, and her
distaste for the sight of me would thereby have been increased. And incidentally it is quite true that it was that
love for her which helped me, by means of the incongruous states of mind which it successively produced in me,
to foresee, more clearly than she herself could, the end of
that love. And yet some such warning I might perhaps
have addressed, by letter or with my own lips, to Gilberte,
after a long enough interval, which would render her,
it is true, less indispensable to me, but would also have
proved to her that she was not so indispensable. Unfortunately certain persons—of good or evil intent—spoke
of me to her in a fashion which must have led her to
think that they were doing so at my request. Whenever
I thus learned that Cottard, my own mother, even M. de
Norpois had by a few ill-chosen words rendered useless all
the sacrifice that I had just been making, wasted all the
advantage of my reserve by giving me, wrongly, the appearance of having emerged from it, I was doubly angry.
In the first place I could no longer reckon from any date
but the present my laborious and fruitful abstention which
these tiresome people had, unknown to me, interrupted
and so brought to nothing. And not only that ; I should

have less pleasure in seeing Gilberte, who would think of me now no longer as containing myself in dignified resignation, but as plotting in the dark for an interview which she had scorned to grant me. I cursed all the idle chatter of people who so often, without any intention of hurting us or of doing us a service, for no reason, for talking's sake, often because we ourselves have not been able to refrain from talking in their presence, and because they are indiscreet (as we ourselves are), do us, at a crucial moment, so much harm. It is true that in the grim operation performed for the eradication of our love they are far from playing a part equal to that played by two persons who are in the habit, from excess of good nature in one and of malice in the other, of undoing everything at the moment when everything is on the point of being settled. But against these two persons we bear no such grudge as against the inopportune Cottards of this world, for the latter of them is the person whom we love and the former is ourself.

Meanwhile, since on almost every occasion of my going to see her Mme. Swann would invite me to come to tea another day, with her daughter, and tell me to reply directly to her, I was constantly writing to Gilberte, and in this correspondence I did not choose the expressions which might, I felt, have won her over, sought only to carve out the easiest channel for the torrent of my tears. For, like desire, regret seeks not to be analysed but to be satisfied. When one begins to love, one spends one's time, not in getting to know what one's love really is, but in making it possible to meet next day. When one abandons love one seeks not to know one's grief but to offer to her who is causing it that expression of it which seems to one the most moving. One says the things which one feels the need of saying, and which the other will not understand, one speaks for oneself alone. I wrote : " I had thought that it would not be possible. Alas, I see now that it is not so difficult." I said also : " I shall probably not see you again ; " I said it while I continued to avoid shewing a coldness which she might think affected, and the words, as I wrote them, made me weep because I felt that they expressed not what I should have liked to believe but what was probably going to happen. For at the next request for a meeting which she would convey to me I should have again, as I had now, the courage not to yield, and, what with one refusal and another, I should gradually come to the moment when, by virtue of not having seen her again, I should not wish to see her. I wept, but I found courage enough to sacrifice, I tasted the sweets of sacrificing the happiness of being with her to the probability of seeming attractive to her one day, a day when, alas, my seeming attractive to her would be immaterial to me. Even the supposition, albeit so far from likely, that at this moment, as she had pretended during the last visit that I had paid her, she loved me, that what I took for the boredom which one feels in the company of a person of whom one has grown tired had been due only to a jealous susceptibility, to a feint of indifference analogous to my own, only rendered my decision less painful. It seemed to me that in years to come, when we had forgotten one another, when I should be able to look back and tell her that this letter which I was now in course of writing had not been for one moment sincere, she would answer, " What, you really did love me, did you ? If you had only known how I waited for that letter, how I hoped that you were coming to see me, how I cried when I read it." The thought, while I was writing it, immediately on my return from her mother's house, that I was perhaps helping to bring about that very misunderstanding, that thought, by the sadness in which it plunged me, by the pleasure of imagining that I was loved by Gilberte, gave me the impulse to continue my letter.

If, at the moment of leaving Mme. Swann, when her tea-party ended, I was thinking of what I was going to write to her daughter, Mme. Cottard, as she departed, had been filled with thoughts of a wholly different order. On her little "tour of inspection" she had not failed to congratulate Mme. Swann on the new "pieces", the recent "acquisitions" which caught the eye in her drawing-room. She could see among them some, though only a very few of the things that Odette had had in the old days in the Rue La Pérouse, for instance her animals carved in precious stones, her fetishes.

For since Mme. Swann had picked up from a friend whose opinion she valued the word "dowdy"—which had opened to her a new horizon because it denoted precisely those things which a few years earlier she had considered "smart"—all those things had, one after another, followed into retirement the gilded trellis that had served as background to her chrysanthemums, innumerable boxes of sweets from Giroux's, and the coroneted note-paper (not to mention the coins of gilt pasteboard littered about on the mantelpieces, which, even before she had come to know Swann, a man of taste had advised her to sacrifice). Moreover in the artistic disorder, the studio-like confusion of the rooms, whose walls were still painted in sombre colours which made them as different as possible from the white-enamelled drawing-rooms in which, a little later, you were to find Mme. Swann installed, the Far East recoiled more and more before the invading forces of the eighteenth century ; and the cushions which, to make me " comfortable ", Mme. Swann heaped up and buffeted into position behind my back were sprinkled with Louis XV garlands and not, as of old, with Chinese dragons. In the room in which she was usually to be found, and of which she would say, " Yes, I like this room ; I use it a great deal. I couldn't live with a lot of horrid vulgar things swearing at me all the time ; this is where I do my work——" though she never stated precisely at what she was working. Was it a picture ? A book, perhaps, for the hobby of writing was beginning to become common among women who liked to " do something ", not to be quite useless. She was surrounded by Dresden pieces (having a fancy for that sort of porcelain, which she would name with an English accent, saying in any connexion : " How pretty that is ; it reminds me of Dresden flowers,"), and dreaded for them even more than in the old days for her grotesque figures and her flower-pots the ignorant handling of her servants who must expiate, every now and then, the anxiety that they had caused her by submitting to outbursts of rage at which Swann, the most courteous and considerate of masters, looked on without being shocked. Not that the clear perception of certain weaknesses in those whom we love in any way diminishes our affection for them ; rather that affection makes us find those weaknesses charming. Rarely nowadays was it in one of those Japanese wrappers that Odette received her familiars, but rather in the bright and billowing silk of a Watteau gown whose flowering foam she

made as though to caress where it covered her bosom, and
in which she immersed herself, looked solemn, splashed
and sported, with such an air of comfort, of a cool skin and
long-drawn breath, that she seemed to look on these garments not as something decorative, a mere setting for
herself, but as necessary, in the same way as her " tub "
or her daily " outing ", to satisfy the requirements of her
style of beauty and the niceties of hygiene. She used
often to say that she would go without bread rather than
give up " art " and " having nice things about her ", and
that the burning of the " Gioconda " would distress her
infinitely more than the destruction, by the same element,
of " millions " of the people she knew. Theories which
seemed paradoxical to her friends, but made her pass
among them as a superior woman, and qualified her to
receive a visit once a week from the Belgian Minister,
so that in the little world whose sun she was everyone
would have been greatly astonished to learn that elsewhere—at the Verdurins', for instance—she was reckoned
a fool. It was this vivacity of expression that made
Mme. Swann prefer men's society to women's. But when
she criticised the latter it was always from the courtesan's
standpoint, singling out the blemishes that might lower
them in the esteem of men, a lumpy figure, a bad complexion, inability to spell, hairy legs, foul breath, pencilled
eyebrows. But towards a woman who had shewn her
kindness or indulgence in the past she was more lenient,
especially if this woman were now in trouble. She would
defend her warmly, saying : " People are not fair to
her. I assure you, she's quite a nice woman really."

It was not only the furniture of Odette's drawing-
room, it was Odette herself that Mme. Cottard and all

those who had frequented the society of Mme. de Crécy would have found it difficult, if they had not seen her for some little time, to recognise. She seemed to be so much younger. No doubt this was partly because she had grown stouter, was in better condition, seemed at once calmer, more cool, more restful, and also because the new way in which she braided her hair gave more breadth to a face which was animated by an application of pink powder, and into which her eyes and profile, formerly too prominent, seemed now to have been reabsorbed. But another reason for this change lay in the fact that, having reached the turning-point of life, Odette had at length discovered, or invented, a physiognomy of her own, an unalterable " character ", a " style of beauty ", and on her incoherent features—which for so long, exposed to every hazard, every weakness of the flesh, borrowing for a moment, at the slightest fatigue, from the years to come, a sort of flickering shadow of anility, had furnished her, well or ill, according to how she was feeling, how she was looking, with a countenance dishevelled, inconstant, formless and attractive—had now set this fixed type, as it were an immortal youthfulness.

Swann had in his room, instead of the handsome photographs that were now taken of his wife, in all of which the same cryptic, victorious expression enabled one to recognise, in whatever dress and hat, her triumphant face and figure, a little old daguerreotype of her, quite plain, taken long before the appearance of this new type, so that the youth and beauty of Odette, which she had not yet discovered when it was taken, appeared to be missing from it. But it is probable that Swann, having remained constant, or having reverted to a different conception of her, enjoyed in the slender young woman with pensive eyes and tired features, caught in a pose between rest and motion, a more Botticellian charm. For he still liked to recognise in his wife one of Botticelli's figures. Odette, who on the other hand sought not to bring out but to make up for, to cover and conceal the points in herself that did not please her, what might perhaps to an artist express her "character" but in her woman's eyes were merely blemishes, would not have that painter mentioned in her presence. Swann had a wonderful scarf of oriental silk, blue and pink, which he had bought because it was exactly that worn by Our Lady in the *Magnificat*. But Mme. Swann refused to wear it. Once only she allowed her husband to order her a dress covered all over with daisies, cornflowers, forget-me-nots and campanulas, like that of the Primavera. And sometimes in the evening, when she was tired, he would quietly draw my attention to the way in which she was giving, quite unconsciously, to her pensive hands the uncontrolled, almost distraught movement of the Virgin who dips her pen into the inkpot that the angel holds out to her, before writing upon the sacred page on which is already traced the word "*Magnificat*". But he added, "Whatever you do, don't say anything about it to her ; if she knew she was doing it, she would change her pose at once."

Save at these moments of involuntary relaxation, in which Swann essayed to recapture the melancholy cadence of Botticelli, Odette seemed now to be cut out in a single figure, wholly confined within a line which, following the contours of the woman, had abandoned the winding paths, the capricious re-entrants and salients, the radial points, the elaborate dispersions of the fashions of former days, but also, where it was her anatomy that went wrong by making unnecessary digressions within or without the ideal circumference traced for it, was able to rectify, by a bold stroke, the errors of nature, to make up, along a whole section of its course, for the failure as well of the human as of the textile element. The pads, the preposterous " bustle " had disappeared, as well as those tailed corsets which, projecting under the skirt and stiffened by rods of whalebone, had so long amplified Odette with an artificial stomach and had given her the appearance of being composed of several incongruous pieces which there was no individuality to bind together. The vertical fall of fringes, the curve of trimmings had made way for the inflexion of a body which made silk palpitate as a siren stirs the waves, gave to cambric a human expression now that it had been liberated, like a creature that had taken shape and drawn breath, from the long chaos and nebulous envelopment of fashions at length dethroned. But Mme. Swann had chosen, had contrived to preserve some vestiges of certain of these, in the very thick of the more recent fashions that had supplanted them. When in the evening, finding myself unable to work and feeling certain that Gilberte had gone to the theatre with friends, I paid a surprise visit to her parents, I used often to find Mme. Swann in an elegant dishabille the skirt of which, of one of those rich dark colours, blood-red or orange, which seemed always as though they meant something very special, because they were no longer the fashion, was crossed diagonally, though not concealed, by a broad band of black lace which recalled the flounces of an earlier day. When on a still chilly afternoon in Spring she had taken me (before my rupture with her daughter) to the Jardin d'Acclimatation, under her coat, which she opened or buttoned up according as the exercise made her feel warm, the dog-toothed border of her blouse suggested a glimpse of the lapel of some non-existent waistcoat such as she had been accustomed to wear, some years earlier, when she had liked their edges to have the same slight indentations ; and her scarf—of that same " Scotch tartan " to which she had remained faithful, but whose tones she had so far softened, red becoming pink and blue lilac, that one might almost have taken it for one of those pigeon's-breast taffetas which were the latest novelty—was knotted in such a way under her chin, without one's being able to make out where it was fastened, that one could not help being reminded of those bonnet-strings which were now no longer worn. She need only "hold out " like this for a little longer and young men attempting to understand her theory of dress would say : " Mme. Swann is quite a period in herself, isn't she ? " As in a fine literary style which overlays with its different forms and so strengthens a tradition which lies concealed among them, so in Mme. Swann's attire those half-hinted memories of waistcoats or of ringlets, sometimes a tendency, at once repressed, towards the " all aboard ", or even a distant and vague allusion to the " chase me " kept alive beneath the concrete form the unfinished likeness of other, older forms which you would not have succeeded, now, in making a tailor or a dressmaker reproduce, but about which your thoughts incessantly hovered, and enwrapped Mme. Swann in a cloak of nobility—perhaps because the sheer uselessness of these fripperies made them seem meant to serve some more than utilitarian purpose, perhaps because of the traces they preserved of vanished years, or else because there was a sort of personality permeating this lady's wardrobe, which gave to the most dissimilar of her costumes a distinct family likeness. One felt that she did not dress simply for the comfort or the adornment of her body ; she was surrounded by her garments as by the delicate and spiritualised machinery of a whole form of civilisation.

When Gilberte, who, as a rule, gave her tea-parties on the days when her mother was " at home ", had for some reason to go out, and I was therefore free to attend Mme. Swann's " kettledrum ", I would find her dressed in one of her lovely gowns, some of which were of taffeta, others of grosgrain, or of velvet, or of *crêpe-de-Chine,* or satin or silk, gowns which, not being loose like those that she generally wore in the house but buttoned up tight as though she were just going out in them, gave to her stay-at-home laziness on those afternoons something alert and energetic. And no doubt the daring simplicity of their cut was singularly appropriate to her figure and to her movements, which her sleeves appeared to be symbolising in colours that varied from day to day : one would have said that there was a sudden determination in the blue velvet, an easy-going good humour in the white taffeta, and that a sort of supreme discretion full of dignity in her way of holding out her arm had, in order to become visible, put on the appearance, dazzling with the smile of one who had made great sacrifices, of the black *crêpe-de-Chine.* But at the same time these animated gowns took from the complication of their trimmings, none of which had any practical value or served any conceivable purpose, something detached, pensive, secret, in harmony with the melancholy which Mme. Swann never failed to shew, at least in the shadows under her eyes and the drooping arches of her hands. Beneath the profusion of sapphire charms, enamelled four-leaf clovers, silver medals, gold medallions, turquoise amulets, ruby chains and topaz chestnuts there would be, on the dress itself, some design carried out in colour which pursued across the surface of an inserted panel a preconceived existence of its own, some row of little satin buttons, which buttoned nothing and could not be unbuttoned, a strip of braid that sought to please the eye with the minuteness, the discretion of a delicate reminder ; and these, as well as the trinkets, had the effect—for otherwise there would have been no possible justification of their presence—of disclosing a secret intention, being a pledge of affection, keeping a secret, ministering to a superstition, commemorating a recovery from sickness, a granted wish, a love affair or a "philippine". And now and then in the blue velvet of the bodice a hint of "slashes", in the Henri II style, in the gown of black satin a slight swelling which, if it was in the sleeves, just below the shoulders, made one think of the "leg of mutton" sleeves of 1830, or if, on the other hand, it was beneath the skirt, with its Louis XV paniers, gave the dress a just perceptible air of being "fancy dress" and at all events, by insinuating beneath the life of the present day a vague reminiscence of the past, blended with the person of Mme. Swann the charm of certain heroines of history or romance. And if I were to draw her attention to this : "I don't play golf," she would answer, "like so many of my friends. So I should have no excuse for going about, as they do, in sweaters."

In the confusion of her drawing-room, on her way from shewing out one visitor, or with a plateful of cakes to "tempt" another, Mme. Swann as she passed by me would take me aside for a moment : "I have special instructions from Gilberte that you are to come to luncheon the day after to-morrow. As I wasn't sure of seeing you here, I was going to write to you if you hadn't come." I continued to resist. And this resistance was costing me steadily less and less, because, however much one may love the poison that is destroying one, when one has compulsorily to do without it, and has had to do without it for some time past, one cannot help attaching a certain value to the peace of mind which one had ceased to know, to the absence of emotion and suffering. If one is not altogether sincere in assuring oneself that one does not wish ever to see again her whom one loves, one would not be a whit more sincere in saying that one would like to see her. For no doubt one can endure her absence only when one promises oneself that it shall not be for long, and thinks of the day on which one shall see her again, but at the same time one feels how much less painful are those daily recurring dreams of a meeting immediate and incessantly postponed than would be an interview which might be followed by a spasm of jealousy, with the result that the news that one is shortly to see her whom one loves would cause a disturbance which would be none too pleasant. What one procrastinates now from day to day is no longer the end of the intolerable anxiety caused by separation, it is the dreaded renewal of emotions which can lead to nothing. How infinitely one prefers to any such interview the docile memory which one can supplement at one's pleasure with dreams, in which she who in reality does not love one seems, far from that, to be making protestations of her love for one, when one is by oneself ; that memory which one can contrive, by blending gradually with it a portion of what one desires, to render as pleasing as one may choose, how infinitely one prefers it to the avoided interview in which one would have to deal with a creature to whom one could no longer dictate at one's pleasure the words that one would like to hear on her lips, but from whom one would meet with fresh coldness, unlooked-for violence. We know, all of us, when we no longer love, that forgetfulness, that even a vague memory do not cause us so much suffering as an ill-starred love. It was of such forgetfulness that in anticipation I preferred, without acknowledging it to myself, the reposeful tranquillity.

Moreover, whatever discomfort there may be in such a course of psychical detachment and isolation grows steadily less for another reason, namely that it weakens while it is in process of healing that fixed obsession which is a state of love. Mine was still strong enough for me to be able to count upon recapturing my old position in Gilberte's estimation, which in view of my deliberate abstention must, it seemed to me, be steadily increasing ; in other words each of those calm and melancholy days on which I did not see her, coming one after the other without interruption, continuing too without prescription (unless some busy-body were to meddle in my affairs), was a day not lost but gained. Gained to no purpose, it might be, for presently they would be able to pronounce that I was healed. Resignation, modulating our habits, allows certain elements of our strength to be indefinitely increased. Those—so wretchedly inadequate—that I had had to support my grief, on the first evening of my rupture with Gilberte, had since multiplied to an incalculable power. Only, the tendency which everything that exists has to prolong its own existence is sometimes interrupted by sudden impulses to which we give way with all the fewer scruples over letting ourselves go since we know for how many days, for how many months even we have been able, and might still be able to abstain. And often it is when the purse in which we hoard our savings is nearly full that we undo and empty it, it is without waiting for the result of our medical treatment and when we have succeeded in growing accustomed to it that we abandon it. So, one day, when Mme. Swann was repeating her familiar statement of what a pleasure it would be to Gilberte to see me, thus putting the happiness of which I had now for so long been depriving myself, as it were within arm's length, I was stupefied by the realisation that it was still possible for me to enjoy that pleasure, and I could hardly wait until next day ; when I had made up my mind to take Gilberte by surprise, in the evening, before dinner.

What helped me to remain patient throughout the long day that followed was another plan that I had made. From the moment in which everything was forgotten, in which I was reconciled to Gilberte, I no longer wished to visit her save as a lover. Every day she should receive from me the finest flowers that grew. And if Mme. Swann, albeit she had no right to be too severe a mother, should forbid my making a daily offering of flowers, I should find other gifts, more precious and less frequent. My parents did not give me enough money for me to be able to buy expensive things. I thought of a big bowl of old Chinese porcelain which had been left to me by aunt Léonie, and of which Mamma prophesied daily that Françoise would come running to her with an " Oh, it's all come to pieces ! " and that that would be the end of it. Would it not be wiser, in that case, to part with it, to sell it so as to be able to give Gilberte all the pleasure I could. I felt sure that I could easily get a thousand francs for it. I had it tied up in paper ; I had grown so used to it that I had ceased altogether to notice it ; parting with it had at least the advantage of making me realise what it was like. I took it with me as I started for the Swanns', and, giving the driver their address, told him to go by the Champs-Elysées, at one end of which was the shop of a big dealer in oriental things, who knew my father. Greatly to my surprise he offered me there and then not one thousand but ten thousand francs for the bowl. I took the notes with rapture. Every day, for a whole year, I could smother Gilberte in roses and lilac. When I left the shop and got into my cab again the driver (naturally enough, since the Swanns lived out by the Bois) instead of taking the ordinary way began to drive me along the Avenue des Champs-Elysées. He had just passed the end of the Rue de Berri when, in the failing light, I thought I saw, close to the Swanns' house but going in the other direction, going away from it, Gilberte, who was walking slowly, though with a firm step, by the side of a young man with whom she was conversing, but whose face I could not distinguish. I stood up in the cab, meaning to tell the driver to stop ; then hesitated. The strolling couple were already some way away, and the parallel lines which their leisurely progress was quietly drawing were on the verge of disappearing in the Elysian gloom. A moment later, I had reached Gilberte's door. I was received by Mme. Swann.

"Oh ! she will be sorry !" was my greeting, "I can't think why she isn't in. She came home just now from a lesson, complaining of the heat, and said she was going out for a little fresh air with another girl." "I fancy I passed her in the Avenue des Champs-Elysées." "Oh, I don't think it can have been. Anyhow, don't mention it to her father ; he doesn't approve of her going out at this time of night. Must you go ? Good bye." I left her, told my driver to go home the same way, but found no trace of the two walking figures. Where had they been ? What were they saying to one another in the darkness so confidentially ?

I returned home, desperately clutching my windfall of ten thousand francs, which would have enabled me to arrange so many pleasant surprises for that Gilberte whom now I had made up my mind never to see again. No doubt my call at the dealer's had brought me happiness by allowing me to expect that in future, whenever I saw my friend, she would be pleased with me and grateful. But if I had not called there, if my cabman had not taken the Avenue des Champs-Elysées, I should not have seen Gilberte with that young man. Thus a single action may have two contradictory effects, and the misfortune that it engenders cancel the good fortune that it has already brought one. There had befallen me the opposite of what so frequently happens. We desire some pleasure, and the material means of obtaining it are lacking. "It is a mistake," Labruyère tells us, "to be in love without an ample fortune." There is nothing for it but to attempt a gradual elimination of our desire for that pleasure. In my case, however, the material means had been forthcoming, but at the same moment, if not by a logical effect, at any rate as a fortuitous consequence of that initial success, my pleasure had been snatched from me. As, for that matter, it seems as though it must always be. As a rule, however, not on the same evening on which we have acquired what makes it possible. Usually, we continue to struggle and to hope for a little longer. But the pleasure can never be realised. If we succeed in overcoming the force of circumstances, nature at once shifts the battle-ground, placing it within ourselves, and effects a gradual change in our heart until it desires something other than what it is going to obtain. And if this transposition has been so rapid that our heart has not had time to change, nature does not, on that account, despair of conquering us, in a manner more gradual, it is true, more subtle, but no less efficacious. It is then, at the last moment, that the possession of our happiness is wrested from us, or rather it is that very possession which nature, with diabolical cleverness, uses to destroy our happiness. After failure in every quarter of the domain of life and action, it is a final incapacity, the mental incapacity for happiness that nature creates in us. The phenomenon of happiness either fails to appear, or at once gives way to the bitterest of reactions.

I put my ten thousand francs in a drawer. But they were no longer of any use to me. I ran through them, as it happened, even sooner than if I had sent flowers every day to Gilberte, for when evening came I was always too wretched to stay in the house and used to go and pour out my sorrows upon the bosoms of women whom I did not love. As for seeking to give any sort of pleasure to Gilberte, I no longer thought of that ; to visit her house again now could only have added to my sufferings. Even the sight of Gilberte, which would have been so exquisite a pleasure only yesterday, would no longer have sufficed me. For I should have been miserable all the time that I was not actually with her. That is how a woman, by every fresh torture that she inflicts on us, increases, often quite unconsciously, her power over us and at the same time our demands upon her. With each injury that she does us, she encircles us more and more completely, doubles our chains—but halves the strength of those which hitherto we had thought adequate to bind her in order that we might retain our own peace of mind. Only yesterday, had I not been afraid of annoying Gilberte, I should have been content to ask for no more than occasional meetings, which now would no longer have contented me and for which I should now have substituted quite different terms. For in this respect love is not like war ; after the battle is ended we renew the fight with keener ardour, which we never cease to intensify the more thoroughly we are defeated, provided always that we are still in a position to give battle. This was not my position with regard to Gilberte. Also I preferred, at first, not to see her mother again. I continued, it is true, to assure myself that Gilberte did not love me, that I had known this for ever so long, that I could see her again if I chose, and, if I did not choose, forget her in course of time. But these ideas, like a remedy which has no effect upon certain complaints, had no power whatsoever to obliterate those two parallel lines which I kept on seeing, traced by Gilberte and the young man as they slowly disappeared along the Avenue des Champs-Elysées. This was a fresh misfortune, which like the rest would gradually lose its force, a fresh image which would one day present itself to my mind's eye completely purged of every noxious element that it now contained, like those deadly poisons which one can handle without danger, or like a crumb of dynamite which one can use to light one's cigarette without fear of an explosion. Meanwhile there was in me another force which was striving with all its might to overpower that unwholesome force which still shewed me, without alteration, the figure of Gilberte walking in the dusk : to meet and to break the shock of the renewed assaults of memory, I had, toiling effectively on the other side, imagination. The former force did indeed continue to shew me that couple walking in the Champs-Elysées, and offered me other disagreeable pictures drawn from the past, as for instance Gilberte shrugging her shoulders when her mother asked her to stay and entertain me. But the other force, working upon the canvas of my hopes, outlined a future far more attractively developed than this poor past which, after all, was so restricted. For one minute in which I saw Gilberte's sullen face, how many were there in which I planned to my own satisfaction all the steps that she was to take towards our reconciliation, perhaps even towards our betrothal. It is true that this force, which my imagination was concentrating upon the future, it was drawing, for all that, from the past. I was still in love with her whom, it is true, I believed that I detested. But whenever anyone told me that I was looking well, or was nicely dressed, I wished that she could have been there to see me. I was irritated by the desire that many people shewed about this time to ask me to their houses, and refused all their invitations. There was a scene at home because I did not accompany my father to an official dinner at which the Bontemps were to be present with their niece Albertine, a young girl still hardly more than a child. So it is that the different periods of our life overlap one another. We scornfully decline, because of one whom we love and who will some day be of so little account, to see another who is of no account to-day, with whom we shall be in love to-morrow, with whom we might, perhaps, had we consented to see her now, have fallen in love a little earlier and who would thus have put a term to our present sufferings, bringing others, it is true, in their place. Mine were steadily growing less. I had the surprise of discovering in my own heart one sentiment one day, another the next, generally inspired by some hope or some fear relative to Gilberte. To the Gilberte whom I kept within me. I ought to have reminded myself that the other, the real Gilberte was perhaps entirely different from mine, knew nothing of the regrets that I ascribed to her, was thinking probably less about me, not merely than I was thinking about her but than I made her be thinking about me when I was closeted alone with my fictitious Gilberte, wondering what really were her feelings with regard to me and so imagining her attention as constantly directed towards myself.

During those periods in which our bitterness of spirit, though steadily diminishing, still persists, a distinction must be drawn between the bitterness which comes to us from our constantly thinking of the person herself and that which is revived by certain memories, some cutting speech, some word in a letter that we have had from her. The various forms which that bitterness can assume we shall examine when we come to deal with another and later love affair; for the present it must suffice to say that, of these two kinds, the former is infinitely the less cruel. That is because our conception of the person, since it dwells always within ourselves, is there adorned with the halo with which we are bound before long to invest her, and bears the marks if not of the frequent solace of hope, at any rate of the tranquillity of a permanent sorrow. (It must also be observed that the image of a person who makes us suffer counts for little if anything in those complications which aggravate the unhappiness of love, prolong it and prevent our recovery, just as in certain maladies the cause is insignificant beyond comparison with the fever which follows it and the time that must elapse before our convalescence.) But if the idea of the person whom we love catches and reflects a ray of light from a mind which is on the whole optimistic, it is not so with those special memories, those cutting words, that inimical letter (I received only one that could be so described from Gilberte) ; you would say that the person herself dwelt in those fragments, few and scattered as they were, and dwelt there multiplied to a power of which she falls ever so far short in the idea which we are accustomed to form of her as a whole. Because the letter has not—as the image of the beloved creature has—been contemplated by us in the melancholy calm of regret ; we have read it, devoured it in the fearful anguish with which we were wrung by an unforeseen misfortune. Sorrows of this sort come to us in another way ; from without ; and it is along the road of the most cruel suffering that they have penetrated to our heart. The picture of our friend in our mind, which we believe to be old, original, authentic, has in reality been refashioned by her many times over. The cruel memory is not itself contemporary with the restored picture, it is of another age, it is one of the rare witnesses to a monstrous past. But inasmuch as this past continues to exist, save in ourself, who have been pleased to substitute for it a miraculous age of gold, a paradise in which all mankind shall be reconciled, those memories, those letters carry us back to reality, and cannot but make us feel, by the sudden pang they give us, what a long way we have been borne from that reality by the baseless hopes engendered daily while we waited for something to happen. Not that the said reality is bound always to remain the same, though that does indeed happen at times. There are in our life any number of women whom we have never wished to see again, and who have quite naturally responded to our in no way calculated silence with a silence as profound. Only in their case as we never loved them, we have never counted the years spent apart from them, and this instance, which would invalidate our whole argument, we are inclined to forget when we are considering the healing effect of isolation, just as people who believe in presentiments forget all the occasions on which their own have not " come true ".

But, after a time, absence may prove efficacious. The desire, the appetite for seeing us again may after all be reborn in the heart which at present contemns us. Only, we must allow time. Now the demands which we ourselves make upon time are no less exorbitant than those of a heart in process of changing. For one thing, time is the very thing that we are least willing to allow, for our own suffering is keen and we are anxious to see it brought to an end. And then, too, the interval of time which the other heart needs to effect its change our own heart will have spent in changing itself also, so that when the goal which we had set ourselves becomes attainable it will have ceased to count as a goal, or to seem worth attaining. This idea, however, that it will be attainable, that what, when it no longer spells any good fortune to us, we shall ultimately secure is not good fortune, this idea embodies a part, but a part only of the truth. Our good fortune accrues to us when we have grown indifferent to it. But the very fact of our indifference will have made us less exacting, and allow us in retrospect to feel convinced that we should have been in raptures over our good fortune had it come at a time when, very probably, it would have seemed to us miserably inadequate. People are not very hard to satisfy nor are they very good judges of matters in which they take no interest. The friendly overtures of a person whom we no longer love, overtures which strike us, in our indifference to her, as excessive, would perhaps have fallen a long way short of satisfying our love. Those tender speeches, that invitation or acceptance, we think only of the pleasure which they would have given us, and not of all those other speeches and meetings by which we should have wished to see them immediately followed, which we should, as likely as not, simply by our avidity for them, have precluded from ever happening. So that we can never be certain that the good fortune which comes to us too late, when we are no longer in love, is altogether the same as that good fortune the want of which made us, at one time, so unhappy. There is only one person who could decide that ; our ego of those days ; he is no longer with us, and were he to, reappear, no doubt that would be quite enough to make our good fortune—whether identical or not—vanish.

Pending these posthumous fulfilments of a dream in which I should not, when the time came, be greatly interested, by dint of my having to invent, as in the days when I still hardly knew Gilberte, speeches, letters in which she implored my forgiveness, swore that she had never loved anyone but myself and besought me to marry her, a series of pleasant images incessantly renewed came by degrees to hold a larger place in my mind than the vision of Gilberte and the young man, which had nothing now to feed upon. At this point I should perhaps have resumed my visits to Mme. Swann but for a dream that came to me, in which one of my friends, who was not, however, one that I could identify, behaved with the utmost treachery towards me and appeared to believe that I had been treacherous to him. Abruptly awakened by the pain which this dream had given me, and finding that it persisted after I was awake, I turned my thoughts back to the dream, racked my brains to discover who could have been the friend whom I had seen in my sleep, the sound of whose name—a Spanish name—was no longer distinct in my ears. Combining Joseph's part with Pharaoh's, I set to work to interpret my dream. I knew that, when one is interpreting a dream, it is often a mistake to pay too much attention to the appearance of the people one saw in it, who may perhaps have been disguised or have exchanged faces, like those mutilated saints on the walls of cathedrals which ignorant archaeologists have restored, fitting the body of one to the head of another and confusing all their attributes and names. Those that people bear in a dream are apt to mislead us. The person with whom we are in love is to be recognised only by the intensity of the pain that we suffer. From mine I learned that, though transformed while I was asleep into a young man, the person whose recent betrayal still hurt me was Gilberte. I remembered then that, the last time I had seen her, on the day when her mother had forbidden her to go out to a dancing-lesson, she had, whether in sincerity or in make-belíeve, declined, laughing in a strange manner, to believe in the genuineness of my feeling for her. And by association this memory brought back to me another. Long before that, it had been Swann who would not believe in my sincerity, nor that I was a suitable friend for Gilberte. In vain had I written to him, Gilberte had brought back my letter and had returned it to me with the same incomprehensible laugh. She had not returned it to me at once : I remembered now the whole of that scene behind the clump of laurels. As soon as one is unhappy one becomes moral. Gilberte's recent antipathy for me seemed to me a judgment delivered on me by life for my conduct that afternoon. Such judgments one imagines one can escape because one looks out for carriages when one is crossing the street, and avoids obvious dangers. But there are others that take effect within us. The accident comes from the side to which one has not been looking, from inside, from the heart. Gilberte's words : "If you like, we might go on wrestling," made me shudder. I imagined her behaving like that, at home perhaps, in the linen-room, with the young man whom I had seen escorting her along the Avenue des Champs-Elysées. And so, just as when, a little time back, I had believed myself to be calmly established in a state of happiness, it had been fatuous in me, now that I had abandoned all thought of happiness, to take for granted that at least I had grown and was going to remain calm. For, so long as our heart keeps enshrined with any permanence the image of another person, it is not only our happiness that may at any moment be destroyed ; when that happiness has vanished, when we have suffered, and, later, when we have succeeded in lulling our sufferings to sleep, the thing then that is as elusive, as precarious as ever our happiness was is our calm. Mine returned to me in the end, for the cloud which, lowering our resistance, tempering our desires, has penetrated, in the train of a dream, the enclosure of our mind, is bound, in course of time, to dissolve, permanence and stability being assured to nothing in this world, not even to grief. Besides, those whose suffering is due to love are, as we say of certain invalids, their own physicians. As consolation can come to them only from the person who is the cause of their grief, and as their grief is an emanation from that person, it is there, in their grief itself, that they must in the end find a remedy : which it will disclose to them at a given moment, for the longer they turn it over in their minds this grief will continue to shew them fresh aspects of the loved, the regretted creature, at one moment so intensely hateful that one has no longer the slightest desire to see her, since before finding enjoyment in her company one would have first to make her suffer, at another so pleasant that the pleasantness in which one has invested her one adds to her own stock of good qualities and finds in it a fresh reason for hope. But even although the anguish that had reawakened in me did at length grow calm, I no longer wished—except just occasionally—to visit Mme. Swann. In the first place because, among those who love and have been forsaken, the state of incessant—even if unconfessed —expectancy in which they live undergoes a spontaneous transformation, and, while to all appearance unchanged, substitutes for its original elements others that are precisely the opposite. The first were the consequences of— a reaction from the painful incidents which had upset us. The tension of waiting for what is yet to come is mingled with fear, all the more since we desire at such moments, should no message come to us from her whom we love, to act for ourselves, and are none too confident of the success of a step which, once we have taken it, we may find it impossible to follow up. But presently, without our having noticed any change, this tension, which still endures, is sustained, we discover, no longer by our recollection of the past but by anticipation of an imaginary future. From that moment it is almost pleasant. Besides, the first state, by continuing for some time, has accustomed us to living in expectation. The suffering that we felt during those last meetings survives in us still, but is already lulled to sleep. We are in no haste to arouse it, especially as we do not see very clearly what to ask for now. The possession of a little more of the woman whom we love would only make more essential to us the part that we did not yet possess, which is bound to remain, whatever happens, since our requirements are begotten of our satisfactions, an irreducible quantity.

Another, final reason came later on to reinforce this, and to make me discontinue altogether my visits to Mme. Swann. This reason, slow in revealing itself, was not that I had now forgotten Gilberte but that I must make every effort to forget her as speedily as possible. No doubt, now that the keen edge of my suffering was dulled, my visits to Mme. Swann had become once again, for what sorrow remained in me, the sedative and distraction which had been so precious to me at first. But what made the sedative efficacious made the distraction impossible, namely that with these visits the memory of Gilberte was intimately blended. The distraction would be of no avail to me unless it was employed to combat a sentiment which the presence of Gilberte no longer nourished, thoughts, interests, passions in which Gilberte should have no part. These states of consciousness, to which the person whom we love remains a stranger, then occupy a place which, however small it may be at first, is always so much reconquered from the love that has been in unchallenged possession of our whole soul. We must seek to encourage these thoughts, to make them grow, while the sentiment which is no more now than a memory dwindles, so that the new elements introduced into our mind contest with that sentiment, wrest from it an ever increasing part of our soul, until at last the victory is complete. I decided that this was the only way in which my love could be killed, and I was still young enough, still courageous enough to undertake the attempt, to subject myself to that most cruel grief which springs from the certainty that, whatever time one may devote to the effort, it will prove successful in the end. The reason I now gave in my letters to Gilberte for refusing to see her was an allusion to some mysterious misunderstanding, wholly fictitious, which was supposed to have arisen between her and myself, and as to which I had hoped at first that Gilberte would insist upon my furnishing her with an explanation. But, as a matter of fact, never, even in the most insignificant relations in life, does a request for enlightenment come from a correspondent who knows that an obscure, untruthful, incriminating sentence has been written on purpose, so that he shall protest against it, and is only too glad to feel, when he reads it, that he possesses—and to keep in his own hands—the initiative in the coming operations. For all the more reason is this so in our more tender relations, in which love is endowed with so much eloquence, indifference with so little curiosity. Gilberte having never appeared to doubt nor sought to learn more about this misunderstanding, it became for me a real entity, to which I referred anew in every letter. And there is in these baseless situations, in the affectation of coldness a sort of fascination which tempts one to persevere in them. By dint of writing : "Now that our hearts are sundered," so that Gilberte might answer : "But they are not. Do explain what you mean," I had gradually come to believe that they were. By constantly repeating, "Life may have changed for us, it will never destroy the feeling that we had for one another," in the hope of hearing myself, one day, say : "But there has been no change, the feeling is stronger now than ever it was," I was living with the idea that life had indeed changed, that we should keep only the memory of a feeling which no longer existed, as certain neurotics, from having at first pretended to be ill, end by becoming chronic invalids. Now, whenever I had to write to Gilberte, I brought my mind back to this imagined change, which, being now tacitly admitted by the silence which she preserved with regard to it in her replies, would in future subsist between us. Then Gilberte ceased to make a point of ignoring it. She too adopted my point of view ; and, as in the speeches at official banquets, when the foreign Sovereign who is being entertained adopts practically the same expressions as have just been used by the Sovereign who is entertaining him, whenever I wrote to Gilberte : " Life may have parted us ; the memory of the days when we knew one another will endure," she never failed to respond : " Life may have parted us ; it cannot make us forget those happy hours which will always be dear to us both," (though we should have found it hard to say why or how " Life " had parted us, or what change had occurred). My sufferings were no longer excessive. And yet, one day when I was telling her in a letter that I had heard of the death of our old barley-sugar woman in the Champs-Elysées, as I wrote the words : " I felt at once that this would distress you, in me it awakened a host of memories," I could not restrain myself from bursting into tears when I saw that I was speaking in the past tense, as though it were of some dead friend, now almost forgotten, of this love of which in spite of myself I had never ceased to think as of a thing still alive, or one that at least might be born again. Nothing can be more affectionate than this sort of correspondence between friends who do not wish to see one another any more. Gilberte's letters to me had all the delicate refinement of those which I used to write to people who did not matter, and shewed me the same apparent marks of affection, which it was so pleasant for me to receive from her.

But, as time went on, every refusal to see her disturbed me less. And as she became less dear to me, my painful memories were no longer strong enough to destroy by their incessant return the growing pleasure which I found in thinking of Florence, or of Venice. I regretted, at such moments, that I had abandoned the idea of diplomacy and had condemned myself to a sedentary existence, in order not to be separated from a girl whom I should not see again and had already almost forgotten. We construct our house of life to suit another person, and when at length it is ready to receive her that person does not come ; presently she is dead to us, and we live on, a prisoner within the walls which were intended only for her. If Venice seemed to my parents to be a long way off, and its climate treacherous, it was at least quite easy for me to go, without tiring myself, and settle down at Balbec. But to do that I should have had to leave Paris, to forego those visits thanks to which, infrequent as they were, I might sometimes hear Mme. Swann telling me about her daughter. Besides, I was beginning to find in them various pleasures in which Gilberte had no part.

When spring drew round, and with it the cold weather, during an icy Lent and the hailstorms of Holy Week, as Mme. Swann began to find it cold in the house, I used often to see her entertaining her guests in her furs, her shivering hands and shoulders hidden beneath the gleaming white carpet of an immense rectangular muff and a cape, both of ermine, which she had not taken off on coming in from her drive, and which suggested the last patches of the snows of winter, more persistent than the rest, which neither the heat of the fire nor the advancing season had succeeded in melting. And the whole truth about these glacial but already flowering weeks was suggested to me in this drawing-room, which soon I should be entering no more, by other more intoxicating forms of whiteness, that for example of the guelder-roses clustering, at the summits of their tall bare stalks, like the rectilinear trees in pre-raphaelite paintings, their balls of blossom, divided yet composite, white as annunciating angels and breathing a fragrance as of lemons. For the mistress of Tansonville knew that April, even an ice-bound April was not barren of flowers, that winter, spring, summer are not held apart by barriers as hermetic as might be supposed by the town-dweller who, until the first hot day, imagines the world as containing nothing but houses that stand naked in the rain. That Mme. Swann was content with the consignments furnished by her Combray gardener, that she did not, by the intervention of her own "special" florist, fill up the gaps left by an insufficiently powerful magic with subsidies borrowed from a precocious Mediterranean shore, I do not for a moment suggest, nor did it worry me at the time. It was enough to fill me with longing for country scenes that, overhanging the loose snow-drifts of the muff in which Mme. Swann kept her hands, the guelder-rose snow-balls (which served very possibly in the mind of my hostess no other purpose than to compose, on the advice of Bergotte, a 'Symphony in White' with her furniture and her garments) reminded me that what the Good Friday music in *Parsifal* symbolised was a natural miracle which one could see performed every year, if one had the sense to look for it, and, assisted by the acid and heady perfume of the other kinds of blossom, which, although their names were unknown to me, had brought me so often to a standstill to gaze at them on my walks round Combray, made Mme. Swann's drawing-room as virginal, as candidly "in bloom", without the least vestige of greenery, as overladen with genuine scents of flowers as was the little lane by Tansonville.

But it was still more than I could endure that these

memories should be recalled to me. There was a risk of their reviving what little remained of my love for Gilberte. Besides, albeit I no longer felt the least distress during these visits to Mme. Swann, I extended the intervals between them and endeavoured to see as little of her as possible. At most, since I continued not to go out of Paris, I allowed myself an occasional walk with her. Fine weather had come at last, and the sun was hot. As I knew that before luncheon Mme. Swann used to go out every day for an hour, and would stroll for a little in the Avenue du Bois, near the Etoile—a spot which, at that time, because of the people who used to collect there to gaze at the " swells " whom they knew only by name, was known as the " Shabby-Genteel Club"—I persuaded my parents, on Sundays, (for on weekdays I was busy all morning), to let me postpone my luncheon until long after theirs, until a quarter past one, and go for a walk before it. During May, that year, I never missed a Sunday, for Gilberte had gone to stay with friends in the country. I used to reach the Arc-de-Triomphe about noon. I kept watch at the entrance to the Avenue, never taking my eyes off the corner of the side-street along which Mme. Swann, who had only a few yards to walk, would come from her house. As by this time many of the people who had been strolling there were going home to luncheon, those who remained were few in number and, for the most part, fashionably dressed. Suddenly, on the gravelled path, unhurrying, cool, luxuriant, Mme. Swann appeared, displaying around her a toilet which was never twice the same, but which I remember as being typically mauve ; then she hoisted and unfurled at the end of its long stalk, just at the moment when her radiance was most complete, the silken banner of a wide parasol of a shade that matched the showering petals of her gown. A whole troop of people escorted her ; Swann himself, four or five fellows from the Club, who had been to call upon her that morning or whom she had met in the street : and their black or grey agglomeration, obedient to her every gesture, performing the almost mechanical movements of a lifeless setting in which Odette was framed, gave to this woman, in whose eyes alone was there any intensity, the air of looking out in front of her, from among all those men, as from a window behind which she had taken her stand, and made her emerge there, frail but fearless, in the nudity of her delicate colours, like the apparition of a creature of a different species, of an unknown race, and of almost martial strength, by virtue of which she seemed by herself a match for all her multiple escort. Smiling, rejoicing in the fine weather, in the sunshine which had not yet become trying, with the air of calm assurance of a creator who has accomplished his task and takes no thought for anything besides ; certain that her clothes —even though the vulgar herd should fail to appreciate them—were the smartest anywhere to be seen, she wore them for herself and for her friends, naturally, without exaggerated attention to them but also without absolute detachment ; not preventing the little bows of ribbon upon her bodice and skirt from floating buoyantly upon the air before her, like separate creatures of whose presence there she was not unconscious, but was indulgent enough to let them play if they chose, keeping their own rhythm, provided that they accompanied her where she led the way ; and even upon her mauve parasol, which, as often as not, she had not yet "put up" when she appeared on the scene, she let fall now and then, as though upon a bunch of Parma violets, a gaze happy and so kindly that, when it was fastened no longer upon her friends but on some inanimate object, her eyes still seemed to smile. She thus kept open, she made her garments occupy that interval of smartness, of which the men with whom she was on the most familiar terms respected both the existence and its necessity, not without shewing a certain deference, as of profane visitors to a shrine, an admission of their own ignorance, an interval over which they recognised that their friend had (as we recognise that a sick man has over the special precautions that he has to take, or a mother over her children's education) a competent jurisdiction. No less than by the court which encircled her and seemed not to observe the passers-by, Mme. Swann by the lateness of her appearance there at once suggested those rooms in which she had spent so long, so leisurely a morning and to which she must presently return for luncheon ; she seemed to indicate their proximity by the unhurrying ease of her progress, like the turn that one takes up and down one's own garden ; of those rooms one would have said that she was carrying about her still the cool, the indoor shade. But for that very reason the sight of her gave me only a stronger sensation of open air and warmth. All the more because, being assured in my own mind that, in accordance with the liturgy, with the ritual in which Mme. Swann was so profoundly versed, her clothes were connected with the time of year and of day by a bond both inevitable and unique, I felt that the flowers upon the stiff straw brim of her hat, the baby-ribbons upon her dress had been even more naturally born of the month of May than the

flowers in gardens and in woods ; and to learn what latest
change there was in weather or season I had not to raise
my eyes higher than to her parasol, open and outstretched
like another, a nearer sky, round, clement, mobile, blue.
For these rites, if they were of sovereign importance, sub-
jugated their glory (and, consequently, Mme. Swann her
own) in condescending obedience to the day, the spring,
the sun, none of which struck me as being sufficiently flattered that so elegant a woman had been graciously pleased
not to ignore their existence, and had chosen on their
account a gown of a brighter, of a thinner fabric, suggesting to me, by the opening of its collar and sleeves, the
moist warmness of the throat and wrists that they exposed,—in a word, had taken for them all the pains that
a great personage takes who, having gaily condescended
to pay a visit to common folk in the country, whom everyone, even the most plebeian, knows, yet makes a point
of donning, for the occasion, suitable attire. On her
arrival I would greet Mme. Swann, she stop me and say
(in English) "Good morning," and smile. We would
walk a little way together. And I learned then that these
canons according to which she dressed, it was for her own
satisfaction that she obeyed them, as though yielding to a
Superior Wisdom of which she herself was High Priestess :
for if it should happen that, feeling too warm, she threw
open or even took off altogether and gave me to carry the
jacket which she had intended to keep buttoned up, I
would discover in the blouse beneath it a thousand details
of execution which had had every chance of remaining
there unperceived, like those parts of an orchestral score
to which the composer has devoted infinite labour albeit
they may never reach the ears of the public : or in the

sleeves of the jacket that lay folded across my arm I
would see, I would drink in slowly, for my own pleasure
or from affection for its wearer, some exquisite detail, a
deliciously tinted strip, a lining of mauve satinette which,
ordinarily concealed from every eye, was yet just as
delicately fashioned as the outer parts, like those gothic
carvings on a cathedral, hidden on the inside of a balus-
trade eighty feet from the ground, as perfect as are the
bas-reliefs over the main porch, and yet never seen by
any living man until, happening to pass that way upon
his travels, an artist obtains leave to climb up there
among them, to stroll in the open air, sweeping the whole
town with a comprehensive gaze, between the soaring
towers.

What enhanced this impression that Mme. Swann was
walking in the Avenue as though along the paths of her
own garden, was—for people ignorant of her habit of
" taking exercise "—that she had come there on foot,
without any carriage following, she whom, once May had
begun, they were accustomed to see, behind the most
brilliant " turn-out ", the smartest liveries in Paris, gently
and majestically seated, like a goddess, in the balmy air of
an immense victoria on eight springs. On foot Mme.
Swann had the appearance—especially as her pace began
to slacken in the heat of the sun—of having yielded to
curiosity, of committing an " exclusive " breach of all the
rules of her code, like those Crowned Heads who, without consulting anyone, accompanied by the slightly scandalised admiration of a suite which dares not venture
any criticism, step out of their boxes during a gala performance and visit the lobby of the theatre, mingling for
a moment or two with the rest of the audience. So be-

tween Mme. Swann and themselves the crowd felt that there existed those barriers of a certain kind of opulence which seem to them the most insurmountable that there are. The Faubourg Saint-Germain may have its barriers also, but these are less " telling " to the eyes and imagination of the " shabby-genteel ". These latter, when in the presence of a real personage, more simple, more easily mistaken for the wife of a small professional or business man, less remote from the people, will not feel the same sense of their own inequality, almost of their unworthiness, as dismays them when they encounter Mme. Swann. Of course women of that sort are not themselves dazzled, as the crowd are, by the brilliance of their apparel, they have ceased to pay any attention to it, but only because they have grown used to it, that is to say have come to look upon it more and more as natural and necessary, to judge their fellow creatures according as they are more or less initiated into these luxurious ways : so that (the grandeur which they allow themselves to display or discover in others being wholly material, easily verified, slowly acquired, the lack of it hard to compensate) if such women place a passer-by in the lowest rank of society, it is by the same instinctive process that has made them appear to him as in the highest, that is to say instinctively, at first sight, and without possibility of appeal. Perhaps that special class of society which included in those days women like Lady Israels, who mixed with the women of the aristocracy, and Mme. Swann, who was to get to know them later on, that intermediate class, inferior to the Faubourg Saint-Germain, since it " ran after " the denizens of that quarter, but superior to everything that was not of the Faubourg Saint-Germain, possessing this

peculiarity that, while already detached from the world
of the merely rich, it was riches still that it represented,
but riches that had been canalised, serving a purpose,
swayed by an idea that were artistic, malleable gold,
chased with a poetic design, taught to smile ; perhaps
that class—in the same form, at least, and with the
same charm—exists no longer. In any event, the women
who were its members would not satisfy to-day what
was the primary condition on which they reigned, since
with advancing age they have lost—almost all of them
—their beauty. Whereas it was (just as much as from
the pinnacle of her noble fortune) from the glorious
zenith of her ripe and still so fragrant summer that
Mme. Swann, majestic, smiling, kind, as she advanced
along the Avenue du Bois, saw like Hypatia, beneath
the slow tread of her feet, worlds revolving. Various young men as they passed looked at her anxiously,
not knowing whether their vague acquaintance with her
(especially since, having been introduced only once, at
the most, to Swann, they were afraid that he might not
remember them) was sufficient excuse for their venturing to take off their hats. And they trembled to think of
the consequences as they made up their minds, asking
themselves whether the gesture, so bold, so sacrilegious a
tempting of providence, would not let loose the catastro-
phic forces of nature or bring down upon them the vengeance of a jealous god. It provoked only, like the winding
of a piece of clockwork, a series of gesticulations from
little, responsive bowing figures, who were none other
than Odette's escort, beginning with Swann himself, who
raised his tall hat lined in green leather with an exquisite
courtesy, which he had acquired in the Faubourg Saint-

Germain, but to which was no longer wedded the indifference that he would at one time have shewn. Its place was now taken (as though he had been to some extent permeated by Odette's prejudices) at once by irritation at having to acknowledge the salute of a person who was none too well dressed and by satisfaction at his wife's knowing so many people, a mixed sensation to which he gave expression by saying to the smart friends who walked by his side : "What ! another ! Upon my word, I can't imagine where my wife picks all these fellows up ! " Meanwhile, having greeted with a slight movement of her head the terrified youth, who had already passed out of sight though his heart was still beating furiously, Mme. Swann turned to me : "Then it's all over ? " she put it to me, "You aren't ever coming to see Gilberte again ? I'm glad you make an exception of me, and are not going to 'drop' me straight away. I like seeing you, but I used to like also the influence you had over my daughter. I'm sure she's very sorry about it, too. However, I mustn't bully you, or you'll make up your mind at once that you never want to set eyes on me again." "Odette, Sagan's trying to speak to you ! " Swann called his wife's attention. And there, indeed, was the Prince, as in some transformation scene at the close of a play, or in a circus, or an old painting, wheeling his horse round so as to face her, in a magnificent heroic pose, and doffing his hat with a sweeping theatrical and, so to speak, allegorical flourish in which he displayed all the chivalrous courtesy of a great noble bowing in token of his respect for Woman, were she incarnate in a woman whom it was impossible for his mother or his sister to know. And at every moment, recognised in the depths of the liquid transparency and of the luminous glaze of the shadow which her parasol cast over her, Mme. Swann was receiving the salutations of the last belated horsemen, who passed as though in a cinematograph taken as they galloped in the blinding glare of the Avenue, men from the clubs, the names of whom, which meant only celebrities to the public, Antoine de Castellane, Adalbert de Montmorency and the rest—were for Mme. Swann the familiar names of friends. And as the average span of life, the relative longevity of our memories of poetical sensations is much greater than that of our memories of what the heart has suffered, long after the sorrows that I once felt on Gilberte's account have faded and vanished, there has survived them the pleasure that I still derive—whenever I close my eyes and read, as it were upon the face of a sundial, the minutes that are recorded between a quarter past twelve and one o'clock in the month of May—from seeing myself once again strolling and talking thus with Mme. Swann beneath her parasol, as though in the coloured shade of a wistaria bower.

I HAD arrived at a state almost of complete indifference to Gilberte when, two years later, I went with my grandmother to Balbec. When I succumbed to the attraction of a strange face, when it was with the help of some other girl that I hoped to discover gothic cathedrals, the palaces and gardens of Italy, I said to myself sadly that this love of ours, in so far as it is love for one particular creature, is not perhaps a very real thing, since if the association of pleasant or unpleasant trains of thought can attach it for a time to a woman so as to make us believe that it has been inspired by her, in a necessary sequence of effect to cause, yet when we detach ourselves, deliberately or unconsciously, from those associations, this love, as though it were indeed a spontaneous thing and sprang from ourselves alone, will revive in order to bestow itself on another woman. At the time, however, of my departure for Balbec, and during the earlier part of my stay there, my indifference was still only intermittent. Often, our life being so careless of chronology, interpolating so many anachronisms in the sequence of our days, I lived still among those—far older days than yesterday or last week—in which I loved Gilberte. And at once not seeing her became as exquisite a torture to me as it had been then. The self that had loved her, which another self had already almost entirely supplanted, rose again in me, stimulated far more often by a trivial than by an important event. For instance, if I may anticipate for a moment my arrival in Normandy, I heard some one who passed me on the sea-front at Balbec refer to the "Secretary to the Ministry of Posts and his family". Now, seeing that as yet I knew nothing of the influence which that family was to exercise over my life, this remark ought to have passed unheeded ; instead, it gave me at once an acute twinge, which a self that had for the most part long since been outgrown in me felt at being parted from Gilberte. Because I had never given another thought to a conversation which Gilberte had had with her father in my hearing, in which allusion was made to the Secretary to the Ministry of Posts and his family. Now our love memories present no exception to the general rules of memory, which in turn are governed by the still more general rules of Habit. And as Habit weakens every impression, what a person recalls to us most vividly is precisely what we had forgotten, because it was of no importance, and had therefore left in full possession of its strength. That is why the better part of our memory exists outside ourself, in a blatter of rain, in the smell of an unaired room or of the first crackling brushwood fire in a cold grate : wherever, in short, we happen upon what our mind, having no use for it, had rejected, the last treasure that the past has in store, the richest, that which when all our flow of tears seems to have dried at the source can make us weep again. Outside ourself, did I say ; rather within ourself, but hidden from our eyes in an oblivion more or less prolonged. It is thanks to this oblivion alone that we can from time to time recover the creature that we were, range ourself face to face with past events as that creature had to face them, suffer afresh because we are no longer ourself but he, and because he loved what leaves us now indifferent. In the broad daylight of our ordinary memory the images of the past turn gradually pale and fade out of sight, nothing remains of them, we shall never find them again. Or rather we should never find them again had not a few words (such as this "Secretary to the Ministry of Posts") been carefully locked away in oblivion, just as an author deposits in the National Library a copy of a book which might otherwise become unobtainable.

But this suffering and this recrudescence of my love for Gilberte lasted no longer than such things last in a dream, and this time, on the contrary, because at Balbec the old Habit was no longer there to keep them alive. And if these two effects of Habit appear to be incompatible, that is because Habit is bound by a diversity of laws. In Paris I had grown more and more indifferent to Gilberte, thanks to Habit. The change of habit, that is to say the temporary cessation of Habit, completed Habit's task when I started for Balbec. It weakens, but it stabilises; it leads to disintegration but it makes the scattered elements last indefinitely. Day after day, for years past, I had begun by modelling my state of mind, more or less effectively, upon that of the day before. At Balbec, a strange bed, to the side of which a tray was brought in the morning that differed from my Paris breakfast tray, could not, obviously, sustain the fancies upon which my love for Gilberte had fed : there are cases (though not, I admit, commonly) in which, one's days being paralysed by a sedentary life, the best way to save time is to change one's place of residence. My journey to Balbec was like the first outing of a convalescent who needed only that to convince him that he was cured.

The journey was one that would now be made, probably, in a motor-car, which would be supposed to render it more interesting. We shall see too that, accomplished in such a way, it would even be in a sense more genuine, since one would be following more nearly, in a closer intimacy, the various contours by which the surface of the earth is wrinkled. But after all the special attraction of the journey lies not in our being able to alight at places on the way and to stop altogether as soon as we grow tired, but in its making the difference between departure and arrival not as imperceptible but as intense as possible, so that we are conscious of it in its totality, intact, as it existed in our mind when imagination bore us from the place in which we were living right to the very heart of a place we longed to see, in a single sweep which seemed miraculous to us not so much because it covered a certain distance as because it united two distinct individualities of the world, took us from one name to another name; and this difference is accentuated (more than in a form of locomotion in which, since one can stop and alight where one chooses, there can scarcely be said to be any point of arrival) by the mysterious operation that is performed in those peculiar places, railway stations, which do not constitute, so to speak, a part of the surrounding town but contain the essence of its personality just as upon their sign-boards they bear its painted name.

But in this respect as in every other, our age is infected with a mania for shewing things only in the environment that properly belongs to them, thereby suppressing the essential thing, the act of the mind which isolated them from that environment. A picture is nowadays " presented " in the midst of furniture, ornaments, hangings of the same period, a second-hand scheme of decoration in the composition of which in the houses of to-day excels that same hostess who but yesterday was so crassly ignorant, but now spends her time poring over records and in libraries ; and among these the masterpiece at which we glance up from the table while we dine does not give us that exhilarating delight which we can expect from it only in a public gallery, which symbolises far better by its bareness, by the absence of all irritating detail, those innermost spaces into which the artist withdrew to create it.

Unhappily those marvellous places which are railway stations, from which one sets out for a remote destination, are tragic places also, for if in them the miracle is accomplished whereby scenes which hitherto have had no existence save in our minds are to become the scenes among which we shall be living, for that very reason we must, as we emerge from the waiting-room, abandon any thought of finding ourself once again within the familiar walls which, but a moment ago, were still enclosing us. We must lay aside all hope of going home to sleep in our own bed, once we have made up our mind to penetrate into the pestiferous cavern through which we may have access to the mystery, into one of those vast, glass-roofed sheds, like that of Saint-Lazare into which I must go to find the train for Balbec, and which extended over the rent bowels of the city one of those bleak and boundless skies, heavy with an accumulation of dramatic menaces, like certain skies painted with an almost Parisian modernity by Mantegna or Veronese, beneath which could be accomplished only some solemn and tremendous act, such as a departure by train or the Elevation of the Cross.

So long as I had been content to look out from the warmth of my own bed in Paris at the Persian church of Balbec, shrouded in driving sleet, no sort of objection to this journey had been offered by my body. Its objections began only when it had gathered that it would have itself to take part in the journey, and that on the evening of my arrival I should be shewn to " my " room which to my body would be unknown. Its revolt was all the more deep-rooted in that on the very eve of my departure I learned that my mother would not be coming with us, my father, who would be kept busy at the Ministry until it was time for him to start for Spain with M. de Norpois, having preferred to take a house in the neighbourhood of Paris. On the other hand, the spectacle of Balbec seemed to me none the less desirable because I must purchase it at the price of a discomfort which, on the contrary, I felt to indicate and to guarantee the reality of the impression which I was going there to seek, an impression the place of which no spectacle of professedly equal value, no " panorama " which I might have gone to see without being thereby precluded from returning home to sleep in my own bed, could possibly have filled. It was not for the first time that I felt that those who love and those who find pleasure are not always the same. I believed myself to be longing fully as much for Balbec as the doctor who was treating me, when he said to me, surprised, on the morning of our departure, to see me look so unhappy ; " I don't mind telling you that if I could only manage a week to go down and get a blow by the sea, I shouldn't wait to be asked twice. You'll be having races, regattas ; you don't know what all ! " But I had already learned the lesson—long before I was taken to hear Berma—that, whatever it might be that I loved, it would never be attained save at the end of a long and heart-rending pursuit, in the course of which I should have first to sacrifice my own pleasure to that paramount good instead of seeking it there.

My grandmother, naturally enough, looked upon our exodus from a somewhat different point of view, and (for she was still as anxious as ever that the presents which were made me should take some artistic form) had planned, so that she might be offering me, of this journey, a "print" that was, at least, in parts "old", that we should repeat, partly by rail and partly by road, the itinerary that Mme. de Sévigné followed when she went from Paris to "L'Orient" by way of Chaulnes and "the Pont-Audemer". But my grandmother had been obliged to abandon this project, at the instance of my father who knew, whenever she organised any expedition with a view to extracting from it the utmost intellectual benefit that it was capable of yielding, what a tale there would be to tell of missed trains, lost luggage, sore throats and broken rules. She was free at least to rejoice in the thought that never, when the time came for us to sally forth to the beach, should we be exposed to the risk of being kept indoors by the sudden appearance of what her beloved Sévigné calls a "beast of a coachload", since we should know not a soul at Balbec, Legrandin having refrained from offering us a letter of introduction to his sister. (This abstention had not been so well appreciated by my aunts Céline and Flora, who, having known as a child that lady, of whom they had always spoken until then, to commemorate this early intimacy, as "Renée de Cambremer", and having had from her and still possessing a number of those little presents which continue to ornament a room or a conversation but to which the feeling between the parties no longer corresponds, imagined that they were avenging the insult offered to us by never uttering again, when they called upon Mme. Legrandin, the name of her daughter, confining themselves to a mutual congratulation, once they were safely out of the house : " I made no reference to you know whom ! " " I think that went home ! ")

And so we were simply to leave Paris by that one twenty-two train which I had too often beguiled myself by looking out in the railway time-table, where its itinerary never failed to give me the emotion, almost the illusion of starting by it, not to feel that I already knew it. As the delineation in our mind of the features of any form of happiness depends more on the nature of the longings that it inspires in us than on the accuracy of the information which we have about it, I felt that I knew this train in all its details, nor did I doubt that I should feel, sitting in one of its compartments, a special delight as the day began to cool, should be contemplating this or that view as the train approached one or another station ; so much so that this train, which always brought to my mind's eye the images of the same towns, which I bathed in the sunlight of those post-meridian hours through which it sped, seemed to me to be different from every other train ; and I had ended—as we are apt to do with a person whom we have never seen but of whom we like to believe that we have won his friendship—by giving a distinct and unalterable cast of countenance to the traveller, artistic, golden-haired, who would thus have taken me with him upon his journey, and to whom I should bid farewell beneath the Cathedral of Saint-Lô, before he hastened to overtake the setting sun.

As my grandmother could not bring herself to do anything so "stupid" as to go straight to Balbec, she was to break the journey half-way, staying the night with one of her friends, from whose house I was to proceed the same evening, so as not to be in the way there and also in order that I might arrive by daylight and see Balbec church, which, we had learned, was at some distance from Balbec-Plage, so that I might not have a chance to visit it later on, when I had begun my course of baths. And perhaps it was less painful for me to feel that the desirable goal of my journey stood between me and that cruel first night on which I should have to enter a new habitation, and consent to dwell there. But I had had first to leave the old; my mother had arranged to "move in", that afternoon, at Saint-Cloud, and had made, or pretended to make all the arrangements for going there directly after she had seen us off at the station, without needing to call again at our own house to which she was afraid that I might otherwise feel impelled at the last moment, instead of going to Balbec, to return with her. In fact, on the pretext of having so much to see to in the house which she had just taken and of being pressed for time, but in reality so as to spare me the cruel ordeal of a long-drawn parting, she had decided not to wait with us until that moment of the signal to start at which, concealed hitherto among ineffective comings and goings and preparations that lead to nothing definite, separation is made suddenly manifest, impossible to endure when it is no longer possibly to be avoided, concentrated in its entirety in one enormous instant of impotent and supreme lucidity.

For the first time I began to feel that it was possible that my mother might live without me, otherwise than for me, a separate life. She was going to stay with my father, whose existence it may have seemed to her that my feeble health, my nervous excitability complicated somewhat and saddened. This separation made me all the more wretched because I told myself that it probably marked for my mother an end of the successive disappointments which I had caused her, of which she had never said a word to me but which had made her realise the difficulty of our taking our holidays together ; and perhaps also the first trial of a form of existence to which she was beginning, now, to resign herself for the future, as the years crept on for my father and herself, an existence in which I should see less of her, in which (a thing that not even in my nightmares had yet been revealed to me) she would already have become something of a stranger, a lady who might be seen going home by herself to a house in which I should not be, asking the porter whether there was not a letter for her from me.

I could scarcely answer the man in the station who offered to take my bag. My mother, to comfort me, tried the methods which seemed to her most efficacious. Thinking it to be useless to appear not to notice my unhappiness, she gently teased me about it :

"Well, and what would Balbec church say if it knew that people pulled long faces like that when they were going to see it ? Surely this is not the enraptured tourist Ruskin speaks of. Besides, I shall know if you rise to the occasion, even when we are miles apart I shall still be with my little man. You shall have a letter to-morrow from Mamma."

"My dear," said my grandmother, "I picture you like

Mme. de Sévigné, your eyes glued to the map, and never losing sight of us for an instant."

Then Mamma sought to distract my mind, asked me what I thought of having for dinner, drew my attention to Françoise, complimented her on a hat and cloak which she did not recognise, in spite of their having horrified her long ago when she first saw them, new, upon my great-aunt, one with an immense bird towering over it, the other decorated with a hideous pattern and jet beads. But the cloak having grown too shabby to wear, Françoise had had it turned, exposing an "inside" of plain cloth and quite a good colour. As for the bird, it had long since come to grief and been thrown away. And just as it is disturbing, sometimes, to find the effects which the most conscious artists attain only by an effort occurring in a folk-song, on the wall of some peasant's cottage where above the door, at the precisely right spot in the composition, blooms a white or yellow rose—so the velvet band, the loop of ribbon which would have delighted one in a portrait by Chardin or Whistler, Françoise had set with a simple but unerring taste upon the hat, which was now charming.

To take a parallel from an earlier age, the modesty and integrity which often gave an air of nobility to the face of our old servant having spread also to the garments which, as a woman reserved but not humbled, who knew how to hold her own and to keep her place, she had put on for the journey so as to be fit to be seen in our company without at the same time seeming or wishing to make herself conspicuous,—Françoise in the cherry-coloured cloth, now faded, of her cloak, and the discreet nap of her fur collar, brought to mind one of those miniatures of

Anne of Brittany painted in Books of Hours by an old master, in which everything is so exactly in the right place, the sense of the whole is so evenly distributed throughout the parts that the rich and obsolete singularity of the costume expresses the same pious gravity as the eyes, lips and hands.

Of thought, in relation to Françoise, one could hardly speak. She knew nothing, in that absolute sense in which to know nothing means to understand nothing, save the rare truths to which the heart is capable of directly attaining. The vast world of ideas existed not for her. But when one studied the clearness of her gaze, the lines of nose and lips, all those signs lacking from so many people of culture in whom they would else have signified a supreme distinction, the noble detachment of a chosen spirit, one was disquieted, as one is by the frank, intelligent eyes of a dog, to which, nevertheless, one knows that all our human concepts must be alien, and was led to ask oneself whether there might not be, among those other humble brethren, our peasant countrymen, creatures who were, like the great ones of the earth, of simple mind, or rather, doomed by a harsh fate to live among the simple-minded, deprived of heavenly light, were yet more naturally, more instinctively akin to the chosen spirits than most educated people, were, so to speak, all members, though scattered, straying, robbed of their heritage of reason, of the celestial family, kinsfolk, that have been lost in infancy, of the loftiest minds to whom—as is apparent from the unmistakable light in their eyes, although they can concentrate that light on nothing—there has been lacking, to endow them with talent, knowledge only.

My mother, seeing that I had difficulty in keeping back my tears, said to me : "'Regulus was in the habit, when things looked grave. . . .' Besides, it isn't nice for Mamma ! What does Mme. de Sévigné say ? Your grandmother will tell you : 'I shall be obliged to draw upon all the courage that you lack.'" And remembering that affection for another distracts one's selfish griefs, she endeavoured to beguile me by telling me that she expected the removal to Saint-Cloud to go without a hitch, that she liked the cab, which she had kept waiting, that the driver seemed civil and the seats comfortable. I made an effort to smile at these trifles, and bowed my head with an air of acquiescence and satisfaction. But they helped me only to depict to myself with more accuracy Mamma's imminent departure, and it was with an agonised heart that I gazed at her as though she were already torn from me, beneath that wide-brimmed straw hat which she had bought to wear in the country, in a flimsy dress which she had put on in view of the long drive through the sweltering midday heat ; hat and dress making her some one else, some one who belonged already to the Villa Montretout, in which I should not see her.

To prevent the choking fits which the journey might otherwise give me the doctor had advised me to take, as we started, a good stiff dose of beer or brandy, so as to begin the journey in a state of what he called "euphoria", in which the nervous system is for a time less vulnerable. I had not yet made up my mind whether I should do this, but I wished at least that my grandmother should admit that, if I did so decide, I should have wisdom and authority on my side. I spoke therefore as if my hesitation were concerned only with where I should go for my drink, to the bar on the platform or to the restaurant-car on the train. But immediately, at the air of reproach which my grandmother's face assumed, an air of not wishing even to entertain such an idea for a moment, "What!" I said to myself, suddenly determining upon this action of going out to drink, the performance of which became necessary as a proof of my independence since the verbal announcement of it had not succeeded in passing unchallenged, "What! You know how ill I am, you know what the doctor ordered, and you treat me like this!"

When I had explained to my grandmother how unwell I felt, her distress, her kindness were so apparent as she replied, "Run along then, quickly; get yourself some beer or a liqueur if it will do you any good," that I flung myself upon her, almost smothering her in kisses. And if after that I went and drank a great deal too much in the restaurant car of the train, that was because I felt that otherwise I should have a more violent attack than usual, which was just what would vex her most. When at the first stop I clambered back into our compartment I told my grandmother how pleased I was to be going to Balbec, that I felt that everything would go off splendidly, that after all I should soon grow used to being without Mamma, that the train was most comfortable, the steward and attendants in the bar so friendly that I should like to make the journey often so as to have opportunities of seeing them again. My grandmother, however, did not appear to feel the same joy as myself at all these good tidings. She answered, without looking me in the face:

"Why don't you try to get a little sleep?" and turned

her gaze to the window, the blind of which, though we had drawn it, did not completely cover the glass, so that the sun could and did slip in over the polished oak of the door and the cloth of the seat (like an advertisement of a life shared with nature far more persuasive than those posted higher upon the walls of the compartment, by the railway company, representing places in the country the names of which I could not make out from where I sat) the same warm and slumberous light which lies along a forest glade.

But when my grandmother thought that my eyes were shut I could see her, now and again, from among the large black spots on her veil, steal a glance at me, then withdraw it, and steal back again, like a person trying to make himself, so as to get into the habit, perform some exercise that hurts him.

Thereupon I spoke to her, but that seemed not to please her either. And yet to myself the sound of my own voice was pleasant, as were the most imperceptible, the most internal movements of my body. And so I endeavoured to prolong it. I allowed each of my inflexions to hang lazily upon its word, I felt each glance from my eyes arrive just at the spot to which it was directed and stay there beyond the normal period. "Now, now, sit still and rest," said my grandmother. "If you can't manage to sleep, read something." And she handed me a volume of Madame de Sévigné which I opened, while she buried herself in the *Mémoires de Madame de Beausergent*. She never travelled anywhere without a volume of each. They were her two favourite authors. With no conscious movement of my head, feeling a keen pleasure in maintaining a posture after I had adopted it, I lay back holding in my hands the volume of Madame de Sévigné which I had allowed to close, without lowering my eyes to it, or indeed letting them see anything but the blue window-blind. But the contemplation of this blind appeared to me an admirable thing, and I should not have troubled to answer anyone who might have sought to distract me from contemplating it. The blue colour of this blind seemed to me, not perhaps by its beauty but by its intense vivacity, to efface so completely all the colours that had passed before my eyes from the day of my birth up to the moment in which I had gulped down the last of my drink and it had begun to take effect, that when compared with this blue they were as drab, as void as must be retrospectively the darkness in which he has lived to a man born blind whom a subsequent operation has at length enabled to see and to distinguish colours. An old ticket-collector came to ask for our tickets. The silvery gleam that shone from the metal buttons of his jacket charmed me in spite of my absorption. I wanted to ask him to sit down beside us. But he passed on to the next carriage, and I thought with longing of the life led by railwaymen for whom, since they spent all their time on the line, hardly a day could pass without their seeing this old collector. The pleasure that I found in staring at the blind, and in feeling that my mouth was half-open, began at length to diminish. I became more mobile ; I even moved in my seat ; I opened the book that my grandmother had given me and turned its pages casually, reading whatever caught my eye. And as I read I felt my admiration for Madame de Sévigné grow.

It is a mistake to let oneself be taken in by the purely

formal details, idioms of the period or social conventions, the effect of which is that certain people believe that they have caught the Sévigné manner when they have said : "Tell me, my dear," or "That Count struck me as being a man of parts," or "Haymaking is the sweetest thing in the world." Mme. de Simiane imagines already that she is being like her grandmother because she can write : "M. de la Boulie is bearing wonderfully, Sir, and is in excellent condition to hear the news of his death," or "Oh, my dear Marquis, how your letter enchanted me ! What can I do but answer it ?" or "Meseems, Sir, that you owe me a letter, and I owe you some boxes of bergamot. I discharge my debt to the number of eight ; others shall follow. . . . Never has the soil borne so many. Apparently for your gratification." And she writes in this style also her letter on bleeding, on lemons and so forth, supposing it to be typical of the letters of Madame de Sévigné. But my grandmother who had approached that lady from within, attracted to her by her own love of kinsfolk and of nature, had taught me to enjoy the real beauties of her correspondence, which are altogether different. They were presently to strike me all the more forcibly inasmuch as Madame de Sévigné is a great artist of the same school as a painter whom I was to meet at Balbec, where his influence on my way of seeing things was immense. I realised at Balbec that it was in the same way as he that she presented things to her readers, in the order of our perception of them, instead of first having to explain them in relation to their several causes. But already that afternoon in the railway carriage, as I read over again that letter in which the moonlight comes :

" I cannot resist the temptation : I put on all my bonnets and veils, though there is no need of them, I walk along this mall, where the air is as sweet as in my chamber ; I find a thousand phantasms, monks white and black, sisters grey and white, linen cast here and there on the ground, men enshrouded upright against the tree-trunks," I was enraptured by what, a little later, I should have described (for does not she draw landscapes in the same way as he draws characters ?) as the Dostoievsky side of Madame de Sévigné's Letters.

When, that evening, after having accompanied my grandmother to her destination and spent some hours in her friend's house, I had returned by myself to the train, at any rate I found nothing to distress me in the night which followed ; this was because I had not to spend it in a room the somnolence of which would have kept me awake ; I was surrounded by the soothing activity of all those movements of the train which kept me company, offered to stay and converse with me if I could not sleep, lulled me with their sounds which I wedded—as I had often wedded the chime of the Combray bells—now to one rhythm now to another (hearing as the whim took me first four level and equivalent semi-quavers, then one semi-quaver furiously dashing against a crotchet) ; they neutralised the centrifugal force of my insomnia by exercising upon it a contrary pressure which kept me in equilibrium and on which my immobility and presently my drowsiness felt themselves to be borne with the same sense of refreshment that I should have had, had I been resting under the protecting vigilance of powerful forces, on the breast of nature and of life, had I been able for a moment to incarnate myself in a fish that sleeps in the sea,

324

driven unheeding by the currents and the tides, or in an eagle outstretched upon the air, with no support but the storm.

Sunrise is a necessary concomitant of long railway journeys, just as are hard-boiled eggs, illustrated papers, packs of cards, rivers upon which boats strain but make no progress. At a certain moment, when I was counting over the thoughts that had filled my mind, in the preceding minutes, so as to discover whether I had just been asleep or not (and when the very uncertainty which made me ask myself the question was to furnish me with an affirmative answer), in the pale square of the window, over a small black wood I saw some ragged clouds whose fleecy edges were of a fixed, dead pink, not liable to change, like the colour that dyes the wing which has grown to wear it, or the sketch upon which the artist's fancy has washed it. But I felt that, unlike them, this colour was due neither to inertia nor to caprice but to necessity and life. Presently there gathered behind it reserves of light. It brightened ; the sky turned to a crimson which I strove, glueing my eyes to the window, to see more clearly, for I felt that it was related somehow to the most intimate life of Nature, but, the course of the line altering, the train turned, the morning scene gave place in the frame of the window to a nocturnal village, its roofs still blue with moonlight, its pond encrusted with the opalescent nacre of night, beneath a firmament still powdered with all its stars, and I was lamenting the loss of my strip of pink sky when I caught sight of it afresh, but red this time, in the opposite window which it left at a second bend in the line, so that I spent my time running from one window to the other to reassemble, to collect on a single canvas the intermittent, antipodean fragments of my fine, scarlet, ever-changing morning, and to obtain a comprehensive view of it and a continuous picture.

The scenery became broken, abrupt, the train stopped at a little station between two mountains. Far down the gorge, on the edge of a hurrying stream, one could see only a solitary watch-house, deep-planted in the water which ran past on a level with its windows. If a person can be the product of a soil the peculiar charm of which one distinguishes in that person, more even than the peasant girl whom I had so desperately longed to see appear when I wandered by myself along the Méséglise way, in the woods of Roussainville, such a person must be the big girl whom I now saw emerge from the house and, climbing a path lighted by the first slanting rays of the sun, come towards the station carrying a jar of milk. In her valley from which its congregated summits hid the rest of the world, she could never see anyone save in these trains which stopped for a moment only. She passed down the line of windows, offering coffee and milk to a few awakened passengers. Purpled with the glow of morning, her face was rosier than the sky. I felt in her presence that desire to live which is reborn in us whenever we become conscious anew of beauty and of happiness. We invariably forget that these are individual qualities, and, substituting for them in our mind a conventional type at which we arrive by striking a sort of mean amongst the different faces that have taken our fancy, the pleasures we have known, we are left with mere abstract images which are lifeless and dull because they are lacking in precisely that element of novelty, different

326

from anything we have known, that element which is proper to beauty and to happiness. And we deliver on life a pessimistic judgment which we suppose to be fair, for we believed that we were taking into account when we formed it happiness and beauty, whereas in fact we left them out and replaced them by syntheses in which there is not a single atom of either. So it is that a well-read man will at once begin to yawn with boredom when anyone speaks to him of a new " good book ", because he imagines a sort of composite of all the good books that he has read and knows already, whereas a good book is something special, something incalculable, and is made up not of the sum of all previous masterpieces but of something which the most thorough assimilation of every one of them would not enable him to discover, since it exists not in their sum but beyond it. Once he has become acquainted with this new work, the well-read man, till then apathetic, feels his interest awaken in the reality which it depicts. So, alien to the models of beauty which my fancy was wont to sketch when I was by myself, this strapping girl gave me at once the sensation of a certain happiness (the sole form, always different, in which we may learn the sensation of happiness), of a happiness that would be realised by my staying and living there by her side. But in this again the temporary cessation of Habit played a great part. I was giving the milk-girl the benefit of what was really my own entire being, ready to taste the keenest joys, which now confronted her. As a rule it is with our being reduced to a minimum that we live, most of our faculties lie dormant because they can rely upon Habit, which knows what there is to be done and has no need of their services.

But on this morning of travel, the interruption of the routine of my existence, the change of place and time had made their presence indispensable. My habits, which were sedentary and not matutinal, played me false, and all my faculties came hurrying to take their place, vieing with one another in their zeal, rising, each of them, like waves in a storm, to the same unaccustomed level, from the basest to the most exalted, from breath, appetite, the circulation of my blood to receptivity and imagination. I cannot say whether, so as to make me believe that this girl was unlike the rest of women, the rugged charm of these barren tracts had been added to her own, but if so she gave it back to them. Life would have seemed an exquisite thing to me if only I had been free to spend it, hour after hour, with her, to go with her to the stream, to the cow, to the train, to be always at her side, to feel that I was known to her, had my place in her thoughts. She would have initiated me into the delights of country life and of the first hours of the day. I signalled to her to give me some of her coffee. I felt that I must be noticed by her. She did not see me ; I called to her. Above her body, which was of massive build, the complexion of her face was so burnished and so ruddy that she appeared almost as though I were looking at her through a lighted window. She had turned and was coming towards me ; I could not take my eyes from her face which grew larger as she approached, like a sun which it was somehow possible to arrest in its course and draw towards one, letting itself be seen at close quarters, blinding the eyes with its blaze of red and gold. She fastened on me her penetrating stare, but while the porters ran along the platform shutting doors the train had begun to move. I saw her leave the station and go down the hill to her home ; it was broad daylight now ; I was speeding away from the dawn. Whether my exaltation had been produced by this girl or had on the other hand been responsible for most of the pleasure that I had found in the sight of her, in the sense of her presence, in either event she was so closely associated with it that my desire to see her again was really not so much a physical as a mental desire, not to allow this state of enthusiasm to perish utterly, not to be separated for ever from the person who, although quite unconsciously, had participated in it. It was not only because this state was a pleasant one. It was principally because (just as increased tension upon a cord or accelerated vibration of a nerve produces a different sound or colour) it gave another tonality to all that I saw, introduced me as an actor upon the stage of an unknown and infinitely more interesting universe ; that handsome girl whom I still could see, while the train gathered speed, was like part of a life other than the life that I knew, separated from it by a clear boundary, in which the sensations that things produced in me were no longer the same, from which to return now to my old life would be almost suicide. To procure myself the pleasure of feeling that I had at least an attachment to this new life, it would suffice that I should live near enough to the little station to be able to come to it every morning for a cup of coffee from the girl. But alas, she must be for ever absent from the other life towards which I was being borne with ever increasing swiftness, a life to the prospect of which I resigned myself only by weaving plans that would enable me to take the same train again some day and to stop at the same station, a project which would have the further advantage of providing with subject matter the selfish, active, practical, mechanical, indolent, centrifugal tendency which is that of the human mind ; for our mind turns readily aside from the effort which is required if it is to analyse in itself, in a general and disinterested manner, a pleasant impression which we have received. And as, on the other hand, we wish to continue to think of that impression, the mind prefers to imagine it in the future tense, which while it gives us no clue as to the real nature of the thing, saves us the trouble of recreating it in our own consciousness and allows us to hope that we may receive it afresh from without.

Certain names of towns, Vezelay or Chartres, Bourges or Beauvais, serve to indicate, by abbreviation, the principal church in those towns. This partial acceptation, in which we are so accustomed to take the word, comes at length—if the names in question are those of places that we do not yet know—to fashion for us a mould of the name as a solid whole, which from that time onwards, whenever we wish it to convey the idea of the town— of that town which we have never seen—will impose on it, as on a cast, the same carved outlines, in the same style of art, will make of the town a sort of vast cathedral. It was, nevertheless, in a railway-station, above the door of a refreshment-room, that I read the name—almost Persian in style—of Balbec. I strode buoyantly through the station and across the avenue that led past it, I asked my way to the beach so as to see nothing in the place but its church and the sea ; people seemed not to understand what I meant. Old Balbec, Balbec-en-Terre, at which I had arrived, had neither beach nor harbour. It was, most certainly, in the sea that the fishermen had found, according to the legend, the miraculous Christ, of which a window in the church that stood a few yards from where I now was recorded the discovery ; it was indeed from cliffs battered by the waves that had been quarried the stone of its nave and towers. But this sea, which for those reasons I had imagined as flowing up to die at the foot of the window, was twelve miles away and more, at Balbec-Plage, and, rising beside its cupola, that steeple, which, because I had read that it was itself a rugged Norman cliff on which seeds were blown and sprouted, round which the sea-birds wheeled, I had always pictured to myself as receiving at its base the last drying foam of the uplifted waves, stood on a Square from which two lines of tramway diverged, opposite a Café which bore, written in letters of gold, the word " Billiards " ; it stood out against a background of houses with the roofs of which no upstanding mast was blended. And the church—entering my mind with the Café, with the passing stranger of whom I had had to ask my way, with the station to which presently I should have to return—made part of the general whole, seemed an accident, a by-product of this summer afternoon, in which its mellow and distended dome against the sky was like a fruit of which the same light that bathed the chimneys of the houses was ripening the skin, pink, glowing, melting-soft. But I wished only to consider the eternal significance of the carvings when I recognised the Apostles, which I had seen in casts in the Trocadéro museum, and which on either side of the Virgin, before the deep bay of the porch, were awaiting me as though to do me reverence. With their benign, blunt, mild faces and bowed shoulders they seemed to be advancing upon me with an air of welcome, singing the

Alleluia of a fine day. But it was evident that their expression was unchanging as that on a dead man's face, and could be modified only by my turning about to look at them in different aspects. I said to myself : "Here I am : this is the Church of Balbec. This square, which looks as though it were conscious of its glory, is the only place in the world that possesses Balbec Church. All that I have seen so far have been photographs of this Church—and of these famous Apostles, this Virgin of the Porch, mere casts only. Now it is the Church itself, the statue itself ; these are they ; they, the unique things —this is something far greater."

It was something less, perhaps, also. As a young man on the day of an examination or of a duel feels the question that he has been asked, the shot that he has fired, to be a very little thing when he thinks of the reserves of knowledge and of valour that he possesses and would like to have displayed, so my mind, which had exalted the Virgin of the Porch far above the reproductions that I had had before my eyes, inaccessible by the vicissitudes which had power to threaten them, intact although they were destroyed, ideal, endowed with universal value, was astonished to see the statue which it had carved a thousand times, reduced now to its own apparent form in stone, occupying, on the radius of my outstretched arm, a place in which it had for rivals an election placard and the point of my stick, fettered to the Square, inseparable from the head of the main street, powerless to hide from the gaze of the Café and of the omnibus office, receiving on its face half of that ray of the setting sun (half, presently, in a few hours' time, of the light of the street lamp) of which the Bank building received the other half, tainted simultaneously with that branch office of a money-lending establishment by the smells from the pastry-cook's oven, subjected to the tyranny of the Individual to such a point that, if I had chosen to scribble my name upon that stone, it was she, the illustrious Virgin whom until then I had endowed with a general existence and an intangible beauty, the Virgin of Balbec, the unique (which meant, alas, the only one) who, on her body coated with the same soot as defiled the neighbouring houses, would have displayed—powerless to rid herself of them—to all the admiring strangers come there to gaze upon her, the marks of my piece of chalk and the letters of my name ; it was she, indeed, the immortal work of art, so long desired, whom I found, transformed, as was the church itself, into a little old woman in stone whose height I could measure and count her wrinkles. But time was passing ; I must return to the station, where I was to wait for my grandmother and Françoise, so that we should all arrive at Balbec-Plage together. I reminded myself of what I had read about Balbec, of Swann's saying : "It is exquisite ; as fine as Siena." And casting the blame for my disappointment upon various accidental causes, such as the state of my health, my exhaustion after the journey, my incapacity for looking at things properly, I endeavoured to console myself with the thought that other towns remained still intact for me, that I might soon, perhaps, be making my way, as into a shower of pearls, into the cool pattering sound that dripped from Quimperlé, cross that green water lit by a rosy glow in which Pont-Aven was bathed ; but as for Balbec, no sooner had I set foot in it than it was as though I had broken open a name which ought to have been kept hermetically closed, and into which, seizing at once the opportunity that I had imprudently given them when I expelled all the images that had been living in it until then, a tramway, a Café, people crossing the square, the local branch of a Bank, irresistibly propelled by some external pressure, by a pneumatic force, had come crowding into the interior of those two syllables which, closing over them, let them now serve as a border to the porch of the Persian church, and would never henceforward cease to contain them.

In the little train of the local railway company which was to take us to Balbec-Plage I found my grandmother, but found her alone—for, imagining that she was sending Françoise on ahead of her, so as to have everything ready before we arrived, but having mixed up her instructions, she had succeeded only in packing off Françoise in the wrong direction, who at that moment was being carried down all unsuspectingly, at full speed, to Nantes, and would probably wake up next morning at Bordeaux. No sooner had I taken my seat in the carriage, filled with the fleeting light of sunset and with the lingering heat of the afternoon (the former enabling me, alas, to see written clearly upon my grandmother's face how much the latter had tired her), than she began : "Well, and Balbec ?" with a smile so brightly illuminated by her expectation of the great pleasure which she supposed me to have been enjoying that I dared not at once confess to her my disappointment. Besides, the impression which my mind had been seeking occupied it steadily less as the place drew nearer to which my body would have to become accustomed. At the end —still more than an hour away—of this journey I was trying to form a picture of the manager of the hotel at Balbec, to whom I, at that moment, did not exist, and I should have liked to be going to present myself to him in more impressive company than that of my grand-mother, who would be certain to ask for a reduction of his terms. The only thing positive about him was his haughty condescension ; his lineaments were still vague.

Every few minutes the little train brought us to a standstill in one of the stations which came before Balbec-Plage, stations the mere names of which, (Incarville, Mar-couville, Doville, Pont-à-Couleuvre, Arambouville, Saint-Mars-le-Vieux, Hermonville, Maineville) seemed to me outlandish, whereas if I had come upon them in a book I should at once have been struck by their affinity to the names of certain places in the neighbourhood of Com-bray. But to the trained ear two musical airs, consisting each of so many notes, several of which are common to them both, will present no similarity whatever if they differ in the colour of their harmony and orchestration. So it was that nothing could have reminded fne less than these dreary names, made up of sand, of space too airy and empty and of salt, out of which the termination " ville " always escaped, as the " fly " seems to spring out from the end of the word " butterfly "—nothing could have reminded me less of those other names, Roussainville or Martinville, which, because I had heard them pro-nounced so often by my great-aunt at table, in the dining-room, had acquired a certain sombre charm in which were blended perhaps extracts of the flavour of " preserves ", the smell of the fire of logs and of the pages of one of Bergotte's books, the colour of the stony front of the house opposite, all of which things still to-day when they rise like a gaseous bubble from the depths of my memory preserve their own specific virtue through all the successive layers of rival interests which must be traversed before they reach the surface.

These were—commanding the distant sea from the crests of their several dunes or folding themselves already for the night beneath hills of a crude green colour and uncomfortable shape, like that of the sofa in one's bedroom in an hotel at which one has just arrived, each composed of a cluster of villas whose line was extended to include a lawn-tennis court and now and then a casino, over which a flag would be snapping in the freshening breeze, like a hollow cough—a series of watering-places which now let me see for the first time their regular visitors, but let me see only the external features of those visitors—lawn-tennis players in white hats, the stationmaster spending all his life there on the spot among his tamarisks and roses, a lady in a straw " boater " who, following the everyday routine of an existence which I should never know, was calling to her dog which had stopped to examine something in the road before going in to her bungalow where the lamp was already lighted for her return—which with these strangely usual and slightingly familiar sights stung my ungreeted eyes and stabbed my exiled heart. But how much were my sufferings increased when we had finally landed in the hall of the Grand Hotel at Balbec, and I stood there in front of the monumental staircase that looked like marble, while my grandmother, regardless of the growing hostility of the strangers among whom we should have to live, discussed " terms " with the manager, a sort of nodding mandarin whose face and voice were alike covered with scars (left by the excision of countless pustules from one and from the other of the divers accents acquired from an alien ancestry and in a cosmopolitan upbringing) who stood there in a smart dinner-jacket, with the air of an expert psychologist, classifying, whenever the "omnibus" discharged a fresh load, the "nobility and gentry" as "geesers" and the "hotel crooks" as nobility and gentry. Forgetting, probably, that he himself was not drawing five hundred francs a month, he had a profound contempt for people to whom five hundred francs—or, as he preferred to put it, "twenty-five louis" was "a lot of money", and regarded them as belonging to a race of pariahs for whom the Grand Hotel was certainly not intended. It is true that even within its walls there were people who did not pay very much and yet had not forfeited the manager's esteem, provided that he was assured that they were watching their expenditure not from poverty so much as from avarice. For this could in no way lower their standing since it is a vice and may consequently be found at every grade of social position. Social position was the one thing by which the manager was impressed, social position, or rather the signs which seemed to him to imply that it was exalted, such as not taking one's hat off when one came into the hall, wearing knickerbockers, or an overcoat with a waist, and taking a cigar with a band of purple and gold out of a crushed morocco case— to none of which advantages could I, alas, lay claim. He would also adorn his business conversation with choice expressions, to which, as a rule, he gave a wrong meaning.

While I heard my grandmother, who shewed no sign

of annoyance at his listening to her with his hat on his head and whistling through his teeth at her, ask him in an artificial voice, " And what are . . . your charges ? . . . Oh ! far too high for my little budget," waiting upon a bench, I sought refuge in the innermost depths of my own consciousness, strove to migrate to a plane of eternal thoughts—to leave nothing of myself, nothing that lived and felt on the surface of my body, anaesthetised as are those of animals which by inhibition feign death when they are attacked—so as not to suffer too keenly in this place, with which my total unfamiliarity was made all the more evident to me when I saw the familiarity that seemed at the same moment to be enjoyed by a smartly dressed lady for whom the manager shewed his respect by taking liberties with the little dog that followed her across the hall, the young " blood " with a feather in his hat who asked, as he came in, " Any letters ? " all these people to whom it was an act of home-coming to mount those stairs of imitation marble. And at the same time the triple frown of Minos, Æacus and Rhadamanthus (beneath which I plunged my naked soul as into an unknown element where there was nothing now to protect it) was bent sternly upon me by a group of gentlemen who, though little versed perhaps in the art of receiving, yet bore the title " Reception Clerks ", while beyond them again, through a closed wall of glass, were people sitting in a reading-room for the description of which I should have had to borrow from Dante alternately the colours in which he paints Paradise and Hell, according as I was thinking of the happiness of the elect who had the right to sit and read there undisturbed, or of the terror which my grandmother would have inspired in me if, in her insensibility to this sort of impression, she had asked me to go in there and wait for her by myself.

My sense of loneliness was further increased a moment later : when I had confessed to my grandmother that I did not feel well, that I thought that we should be obliged to return to Paris, she had offered no protest, saying merely that she was going out to buy a few things which would be equally useful whether we left or stayed (and which, I afterwards learned, were all for my benefit, Françoise having gone off with certain articles which I might need) ; while I waited for her I had taken a turn through the streets, packed with a crowd of people who imparted to them a sort of indoor warmth, streets in which were still open the hairdresser's shop and the pastry-cook's, the latter filled with customers eating ices, opposite the statue of Duguay-Trouin. This crowd gave me just about as much pleasure as a photograph of it in one of the " illustrateds " might give a patient who was turning its pages in the surgeon's waiting-room. I was astonished to find that there were people so different from myself that this stroll through the town had actually been recommended to me by the manager as a distraction, and also that the torture chamber which a new place of residence is could appear to some people a " continuous amusement ", to quote the hotel prospectus, which might, it was true, exaggerate, but was, for all that, addressed to a whole army of clients to whose tastes it must appeal. True, it invoked, to make them come to the Grand Hotel, Balbec, not only the " exquisite fare " and the " fairy-like view across the Casino gardens," but also the " ordinances of her Majesty Queen Fashion, which no one may break with impunity, or without being taken for a Bœotian, a charge that no well-bred man would willingly incur." The need that I now had of my grandmother was enhanced by my fear that I had shattered another of her illusions. She must be feeling discouraged, feeling that if I could not stand the fatigue of this journey there was no hope that any change of air could ever do me good. I decided to return to the hotel and to wait for her there : the manager himself came forward and pressed a button, and a person whose acquaintance I had not yet made, labelled " LIFT " (who at that highest point in the building, which corresponded to the lantern in a Norman church, was installed like a photographer in his darkroom or an organist in his loft) came rushing down towards me with the agility of a squirrel, tamed, active, caged. Then, sliding upwards again along a steel pillar, he bore me aloft in his train towards the dome of this temple of Mammon. On each floor, on either side of a narrow communicating stair, opened out fanwise a range of shadowy galleries, along one of which, carrying a bolster, a chambermaid came past. I lent to her face, which the gathering dusk made featureless, the mask of my most impassioned dreams of beauty, but read in her eyes as they turned towards me the horror of my own nonentity. Meanwhile, to dissipate, in the course of this interminable assent, the mortal anguish which I felt in penetrating thus in silence the mystery of this chiaroscuro so devoid of poetry, lighted by a single vertical line of little windows which were those of the solitary water-closet on each landing, I addressed a few words to the young organist, artificer of my journey and my partner in captivity, who continued to manipulate the registers of his instrument and to finger the stops. I apologised for taking up so much room, for giving him so much trouble, and asked whether I was not obstructing him in the practice of an art to which, so as to flatter the performer, I did more than display curiosity, I confessed my strong attachment. But he vouchsafed no answer, whether from astonishment at my words, preoccupation with what he was doing, regard for convention, hardness of hearing, respect for holy ground, fear of danger, slowness of understanding, or by the manager's orders.

There is perhaps nothing that gives us so strong an impression of the reality of the external world as the difference in the positions, relative to ourself, of even a quite unimportant person before we have met him and after. I was the same man who had taken, that afternoon, the little train from Balbec to the coast, I carried in my body the same consciousness. But on that consciousness, in the place where, at six o'clock, there had been, with the impossibility of forming any idea of the manager, the Grand Hotel or its occupants, a vague and timorous impatience for the moment at which I should reach my destination, were to be found now the pustules excised from the face of the cosmopolitan manager (he was, as a matter of fact, a naturalised Monegasque, although—as he himself put it, for he was always using expressions which he thought distinguished without noticing that they were incorrect—" of Rumanian originality "), his action in ringing for the lift, the lift-boy himself, a whole frieze of puppet-show characters issuing from that Pandora's box which was the Grand Hotel, undeniable, irremovable, and, like everything that is realised, sterilising. But at least this change, which I had done nothing to bring about,

341

proved to me that something had happened which was external to myself—however devoid of interest that thing
might be—and I was like a traveller who, having had the
sun in his face when he started, concludes that he has been
for so many hours on the road when he finds the sun behind him. I was half dead with exhaustion, I was burning with fever ; I would gladly have gone to bed, but I
had no night-things. I should have liked at least to lie
down for a little while on the bed, but what good would
that have done me, seeing that I should not have been
able to find any rest there for that mass of sensations
which is for each of us his sentient if not his material
body, and that the unfamiliar objects which encircled
that body, forcing it to set its perceptions on the permanent footing of a vigilant and defensive guard, would
have kept my sight, my hearing, all my senses in a position
as cramped and comfortless (even if I had stretched out
my legs) as that of Cardinal La Balue in the cage in
which he could neither stand nor sit. It is our noticing
them that puts things in a room, our growing used to
them that takes them away again and clears a space for
us. Space there was none for me in my bedroom (mine
in name only) at Balbec ; it was full of things which did
not know me, which flung back at me the distrustful look
that I had cast at them, and, without taking any heed of
my existence, shewed that I was interrupting the course
of theirs. The clock—whereas at home I heard my clock
tick only a few seconds in a week, when I was coming
out of some profound meditation—continued without a
moment's interruption to utter, in an unknown tongue, a
series of observations which must have been most uncomplimentary to myself, for the violet curtains listened

to them without replying, but in an attitude such as people adopt who shrug their shoulders to indicate that the sight of a third person irritates them. They gave to this room with its lofty ceiling a semi-historical character which might have made it a suitable place for the assassination of the Duc de Guise, and afterwards for parties of tourists personally conducted by one of Messrs. Thomas Cook and Son's guides, but for me to sleep in—no. I was tormented by the presence of some little bookcases with glass fronts which ran along the walls, but especially by a large mirror with feet which stood across one corner, for I felt that until it had left the room there would be no possibility of rest for me there. I kept raising my eyes—which the things in my room in Paris disturbed no more than did my eyelids themselves, for they were merely extensions of my organs, an enlargement of myself—towards the fantastically high ceiling of this belvedere planted upon the summit of the hotel which my grandmother had chosen for me ; and in that region more intimate than those in which we see and hear, that region in which we test the quality of odours, almost in the very heart of my inmost self, the smell of flowering grasses next launched its offensive against my last feeble line of trenches, where I stood up to it, not without tiring myself still further, with the futile incessant defence of an anxious sniffing. Having no world, no room, no body now that was not menaced by the enemies thronging round me, invaded to the very bones by fever, I was utterly alone ; I longed to die. Then my grandmother came in, and to the expansion of my ebbing heart there opened at once an infinity of space.

She was wearing a loose cambric gown which she put

on at home whenever any of us was ill (because she felt
more comfortable in it, she used to say, for she always
ascribed to her actions a selfish motive), and which was,
for tending us, for watching by our beds, her servant's
livery, her nurse's uniform, her religious habit. But
whereas the trouble that servants, nurses, religious take,
their kindness to us, the merits that we discover in them
and the gratitude that we owe them all go to increase the
impression that we have of being, in their eyes, some one
different, of feeling that we are alone, keeping in our own
hands the control over our thoughts, our will to live, I
knew, when I was with my grandmother, that, however
great the misery that there was in me, it would be received
by her with a pity still more vast ; that everything that
was mine, my cares, my wishes, would be, in my grandmother, supported upon a desire to save and prolong my
life stronger than was my own ; and my thoughts were
continued in her without having to undergo any deflec-
tion, since they passed from my mind into hers without
change of atmosphere or of personality. And—like a man
who tries to fasten his necktie in front of a glass and forgets that the end which he sees reflected is not on the side
to which he raises his hand, or like a dog that chases
along the ground the dancing shadow of an insect in the
air—misled by her appearance in the body as we are apt
to be in this world where we have no direct perception of
people's souls, I threw myself into the arms of my grandmother and clung with my lips to her face as though I
had access thus to that immense heart which she opened
to me. And when I felt my mouth glued to her cheeks,
to her brow, I drew from them something so beneficial,

so nourishing that I lay in her arms as motionless, as solemn, as calmly gluttonous as a babe at the breast.

At last I let go, and lay and gazed, and could not tire of gazing at her large face, as clear in its outline as a fine cloud, glowing and serene, behind which I could discern the radiance of her tender love. And everything that received, in however slight a degree, any share of her sensations, everything that could be said to belong in any way to her was at once so spiritualised, so sanctified that with outstretched hands I smoothed her dear hair, still hardly grey, with as much respect, precaution, comfort as if I had actually been touching her goodness. She found a similar pleasure in taking any trouble that saved me one, and in a moment of immobility and rest for my weary limbs something so delicious that when, having seen that she wished to help me with my undressing and to take my boots off, I made as though to stop her and began to undress myself, with an imploring gaze she arrested my hands as they fumbled with the top buttons of my coat and boots.

" Oh, do let me ! " she begged. " It is such a joy for your Granny. And be sure you knock on the wall if you want anything in the night. My bed is just on the other side, and the partition is quite thin. Just give a knock now, as soon as you are ready, so that we shall know where we are."

And, sure enough, that evening I gave three knocks— a signal which, the week after, when I was ill, I repeated every morning for several days, because my grandmother wanted me to have some milk early. Then, when I thought that I could hear her stirring, so that she should

345

not be kept waiting but might, the moment she had brought me the milk, go to sleep again, I ventured on three little taps, timidly, faintly, but for all that distinctly, for if I was afraid of disturbing her, supposing that I had been mistaken and that she was still asleep, I should not have wished her either to lie awake listening for a summons which she had not at once caught and which I should not have the courage to repeat. And scarcely had I given my taps than I heard three others, in a different intonation from mine, stamped with a calm authority, repeated twice over so that there should be no mistake, and saying to me plainly : "Don't get excited ; I heard you ; I shall be with you in a minute !" and shortly afterwards my grandmother appeared. I explained to her that I had been afraid that she would not hear me, or might think that it was some one in the room beyond who was tapping ; at which she smiled :

"Mistake my poor chick's knocking for anyone else ! Why, Granny could tell it among a thousand ! Do you suppose there's anyone else in the world who's such a silly-billy, with such feverish little knuckles, so afraid of waking me up and of not making me understand ? Even if he just gave the least scratch, Granny could tell her mouse's sound at once, especially such a poor miserable little mouse as mine is. I could hear it just now, trying to make up its mind, and rustling the bedclothes, and going through all its tricks."

She pushed open the shutters ; where a wing of the hotel jutted out at right angles to my window, the sun was already installed upon the roof, like a slater who is up betimes, and starts early and works quietly so as not to rouse the sleeping town, whose stillness seems to enhance his activity. She told me what o'clock, what sort of day it was ; that it was not worth while my getting up and coming to the window, that there was a mist over the sea ; if the baker's shop had opened yet ; what the vehicle was that I could hear passing. All that brief, trivial curtain-raiser, that negligible *introit* of a new day, performed without any spectator, a little scrap of life which was only for our two selves, which I should have no hesitation in repeating, later on, to Françoise or even to strangers, speaking of the fog " which you could have cut with a knife " at six o'clock that morning, with the ostentation of one who was boasting not of a piece of knowledge that he had acquired but of a mark of affection shewn to himself alone ; dear morning moment, opened like a symphony by the rhythmical dialogue of my three taps, to which the thin wall of my bedroom, steeped in love and joy, grown melodious, immaterial, singing like the angelic choir, responded with three other taps, eagerly awaited, repeated once and again, in which it contrived to waft to me the soul of my grandmother, whole and perfect, and the promise of her coming, with a swiftness of annunciation and melodic accuracy. But on this first night after our arrival, when my grandmother had left me, I began again to feel as I had felt, the day before, in Paris, at the moment of leaving home. Perhaps this fear that I had—and shared with so many of my fellow-men— of sleeping in a strange room, perhaps this fear is only the most humble, obscure, organic, almost unconscious form of that great and desperate resistance set up by the things that constitute the better part of our present life towards our mentally assuming, by accepting it as true, the formula of a future in which those things are to have no part ; a

resistance which was at the root of the horror that I had
so often been made to feel by the thought that my parents
must, one day, die, that the stern necessity of life might
oblige me to live remote from Gilberte, or simply to settle
permanently in a place where I should never see any of
my old friends ; a resistance which was also at the root
of the difficulty that I found in imagining my own death,
or a survival such as Bergotte used to promise to mankind
in his books, a survival in which I should not be allowed
to take with me my memories, my frailties, my character,
which did not easily resign themselves to the idea of ceasing to be, and desired for me neither annihilation nor an
eternity in which they would have no part.

When Swann had said to me, in Paris one day when I
felt particularly unwell : " You ought to go off to one of
those glorious islands in the Pacific ; you'd never come
back again if you did." I should have liked to answer :
" But then I shall not see your daughter any more ; I shall
be living among people and things she has never seen."
And yet my better judgment whispered : " What difference can that make, since you are not going to be affected by it ? When M. Swann tells you that you will
not come back he means by that that you will not want to
come back, and if you don't want to that is because you
will be happier out there." For my judgment was aware
that Habit—Habit which was even now setting to work
to make me like this unfamiliar lodging, to change the
position of the mirror, the shade of the curtains, to stop
the clock—undertakes as well to make dear to us the
companions whom at first we disliked, to give another appearance to their faces, to make attractive the sound of
their voices, to modify the inclinations of their hearts. It

is true that these new friendships for places and people are based upon forgetfulness of the old ; but what my better judgment was thinking was simply that I could look without apprehension along the vista of a life in which I should be for ever separated from people all memory of whom I should lose, and it was by way of consolation that my mind was offering to my heart a promise of oblivion which succeeded only in sharpening the edge of its despair. Not that the heart also is not bound in time, when separation is complete, to feel the anodyne effect of habit ; but until then it will continue to suffer. And our dread of a future in which we must forego the sight of faces, the sound of voices that we love, friends from whom we derive to-day our keenest joys, this dread, far from being dissipated, is intensified, if to the grief of such a privation we reflect that there will be added what seems to us now in anticipation an even more cruel grief ; not to feel it as a grief at all—to remain indifferent ; for if that should occur, our ego would have changed, it would then be not merely the attractiveness of our family, our mistress, our friends that had ceased to environ us, but our affection for them ; it would have been so completely eradicated from our heart, in which to-day it is a conspicuous element, that we should be able to enjoy that life apart from them the very thought of which to-day makes us recoil in horror ; so that it would be in a real sense the death of ourself, a death followed, it is true, by resurrection but in a different ego, the life, the love of which are beyond the reach of those elements of the existing ego that are doomed to die. It is they—even the meanest of them, such as our obscure attachments to the dimensions, to the atmosphere of a bedroom—that grow stubborn and refuse, in acts of rebellion which we must recognise to be a secret, partial, tangible and true aspect of our resistance to death, of the long resistance, desperate and daily renewed, to a fragmentary and gradual death such as interpolates itself throughout the whole course of our life, tearing away from us at every moment a shred of ourself, dead matter on which new cells will multiply, and grow. And for a neurotic nature such as mine, one that is to say in which the intermediaries, the nerves, perform their functions badly—fail to arrest on its way to the consciousness, allow indeed to penetrate there, distinct, exhausting, innumerable, agonising, the plaint of those most humble elements of the personality which are about to disappear—the anxiety and alarm which I felt as I lay outstretched beneath that strange and too lofty ceiling were but the protest of an affection that survived in me for a ceiling that was familiar and low. Doubtless this affection too would disappear, and another have taken its place (when death, and then another life, would, in the guise of Habit, have performed their double task) ; but until its annihilation, every night it would suffer afresh, and on this first night especially, confronted with a future already realised in which there would no longer be any place for it, it rose in revolt, it tortured me with the sharp sound of its lamentations whenever my straining eyes, powerless to turn from what was wounding them, endeavoured to fasten their gaze upon that inaccessible ceiling.

But next morning !—after a servant had come to call me, and had brought me hot water, and while I was washing and dressing myself and trying in vain to find the things that I wanted in my trunk, from which I extracted, pell-mell, only a lot of things that were of no use whatever, what a joy it was to me, thinking already of the delights of luncheon and of a walk along the shore, to see in the window, and in all the glass fronts of the bookcases as in the portholes of a ship's cabin, the open sea, naked, unshadowed, and yet with half of its expanse in shadow, bounded by a thin and fluctuant line, and to follow with my eyes the waves that came leaping towards me, one behind another, like divers along a springboard. Every other moment, holding in one hand the starched, unyielding towel, with the name of the hotel printed upon it, with which I was making futile efforts to dry myself, I returned to the window to gaze once more upon that vast amphitheatre, dazzling, mountainous, and upon the snowy crests of its emerald waves, here and there polished and translucent, which with a placid violence, a leonine bending of the brows, let their steep fronts, to which the sun now added a smile without face or features, run forward to their goal, totter and melt and be no more. Window in which I was, henceforward, to plant myself every morning, as at the pane of a mail coach in which one has slept, to see whether, in the night, a long sought mountain-chain has come nearer or withdrawn—only here it was those hills of the sea which, before they come dancing back towards us, are apt to retire so far that often it was only at the end of a long and sandy plain that I would distinguish, miles it seemed away, their first undulations upon a background transparent, vaporous, bluish, like the glaciers that one sees in the backgrounds of the Tuscan Primitives. On other mornings it was quite close at hand that the sun was smiling upon those waters of a green as tender as that preserved in Alpine pastures (among mountains on which the sun spreads himself here and there like a lazy giant who may at any moment come leaping gaily down their craggy sides) less by the moisture of their soil than by the liquid mobility of their light. Anyhow, in that breach which shore and water between them drive through all the rest of the world, for the passage, the accumulation there of light, it is light above all, according to the direction from which it comes and along which our eyes follow it, it is light that shifts and fixes the undulations of the sea. Difference of lighting modifies no less the orientation of a place, constructs no less before our eyes new goals which it inspires in us the yearning to attain, than would a distance in space actually traversed in the course of a long journey. When, in the morning, the sun came from behind the hotel, disclosing to me the sands bathed in light as far as the first bastions of the sea, it seemed to be shewing me another side of the picture, and to be engaging me on the pursuit, along the winding path of its rays, of a journey motionless but ever varied amid all the fairest scenes of the diversified landscape of the hours. And on this first morning the sun pointed out to me far off with a jovial finger those blue peaks of the sea, which bear no name upon any geographer's chart, until, dizzy with its sublime excursion over the thundering and chaotic surface of their crests and avalanches, it came back to take shelter from the wind in my bedroom, swaggering across the unmade bed and scattering its riches over the splashed surface of the basin-stand, and into my open trunk, where by its very splendour and ill-matched luxury it added still further to the general effect of disorder. Alas, that wind from the sea ; an hour later, in the great dining-room— while we were having our luncheon, and from the leathern

gourd of a lemon were sprinkling a few golden drops on
to a pair of soles which presently left on our plates the
plumes of their picked skeletons, curled like stiff feathers
and resonant as cithers,—it seemed to my grandmother
a cruel deprivation not to be able to feel its life-giving
breath on her cheek, on account of the window, transparent but closed, which like the front of a glass case in a
museum divided us from the beach while allowing us to
look out upon its whole extent, and into which the sky entered so completely that its azure had the effect of being
the colour of the windows and its white clouds only so
many flaws in the glass. Imagining that I was "seated
upon the mole" or at rest in the "boudoir" of which
Baudelaire speaks I asked myself whether his "Sun's rays
upon the sea" were not—a very different thing from the
evening ray, simple and superficial as the wavering stroke
of a golden pencil—just what at that moment was scorching the sea topaz-brown, fermenting it, turning it pale and
milky like foaming beer, like milk, while now and then
there hovered over it great blue shadows which some god
seemed, for his pastime, to be shifting to and fro by moving a mirror in the sky. Unfortunately, it was not only
in its outlook that it differed from our room at Combray,
giving upon the houses over the way, this dining-room at
Balbec, bare-walled, filled with a sunlight green as the
water in a marble font, while a few feet away the full
tide and broad daylight erected as though before the gates
of the heavenly city an indestructible and moving ram-
part of emerald and gold. At Combray, since we were
known to everyone, I took heed of no one. In life at the
seaside one knows only one's own party. I was not yet
old enough, I was still too sensitive to have outgrown the

desire to find favour in the sight of other people and to possess their hearts. Nor had I acquired the more noble indifference which a man of the world would have felt, with regard to the people who were eating their luncheon in the room, nor to the boys and girls who strolled past the window, with whom I was pained by the thought that I should never be allowed to go on expeditions, though not so much pained as if my grandmother, contemptuous of social formalities and concerned about nothing but my health, had gone to them with the request, humiliating for me to overhear, that they would consent to let me accompany them. Whether they were returning to some villa beyond my ken, or had emerged from it, racquet in hand, on their way to some lawn-tennis court, or were mounted on horses whose hooves trampled and tore my heart, I gazed at them with a passionate curiosity, in that blinding light of the beach by which social distinctions are altered, I followed all their movements through the transparency of that great bay of glass which allowed so much light to flood the room. But it intercepted the wind, and this seemed wrong to my grandmother, who, unable to endure the thought that I was losing the benefit of an hour in the open air, surreptitiously unlatched a pane and at once set flying, with the bills of fare, the newspapers, veils and hats of all the people at the other tables; she herself, fortified by the breath of heaven, remained calm and smiling like Saint Blandina, amid the torrent of invective which, increasing my sense of isolation and misery, those scornful, dishevelled, furious visitors combined to pour on us.

To a certain extent—and this, at Balbec, gave to the population, as a rule monotonously rich and cosmopolitan, of that sort of smart and "exclusive" hotel, a quite distinctive local character—they were composed of eminent persons from the departmental capitals of that region of France, a chief magistrate from Caen, a leader of the Cherbourg bar, a big solicitor from Le Mans, who annually, when the holidays came round, starting from the various points over which, throughout the working year, they were scattered like snipers in a battle or draughtsmen upon a board, concentrated their forces upon this hotel. They always reserved the same rooms, and with their wives, who had pretensions to aristocracy, formed a little group, which was joined by a leading barrister and a leading doctor from Paris, who on the day of their departure would say to the others :

"Oh, yes, of course ; you don't go by our train. You are fortunate, you will be home in time for luncheon."

"Fortunate, do you say ? You, who live in the Capital, in 'Paris, the great town', while I have to live in a wretched county town of a hundred thousand souls (it is true, we managed to muster a hundred and two thousand at the last census, but what is that compared to your two and a half millions ?) going back, too, to asphalt streets and all the bustle and gaiety of Paris life."

They said this with a rustic burring of their 'r's, but without bitterness, for they were leading lights each in his own province, who could like other people have gone to Paris had they chosen—the chief magistrate of Caen had several times been offered a judgeship in the Court of Appeal—but had preferred to stay where they were, from love of their native towns or of obscurity or of fame, or because they were reactionaries, and enjoyed being on friendly terms with the country houses of the neighbourhood. Besides several of them were not going back at once to their county towns.

For—inasmuch as the Bay of Balbec was a little world apart in the midst of a great world, a basketful of the seasons in which were clustered in a ring good days and bad, and the months in their order, so that not only, on days when one could make out Rivebelle, which was in itself a sign of coming storms, could one see the sunlight on the houses there while Balbec was plunged in darkness, but later on, when the cold weather had reached Balbec, one could be certain of finding on that opposite shore two or three supplementary months of warmth— those of the regular visitors to the Grand Hotel whose holidays began late or lasted long, gave orders, when rain and fog came and Autumn was in the air, for their boxes to be packed and embarked, and set sail across the Bay to find summer again at Rivebelle or Costedor. This little group in the Balbec hotel looked with distrust upon each new arrival, and while affecting to take not the least interest in him, hastened, all of them, to ply with questions their friend the head waiter. For it was the same head waiter—Aimé—who returned every year for the season, and kept their tables for them; and their good ladies, having heard that his wife was "expecting", would sit after meals working each at one of the "little things", stopping only to put up their glasses and stare at us, my grandmother and myself, because we were eating hard-boiled eggs in salad, which was considered common, and was, in fact, "not done" in the best society of Alençon. They affected an attitude of contemptuous irony with regard to a Frenchman who was called "His Majesty" and had indeed proclaimed himself King of a small island in the South Seas, inhabited by a few savages. He was staying in the hotel with his pretty mistress, whom, as she crossed the beach to bathe, the little boys would greet with "Three cheers for the Queen!" because she would reward them with a shower of small silver. The chief magistrate and the barrister went so far as to pretend not to see her, and if any of their friends happened to look at her, felt bound to warn him that she was only a little shop-girl.

"But I was told that at Ostend they used the royal bathing machine."

"Well, and why not? It's on hire for twenty francs. You can take it yourself, if you care for that sort of thing. Anyhow, I know for a fact that the fellow asked for an audience, when he was there, with the King, who sent back word that he took no cognisance of any Pantomime Princes."

"Really, that's interesting! What queer people there are in the world, to be sure!"

And I dare say it was all quite true: but it was also from resentment of the thought that, to many of their fellow-visitors, they were themselves simply respectable but rather common people who did not know this King and Queen so prodigal with their small change, that the solicitor, the magistrate, the barrister, when what they were pleased to call the "Carnival" went by, felt so much annoyance, and expressed aloud an indignation that was quite understood by their friend the head waiter who, obliged to shew proper civility to these generous if not authentic Sovereigns, still, while he took their orders, would dart from afar at his old patrons a covert but speaking glance. Perhaps there was also something of the same resentment at being erroneously supposed to be less and unable to explain that they were more smart, underlining the "fine specimen" with which they qualified a young "blood", the consumptive and dissipated son of an industrial magnate, who appeared every day in a new suit of clothes with an orchid in his buttonhole, drank champagne at luncheon, and then strolled out of the hotel, pale, impassive, a smile of complete indifference on his lips, to the casino to throw away at the baccarat table enormous sums, "which he could ill afford to lose," as the solicitor said with a resigned air to the chief magistrate, whose wife had it "on good authority" that this "detrimental" young man was bringing his parents' grey hair in sorrow to the grave.

On the other hand, the barrister and his friends could not exhaust their flow of sarcasm on the subject of a wealthy old lady of title, because she never moved anywhere without taking her whole household with her. Whenever the wives of the solicitor and the magistrate saw her in the dining-room at meal-times they put up their glasses and gave her an insolent scrutiny, as minute and distrustful as if she had been some dish with a pretentious name but a suspicious appearance which, after the negative result of a systematic study, must be sent away with a lofty wave of the hand and a grimace of disgust.

No doubt by this behaviour they meant only to shew that, if there were things in the world which they themselves lacked—in this instance, certain prerogatives which the old lady enjoyed, and the privilege of her acquaintance—it was not because they could not, but because they did not choose to acquire them. But they had succeeded in convincing themselves that this really was what they

THE HOTEL

felt ; and it was the suppression of all desire for, of all
curiosity as to forms of life which were unfamiliar, of all
hope of pleasing new people (for which, in the women,
had been substituted a feigned contempt, an artificial
brightness) that had the awkward result of obliging them
to label their discontent satisfaction, and lie everlastingly
to themselves, for which they were greatly to be pitied.
But everyone else in the hotel was no doubt behaving in
a similar fashion, though his behaviour might take a different form, and sacrificing, if not to self-importance, at
any rate to certain inculcated principles and mental habits
the thrilling delight of mixing in a strange kind of life.
Of course, the atmosphere of the microcosm in which the
old lady isolated herself was not poisoned with virulent
bitterness, as was that of the group in which the wives of
the solicitor and magistrate sat chattering with impotent
rage. It was indeed embalmed with a delicate and old
world fragrance which, however, was none the less artificial. For at heart the old lady would probably have
found in attracting, in attaching to herself (and, with that
object, recreating herself) the mysterious sympathy of
new friends a charm which is altogether lacking from the
pleasure that is to be derived from mixing only with the
people of one's own world, and reminding oneself that,
one's own being the best of all possible worlds, the ill-
informed contempt of " outsiders " may be disregarded.
Perhaps she felt that—were she to arrive *incognito* at the
Grand Hotel, Balbec, she would, in her black stuff gown
and old-fashioned bonnet, bring a smile to the lips of
some old reprobate, who from the depths of his rocking
chair would glance up and murmur, " What a scare-
crow ! " or, still worse, to those of some man of repute

who had, like the magistrate, kept between his pepper-and-salt whiskers a rosy complexion and a pair of sparkling eyes such as she liked to see, and would at once bring the magnifying lens of the conjugal glasses to bear upon so quaint a phenomenon ; and perhaps it was in unconfessed dread of those first few minutes, which, though one knows that they will be but a few minutes, are none the less terrifying, like the first plunge of one's head under water, that this old lady sent down in advance a servant, who would inform the hotel of the personality and habits of his mistress, and, cutting short the manager's greetings, made, with an abruptness in which there was more timidity than pride, for her room, where her own curtains, substituted for those that draped the hotel windows, her own screens and photographs set up so effectively between her and the outside world, to which otherwise she would have had to adapt herself, the barrier of her private life that it was her home (in which she had comfortably stayed) that travelled rather than herself.

Thenceforward, having placed between herself, on the one hand, and the staff of the hotel and its decorators on the other the servants who bore instead of her the shock of contact with all this strange humanity, and kept up around their mistress her familiar atmosphere, having set her prejudices between herself and the other visitors, indifferent whether or not she gave offence to people whom her friends would not have had in their houses, it was in her own world that she continued to live, by correspondence with her friends, by memories, by her intimate sense of and confidence in her own position, the quality of her manners, the competence of her politeness. And every day, when she came downstairs to go for a drive in her own carriage, the lady's-maid who came after her carrying her wraps, the footman who preceded her seemed like sentries who, at the gate of an embassy, flying the flag of the country to which she belonged, assured to her upon foreign soil the privilege of extra-territoriality. She did not leave her room until late in the afternoon on the day following our arrival, so that we did not see her in the dining-room, into which the manager, since we were strangers there, conducted us, taking us under his wing, as a corporal takes a squad of recruits to the master-tailor, to have them fitted ; we did see however, a moment later, a country gentleman and his daughter, of an obscure but very ancient Breton family, M. and Mlle. de Stermaria, whose table had been allotted to us, in the belief that they had gone out and would not be back until the evening. Having come to Balbec only to see various country magnates whom they knew in that neighbourhood, they spent in the hotel dining-room, what with the invitations they accepted and the visits they paid, only such time as was strictly unavoidable. It was their stiffness that preserved them intact from all human sympathy, from interesting at all the strangers seated round about them, among whom M. de Stermaria kept up the glacial, preoccupied, distant, rude, punctilious and distrustful air that we assume in a railway refreshment-room, among fellow-passengers whom we have never seen before and will never see again, and with whom we can conceive of no other relations than to defend from their onslaught our " portion " of cold chicken and our corner seat in the train. No sooner had we begun our luncheon than we were asked to leave the table, on the instructions of M.

de Stermaria who had just arrived and, without the faintest attempt at an apology to us, requested the head waiter, in our hearing to " see that such a mistake did not occur again," for it was repugnant to him that " people whom he did not know " should have taken his table.

And certainly into the feeling which impelled a young actress (better known, though, for her smart clothes, her smart sayings, her collection of German porcelain, than in the occasional parts that she had played at the Odéon) her lover, an immensely rich young man for whose sake she had acquired her culture, and two sprigs of aristocracy at that time much in the public eye to form a little band apart, to travel only together, to come down to luncheon —when at Balbec—very late, after everyone had finished ; to spend the whole day in their sitting-room playing cards, there entered no sort of ill-humour against the rest of us but simply the requirements of the taste that they had formed for a certain type of conversation, for certain refinements of good living, which made them find pleasure in spending their time, in taking their meals only by themselves, and would have rendered intolerable a life in common with people who had not been initiated into those mysteries. Even at a dinner or a card table, each of them had to be certain that, in the diner or partner who sat opposite to him, there was, latent and not yet made use of, a certain brand of knowledge which would enable him to identify the rubbish with which so many houses in Paris were littered as genuine mediaeval or renaissance " pieces " and, whatever the subject of discussion, to apply the critical standards common to all their party whereby they distinguished good work from bad. Probably it was only—at such moments—by some infrequent,

amusing interruption flung into the general silence of
meal or game, or by the new and charming frock which
the young actress had put on for luncheon or for poker,
that the special kind of existence in which these four
friends desired, above all things, to remain plunged was
made apparent. But by engulfing them thus in a system
of habits which they knew by heart it sufficed to protect
them from the mystery of the life that was going on all
round them. All the long afternoon, the sea was sus-
pended there before their eyes only as a canvas of
attractive colouring might hang on the wall of a wealthy
bachelor's flat and it was only in the intervals between
the "hands" that one of the players, finding nothing
better to do, raised his eyes to it to seek from it some
indication of the weather or the time, and to remind
the others that tea was ready. And at night they did
not dine in the hotel, where, hidden springs of electricity flooding the great dining-room with light, it became
as it were an immense and wonderful aquarium against
whose wall of glass the working population of Balbec, the fishermen and also the tradesmen's families, clustering invisibly in the outer darkness, pressed their faces
to watch, gently floating upon the golden eddies within,
the luxurious life of its occupants, a thing as extraordinary
to the poor as the life of strange fishes or molluscs : (an
important social question, this ; whether the wall of glass
will always protect the wonderful creatures at their feast-
ing, whether the obscure folk who watch them hungrily
out of the night will not break in some day to gather them
from their aquarium and devour them.) Meanwhile
there may have been, perhaps, among the gazing crowd, a
motionless, formless mass there in the dark, some writer,

some student of human ichthyology who, as he watched the jaws of old feminine monstrosities close over a mouthful of food which they proceeded then to absorb, was amusing himself by classifying them according to their race, by their innate characteristics as well as by those acquired characteristics which bring it about that an old Serbian lady whose buccal protuberance is that of a great sea-fish, because from her earliest years she has moved in the fresh waters of the Faubourg Saint-Germain, eats her salad for all the world like a La Rochefoucauld.

At that hour one could see the three young men in dinner-jackets, waiting for the young woman, who was as usual late but presently, wearing a dress that was almost always different and one of a series of scarves, chosen to gratify some special instinct in her lover, after having from her landing rung for the lift, would emerge from it like a doll coming out of its box. And then all four, because they found that the international phenomenon of the " Palace ", planted on Balbec soil, had blossomed there in material splendour rather than in food that was fit to eat, bundled into a carriage and went to dine, a mile off, in a little restaurant that was well spoken of, where they held with the cook himself endless discussions of the composition of their meal and the cooking of its various dishes. During their drive, the road bordered with apple-trees that led out of Balbec was no more to them than the distance that must be traversed—barely distinguishable in the darkness from that which separated their homes in Paris from the Café Anglais or the Tour d'Argent—before they could arrive at the fashionable little restaurant where, while the young man's friends envied him because he had such a smartly dressed mistress, the latter's scarves were spread about the little company like a fragrant, flow-ing veil, but one that kept it apart from the outer world.

Alas for my peace of mind, I had none of the detach-ment that all these people shewed. To many of them I gave constant thought ; I should have liked not to pass unobserved by a man with a receding brow and eyes that dodged between the blinkers of his prejudices and his education, the great nobleman of the district, who was none other than the brother-in-law of Legrandin, and came every now and then to see somebody at Balbec and on Sundays, by reason of the weekly garden-party that his wife and he gave, robbed the hotel of a large number of its occupants, because one or two of them were invited to these entertainments and the others, so as not to appear to have been not invited, chose that day for an expedition to some distant spot. He had had, as it happened, an ex-ceedingly bad reception at the hotel on the first day of the season, when the staff, freshly imported from the Riviera, did not yet know who or what he was. Not only was he not wearing white flannels, but, with old-fashioned French courtesy and in his ignorance of the ways of smart hotels, on coming into the hall in which there were ladies sitting, he had taken off his hat at the door, the effect of which had been that the manager did not so much as raise a finger to his own in acknowledgment, concluding that this must be some one of the most humble extraction, what he called " sprung from the ordinary." The solicitor's wife, alone, had felt herself attracted by the stranger, who ex-haled all the starched vulgarity of the really respectable, and had declared, with the unerring discernment and the indisputable authority of a person from whom the highest society of Le Mans held no secrets, that one could see at a glance that one was in the presence of a gentleman of great distinction, of perfect breeding, a striking contrast to the sort of people one usually saw at Balbec, whom she condemned as impossible to know so long as she did not know them. This favourable judgment which she had pronounced on Legrandin's brother-in-law was based perhaps on the spiritless appearance of a man about whom there was nothing to intimidate anyone ; perhaps also she had recognised in this gentleman farmer with the gait of a sacristan the Masonic signs of her own inveterate clericalism.

It made no difference my knowing that the young fellows who went past the hotel every day on horseback were the sons of the questionably solvent proprietor of a linen-drapery to whom my father would never have dreamed of speaking ; the glamour of "seaside life" exalted them in my eyes to equestrian statues of demi-gods, and the best thing that I could hope for was that they would never allow their proud gaze to fall upon the wretched boy who was myself, who left the hotel dining-room only to sit humbly upon the sands. I should have been glad to arouse some response even from the adventurer who had been king of a desert island in the South Seas, even of the young consumptive, of whom I liked to think that he was hiding beneath his insolent exterior a shy and tender heart, which would perhaps have lavished on me, and on me alone, the treasures of its affection. Besides (unlike what one generally says of the people one meets when travelling) just as being seen in certain company can invest us, in a watering-place to which we shall return another year, with a coefficient that has no equivalent in our true social life, so there is nothing—not which we keep so resolutely at a distance, but—which we cultivate with such assiduity after our return to Paris as the friendships that we have formed by the sea. I was anxious about the opinion that might be held of me by all these temporary or local celebrities whom my tendency to put myself in the place of other people and to reconstruct what was in their minds had made me place not in their true rank, that which they would have held in Paris, for instance, and which would have been quite low, but in that which they must imagine to be, and which indeed was their rank at Balbec, where the want of a common denominator gave them a sort of relative superiority and an individual interest. Alas, none of these people's contempt for me was so unbearable as that of M. de Stermaria.

For I had noticed his daughter, the moment she came into the room, her pretty features, her pallid, almost blue complexion, what there was peculiar in the carriage of her tall figure, in her gait, which suggested to me—and rightly —her long descent, her aristocratic upbringing, all the more vividly because I knew her name, like those expressive themes composed by musicians of genius which paint in splendid colours the glow of fire, the rush of water, the peace of fields and woods, to audiences who, having first let their eyes run over the programme, have their imaginations trained in the right direction. The label " Centuries of Breeding ", by adding to Mlle. de Stermaria's charms the idea of their origin, made them more desirable also, advertising their rarity as a high price enhances the value of a thing that has already taken our fancy. And its stock of heredity gave to her complexion, in which so many selected juices had been blended, the savour of an exotic fruit or of a famous vintage.

And then mere chance put into our hands, my grandmother's and mine, the means of giving ourselves an immediate distinction in the eyes of all the other occupants of the hotel. On that first afternoon, at the moment when the old lady came downstairs from her room, producing, thanks to the footman who preceded her, the maid who came running after her with a book and a rug that had been left behind, a marked effect upon all who beheld her and arousing in each of them a curiosity from which it was evident that none was so little immune as M. de Stermaria, the manager leaned across to my grandmother and, from pure kindness of heart (as one might point out the Shah, or Queen Ranavalo to an obscure onlooker who could obviously have no sort of connexion with so mighty a potentate, but might be interested, all the same, to know that he had been standing within a few feet of one) whispered in her ear, " The Marquise de Villeparisis ! " while at the same moment the old lady, catching sight of my grandmother, could not repress a start of pleased surprise.

It may be imagined that the sudden appearance, in the guise of a little old woman, of the most powerful of fairies would not have given me so much pleasure, destitute as I was of any means of access to Mlle. de Stermaria, in a strange place where I knew no one : no one, that is to say, for any practical purpose. Aesthetically the number of types of humanity is so restricted that we must constantly, wherever we may be, have the pleasure of seeing people we know, even without looking for them in the works of the old masters, like Swann. Thus it happened that in the first few days of our visit to Balbec I had succeeded in finding Legrandin, Swann's hall porter and Mme. Swann herself, transformed into a waiter, a foreign visitor whom I never saw again and a bathing superintendent. And a sort of magnetism attracts and retains so inseparably, one after another, certain characteristics, facial and mental, that when nature thus introduces a person into a new body she does not mutilate him unduly. Legrandin turned waiter kept intact his stature, the outline of his nose, part of his chin ; Mme. Swann, in the masculine gender and the calling of a bathing superintendent, had been accompanied not only by familiar features, but even by the way she had of speaking. Only, she could be of little if any more use to me, standing upon the beach there in the red sash of her office, and hoisting at the first gust of wind the flag which forbade us to bathe (for these superintendents are prudent men, and seldom know how to swim) than she would have been in that fresco of the *Life of Moses* in which Swann had long ago identified her in the portrait of Jethro's Daughter. Whereas this Mme. de Villeparisis was her real self, she had not been the victim of an enchantment which had deprived her of her power, but was capable, on the contrary, of putting at the service of my power an enchantment which would multiply it an hundred fold, and thanks to which, as though I had been swept through the air on the wings of a fabulous bird, I was to cross in a few moments the infinitely wide (at least, at Balbec) social gulf which separated me from Mlle. de Stermaria.

Unfortunately, if there was one person in the world who, more than anyone else, lived shut up in a little world of her own, it was my grandmother. She would not, indeed, have despised me, she would simply not have understood what I meant had she been told that I attached importance to the opinions, that I felt an interest in the persons of people the very existence of whom she had never noticed and would, when the time came to leave Balbec, retain no impression of their names. I dared not confess to her that if these same people had seen her talking to Mme. de Villeparisis, I should have been immensely gratified, because I felt that the Marquise counted for much in the hotel and that her friendship would have given us a position in the eyes of Mlle. de Stermaria. Not that my grandmother's friend represented to me, in any sense of the word, a member of the aristocracy : I was too well used to her name, which had been familiar to my ears before my mind had begun to consider it, when as a child I had heard it occur in conversation at home : while her title added to it only a touch of quaintness—as some uncommon Christian name would have done, or as in the names of streets, among which we can see nothing more noble in the Rue Lord Byron, in the plebeian and even squalid Rue Rochechouart, or in the Rue Grammont than in the Rue Léonce Reynaud or the Rue Hippolyte Lebas. Mme. de Villeparisis no more made me think of a person who belonged to a special world than did her cousin Mac-Mahon, whom I did not clearly distinguish from M. Carnot, likewise President of the Republic, or from Raspail, whose photograph Françoise had bought with that of Pius IX. It was one of my grandmother's principles that, when away from home, one should cease to have any social intercourse, that one did not go to the seaside to meet people, having plenty of time for that sort of thing in Paris, that they would make one waste on being merely polite, in pointless conversation, the precious time which ought all to be spent in the open air, beside the waves ; and finding it convenient to assume that this view was shared by everyone else, and that it authorised, between old friends whom chance brought face to face in the same hotel, the fiction of a mutual *incognito*, on hearing her friend's name from the manager she merely looked the other way, and pretended not to see Mme. de Villeparisis, who, realising that my grandmother did not want to be recognised, looked also into the void. She went past, and I was left in my isolation like a shipwrecked mariner who has seen a vessel apparently coming towards him which has then, without lowering a boat, vanished under the horizon.

She, too, had her meals in the dining-room, but at the other end of it. She knew none of the people who were staying in the hotel, or who came there to call, not even M. de Cambremer ; in fact, I noticed that he gave her no greeting, one day when, with his wife, he had accepted an invitation to take luncheon with the barrister, who drunken with the honour of having the nobleman at his table avoided his friends of every day, and confined himself to a distant twitch of the eyelid, so as to draw their attention to this historic event but so discreetly that his signal could not be interpreted by them as an invitation to join the party.

"Well, I hope you've got on your best clothes ; I hope you feel smart enough," was the magistrate's wife's greeting to him that evening.

"Smart? Why should I ?" asked the barrister, concealing his rapture in an exaggerated astonishment. "Because of my guests, do you mean ?" he went on, feeling that it was impossible to keep up the farce any longer.

" But what is there smart about having a few friends in to luncheon ?   After all, they must feed somewhere ! "

" But it is smart !   They are the *de* Cambremers, aren't they ?   I recognised them at once.   She is a Marquise.   And quite genuine, too.   Not through the females."

" Oh, she's a very simple soul, she is charming, no stand-offishness about her.   I thought you were coming to join us.   I was making signals to you. . .   I would have introduced you ! " he asserted, tempering with a hint of irony the vast generosity of the offer, like Ahasuerus when he says to Esther :

> Of all my Kingdom must I give you half !

" No, no, no, no !   We lie hidden, like the modest violet."

" But you were quite wrong, I assure you," replied the barrister, growing bolder now that the danger point was passed.   " They weren't going to eat you.   I say, aren't we going to have our little game of bezique ? "

" Why, of course !   We were afraid to suggest it, now that you go about entertaining Marquises."

" Oh, get along with you ; there's nothing so very wonderful about them.   Why, I'm dining there to-morrow.   Would you care to go instead of me ?   I mean it.   Honestly, I'd just as soon stay here."

" No, no !   I should be removed from the bench as a Reactionary," cried the chief magistrate, laughing till the tears stood in his eyes at his own joke.   " But you go to Féterne too, don't you ? " he went on, turning to the solicitor.

"Oh, I go there on Sundays—in at one door and out at the other. But I don't have them here to luncheon, like the Leader."

M. de Stermaria was not at Balbec that day, to the barrister's great regret. But he managed to say a word in season to the head waiter :

"Aimé, you can tell M. de Stermaria that he's not the only nobleman you've had in here. You saw the gentleman who was with me to-day at luncheon ? Eh ? A small moustache, looked like a military man. Well, that was the Marquis de Cambremer ! "

"Was it indeed ? I'm not surprised to hear it."

"That will shew him that he's not the only man who's got a title. That will teach him ! It's not a bad thing to take 'em down a peg or two, those noblemen. I say, Aimé, don't say anything to him unless you like : I mean to say, it's no business of mine ; besides, they know each other already."

And next day M. de Stermaria, who remembered that the barrister had once held a brief for one of his friends, came up and introduced himself.

"Our friends in common, the de Cambremers, were anxious that we should meet ; the days didn't fit ; I don't know quite what went wrong—" stammered the barrister, who, like most liars, imagined that other people do not take the trouble to investigate an unimportant detail which, for all that, may be sufficient (if chance puts you in possession of the humble facts of the case, and they contradict it) to shew the liar in his true colours and to inspire a lasting mistrust.

Then as at all times, but more easily now that her father had left her and was talking to the barrister, I was gazing at Mlle. de Stermaria. No less than the bold and always graceful originality of her attitudes, as when, leaning her elbows on the table, she raised her glass in both hands over her outstretched arms, the dry flame of a glance at once extinguished, the ingrained, congenital hardness that one could feel, ill-concealed by her own personal inflexions, in the sound of her voice, which had shocked my grandmother ; a sort of atavistic starting point to which she recoiled whenever, by glance or utterance, she had succeeded in expressing a thought of her own ; all of these qualities carried the mind of him who watched her back to the line of ancestors who had bequeathed to her that inadequacy of human sympathy, those blanks in her sensibility, that short measure of humanity which was at every moment running out. But from a certain look which flooded for a moment the wells —instantly dry again—of her eyes, a look in which I could discern that almost obsequious docility which the predominance of a taste for sensual pleasures gives to the proudest of women, who will soon come to recognise but one form of personal distinction, that namely which any man enjoys who can make her feel those pleasures, an actor, an acrobat even, for whom, perhaps, she will one day leave her husband ; —from a certain rosy tint, warm and sensual, which flushed her pallid cheeks, like the colour that stained the hearts of the white water-lilies in the Vivonne, I thought I could discern that she would readily have consented to my coming to seek in her the savour of that life of poetry and romance which she led in Brittany, a life to which, whether from over-familiarity or from innate superiority, or from disgust at the penury or the avarice of her family, she seemed not to attach any great value, but which, for all that, she held enclosed in her body. In the meagre stock of will-power that had been transmitted to her, and gave an element of weakness to her expression, she would not perhaps have found the strength to resist. And, crowned by a feather that was a trifle old-fashioned and pretentious, the grey felt hat which she invariably wore at meals made her all the more attractive to me, not because it was in harmony with her pearly or rosy complexion, but because, by making me suppose her to be poor, it brought her closer to myself. Obliged by her father's presence to adopt a conventional attitude, but already bringing to the perception and classification of the people who passed before her eyes other principles than his, perhaps she saw in me not my humble rank, but the right sex and age. If one day M. de Stermaria had gone out leaving her behind, if, above all, Mme. de Villeparisis, by coming to sit at our table, had given her an opinion of me which might have emboldened me to approach her, perhaps then we might have contrived to exchange a few words, to arrange a meeting, to form a closer tie. And for a whole month during which she would be left alone, without her parents, in her romantic Breton castle, we should perhaps have been able to wander by ourselves at evening, she and I together in the dusk which would shew in a softer light above the darkening water pink briar roses, beneath oak trees beaten and stunted by the hammering of the waves. Together we should have roamed that isle impregnated with so intense a charm for me because it had enclosed the everyday life of Mlle. de Stermaria and lay at rest in her remembering eyes. For it seemed to me that I should not really have possessed her save there, when I should have traversed

those regions which enveloped her in so many memories—
a veil which my desire sought to tear apart, one of those
veils which nature interposes between woman and her
pursuers (with the same intention as when, for all of us,
she places the act of reproduction between ourselves and
our keenest pleasure, and for insects, places before the
nectar the pollen which they must carry away with them)
in order that, tricked by the illusion of possessing her
thus more completely, they may be forced to occupy first
the scenes among which she lives, and which, of more
service to their imagination than sensual pleasure can be,
yet would not without that pleasure have had the power to
attract them.

But I was obliged to take my eyes from Mlle. de Stermaria, for already, considering no doubt that making the
acquaintance of an important person was a brief, inquisi-
tive act which was sufficient in itself, and to bring out all
the interest that was latent in it required only a hand-
shake and a penetrating stare, without either immediate
conversation or any subsequent relations, her father had
taken leave of the barrister and returned to sit down fac-
ing her, rubbing his hands like a man who has just made
a valuable acquisition. As for the barrister, once the first
emotion of this interview had subsided, then, as on other
days, he could be heard every minute addressing the
head waiter :

"But I am not a king, Aimé ; go and attend to the
king ! I say, Chief, those little trout don't look at all bad,
do they ? We must ask Aimé to let us have some.
Aimé, that little fish you have over there looks to me
highly commendable : will you bring us some, please,
Aimé, and don't be sparing with it."

He would repeat the name "Aimé" all day long, one result of which was that when he had anyone to dinner the guest would remark "I can see, you are quite at home in this place," and would feel himself obliged to keep on saying "Aimé" also, from that tendency, combining elements of timidity, vulgarity and silliness, which many people have, to believe that it is smart and witty to copy to the letter what is said by the company in which they may happen to be. The barrister repeated the name incessantly, but with a smile, for he felt that he was exhibiting at once the good terms on which he stood with the head waiter and his own superior station. And the head waiter, whenever he caught the sound of his own name, smiled too, as though touched and at the same time proud, shewing that he was conscious of the honour and could appreciate the pleasantry.

Terrifying as I always found these meals, in the vast restaurant, generally full, of the mammoth hotel, they became even more terrifying when there arrived for a few days the Proprietor (or he may have been only the General Manager, appointed by a board of directors) not only of this "palace" but of seven or eight more besides, situated at all the four corners of France, in each of which, travelling continuously, he would spend a week now and again. Then, just after dinner had begun, there appeared every evening in the doorway of the dining-room this small man with white hair and a red nose, astonishingly neat and impassive, who was known, it appeared, as well in London as at Monte Carlo, as one of the leading hotel-keepers in Europe. Once when I had gone out for a moment at the beginning of dinner, as I came in again I passed close by him, and he bowed to me, but with a cold-

ness in which I could not distinguish whether it should be
attributed to the reserve of a man who could never forget
what he was, or to his contempt for a customer of so little
importance. To those whose importance was considerable the Managing Director would bow, with quite as
much coldness but more deeply, lowering his eyelids with
a reverence that was almost offended modesty, as though
he had found himself confronted, at a funeral, with the
father of the deceased or with the Blessed Sacrament.
Except for these icy and infrequent salutations, he made
not the slightest movement, as if to shew that his glittering eyes, which appeared to be starting out of his head,
saw everything, controlled everything, assured to us in
the "Hotel dinner" perfection in every detail as well
as a general harmony. He felt, evidently, that he was
more than the producer of a play, than the conductor
of an orchestra, nothing less than a general in supreme
command. Having decided that a contemplation carried to its utmost intensity would suffice to assure him
that everything was in readiness, that no mistake had
been made which could lead to disaster,—to invest him,
in a word, with full responsibility, he abstained not
merely from any gesture but even from moving his eyes,
which, petrified by the intensity of their gaze, took in
and directed everything that was going on. I felt that
even the movements of my spoon did not escape him,
and were he to vanish after the soup, for the whole
of dinner the review that he had held would have taken
away my appetite. His own was exceedingly good, as
one could see at luncheon, which he took like an ordinary guest of the hotel at a table that anyone else might
have had in the public dining-room. His table had

this peculiarity only, that by his side, while he was eating, the other manager, the resident one, remained standing all the time to make conversation. For being subordinate to this Managing Director he was anxious to please a man of whom he lived in constant fear. My fear of him diminished during these luncheons, for being then lost in the crowd of visitors he would exercise the discretion of a general sitting in a restaurant where there are also private soldiers, in not seeming to take any notice of them. Nevertheless when the porter, from among a cluster of pages, announced to me : "He leaves to-morrow morning for Dinard. Then he's going down to Biarritz, and after that to Cannes," I began to breathe more freely.

My life in the hotel was rendered not only dull because I had no friends there but uncomfortable because Françoise had made so many. It might be thought that they would have made things easier for us in various respects. Quite the contrary. The proletariat, if they succeeded only with great difficulty in being treated as people she knew by Françoise, and could not succeed at all unless they fulfilled the condition of shewing the utmost politeness to her, were, on the other hand, once they had reached the position, the only people who "counted". Her time-honoured code taught her that she was in no way bound to the friends of her employers, that she might, if she was busy, shut the door without ceremony in the face of a lady who had come to call on my grandmother. But towards her own acquaintance, that is to say, the select handful of the lower orders whom she admitted to an unconquerable intimacy, her actions were regulated by the most subtle and most stringent of protocols. Thus Françoise having made the acquaintance of the man in the coffee-shop and of a little maid who did dressmaking for a Belgian lady, no longer came upstairs immediately after luncheon to get my grandmother's things ready, but came an hour later, because the coffee man had wanted to make her a cup of coffee or a *tisane* in his shop, or the maid had invited her to go and watch her sew, and to refuse either of them would have been impossible, and one of the things that were not done. Moreover, particular attention was due to the little sewing-maid, who was an orphan and had been brought up by strangers to whom she still went occasionally for a few days' holiday. Her unusual situation aroused Françoise's pity, and also a benevolent contempt. She, who had a family, a little house that had come to her from her parents, with a field in which her brother kept his cows, how could she regard so uprooted a creature as her equal ? And since this girl hoped, on Assumption Day, to be allowed to pay her benefactors a visit, Françoise kept on repeating : "She does make me laugh! She says, 'I hope to be going home for the Assumption.' 'Home !' says she ! It isn't just that it's not her own place, they're people who took her in from nowhere, and the creature says 'home' just as if it really was her home. Poor girl ! What a wretched state she must be in, not to know what it is to have a home." Still, if Françoise had associated only with the ladies'-maids brought to the hotel by other visitors, who fed with her in the " service " quarters and, seeing her grand lace cap and her handsome profile, took her perhaps for some lady of noble birth, whom " reduced circumstances ", or a personal attachment had driven to serve as companion to my grandmother, if in a word Françoise had known only people who did not belong to the hotel, no great harm would have been done, since she could not have prevented them from doing us any service, for the simple reason that in no circumstances, even without her knowledge, would it have been possible for them to serve us at all. But she had formed connexions also with one of the wine waiters, with a man in the kitchen, and with the head chambermaid of our landing. And the result of this in our every day life was that Françoise, who on the day of her arrival, when she still did not know anyone, would set all the bells jangling for the slightest thing, at an hour when my grandmother and I would never have dared to ring, and if we offered some gentle admonition answered : "Well, we're paying enough for it, aren't we ? " as though it were she herself that would have to pay ; nowadays, since she had made friends with a personage in the kitchen, which had appeared to us to augur well for our future comfort, were my grandmother or I to complain of cold feet, Françoise, even at an hour that was quite normal, dared not ring ; she assured us that it would give offence because they would have to light the furnace again, or because it would interrupt the servants' dinner and they would be annoyed. And she ended with a formula that, in spite of the ambiguous way in which she uttered it, was none the less clear, and put us plainly in the wrong : "The fact is . . ." We did not insist, for fear of bringing upon ourselves another, far more serious : " It's a matter . . . ! " So that it amounted to this, that we could no longer have any hot water because Françoise had become a friend of the man who would have to heat it.

In the end we too formed a connexion, in spite of but

through my grandmother, for she and Mme. de Villeparisis came in collision one morning in a doorway and
were obliged to accost each other, not without having first
exchanged gestures of surprise and hesitation, performed
movements of recoil and uncertainty, and finally uttered
protestations of joy and greeting, as in some of Molière's
plays, where two actors who have been delivering long
soliloquies from opposite sides of the stage, a few feet
apart, are supposed not to have seen each other yet, and
then suddenly catch sight of each other, cannot believe
their eyes, break off what they are saying and finally address each other (the chorus having meanwhile kept the
dialogue going) and fall into each other's arms. Mme. de
Villeparisis was tactful, and made as if to leave my grandmother to herself after the first greetings, but my grandmother insisted on her staying to talk to her until luncheon, being anxious to discover how her friend managed
to get her letters sent up to her earlier than we got ours,
and to get such nice grilled things (for Mme. de Villeparisis, a great epicure, had the poorest opinion of the
hotel kitchen which served us with meals that my grandmother, still quoting Mme. de Sévigné, described as "of
a magnificence to make you die of hunger.") And the
Marquise formed the habit of coming every day, until
her own meal was ready, to sit down for a moment at our
table in the dining-room, insisting that we should not rise
from our chairs or in any way put ourselves out. At the
most we would linger, as often as not, in the room after
finishing our luncheon, to talk to her, at that sordid moment when the knives are left littering the tablecloth
among crumpled napkins. For my own part, so as to
preserve (in order that I might be able to enjoy Balbec)

the idea that I was on the uttermost promontory of the earth, I compelled myself to look farther afield, to notice only the sea, to seek in it the effects described by Baudelaire and to let my gaze fall upon our table only on days when there was set on it some gigantic fish, some marine monster, which unlike the knives and forks was contemporary with the primitive epochs in which the Ocean first began to teem with life, in the Cimmerians' time, a fish whose body with its numberless vertebrae, its blue veins and red, had been constructed by nature, but according to an architectural plan, like a polychrome cathedral of the deep.

As a barber, seeing an officer whom he is accustomed to shave with special deference and care recognise a customer who has just entered the shop and stop for a moment to talk to him, rejoices in the thought that these are two men of the same social order, and cannot help smiling as he goes to fetch the bowl of soap, for he knows that in his establishment, to the vulgar routine of a mere barber's-shop, are being added social, not to say aristocratic pleasures, so Aimé, seeing that Mme. de Villeparisis had found in us old friends, went to fetch our finger-bowls with precisely the smile, proudly modest and knowingly discreet, of a hostess who knows when to leave her guests to themselves. He suggested also a pleased and loving father who looks on, without interfering, at the happy pair who have plighted their troth at his hospitable board. Besides, it was enough merely to utter the name of a person of title for Aimé to appear pleased, unlike Françoise, before whom you could not mention Count So-and-so without her face darkening and her speech becoming dry and sharp, all of which meant that she worshipped the aris-

tocracy not less than Aimé but far more. But then Françoise had that quality which in others she condemned as
the worst possible fault ; she was proud. She was not
of that friendly and good-humoured race to which Aimé
belonged. They feel, they exhibit an intense delight when
you tell them a piece of news which may be more or less
sensational but is at any rate new, and not to be found in
the papers. Françoise declined to appear surprised. You
might have announced in her hearing that the Archduke
Rudolf—not that she had the least suspicion of his having
ever existed—was not, as was generally supposed, dead,
but " alive and kicking " ; she would have answered only
" Yes," as though she had known it all the time. It may,
however, have been that if even from our own lips, from
us whom she so meekly called her masters, who had so
nearly succeeded in taming her, she could not, without having to check an angry start, hear the name of a noble,
that was because the family from which she had sprung
occupied in its own village a comfortable and independent
position, and was not to be threatened in the consideration
which it enjoyed save by those same nobles, in whose
households, meanwhile, from his boyhood, an Aimé would
have been domiciled as a servant, if not actually brought
up by their charity. Of Françoise, then, Mme. de
Villeparisis must ask pardon, first, for her nobility.
But (in France, at any rate) that is precisely the talent,
in fact the sole occupation of our great gentlemen and
ladies. Françoise, following the common tendency of
servants, who pick up incessantly from the conversation of
their masters with other people fragmentary observations
from which they are apt to draw erroneous inductions, as
the human race generally does with respect to the

habits of animals, was constantly discovering that some-body had "failed" us, a conclusion to which she was easily led, not so much, perhaps, by her extravagant love for us, as by the delight that she took in being disagreeable to us. But having once established, without possibility of error, the endless little attentions paid to us, and paid to herself also by Mme. de Villeparisis, Françoise forgave her for being a Marquise, and, as she had never ceased to be proud of her because she was one, preferred her thenceforward to all our other friends. It must be added that no one else took the trouble to be so continually nice to us. Whenever my grandmother remarked on a book that Mme. de Villeparisis was reading, or said she had been admiring the fruit which some one had just sent to our friend, within an hour the footman would come to our rooms with book or fruit. And the next time we saw her, in response to our thanks, she would say only, seeming to seek some excuse for the meagreness of her present in some special use to which it might be put : "It's nothing wonderful, but the newspapers come so late here, one must have something to read." Or, "It is always wiser to have fruit one can be quite certain of, at the seaside."—"But I don't believe I've ever seen you eating oysters," she said to us, increasing the sense of disgust which I felt at that moment, for the living flesh of the oyster revolted me even more than the gumminess of the stranded jelly-fish defiled for me the beach at Balbec ; "they are de-licious down here ! Oh, let me tell my maid to fetch your letters when she goes for mine. What, your daugh-ter writes *every day* ? But what on earth can you find to say to each other ? " My grandmother was silent, but it may be assumed that her silence was due to

scorn, in her who used to repeat, when she wrote to
Mamma, the words of Mme. de Sévigné : "As soon
as I have received a letter, I want another at once ; I
cannot breathe until it comes. There are few who are
worthy to understand what I mean." And I was afraid
of her applying to Mme. de Villeparisis the conclusion :
"I seek out those who are of the chosen few, and I
avoid the rest." She fell back upon praise of the fruit
which Mme. de Villeparisis had sent us the day before.
And this had been, indeed, so fine that the manager, in
spite of the jealousy aroused by our neglect of his official
offerings, had said to me : "I am like you ; I'm madder
about fruit than any other kind of dessert." My grandmother told her friend that she had enjoyed them all the
more because the fruit which we got in the hotel was
generally horrid. "I cannot," she went on, "say, like
Mme. de Sévigné, that if we should take a sudden fancy
for bad fruit we should be obliged to order it from Paris."
"Oh yes, of course, you read Mme. de Sévigné. I saw
you with her letters the day you came." (She forgot that
she had never officially seen my grandmother in the hotel
until their collision in the doorway.) "Don't you find it
rather exaggerated, her constant anxiety about her daughter ? She refers to it too often to be really sincere. She
is not natural." My grandmother felt that any discussion
would be futile, and so as not to be obliged to speak of the
things she loved to a person incapable of understanding
them, concealed by laying her bag upon them the
Mémoires de Mme. de Beausergent.

Were she to encounter Françoise at the moment (which
Françoise called "the noon") when, wearing her fine
cap and surrounded with every mark of respect, she was

coming downstairs to " feed with the service ", Mme. Villeparisis would stop her to ask after us. And Françoise,
when transmitting to us the Marquise's message : " She
said to me, ' You'll be sure and bid them good day,' she
said," counterfeited the voice of Mme. de Villeparisis,
whose exact words she imagined herself to be quoting
textually, whereas she was really corrupting them no less
than Plato corrupts the words of Socrates or Saint John
the words of Jesus. Françoise, as was natural, was
deeply touched by these attentions. Only she did not believe my grandmother, but supposed that she must be
lying in the interest of her class (the rich always combining thus to support one another) when she assured
us that Mme. de Villeparisis had been lovely as a young
woman. It was true that of this loveliness only the
faintest trace remained, from which no one—unless he
happened to be a great deal more of an artist than Françoise—would have been able to restore her ruined beauty.
For in order to understand how beautiful an elderly woman can once have been one must not only study but
interpret every line of her face.

" I must remember, some time, to ask her whether I'm
not right, after all, in thinking that there is some connexion with the Guermantes," said my grandmother, to
my great indignation. How could I be expected to believe in a common origin uniting two names which had
entered my consciousness, one through the low and shame-
ful gate of experience, the other by the golden gate of
imagination ?

We had several times, in the last few days, seen driving past us in a stately equipage, tall, auburn, handsome, with a rather prominent nose, the Princesse de

Luxembourg, who was staying in the neighbourhood for a few weeks. Her carriage had stopped outside the hotel, a footman had come in and spoken to the manager, had gone back to the carriage and had reappeared with the most amazing armful of fruit (which combined in a single basket, like the bay itself, different seasons) with a card : " La Princesse de Luxembourg ", on which were scrawled a few words in pencil. For what princely traveller sojourning here *incognito,* could they be intended, those glaucous plums, luminous and spherical as was at that moment the circumfluent sea, transparent grapes clustering on a shrivelled stick, like a fine day in autumn, pears of a heavenly ultramarine ? For it could not be on my grandmother's friend that the Princess had meant to pay a call. And yet on the following evening Mme. de Villeparisis sent us the bunch of grapes, cool, liquid, golden ; plums too and pears which we remembered, though the plums had changed, like the sea at our dinner-hour, to a dull purple, and on the ultramarine surface of the pears there floated the forms of a few rosy clouds. A few days later we met Mme. de Villeparisis as we came away from the symphony concert that was given every morning on the beach. Convinced that the music to which I had been listening (the Prelude to *Lohengrin,* the Overture to *Tannhäuser* and suchlike) expressed the loftiest of truths, I was trying to elevate myself, as far as I could, so as to attain to a comprehension of them, I was extracting from myself so as to understand them, and was attributing to them, all that was best and most profound in my own nature at that time.

Well, as we came out of the concert, and, on our way

back to the hotel, had stopped for a moment on the front, my grandmother and I, for a few words with Mme. de Villeparisis who told us that she had ordered some *croque-monsieurs* and a dish of creamed eggs for us at the hotel, I saw, a long way away, coming in our direction, the Princesse de Luxembourg, half leaning upon a parasol in such a way as to impart to her tall and wonderful form that slight inclination, to make it trace that arabesque dear to the women who had been beautiful under the Empire, and knew how, with drooping shoulders, arched backs, concave hips and bent limbs, to make their bodies float as gently as a silken scarf about the rigidity of the invisible stem which might be supposed to have been passed diagonally through them. She went out every morning for a turn on the beach almost at the time when everyone else, after bathing, was climbing home to luncheon, and as hers was not until half past one she did not return to her villa until long after the hungry bathers had left the scorching " front " a desert. Mme. de Villeparisis presented my grandmother and would have presented me, but had first to ask me my name, which she could not remember. She had, perhaps, never known it, or if she had must have forgotten years ago to whom my grandmother had married her daughter. My name, when she did hear it, appeared to impress Mme. de Villeparisis considerably. Meanwhile the Princesse de Luxembourg had given us her hand and, now and again, while she conversed with the Marquise, turned to bestow a kindly glance on my grandmother and myself, with that embryonic kiss which we put into our smiles when they are addressed to a baby out with its " Nana ". Indeed, in her anxiety not to appear to be a denizen of a higher sphere than ours, she had probably miscalculated the distance there was indeed between us, for by an error in adjustment she made her eyes beam with such benevolence that I could see the moment approaching when she would put out her hand and stroke us, as if we were two nice beasts and had poked our heads out at her through the bars of our cage in the Gardens. And, immediately, as it happened, this idea of caged animals and the Bois de Boulogne received striking confirmation. It was the time of day at which the beach is crowded by itinerant and clamorous vendors, hawking cakes and sweets and biscuits. Not knowing quite what to do to shew her affection for us, the Princess hailed the next that came by; he had nothing left but one rye-cake, of the kind one throws to the ducks. The Princess took it and said to me : " For your grandmother." And yet it was to me that she held it out, saying with a friendly smile, " You shall give it to her yourself ! " thinking that my pleasure would thus be more complete if there were no intermediary between myself and the animals. Other vendors came up ; she stuffed my pockets with everything that they had, tied up in packets, comfits, sponge-cakes, sugar-sticks. " You will eat some yourself," she told me, " and give some to your grandmother," and she had the vendors paid by the little negro page, dressed in red satin, who followed her everywhere and was a nine days' wonder upon the beach. Then she said good-bye to Mme. de Villeparisis and held out her hand to us with the intention of treating us in the same way as she treated her friend, as people whom she knew, and of bringing herself within our reach. But this time she must have reckoned our level as not quite so low in the scale of creation, for her and our equality was indicated by the Princess to my grandmother by that tender and maternal smile which a woman gives a little boy when she says good-bye to him as though to a grown-up person. By a miraculous stride in evolution, my grandmother was no longer a duck or an antelope, but had already become what the anglophil Mme. Swann would have called a "baby". Finally, having taken leave of us all, the Princess resumed her stroll along the basking "front", curving her splendid shape which, like a serpent coiled about a wand, was interlaced with the white parasol patterned in blue which Mme. de Luxembourg held, unopened, in her hand. She was my first Royalty—I say my first, for strictly speaking Princesse Mathilde did not count. The second, as we shall see in due course, was to astonish me no less by her indulgence. One of the ways in which our great nobles, kindly intermediaries between commoners and kings, can befriend us was revealed to me next day when Mme. de Villeparisis reported : "She thought you quite charming. She is a woman of the soundest judgment, the warmest heart. Not like so many Queens and people ! She has real merit." And Mme. de Villeparisis went on in a tone of conviction, and quite thrilled to be able to say it to us : "I am sure she would be delighted to see you again."

But on that previous morning, after we had parted from the Princesse de Luxembourg, Mme. de Villeparisis said a thing which impressed me far more and was not prompted merely by friendly feeling.

"Are you," she had asked me, "the son of the Permanent Secretary at the Ministry ? Indeed ! I am told your father is a most charming man. He is having a splendid holiday just now."

A few days earlier we had heard, in a letter from Mamma, that my father and his friend M. de Norpois had lost their luggage.

"It has been found ; as a matter of fact, it was never really lost, I can tell you what happened," explained Mme. de Villeparisis, who, without our knowing how, seemed to be far better informed than ourselves of the course of my father's travels. "I think your father is now planning to come home earlier, next week, in fact, as he will probably give up the idea of going to Algeçiras. But he is anxious to devote a day longer to Toledo ; it seems, he is an admirer of a pupil of Titian,—I forget the name—whose work can only be seen properly there."

I asked myself by what strange accident, in the impartial glass through which Mme. de Villeparisis considered, from a safe distance, the bustling, tiny, purposeless agitation of the crowd of people whom she knew, there had come to be inserted at the spot through which she observed my father a fragment of prodigious magnifying power which made her see in such high relief and in the fullest detail everything that there was attractive about him, the contingencies that were obliging him to return home, his difficulties with the customs, his admiration for El Greco, and, altering the scale of her vision, shewed her this one man so large among all the rest quite small, like that Jupiter to whom Gustave Moreau gave, when he portrayed him by the side of a weak mortal, a superhuman stature.

My grandmother bade Mme. de Villeparisis good-bye,

so that we might stay and imbibe the fresh air for a little while longer outside the hotel, until they signalled to us through the glazed partition that our luncheon was ready. There were sounds of tumult. The young mistress of the King of the Cannibal Island had been down to bathe and was now coming back to the hotel.

" Really and truly, it's a perfect plague : it's enough to make one decide to emigrate ! " cried the barrister, who had happened to cross her path, in a towering rage.

Meanwhile the solicitor's wife was following the bogus Queen with eyes that seemed ready to start from their sockets.

" I can't tell you how angry Mme. Blandais makes me when she stares at those people like that," said the barrister to the chief magistrate, " I feel I want to slap her. That is just the way to make the wretches appear important ; and of course that's the very thing they want, that people should take an interest in them. Do ask her husband to tell her what a fool she's making of herself. I swear I won't go out with them again if they stop and gape at those masqueraders."

As to the coming of the Princesse de Luxembourg, whose carriage, on the day on which she left the fruit, had drawn up outside the hotel, it had not passed unobserved by the little group of wives, the solicitor's, the barrister's and the magistrate's, who had for some time past been most concerned to know whether she was a genuine Marquise and not an adventuress, that Mme. de Villeparisis whom everyone treated with so much respect, which all these ladies were burning to hear that she did not deserve. Whenever Mme. de Villeparisis passed through the hall the chief magistrate's wife, who scented

irregularities everywhere, would raise her eyes from her
" work " and stare at the intruder in a way that made her
friends die with laughter.

" Oh, well, you know," she explained with lofty condescension, " I always begin by believing the worst. I will
never admit that a woman is properly married until she
has shewn me her birth certificate and her marriage lines.
But there's no need to alarm yourselves ; just wait till
I've finished my little investigation."

And so, day after day the ladies would come together,
and, laughingly, ask one another : " Any news ? "

But on the evening after the Princesse de Luxembourg's
call the magistrate's wife laid a finger on her lips.

" I've discovered something."

" Oh, isn't Mme. Poncin simply wonderful ? I never
saw anyone. . . . But do tell us ! What has happened ? "

" Just listen to this. A woman with yellow hair and six
inches of paint on her face and a carriage like a—you
could *smell* it a mile off ; which only a creature like that
would dare to have—came here to-day to call on the
Marquise, by way of ! "

" Oh-yow-yow ! Tut-tut-tut-tut. Did you ever !
Why, it must be that woman we saw—you remember,
Leader,—we said at the time we didn't at all like the look
of her, but we didn't know that it was the ' Marquise '
she'd come to see. A woman with a nigger-boy, you
mean ? "

" That's the one."

" D'you mean to say so ? You don't happen to know
her name ? "

" Yes, I made a mistake on purpose ; I picked up her
card ; she *trades* under the name of the ' Princesse de

Luxembourg'! Wasn't I right to have my doubts about her? It's a nice thing to have to mix promiscuously with a Baronne d'Ange like that?" The barrister quoted Mathurin Régnier's *Macette* to the chief magistrate.

It must not, however, be supposed that this misunderstanding was merely temporary, like those that occur in the second act of a farce to be cleared up before the final curtain. Mme. de Luxembourg, a niece of the King of England and of the Emperor of Austria, and Mme. de Villeparisis, when one called to take the other for a drive, did look like nothing but two " old trots " of the kind one has always such difficulty in avoiding at a watering place. Nine tenths of the men of the Faubourg Saint-Germain appear to the average man of the middle class simply as alcoholic wasters (which, individually, they not infrequently are) whom, therefore, no respectable person would dream of asking to dinner. The middle class fixes its standard, in this respect, too high, for the failings of these men would never prevent their being received with every mark of esteem in houses which it, the middle class, may never enter. And so sincerely do they believe that the middle class knows this that they affect a simplicity in speaking of their own affairs and a tone of disparagement of their friends, especially when they are " at the coast ", which make the misunderstanding complete. If, by any chance, a man of the fashionable world is kept in touch with "business people " because, having more money than he knows what to do with, he finds himself elected chairman of all sorts of important financial concerns, the business man who at last sees a nobleman worthy, he considers, to rank with " big business ", would take his oath that such a man can have no dealings with the Marquis ruined by gambling whom the said business man supposes to be all the more destitute of friends the more friendly he makes himself. And he cannot get over his surprise when the Duke, Chairman of the Board of Directors of the colossal undertaking, arranges a marriage for his son with the daughter of that very Marquis, who may be a gambler but who bears the oldest name in France, just as a Sovereign would sooner see his son marry the daughter of a dethroned King than that of a President still in office. That is to say, the two worlds take as fantastic a view of one another as the inhabitants of a town situated at one end of Balbec Bay have of the town at the other end : from Rivebelle you can just see Marcouville l'Orgueilleuse ; but even that is deceptive, for you imagine that you are seen from Marcouville, where, as a matter of fact, the splendours of Rivebelle are almost wholly invisible.